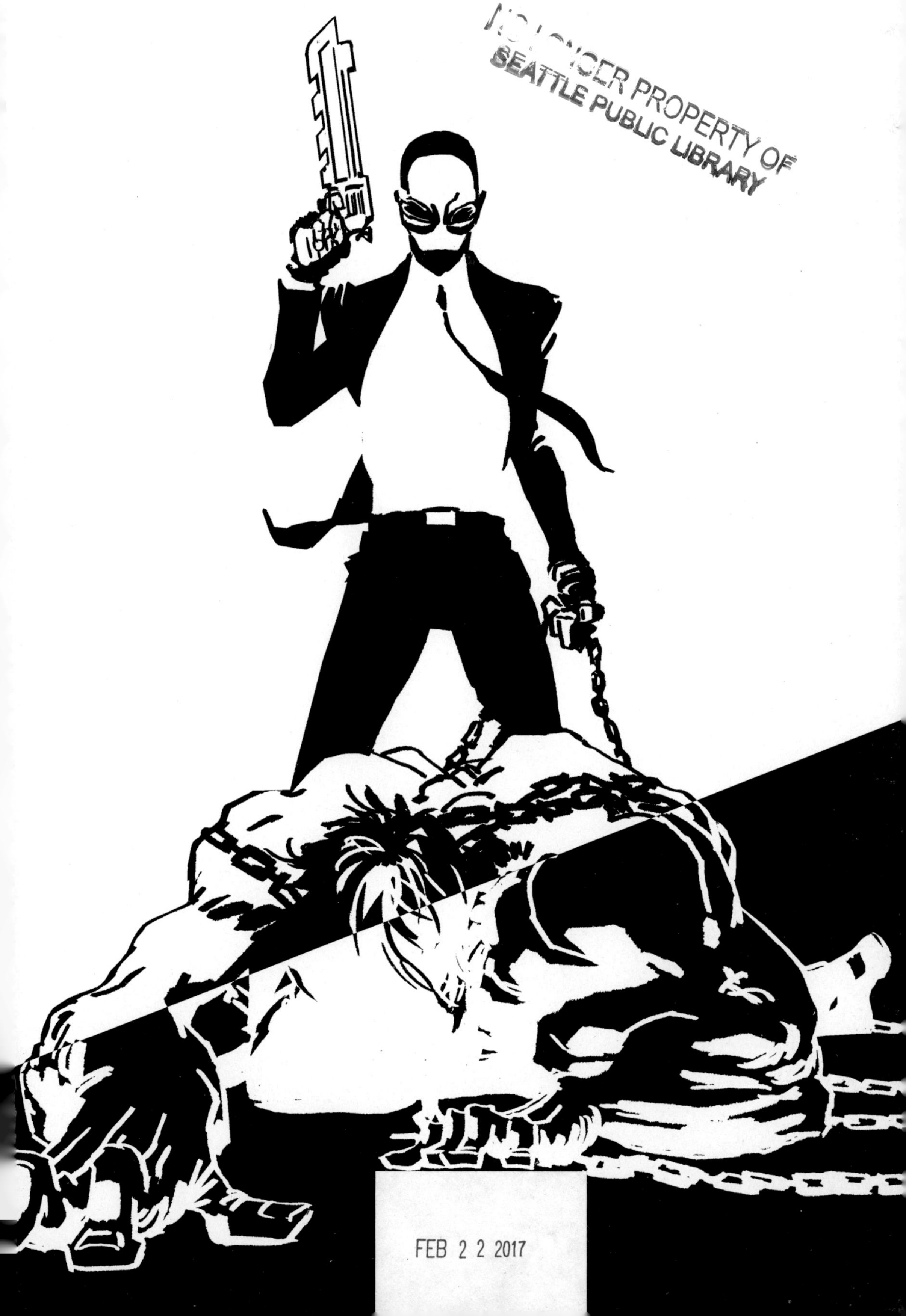

IMAGE COMICS, INC.

IMAGECOMICS.COM

COLLECTION DESIGN BY
JEFF POWELL

ISBN 978-1-63215-900-7

RENATO JONES: THE ONE%, SEASON ONE. First Printing. January 2017. Published by Image Comics, Inc. Office of publication: 2701 NW Vaughn St., Ste. 780, Portland, OR 97210. Copyright © 2017 Kaare Andrews. All rights reserved. Originally published in single magazine form as RENATO JONES: THE ONE% #1-5. RENATO JONES™ (including all prominent characters featured herein), its logo and all character likenesses are trademarks of Kaare Andrews, unless otherwise noted. Image Comics® and its logos are registered trademarks of Image Comics, Inc. No part of this publication may be reproduced or transmitted, in any form or by any means (except for short excerpts for review purposes) without the express written permission of Image Comics, Inc. All names, characters, events and locales in this publication are entirely fictional. Any resemblance to actual persons (living or dead), events or places, without satiric intent, is coincidental. PRINTED IN THE U.S.A. For information regarding the CPSIA on this printed material call: 203-595-3636 and provide reference # RICH – 718999. For international rights inquiries, contact: foreignlicensing@imagecomics.com.

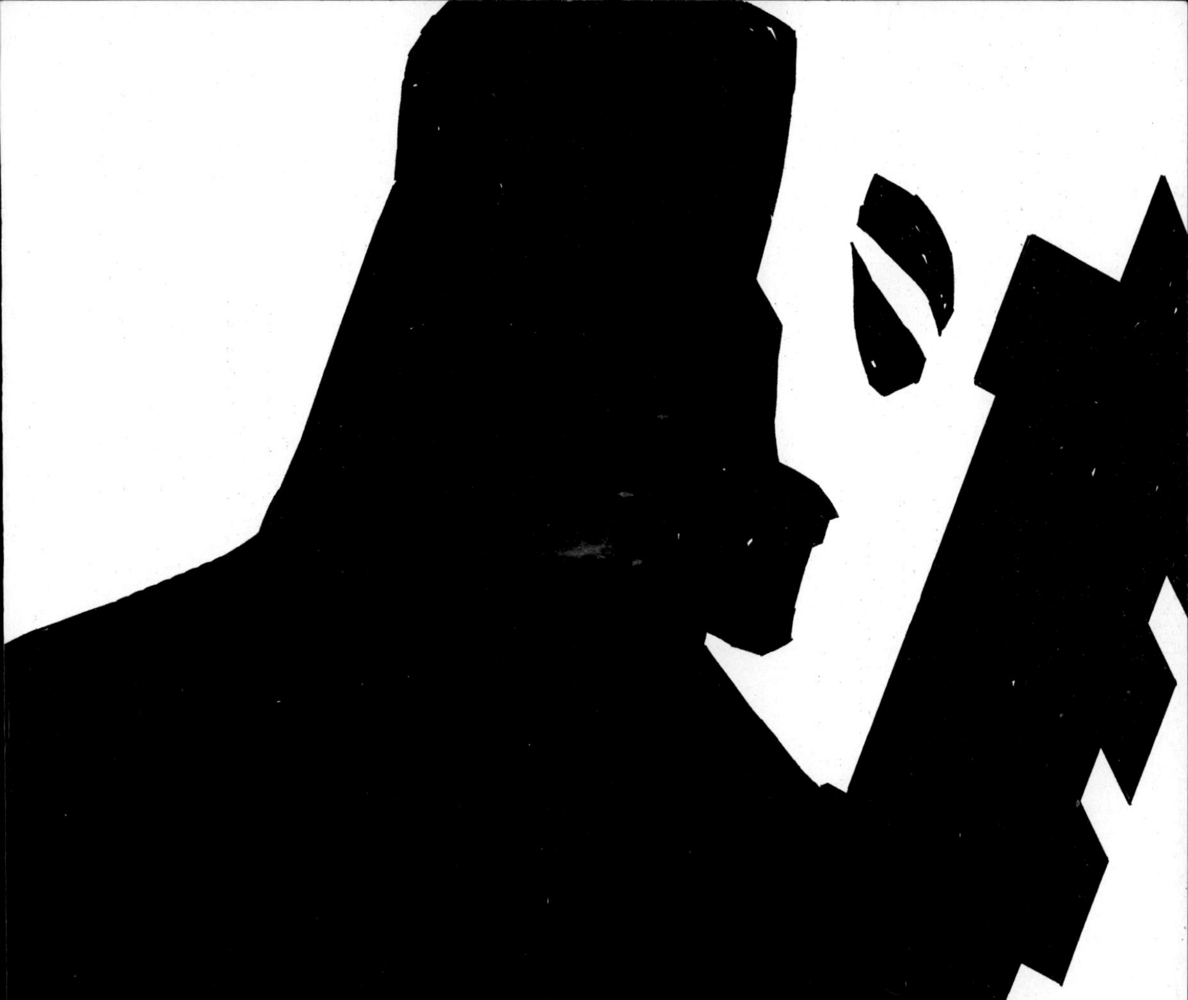

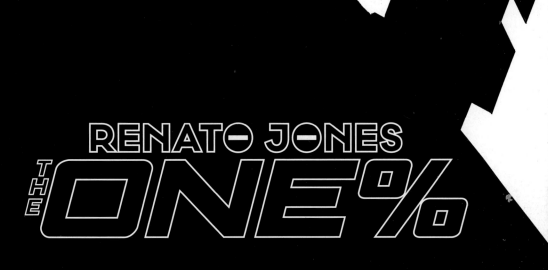

RENATO JONES

THE ONE%

CREATED, WRITTEN, DRAWN AND OWNED BY

KAARE KYLE ANDREWS

LETTERED BY
JEFF POWELL

EDITED BY
SEBASTIAN GIRNER

FLATS
ALICE ITO

INSPIRATION
NICOLE ANDREWS

So you want to be a comicbook creator?

In a world of remakes and remixes, reimaginings and reboots, you have your own ideas. Redoing isn't doing enough. Reworking isn't working for you.

So create.

Create with fire and blood. Spit into the sky and birth something new.

You're not chasing money or fame. You're chasing life.

Likes and retweets in the sea of social media sludge, a programmer's trick to make you think you matter. Well, let me tell you something, friend.

YOU MATTER.

WHAT YOU HAVE TO SAY MATTERS.

WHAT'S IN YOU MATTERS.

So let it out.

Create.

Shore yourself up against the storm to come. Because they will come for you. When you dare to matter…

Those too afraid to live their dreams will try to kill yours. To make things even. A blood sacrifice to false gods.

But as they tear your pages apart, remember to smile. It's not your dreams in their filthy hands, it's simply paper.

And you have so much more to say, so much more than they can ever tear away.

Keep creating.

Create until you've built a pile of life so high, the dead can't reach you.

I'll meet you there.

Wait for me, will you? I just have a few things to do…

— Kaare

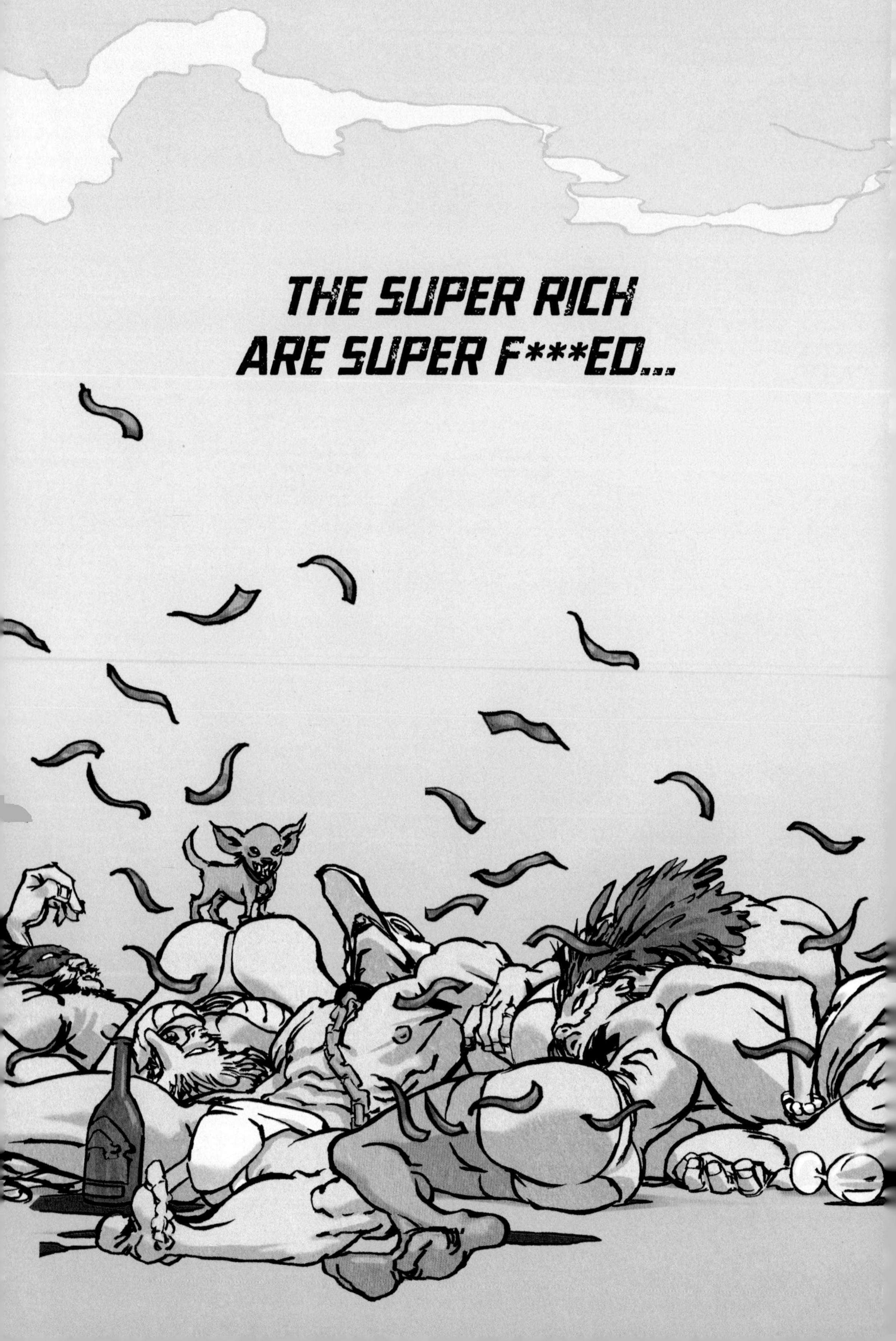
THE SUPER RICH
ARE SUPER F***ED...

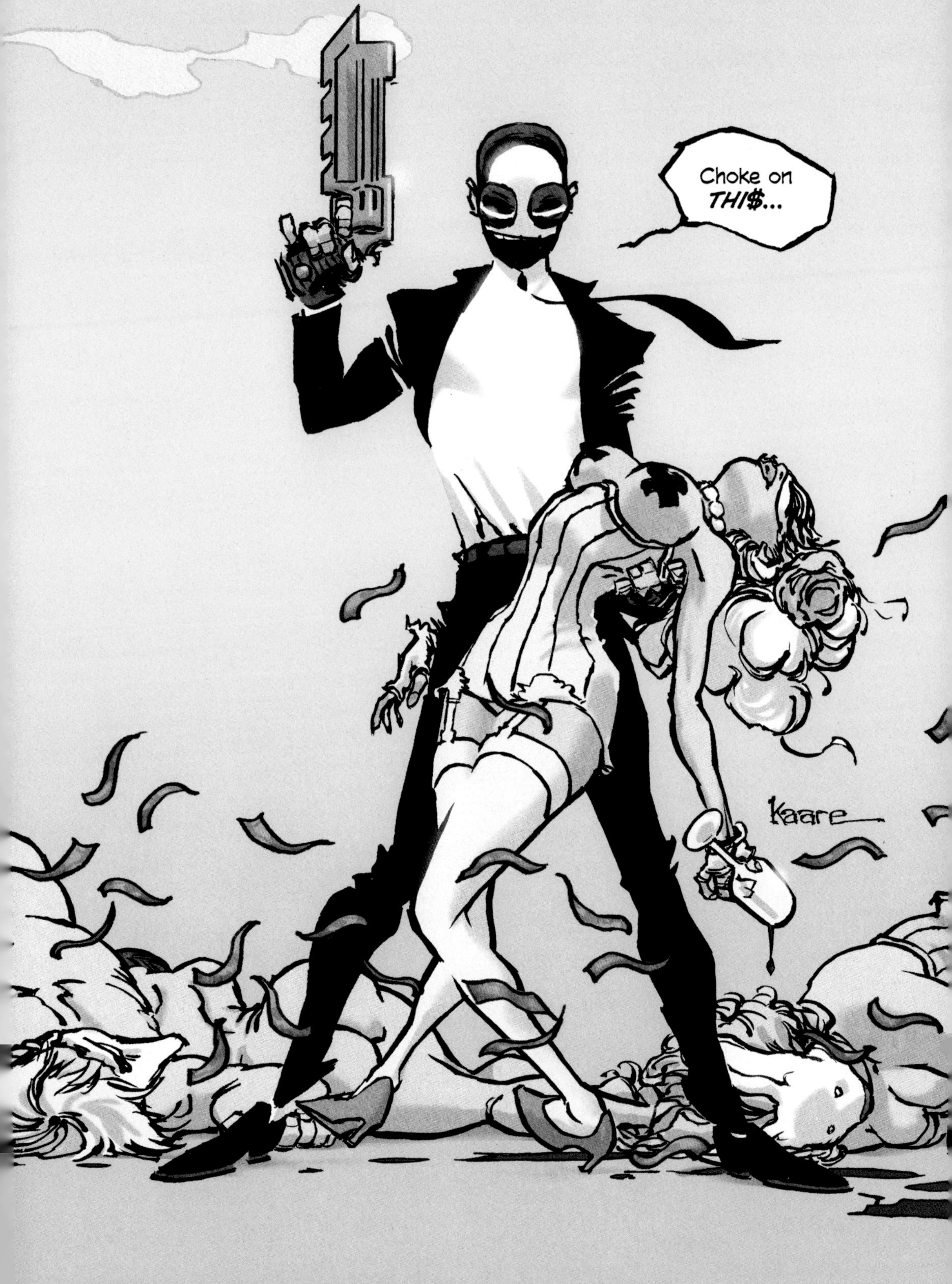
Choke on THI$...
Kaare

1

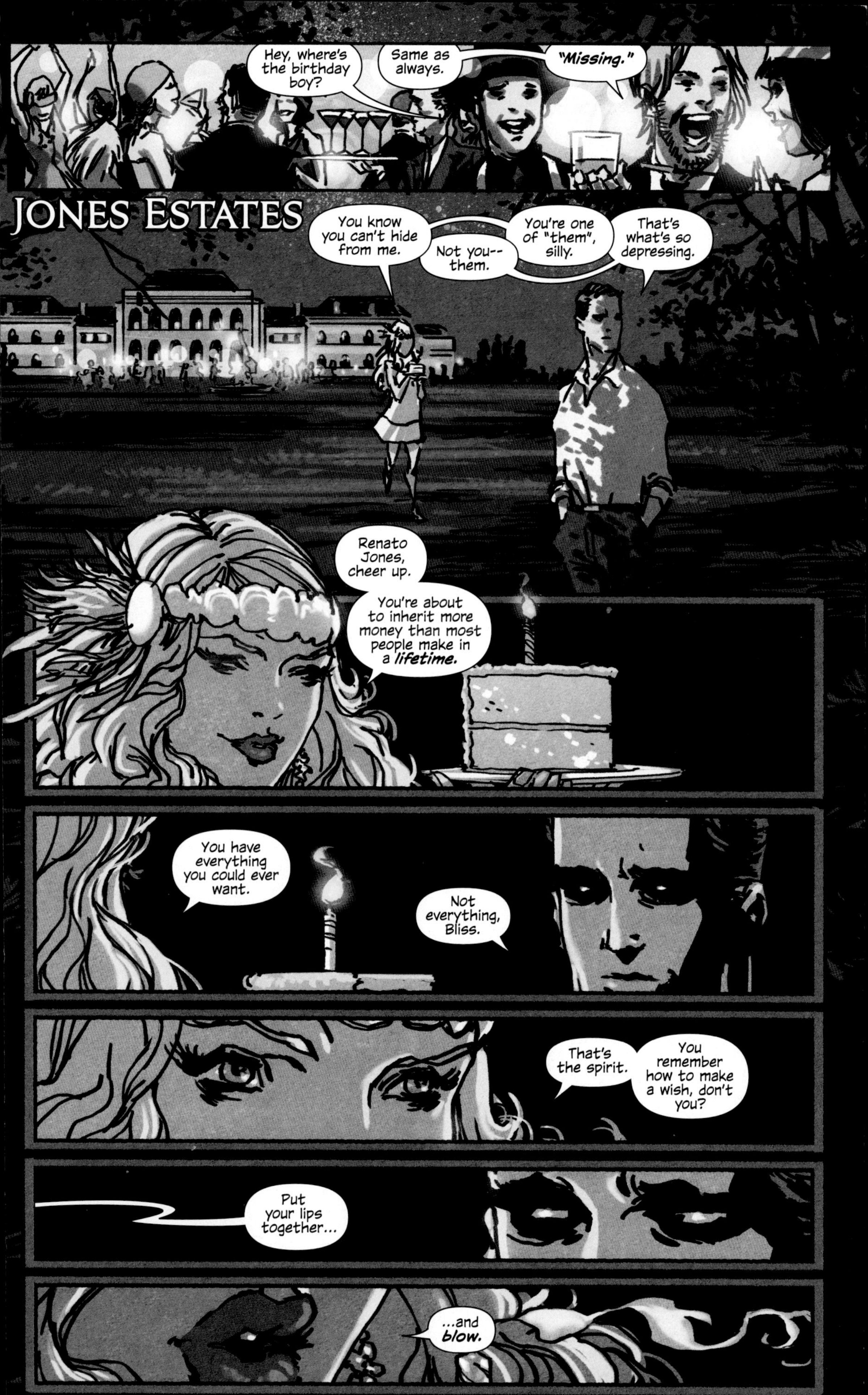
Hey, where's the birthday boy?
Same as always.
"Missing."
JONES ESTATES
You know you can't hide from me.
Not you--them.
You're one of "them", silly.
That's what's so depressing.
Renato Jones, cheer up.
You're about to inherit more money than most people make in a lifetime.
You have everything you could ever want.
Not everything, Bliss.
That's the spirit.
You remember how to make a wish, don't you?
Put your lips together...
...and blow.

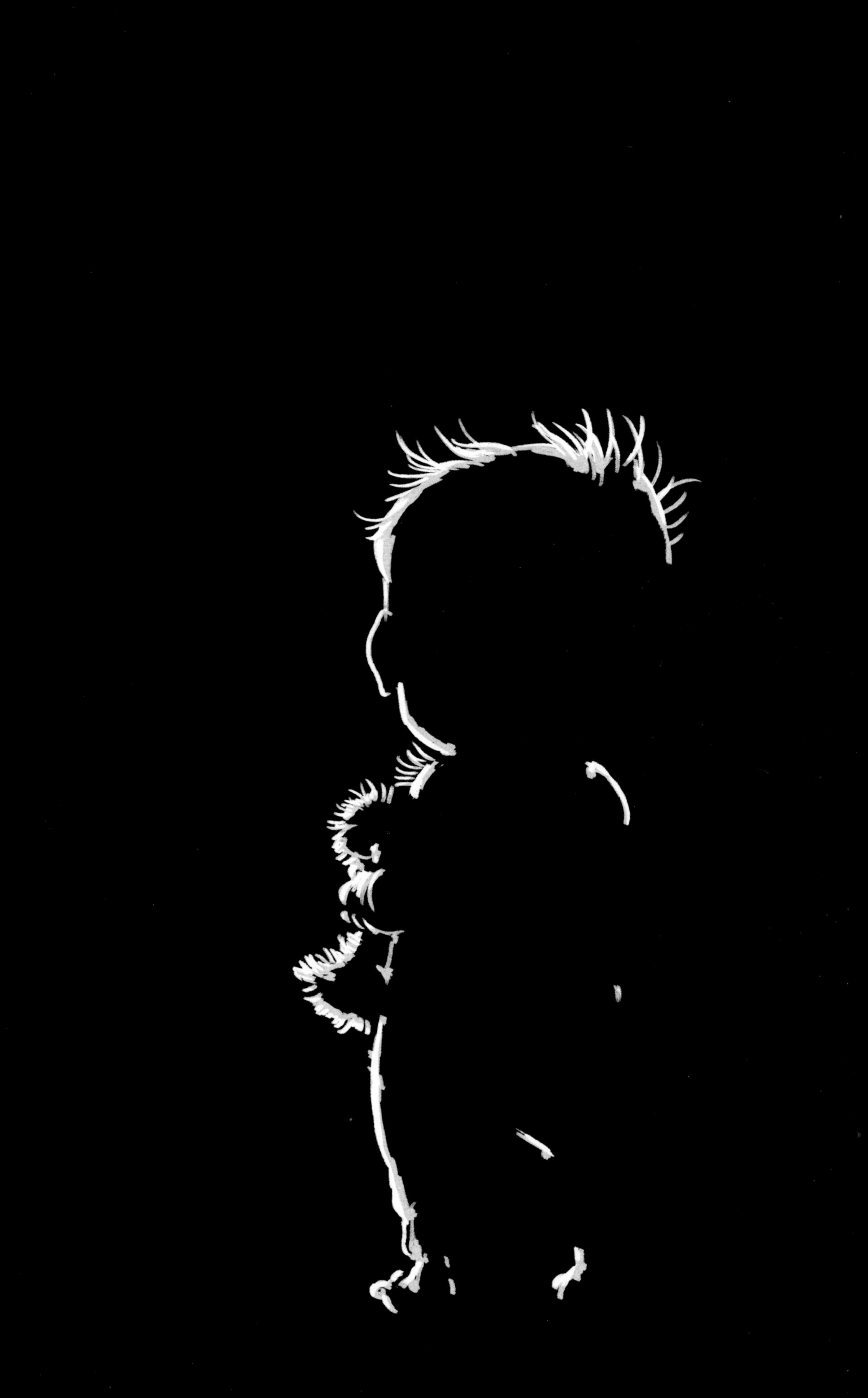

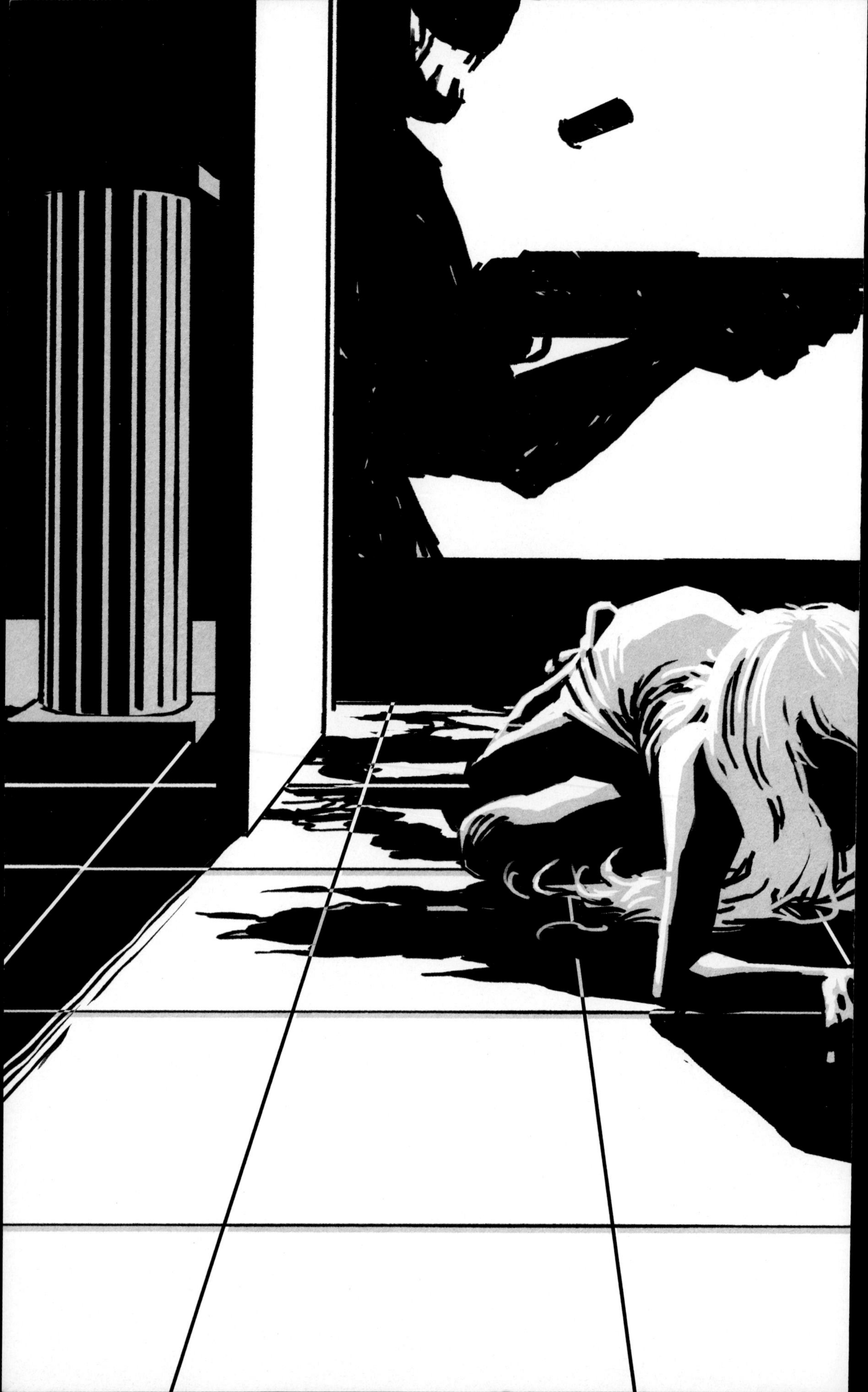

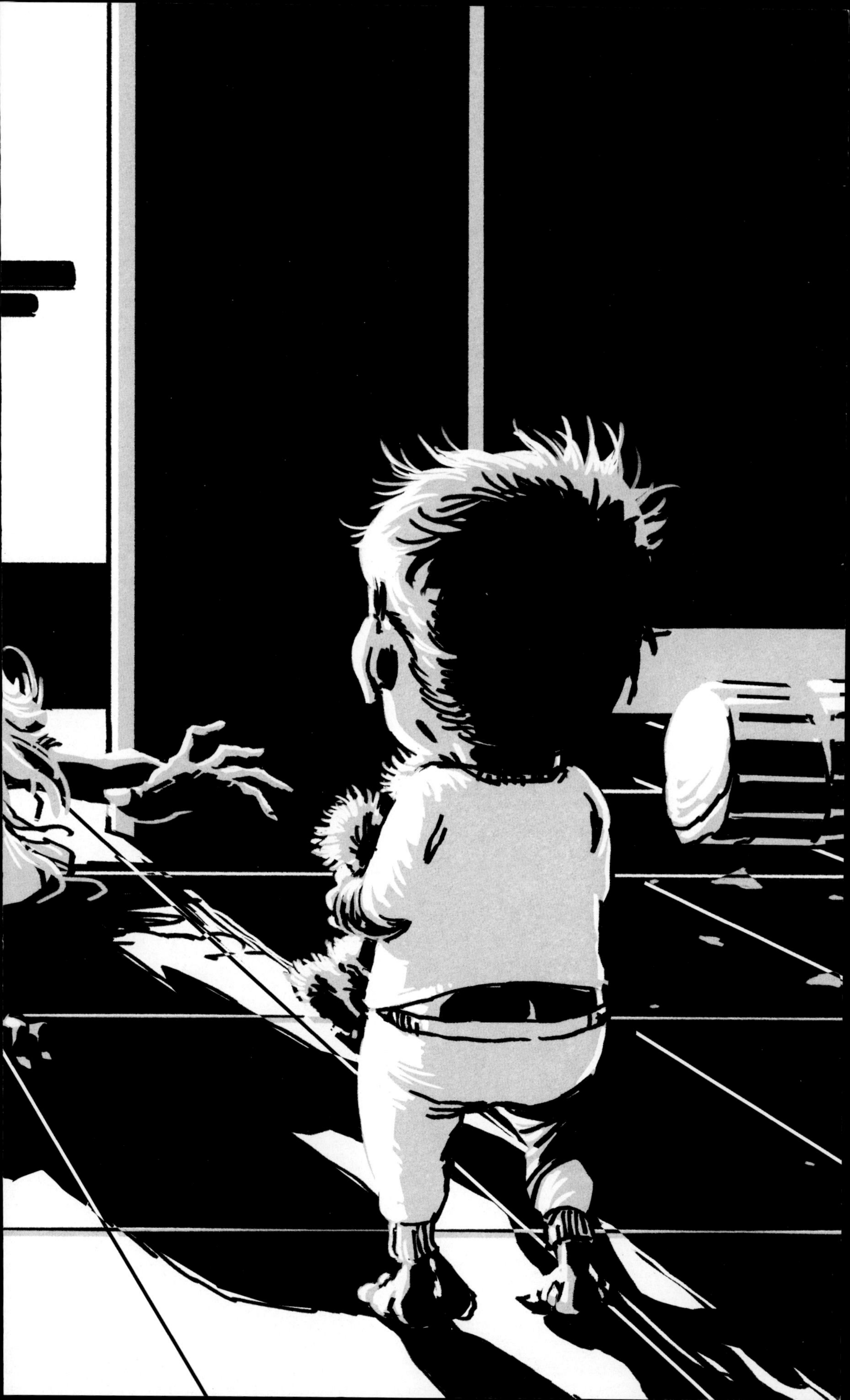

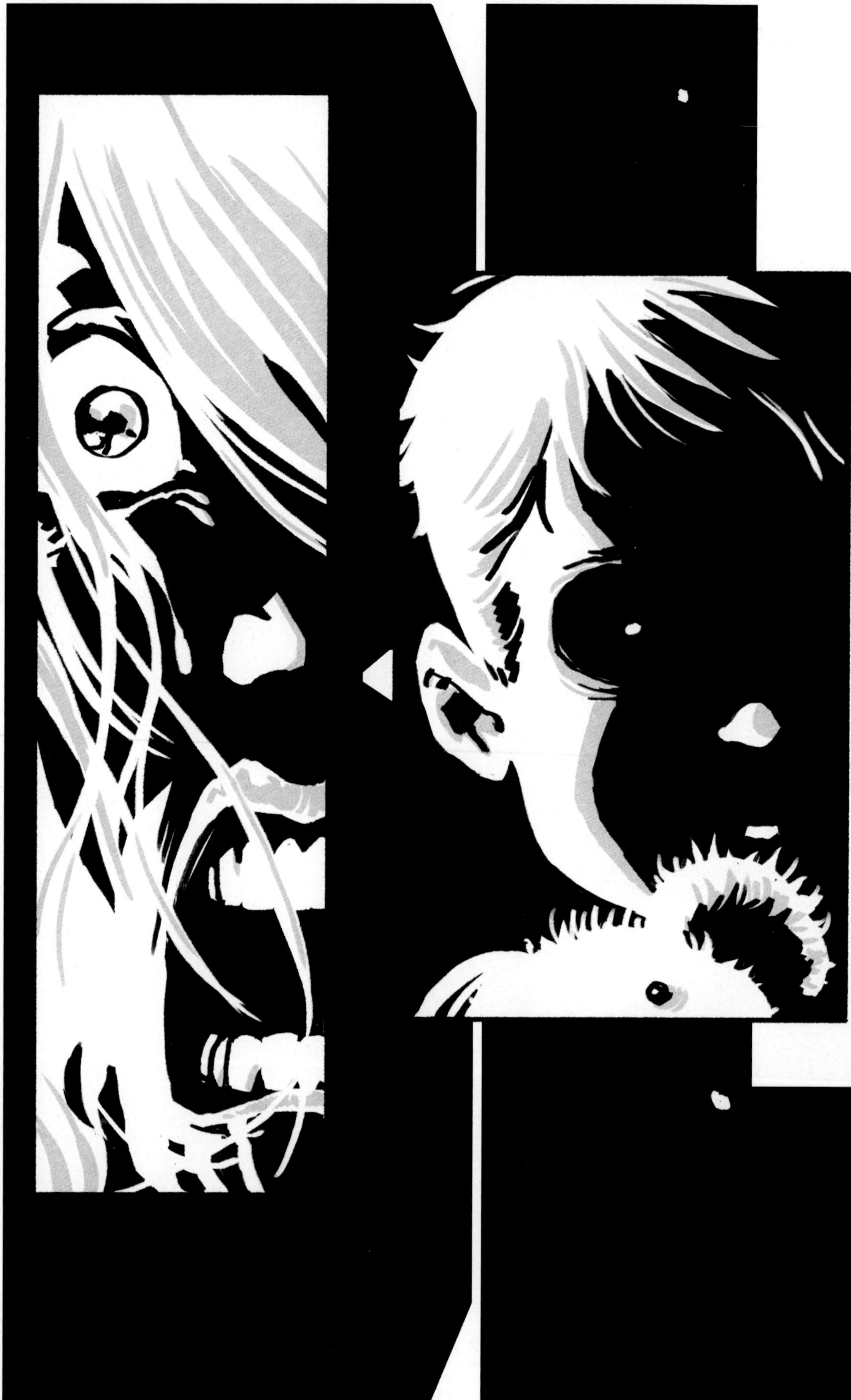

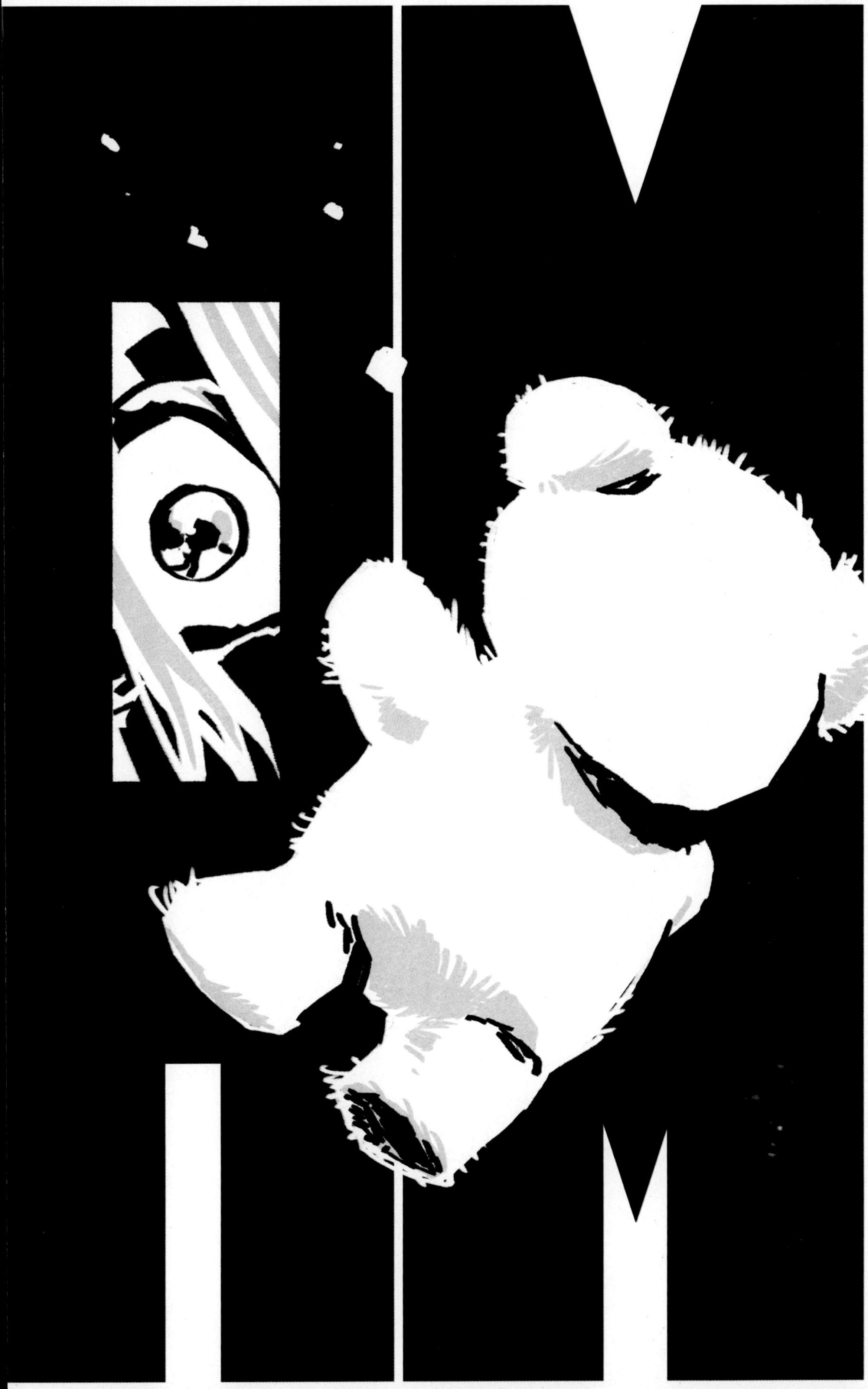

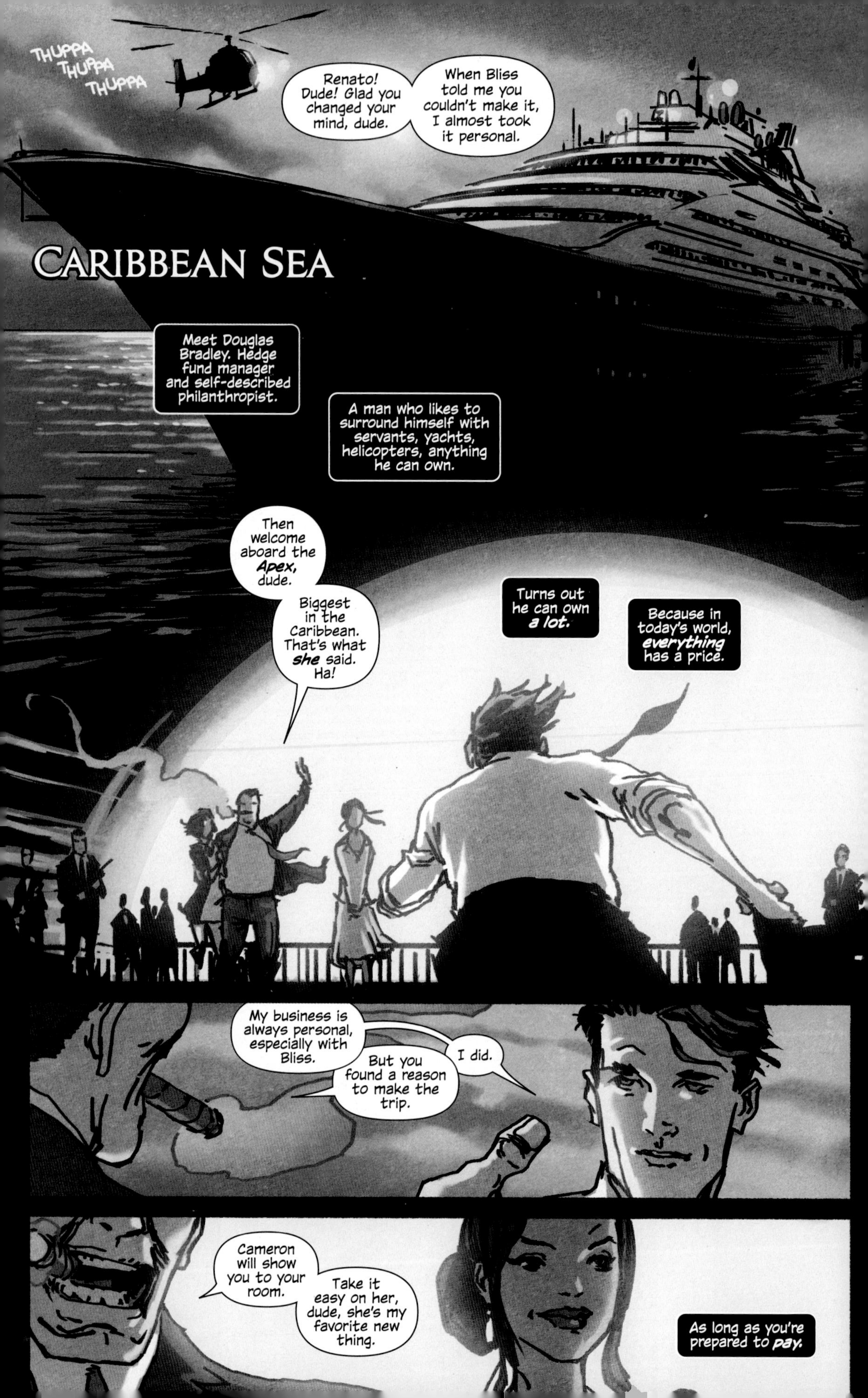
THUPPA THUPPA THUPPA
Renato! Dude! Glad you changed your mind, dude.
When Bliss told me you couldn't make it, I almost took it personal.
CARIBBEAN SEA
Meet Douglas Bradley. Hedge fund manager and self-described philanthropist.
A man who likes to surround himself with servants, yachts, helicopters, anything he can own.
Then welcome aboard the ***Apex,*** dude.
Biggest in the Caribbean. That's what ***she*** said. Ha!
Turns out he can own ***a lot.***
Because in today's world, ***everything*** has a price.
My business is always personal, especially with Bliss.
I did.
But you found a reason to make the trip.
Cameron will show you to your room.
Take it easy on her, dude, she's my favorite new thing.
As long as you're prepared to ***pay.***

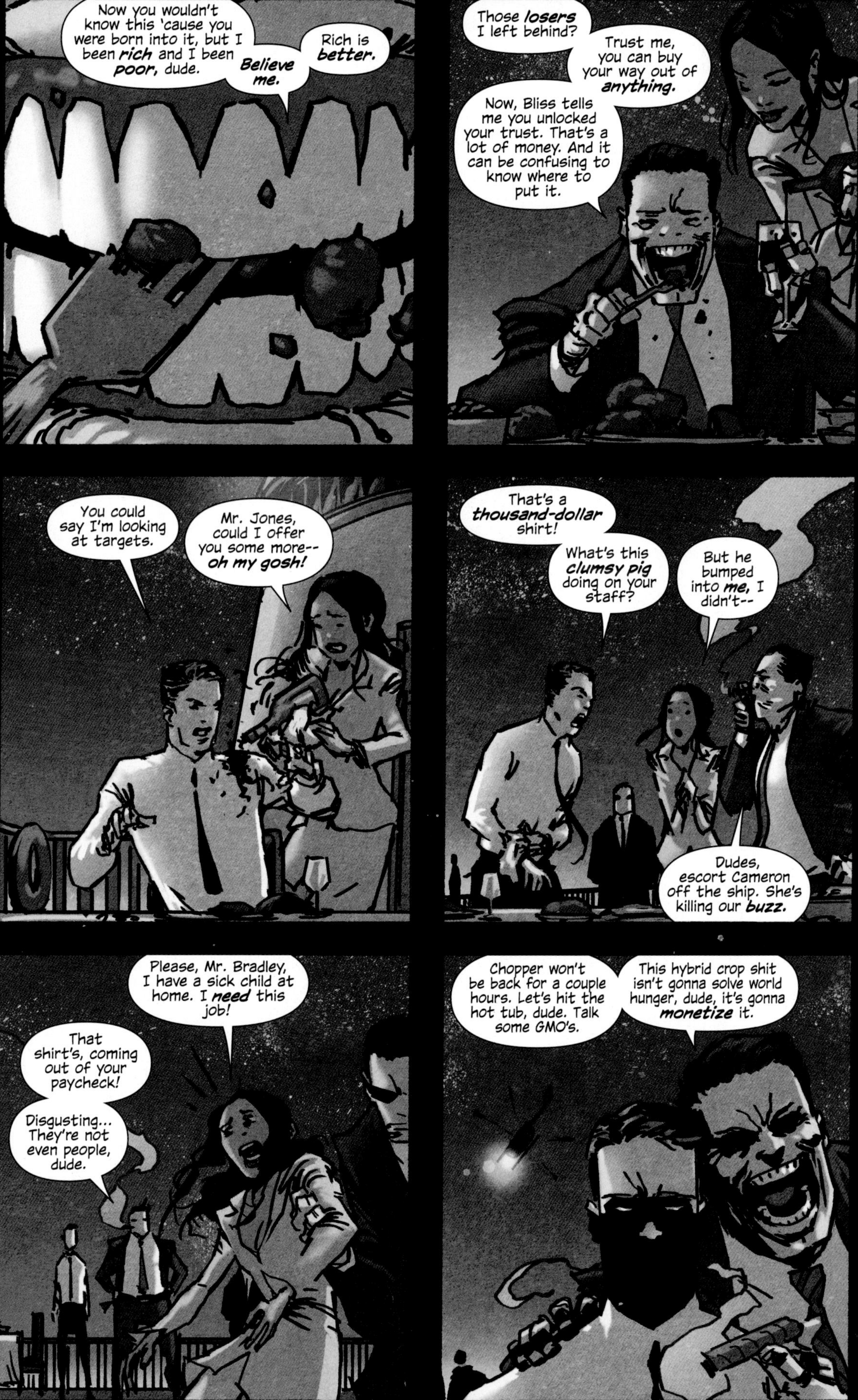

Now you wouldn't know this 'cause you were born into it, but I been rich and I been poor, dude.
Believe me.
Rich is better.
Those losers I left behind?
Trust me, you can buy your way out of anything.
Now, Bliss tells me you unlocked your trust. That's a lot of money. And it can be confusing to know where to put it.
You could say I'm looking at targets.
Mr. Jones, could I offer you some more-- oh my gosh!
That's a thousand-dollar shirt!
What's this clumsy pig doing on your staff?
But he bumped into me, I didn't--
Dudes, escort Cameron off the ship. She's killing our buzz.
Please, Mr. Bradley, I have a sick child at home. I need this job!
That shirt's, coming out of your paycheck!
Disgusting... They're not even people, dude.
Chopper won't be back for a couple hours. Let's hit the hot tub, dude. Talk some GMO's.
This hybrid crop shit isn't gonna solve world hunger, dude, it's gonna monetize it.

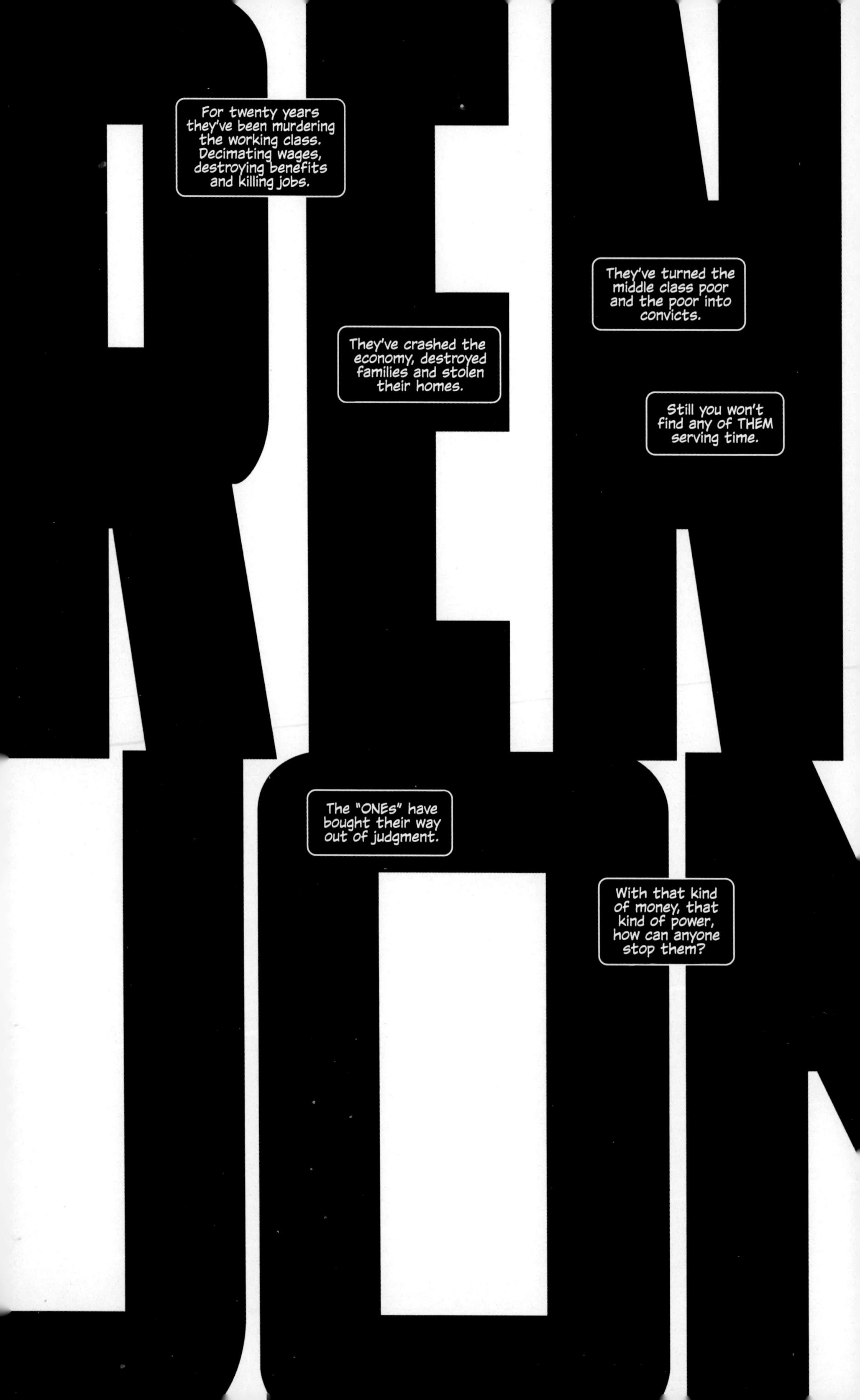
For twenty years they've been murdering the working class. Decimating wages, destroying benefits and killing jobs.
They've crashed the economy, destroyed families and stolen their homes.
They've turned the middle class poor and the poor into convicts.
Still you won't find any of THEM serving time.
The "ONEs" have bought their way out of judgment.
With that kind of money, that kind of power, how can anyone stop them?

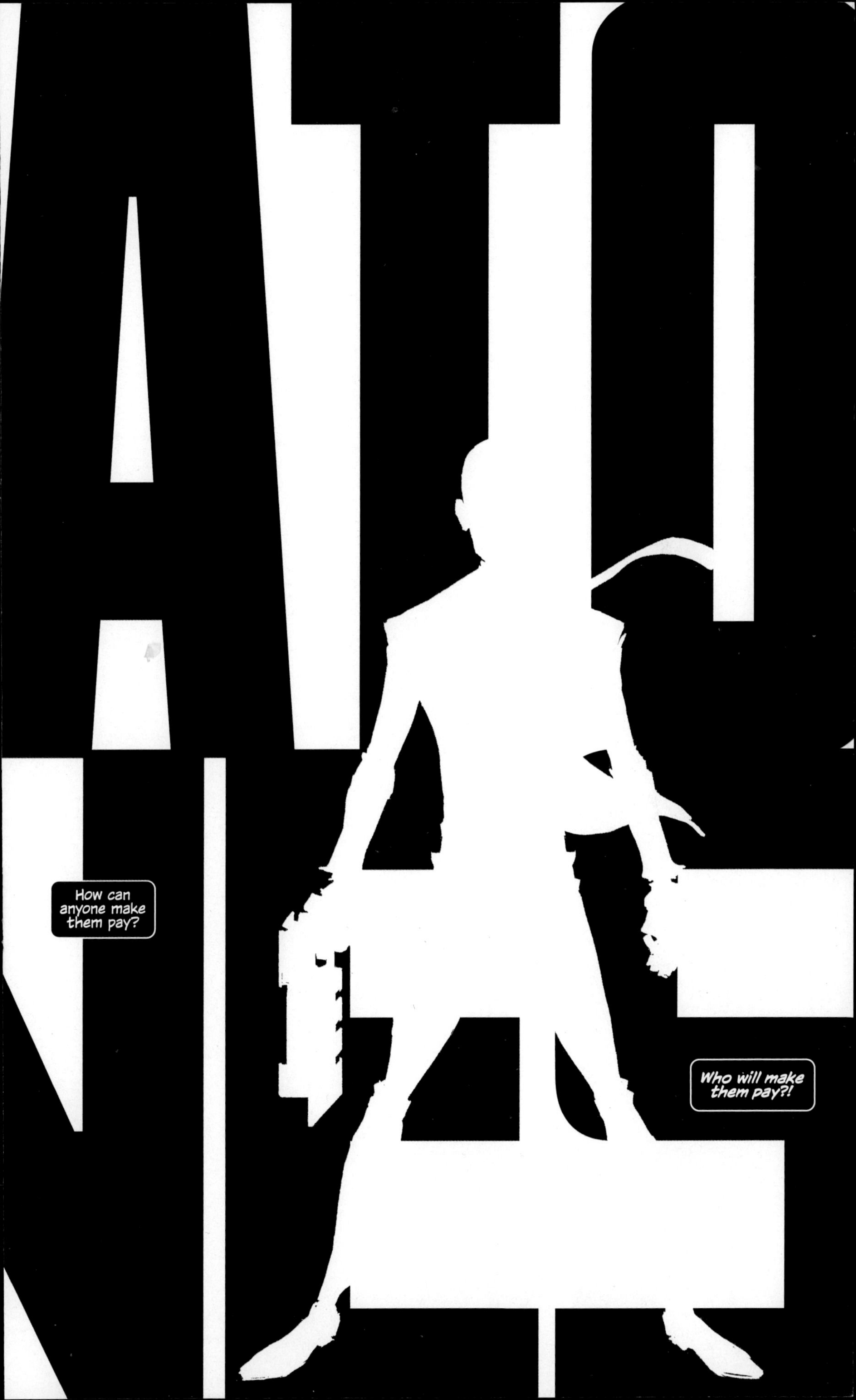
How can anyone make them pay?
Who will make them pay?!

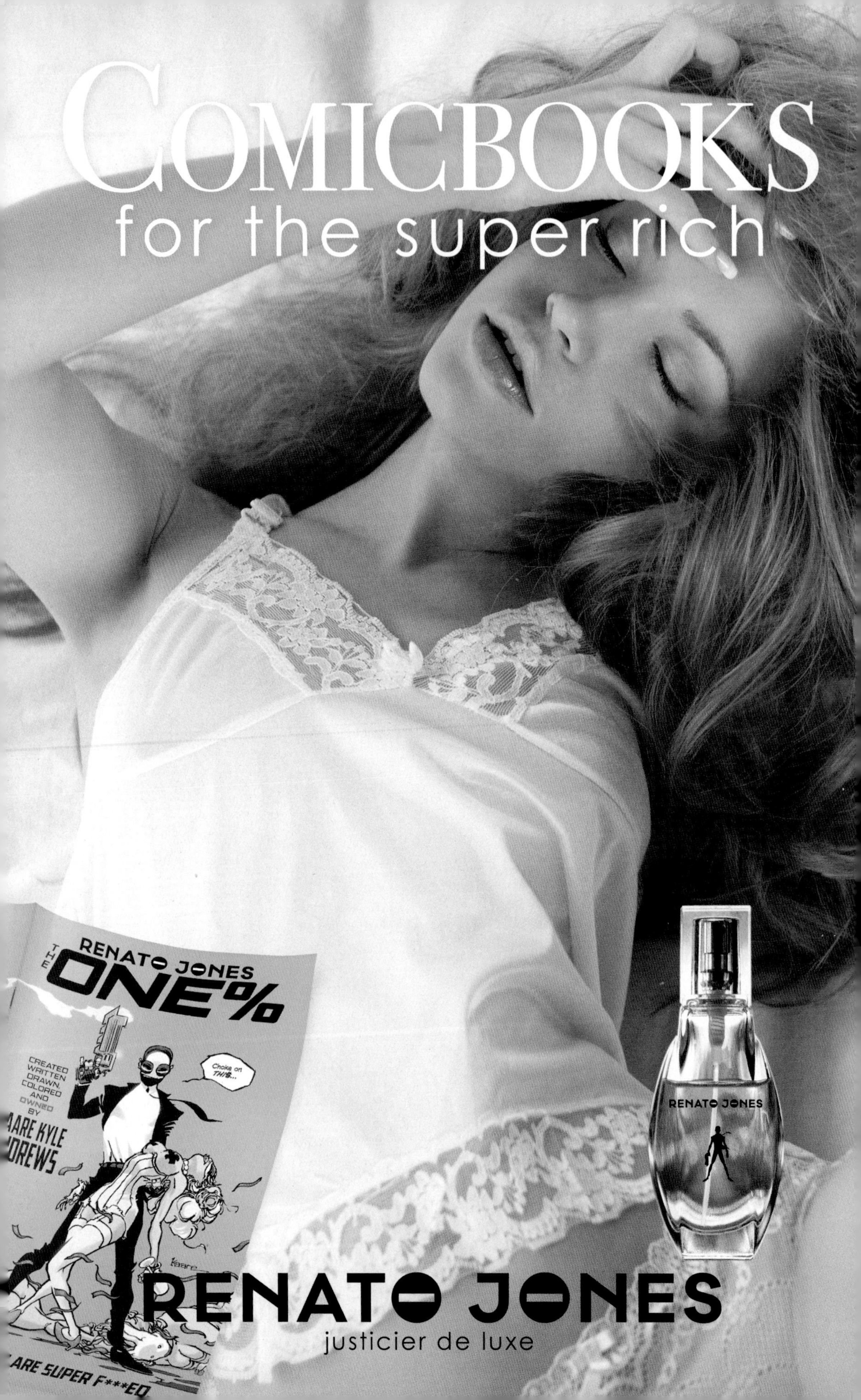

COMICBOOKS
for the super rich
RENATO JONES
THE ONE%
CREATED WRITTEN DRAWN, COLORED AND OWNED BY
Choke on THIS...
ARE SUPER F***ED
RENATO JONES
RENATO JONES
justicier de luxe

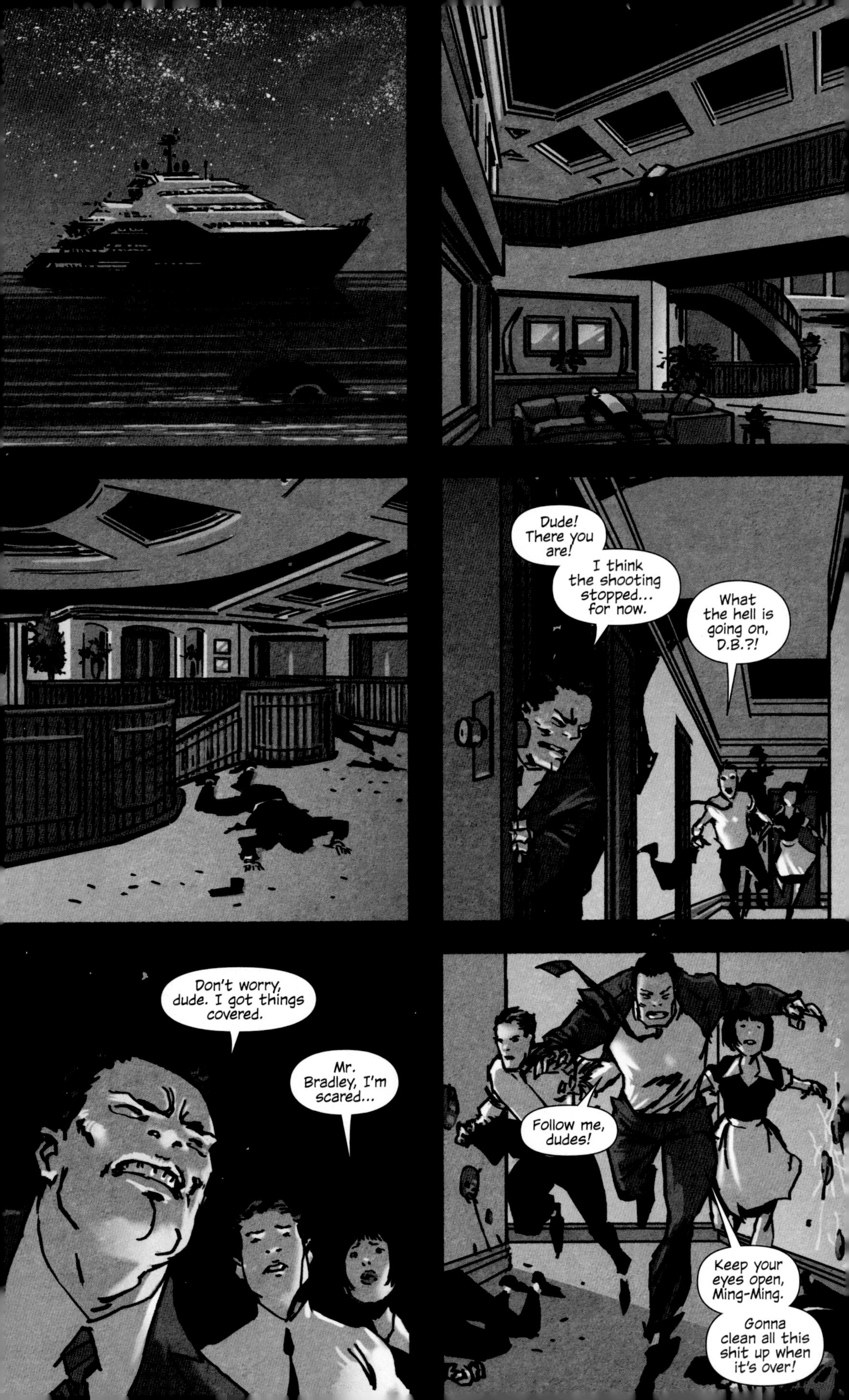
Dude! There you are!
I think the shooting stopped... for now.
What the hell is going on, D.B.?!
Don't worry, dude. I got things covered.
Mr. Bradley, I'm scared...
Follow me, dudes!
Keep your eyes open, Ming-Ming.
Gonna clean all this shit up when it's over!

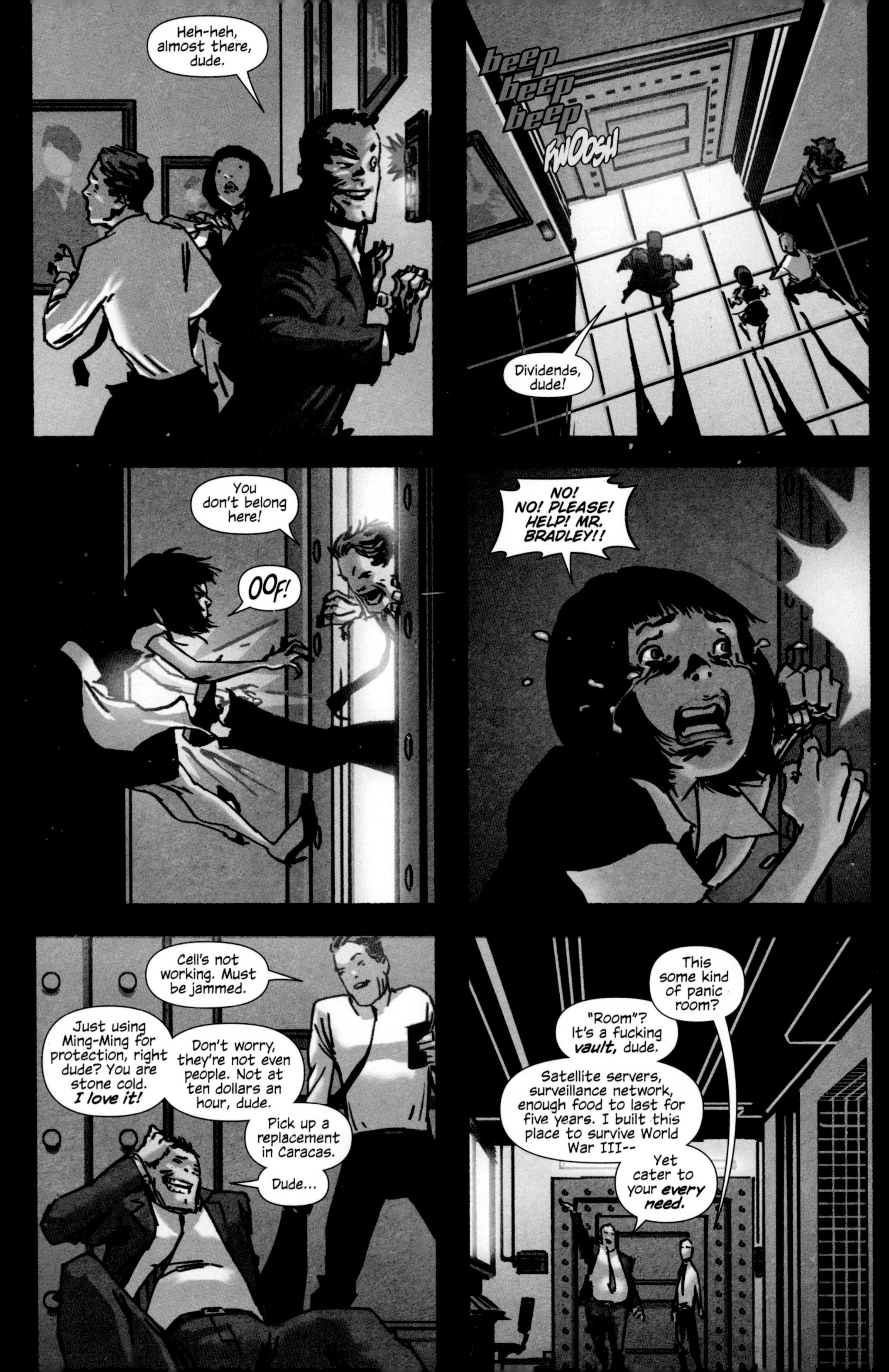

Heh-heh, almost there, dude.
beep beep beep
FWOOSH
Dividends, dude!
You don't belong here!
OOF!
NO! NO! PLEASE! HELP! MR. BRADLEY!!
Cell's not working. Must be jammed.
Just using Ming-Ming for protection, right dude? You are stone cold. I love it!
Don't worry, they're not even people. Not at ten dollars an hour, dude.
Pick up a replacement in Caracas.
Dude...
This some kind of panic room?
"Room"? It's a fucking vault, dude.
Satellite servers, surveillance network, enough food to last for five years. I built this place to survive World War III--
Yet cater to your every need.

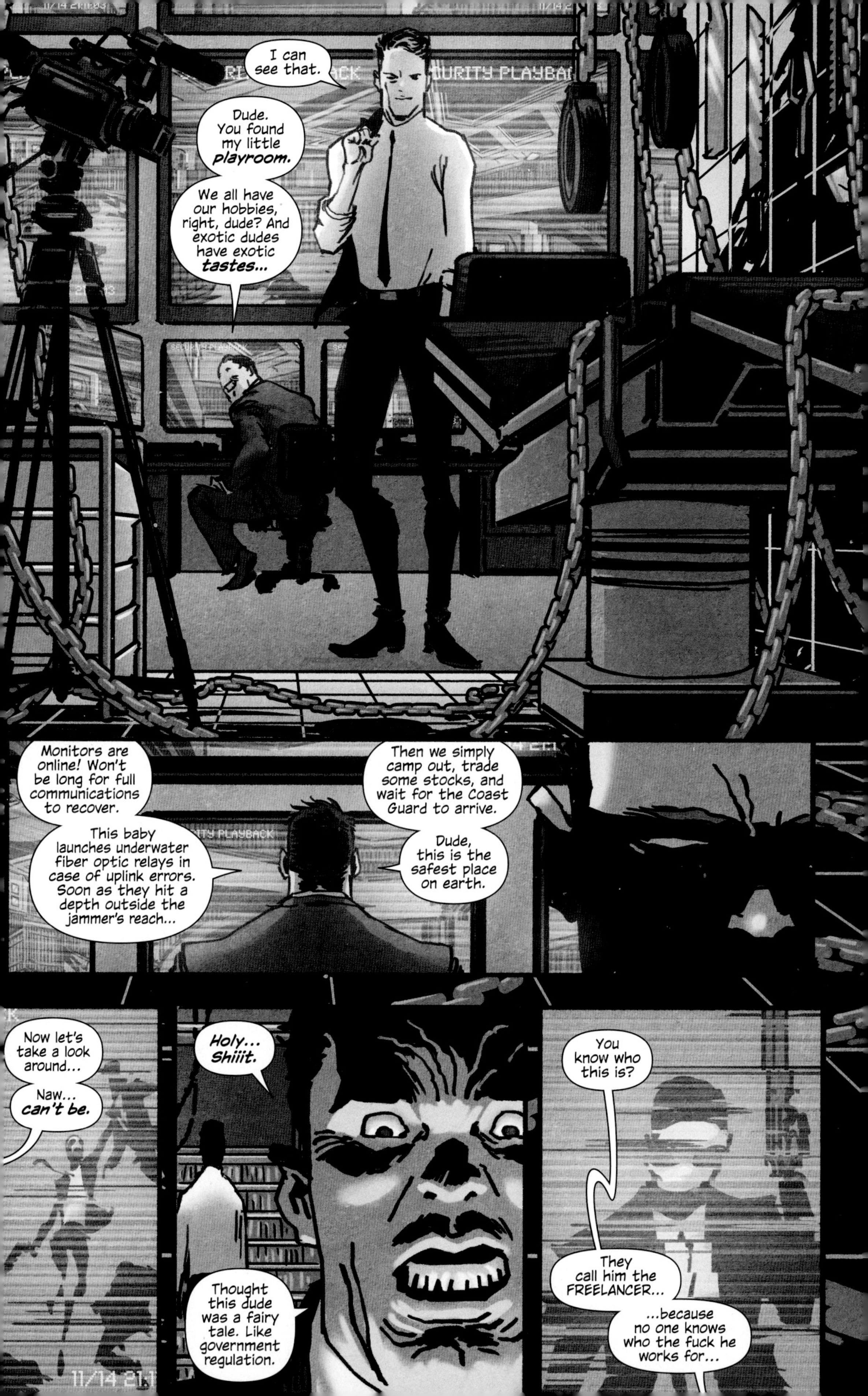
I can see that.
Dude. You found my little *playroom.*
We all have our hobbies, right, dude? And exotic dudes have exotic *tastes...*
SECURITY PLAYBACK
Monitors are online! Won't be long for full communications to recover.
This baby launches underwater fiber optic relays in case of uplink errors. Soon as they hit a depth outside the jammer's reach...
Then we simply camp out, trade some stocks, and wait for the Coast Guard to arrive.
Dude, this is the safest place on earth.
Now let's take a look around...
Naw... *can't be.*
Holy... Shiiit.
Thought this dude was a fairy tale. Like government regulation.
You know who this is?
They call him the FREELANCER...
...because no one knows who the fuck he works for...

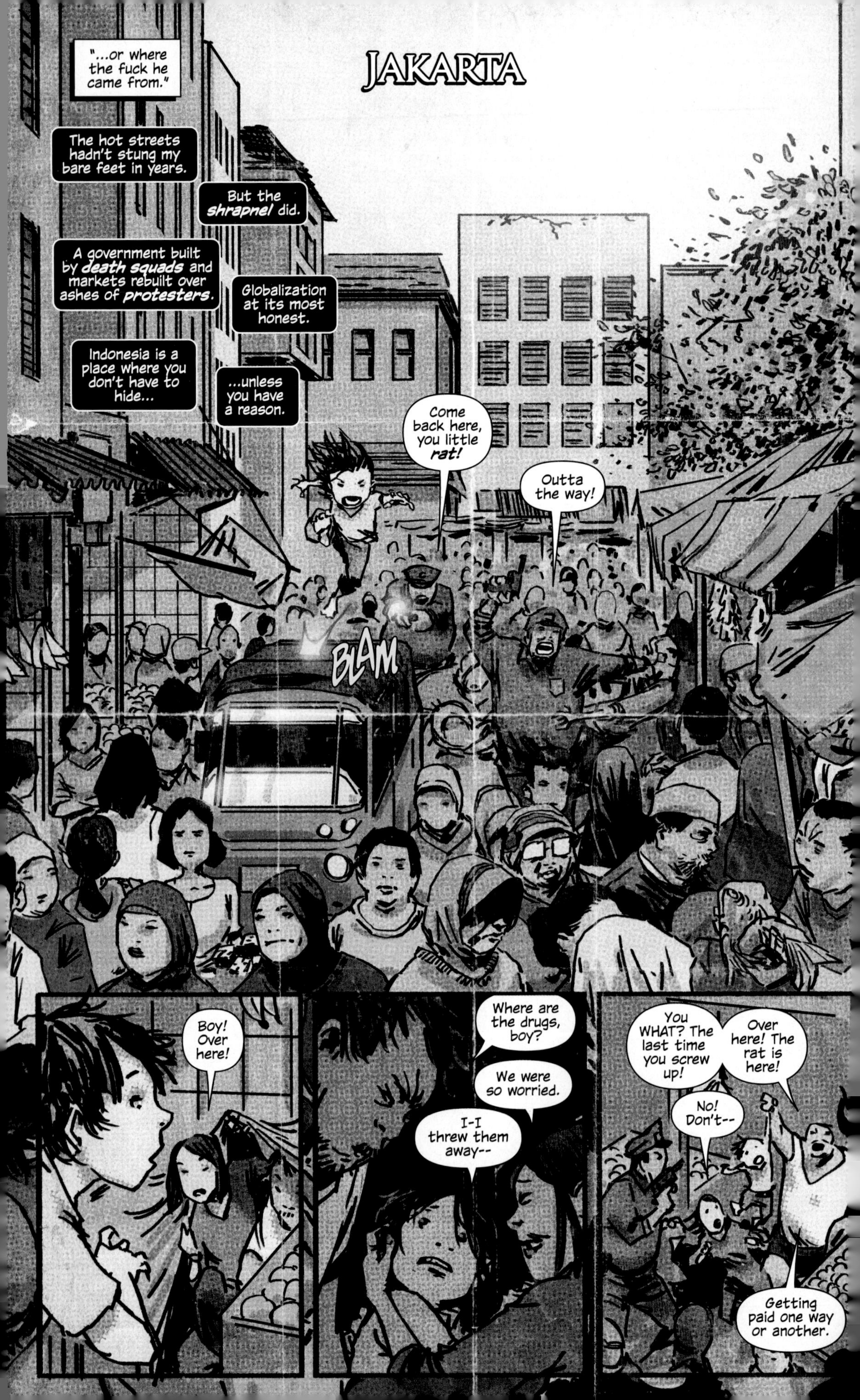

JAKARTA
"...or where the fuck he came from."
The hot streets hadn't stung my bare feet in years.
But the shrapnel did.
A government built by death squads and markets rebuilt over ashes of protesters.
Globalization at its most honest.
Indonesia is a place where you don't have to hide...
...unless you have a reason.
Come back here, you little rat!
Outta the way!
BLAM
Boy! Over here!
Where are the drugs, boy?
We were so worried.
I-I threw them away--
You WHAT? The last time you screw up!
Over here! The rat is here!
No! Don't--
Getting paid one way or another.

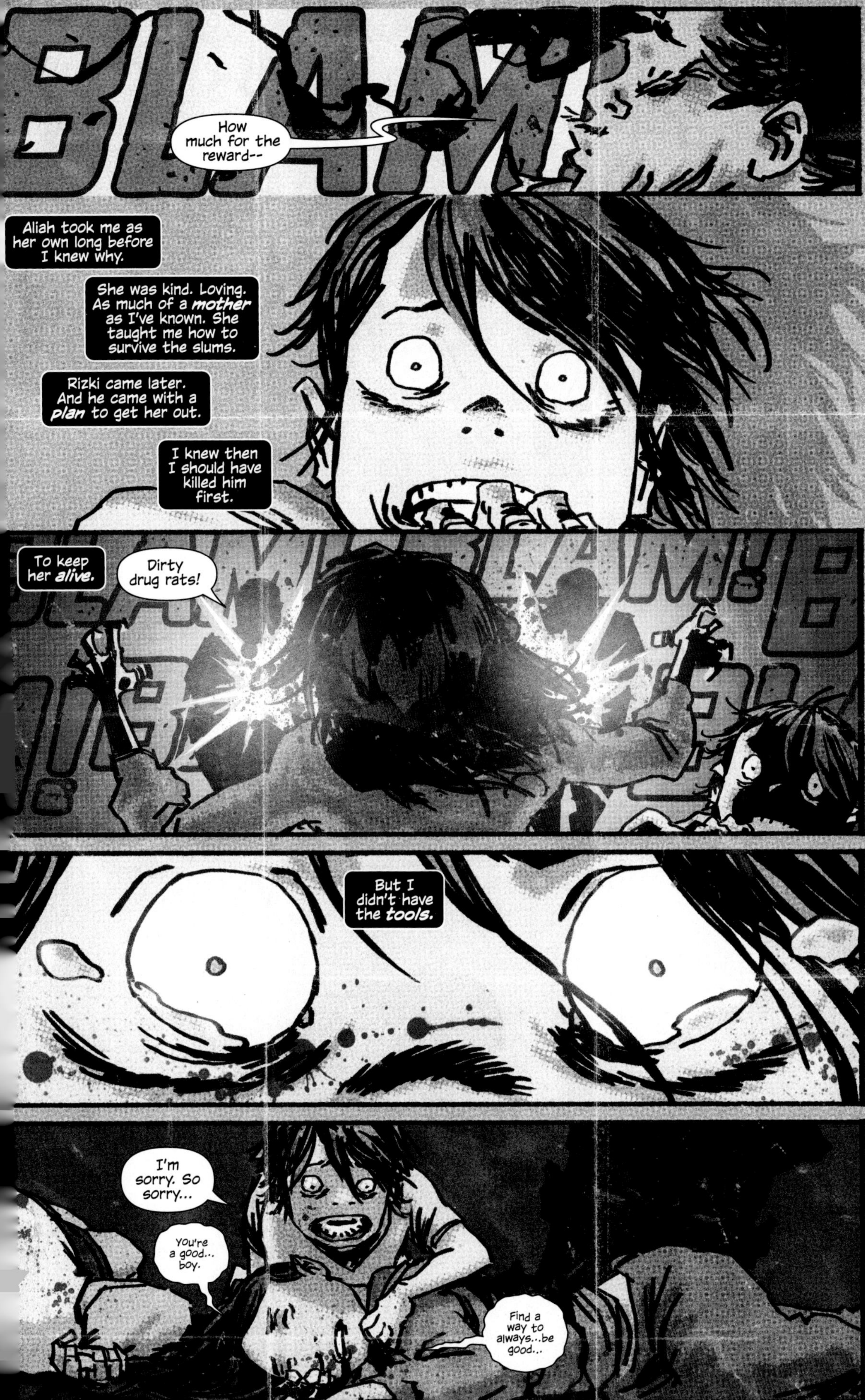
BLAM!
How much for the reward--
Aliah took me as her own long before I knew why.
She was kind. Loving. As much of a *mother* as I've known. She taught me how to survive the slums.
Rizki came later. And he came with a *plan* to get her out.
I knew then I should have killed him first.
To keep her *alive.*
Dirty drug rats!
But I didn't have the *tools.*
I'm sorry. So sorry...
You're a good... boy.
Find a way to always...be good...

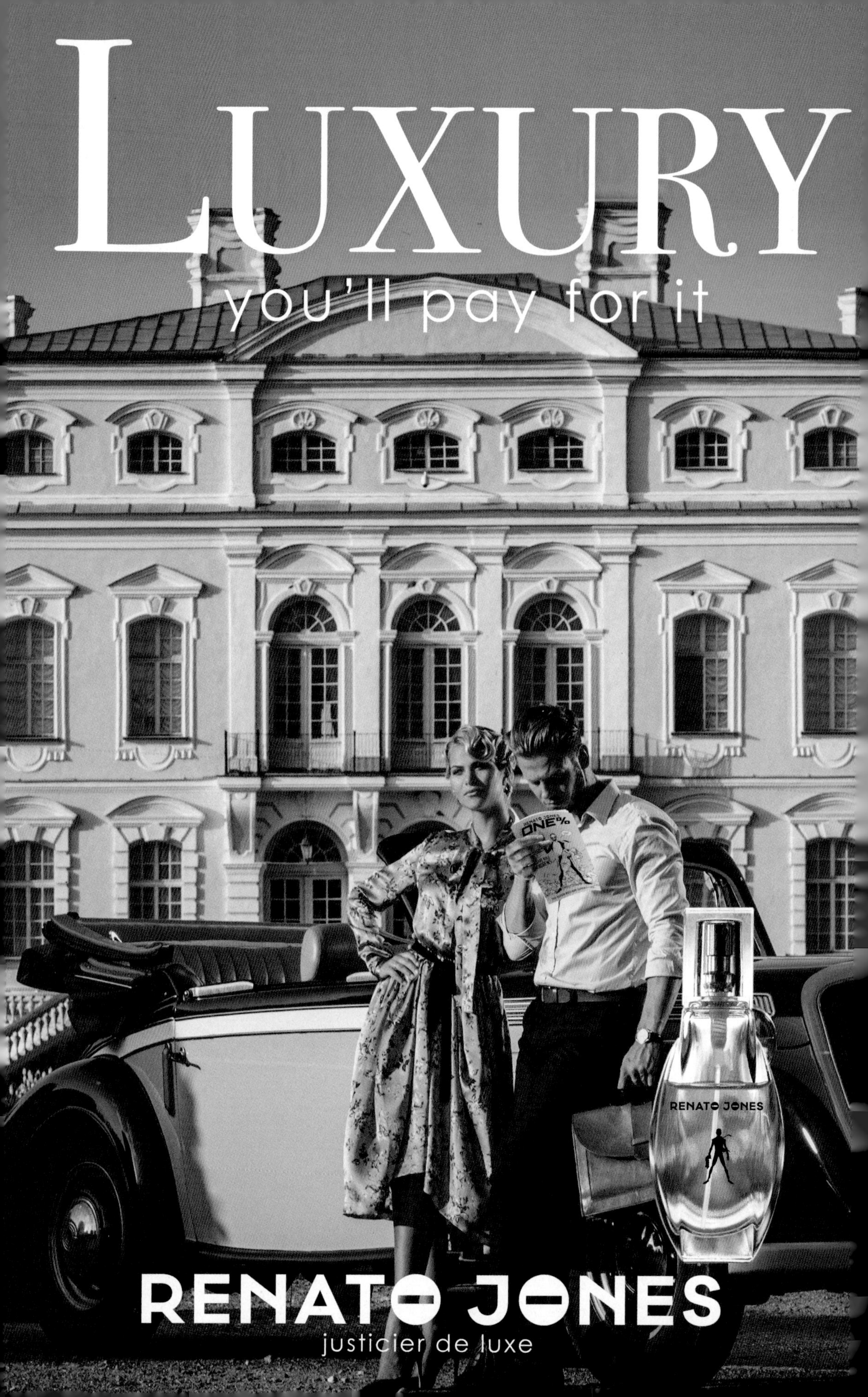
LUXURY
you'll pay for it
RENATO JONES
RENATO JONES
justicier de luxe

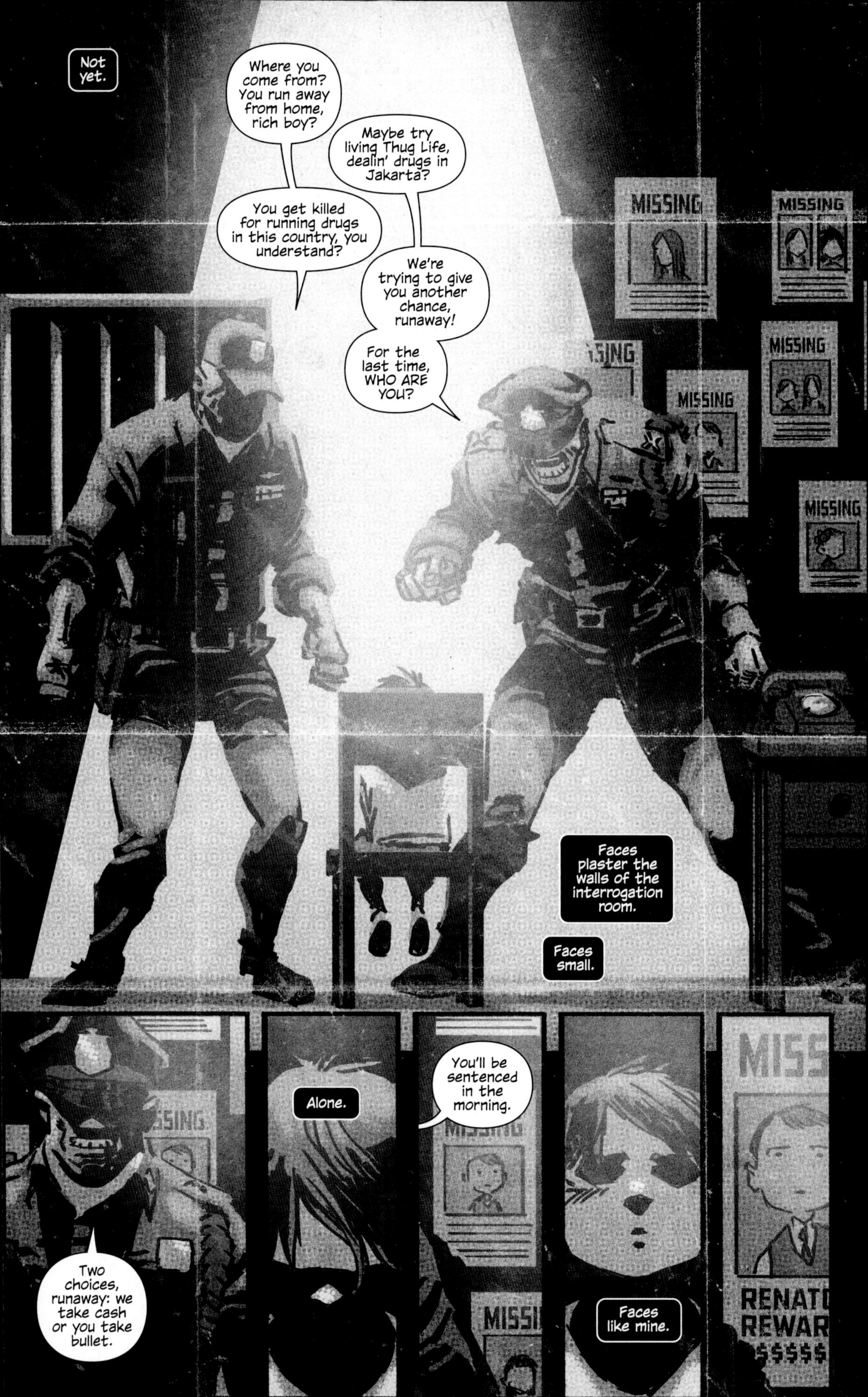
Not yet.
Where you come from? You run away from home, rich boy?
Maybe try living Thug Life, dealin' drugs in Jakarta?
You get killed for running drugs in this country, you understand?
We're trying to give you another chance, runaway!
For the last time, WHO ARE YOU?
MISSING
MISSING
MISSING
MISSING
MISSING
Faces plaster the walls of the interrogation room.
Faces small.
Two choices, runaway: we take cash or you take bullet.
Alone.
You'll be sentenced in the morning.
Faces like mine.
RENATO
REWAR
$$$$$

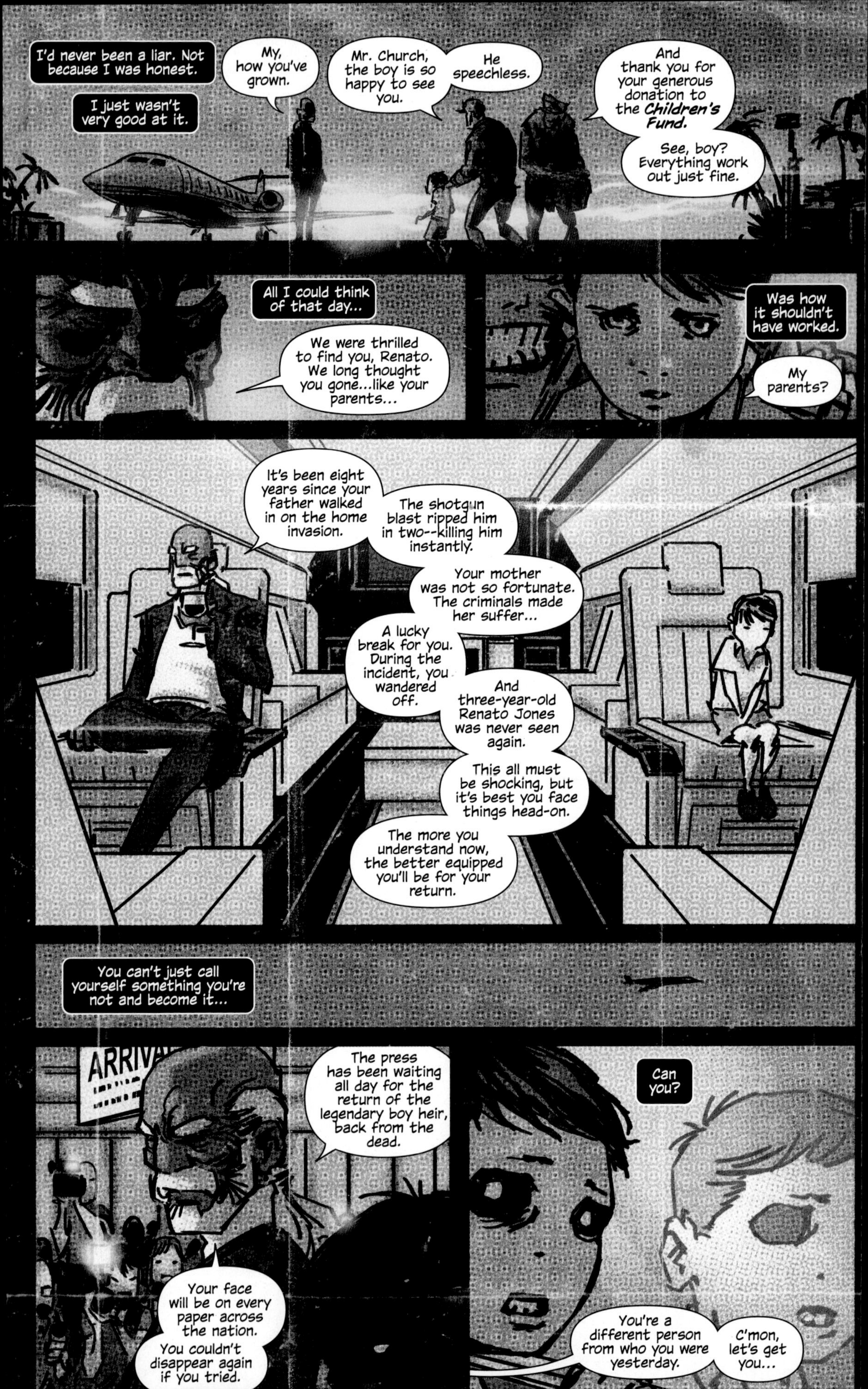
I'd never been a liar. Not because I was honest.
I just wasn't very good at it.
My, how you've grown.
Mr. Church, the boy is so happy to see you.
He speechless.
And thank you for your generous donation to the Children's Fund.
See, boy? Everything work out just fine.
All I could think of that day...
We were thrilled to find you, Renato. We long thought you gone...like your parents...
Was how it shouldn't have worked.
My parents?
It's been eight years since your father walked in on the home invasion.
The shotgun blast ripped him in two--killing him instantly.
Your mother was not so fortunate. The criminals made her suffer...
A lucky break for you. During the incident, you wandered off.
And three-year-old Renato Jones was never seen again.
This all must be shocking, but it's best you face things head-on.
The more you understand now, the better equipped you'll be for your return.
You can't just call yourself something you're not and become it...
ARRIVA
The press has been waiting all day for the return of the legendary boy heir, back from the dead.
Your face will be on every paper across the nation.
You couldn't disappear again if you tried.
Can you?
You're a different person from who you were yesterday.
C'mon, let's get you...

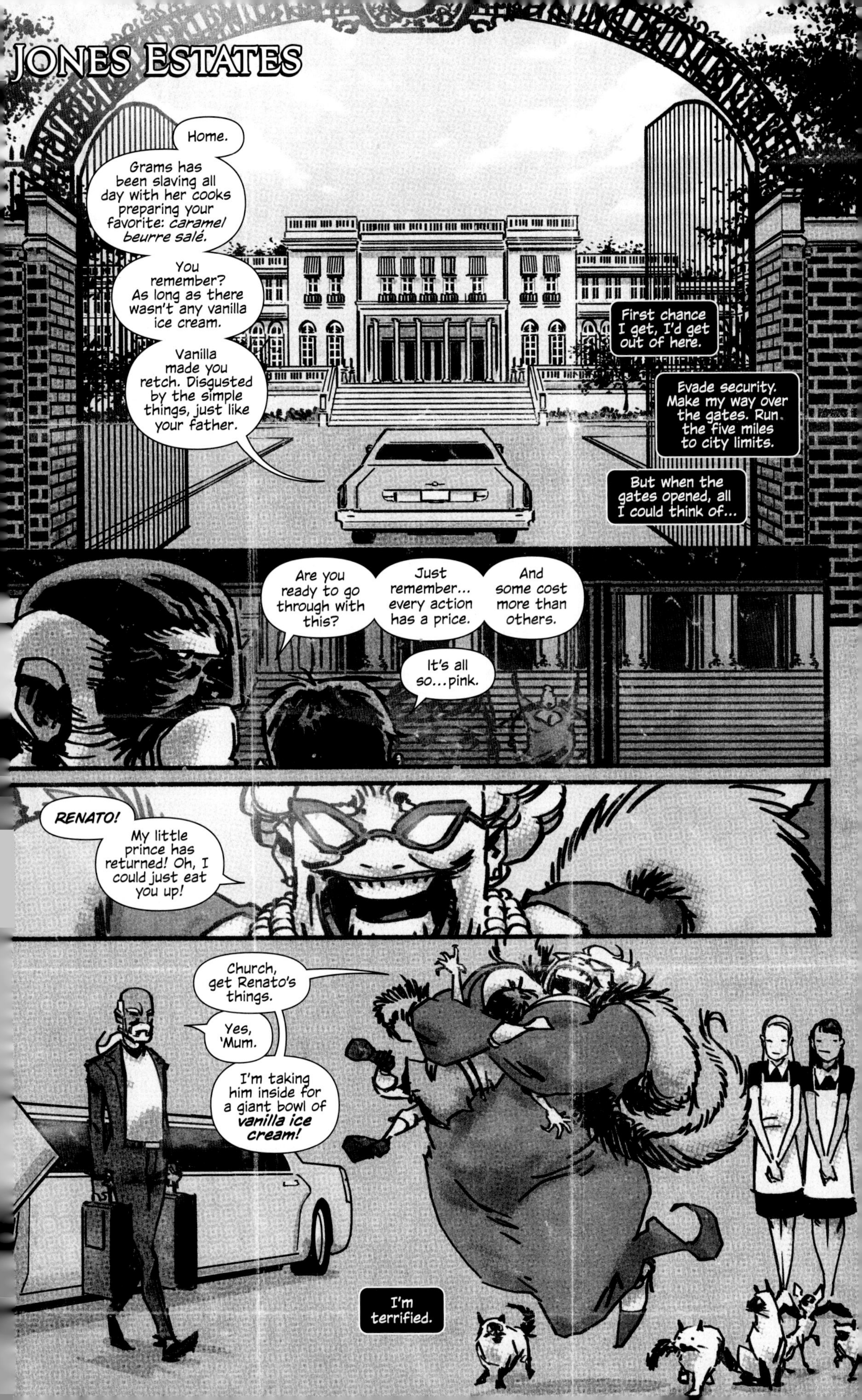
JONES ESTATES
Home.
Grams has been slaving all day with her cooks preparing your favorite: *caramel beurre salé.*
You remember? As long as there wasn't any vanilla ice cream.
Vanilla made you retch. Disgusted by the simple things, just like your father.
First chance I get, I'd get out of here.
Evade security. Make my way over the gates. Run the five miles to city limits.
But when the gates opened, all I could think of...
Are you ready to go through with this?
Just remember... every action has a price.
And some cost more than others.
It's all so...pink.
RENATO!
My little prince has returned! Oh, I could just eat you up!
Church, get Renato's things.
Yes, 'Mum.
I'm taking him inside for a giant bowl of ***vanilla ice cream!***
I'm terrified.

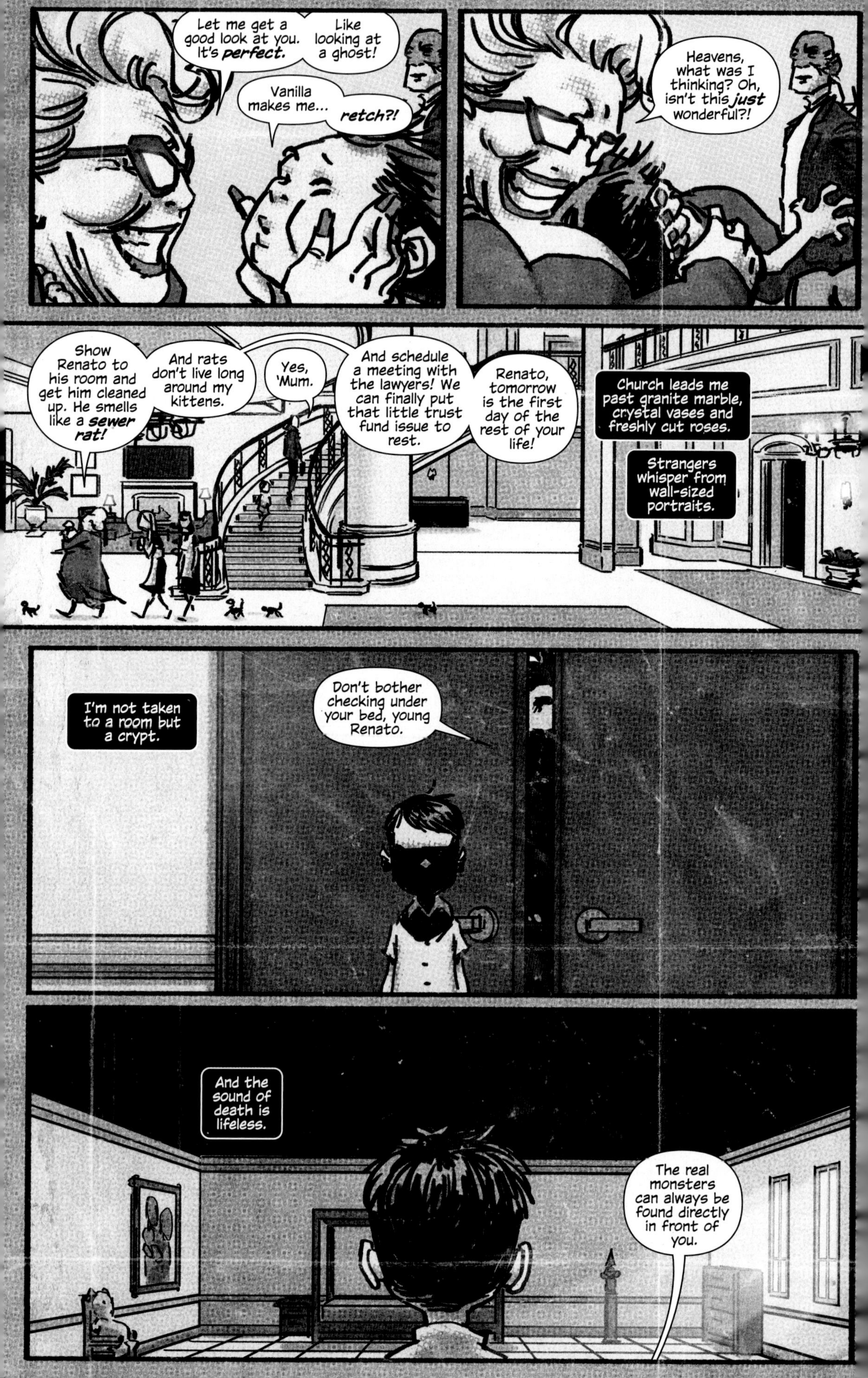

Let me get a good look at you. It's *perfect.*
Like looking at a ghost!
Vanilla makes me... *retch?!*
Heavens, what was I thinking? Oh, isn't this *just* wonderful?!
Show Renato to his room and get him cleaned up. He smells like a *sewer rat!*
And rats don't live long around my kittens.
Yes, 'Mum.
And schedule a meeting with the lawyers! We can finally put that little trust fund issue to rest.
Renato, tomorrow is the first day of the rest of your life!
Church leads me past granite marble, crystal vases and freshly cut roses.
Strangers whisper from wall-sized portraits.
I'm not taken to a room but a crypt.
Don't bother checking under your bed, young Renato.
And the sound of death is lifeless.
The real monsters can always be found directly in front of you.

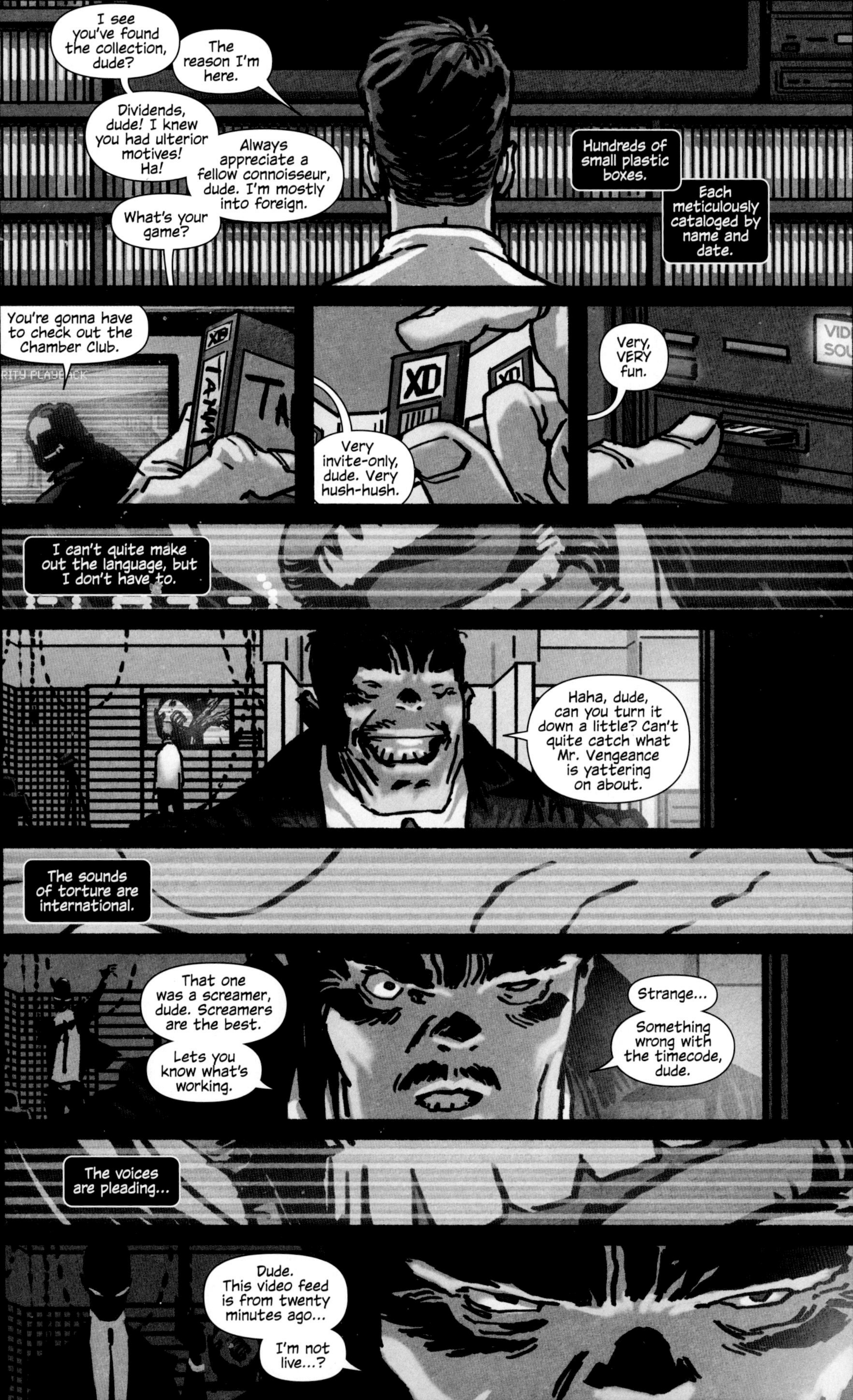
I see you've found the collection, dude?
The reason I'm here.
Dividends, dude! I knew you had ulterior motives! Ha!
Always appreciate a fellow connoisseur, dude. I'm mostly into foreign.
What's your game?
Hundreds of small plastic boxes.
Each meticulously cataloged by name and date.
You're gonna have to check out the Chamber Club.
Very invite-only, dude. Very hush-hush.
Very, VERY fun.
I can't quite make out the language, but I don't have to.
Haha, dude, can you turn it down a little? Can't quite catch what Mr. Vengeance is yattering on about.
The sounds of torture are international.
That one was a screamer, dude. Screamers are the best.
Lets you know what's working.
Strange...
Something wrong with the timecode, dude.
The voices are pleading...
Dude. This video feed is from twenty minutes ago...
I'm not live...?

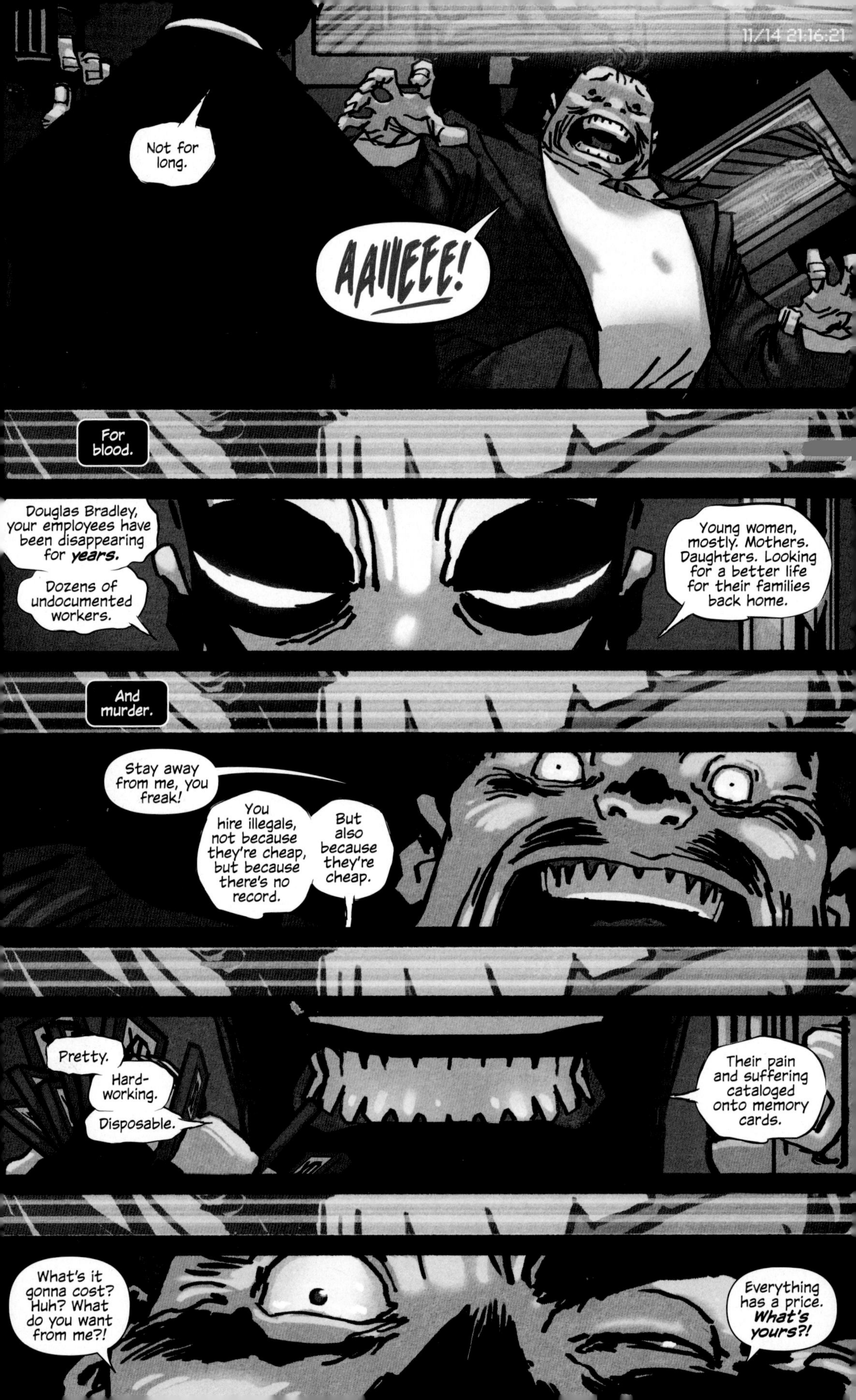
11/14 21:16:21
Not for long.
AAIIEEE!
For blood.
Douglas Bradley, your employees have been disappearing for **years.**
Dozens of undocumented workers.
Young women, mostly. Mothers. Daughters. Looking for a better life for their families back home.
And murder.
Stay away from me, you freak!
You hire illegals, not because they're cheap, but because there's no record.
But also because they're cheap.
Pretty.
Hard-working.
Disposable.
Their pain and suffering cataloged onto memory cards.
What's it gonna cost? Huh? What do you want from me?!
Everything has a price. ***What's yours?!***

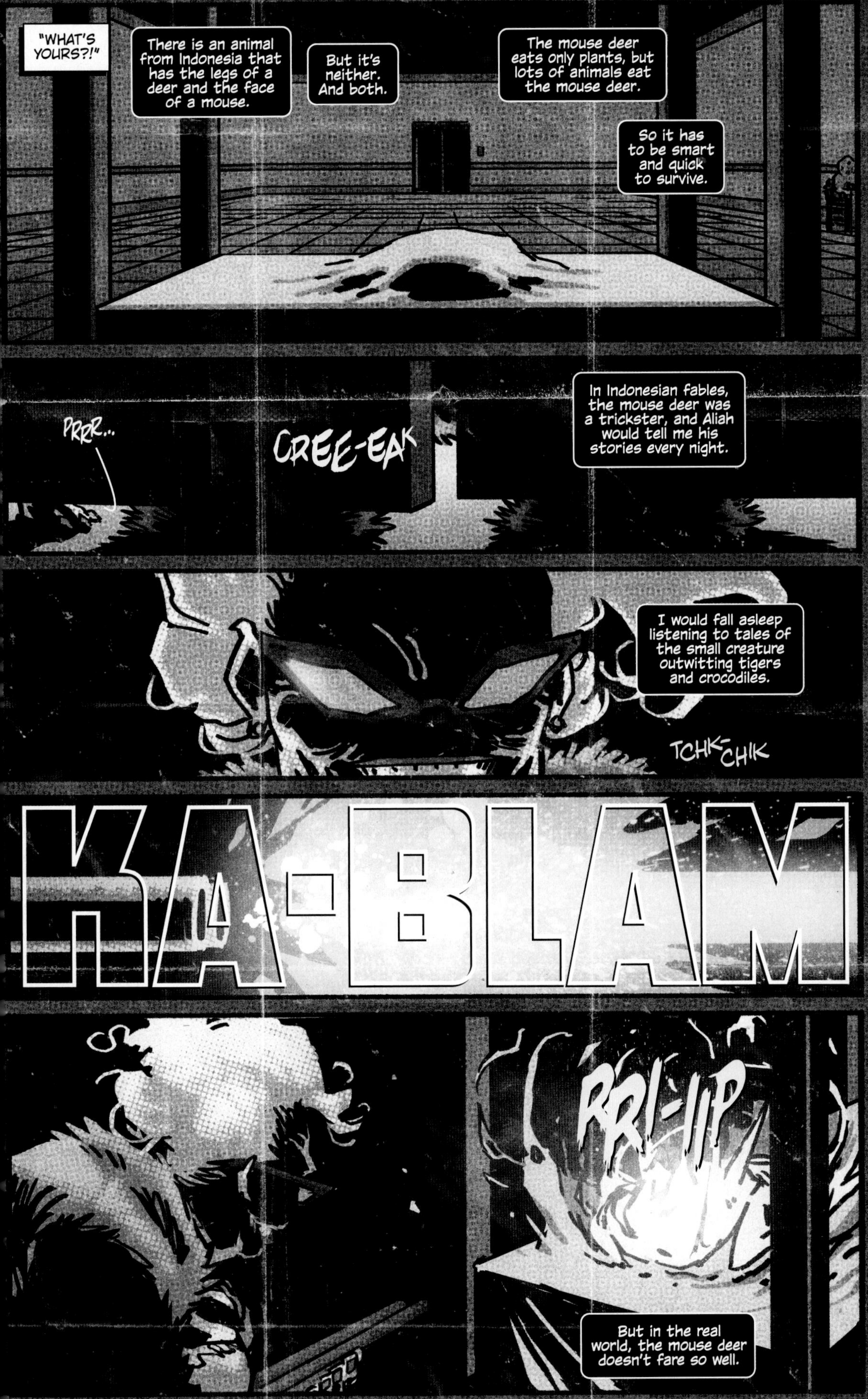
"WHAT'S YOURS?!"
There is an animal from Indonesia that has the legs of a deer and the face of a mouse.
But it's neither. And both.
The mouse deer eats only plants, but lots of animals eat the mouse deer.
So it has to be smart and quick to survive.
PRRR...
CREE-EAK
In Indonesian fables, the mouse deer was a trickster, and Aliah would tell me his stories every night.
I would fall asleep listening to tales of the small creature outwitting tigers and crocodiles.
TCHK-CHIK
KA-BLAM
RRI-IIP
But in the real world, the mouse deer doesn't fare so well.

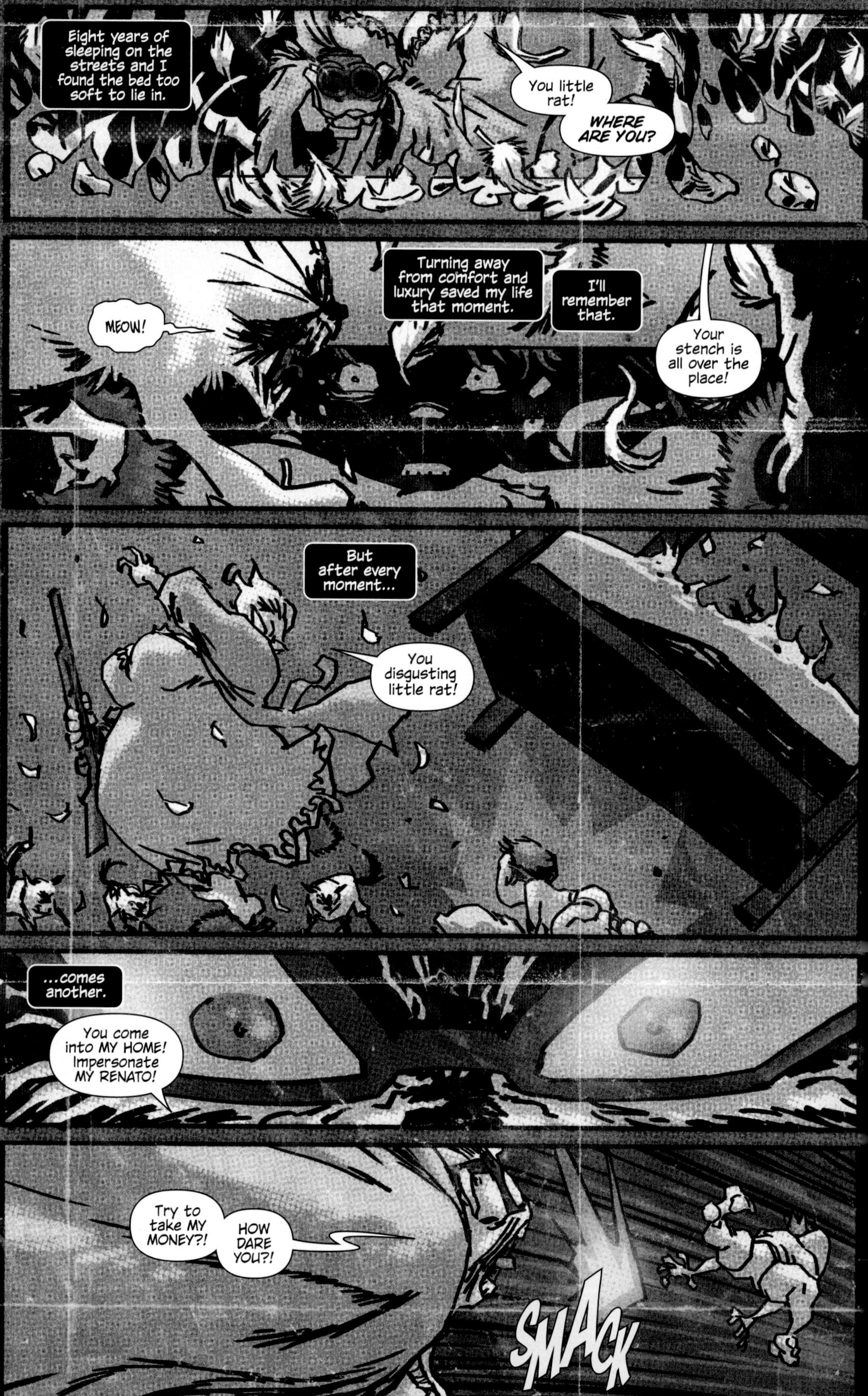
Eight years of sleeping on the streets and I found the bed too soft to lie in.
You little rat!
WHERE ARE YOU?
Turning away from comfort and luxury saved my life that moment.
I'll remember that.
MEOW!
Your stench is all over the place!
But after every moment...
You disgusting little rat!
...comes another.
You come into MY HOME! Impersonate MY RENATO!
Try to take MY MONEY?!
HOW DARE YOU?!
SMACK

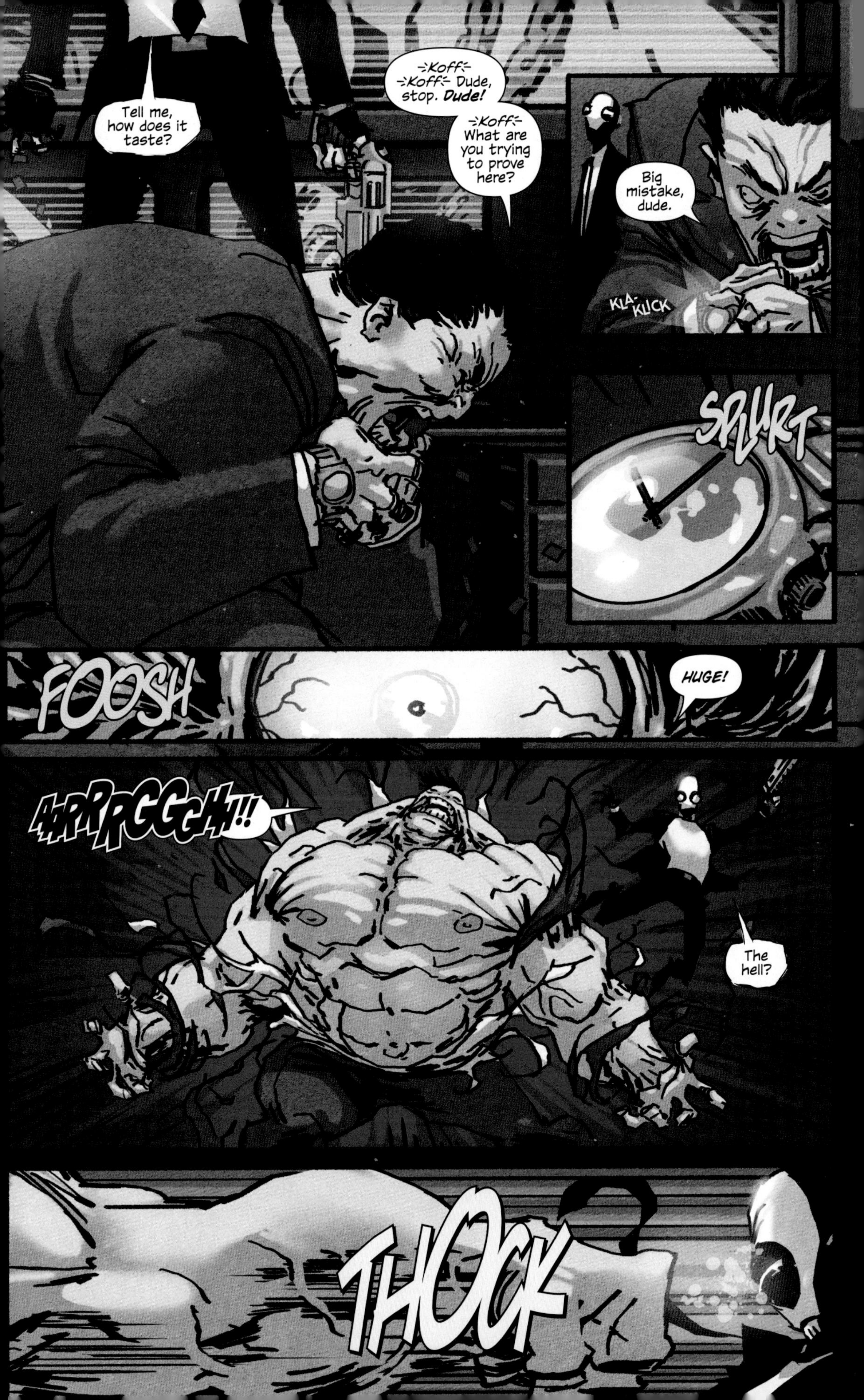
Tell me, how does it taste?
-Koff- -Koff- Dude, stop. Dude!
-Koff- What are you trying to prove here?
Big mistake, dude.
KLA-KLICK
SPLURT
FOOSH
HUGE!
AARRRGGGHH!!
The hell?
THOCK

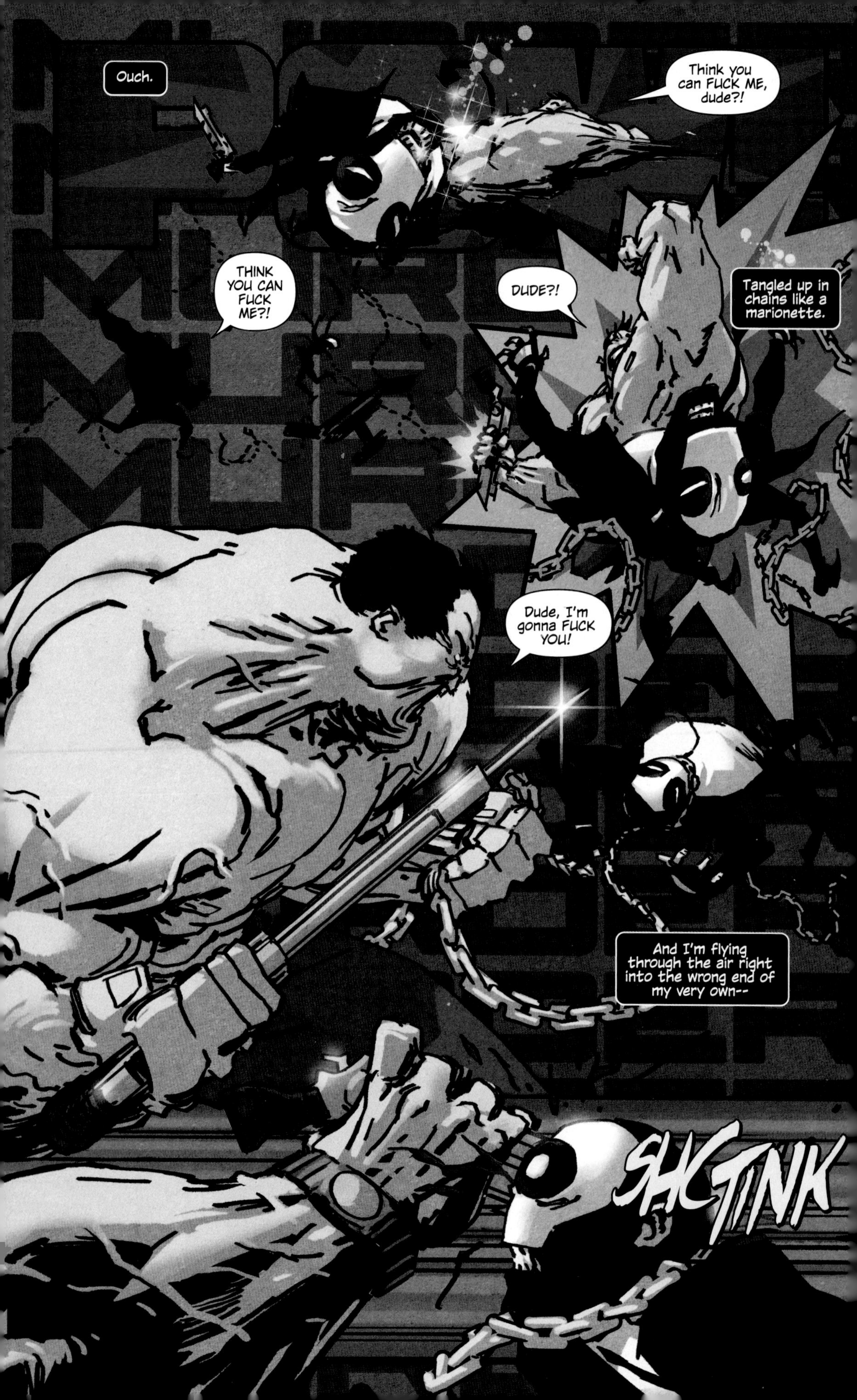
Ouch.
Think you can FUCK ME, dude?!
THINK YOU CAN FUCK ME?!
DUDE?!
Tangled up in chains like a marionette.
Dude, I'm gonna FUCK YOU!
And I'm flying through the air right into the wrong end of my very own--
SHCTINK

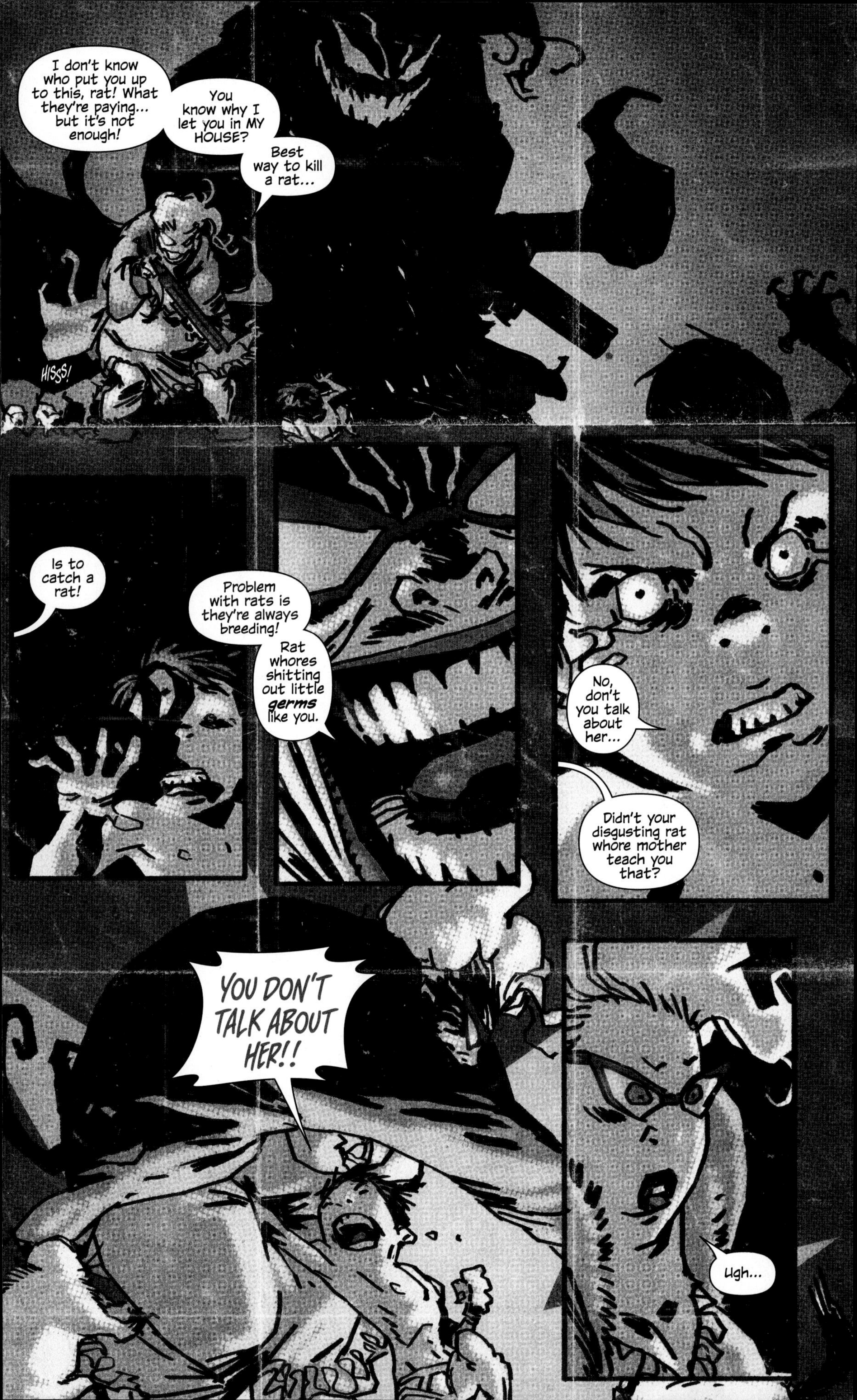
I don't know who put you up to this, rat! What they're paying... but it's not enough!
You know why I let you in MY HOUSE?
Best way to kill a rat...
HISSS!
Is to catch a rat!
Problem with rats is they're always breeding!
Rat whores shitting out little germs like you.
No, don't you talk about her...
Didn't your disgusting rat whore mother teach you that?
YOU DON'T TALK ABOUT HER!!
Ugh...

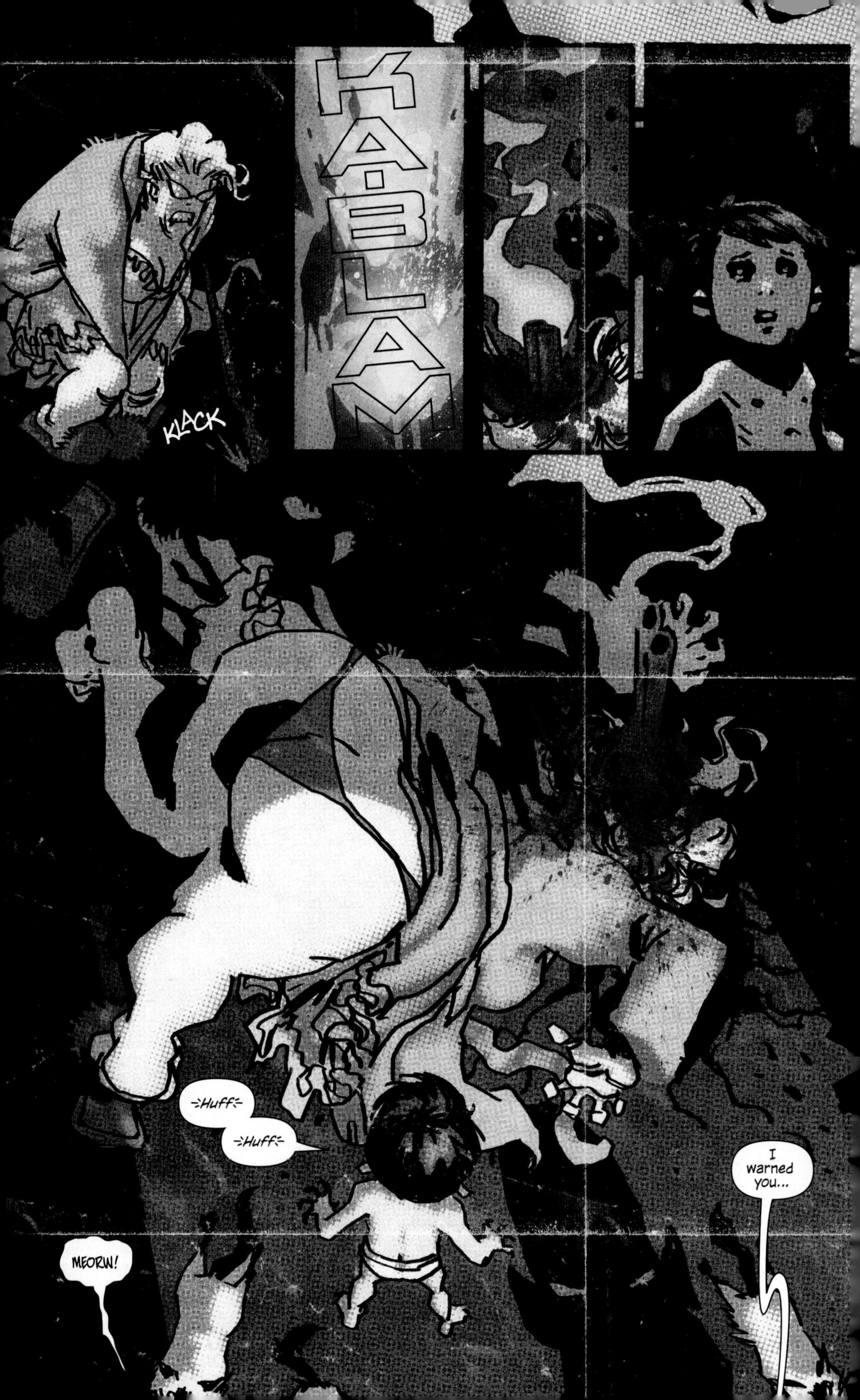
KLACK
KABLAM
-Huff-
-Huff-
I warned you...
MEORW!

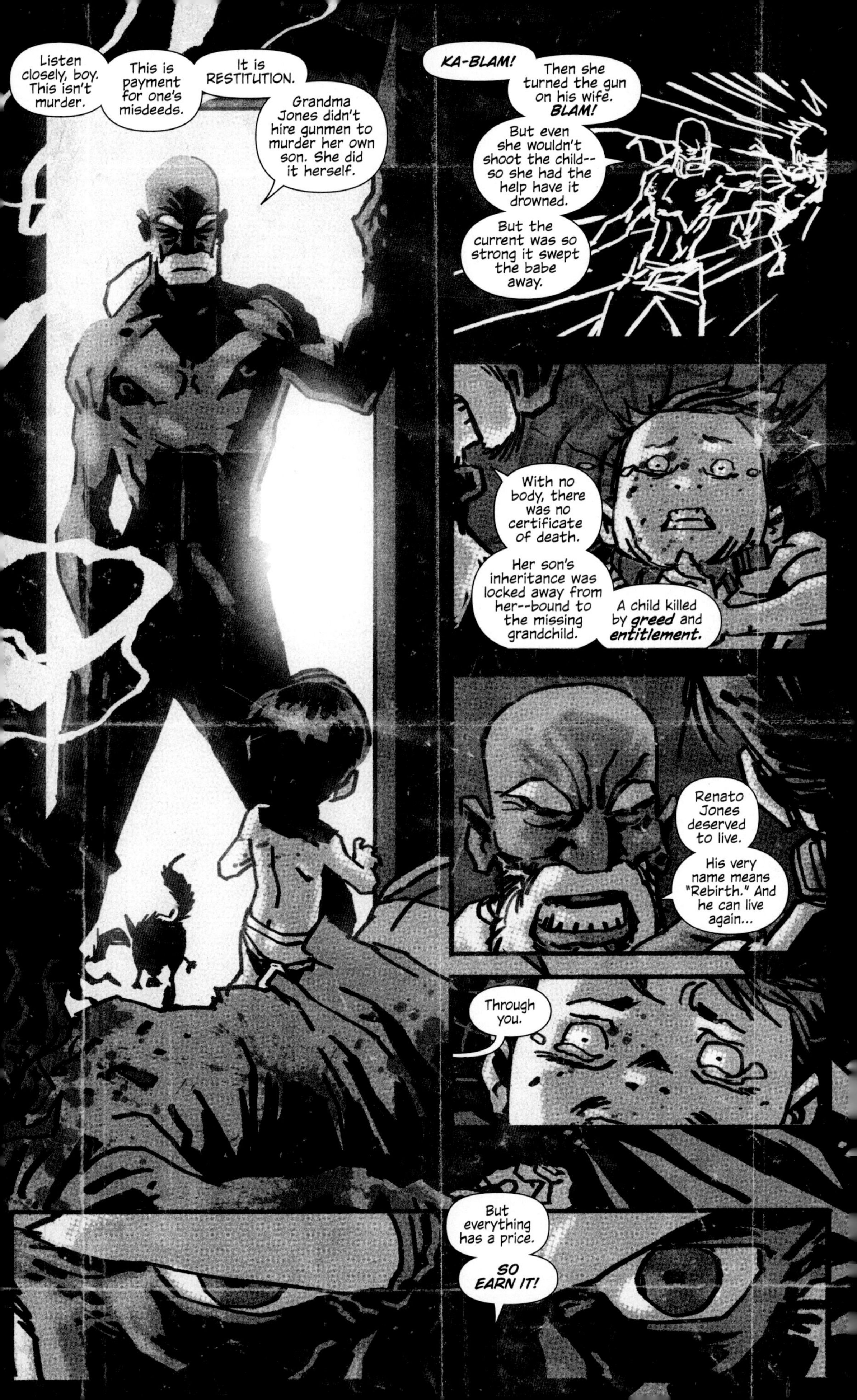

Listen closely, boy. This isn't murder.
This is payment for one's misdeeds.
It is RESTITUTION.
Grandma Jones didn't hire gunmen to murder her own son. She did it herself.
KA-BLAM!
Then she turned the gun on his wife. BLAM!
But even she wouldn't shoot the child--so she had the help have it drowned.
But the current was so strong it swept the babe away.
With no body, there was no certificate of death.
Her son's inheritance was locked away from her--bound to the missing grandchild.
A child killed by greed and entitlement.
Renato Jones deserved to live.
His very name means "Rebirth." And he can live again...
Through you.
But everything has a price.
SO EARN IT!

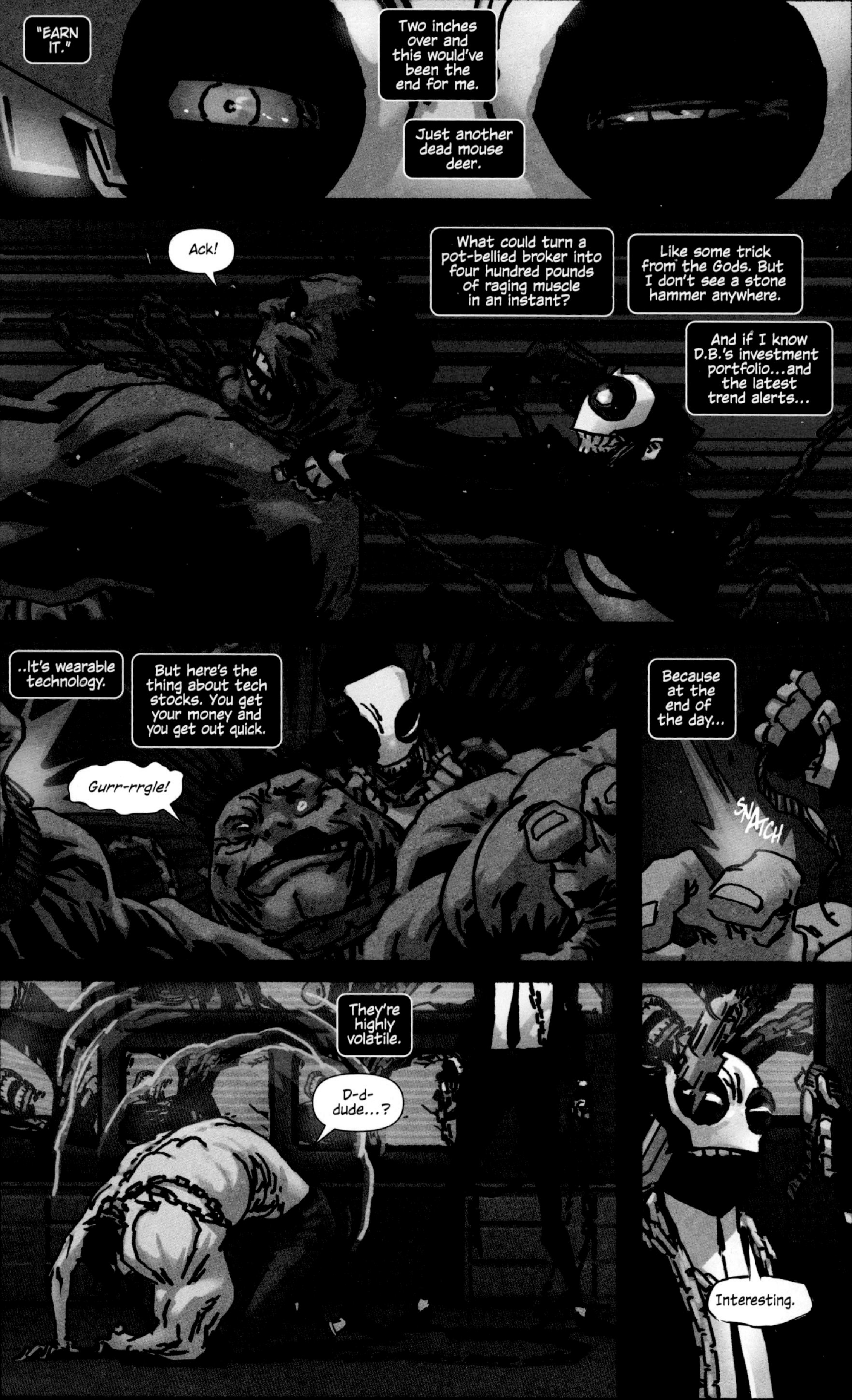
"EARN IT."
Two inches over and this would've been the end for me.
Just another dead mouse deer.
Ack!
What could turn a pot-bellied broker into four hundred pounds of raging muscle in an instant?
Like some trick from the Gods. But I don't see a stone hammer anywhere.
And if I know D.B.'s investment portfolio...and the latest trend alerts...
..It's wearable technology.
But here's the thing about tech stocks. You get your money and you get out quick.
Gurr-rrgle!
Because at the end of the day...
SNATCH
They're highly volatile.
D-d-dude...?
Interesting.

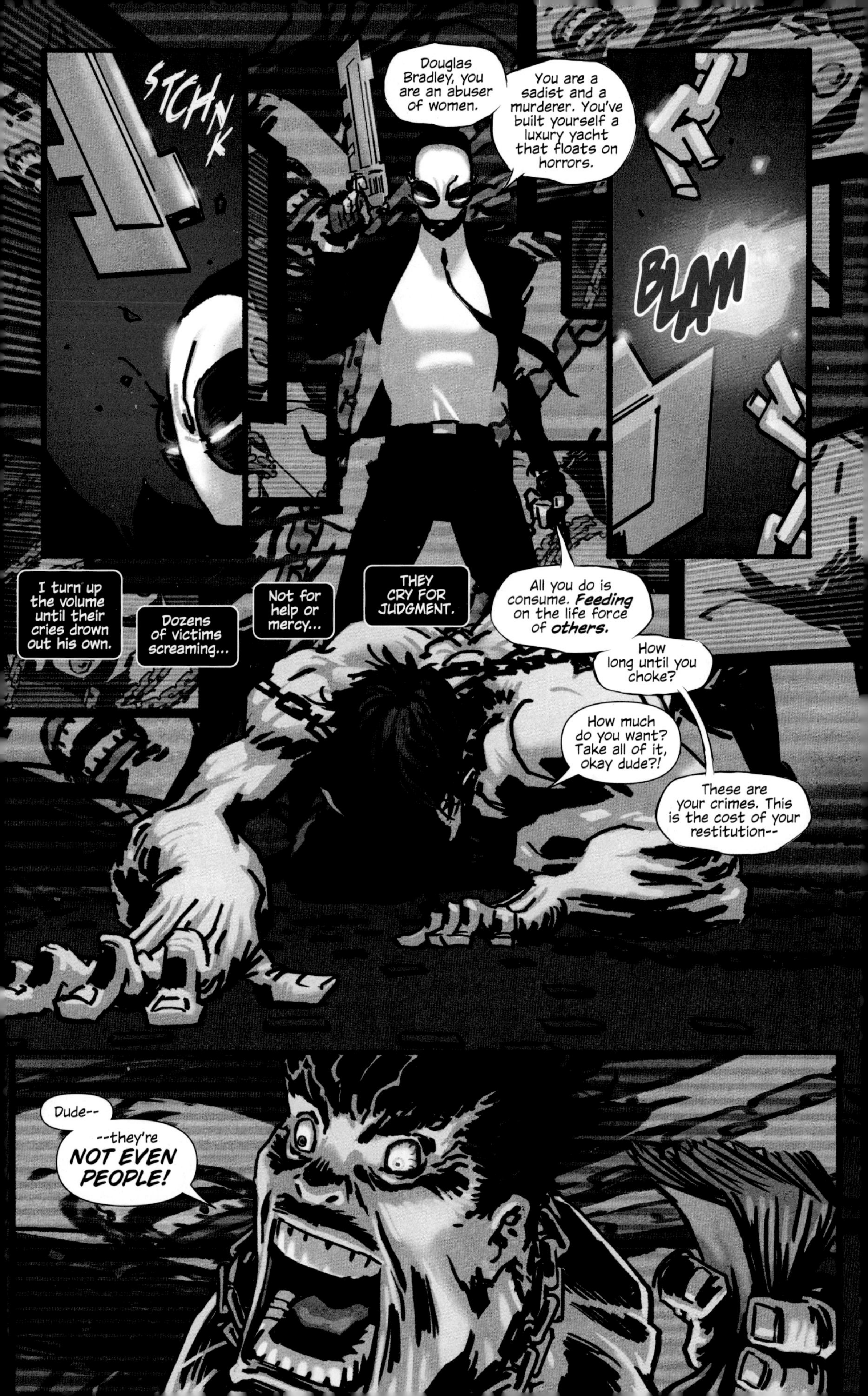
STCHANK
Douglas Bradley, you are an abuser of women.
You are a sadist and a murderer. You've built yourself a luxury yacht that floats on horrors.
BLAM
I turn up the volume until their cries drown out his own.
Dozens of victims screaming...
Not for help or mercy...
THEY CRY FOR JUDGMENT.
All you do is consume. ***Feeding*** on the life force of ***others.***
How long until you choke?
How much do you want? Take all of it, okay dude?!
These are your crimes. This is the cost of your restitution--
Dude--
--they're ***NOT EVEN PEOPLE!***

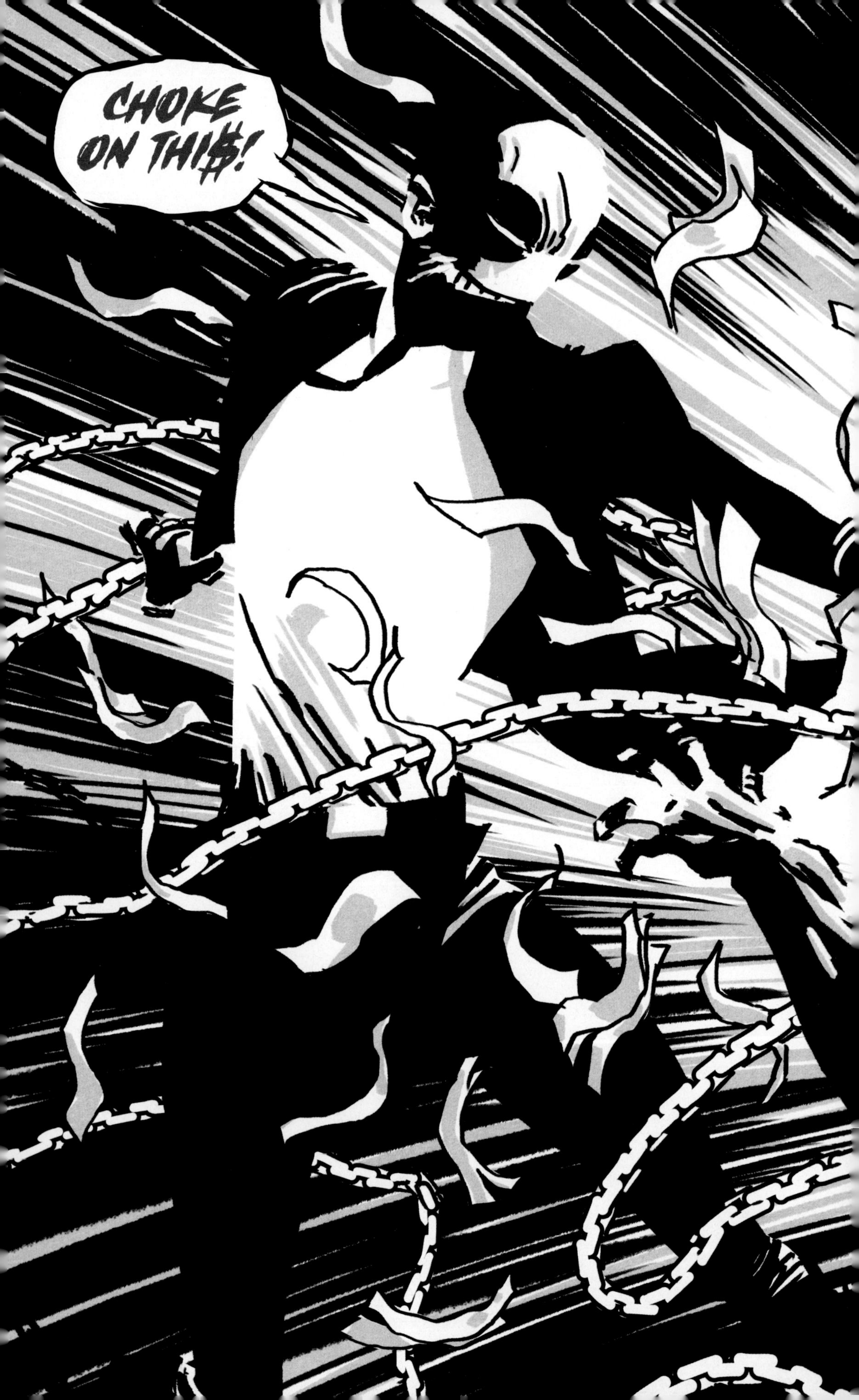
CHOKE ON THI$!

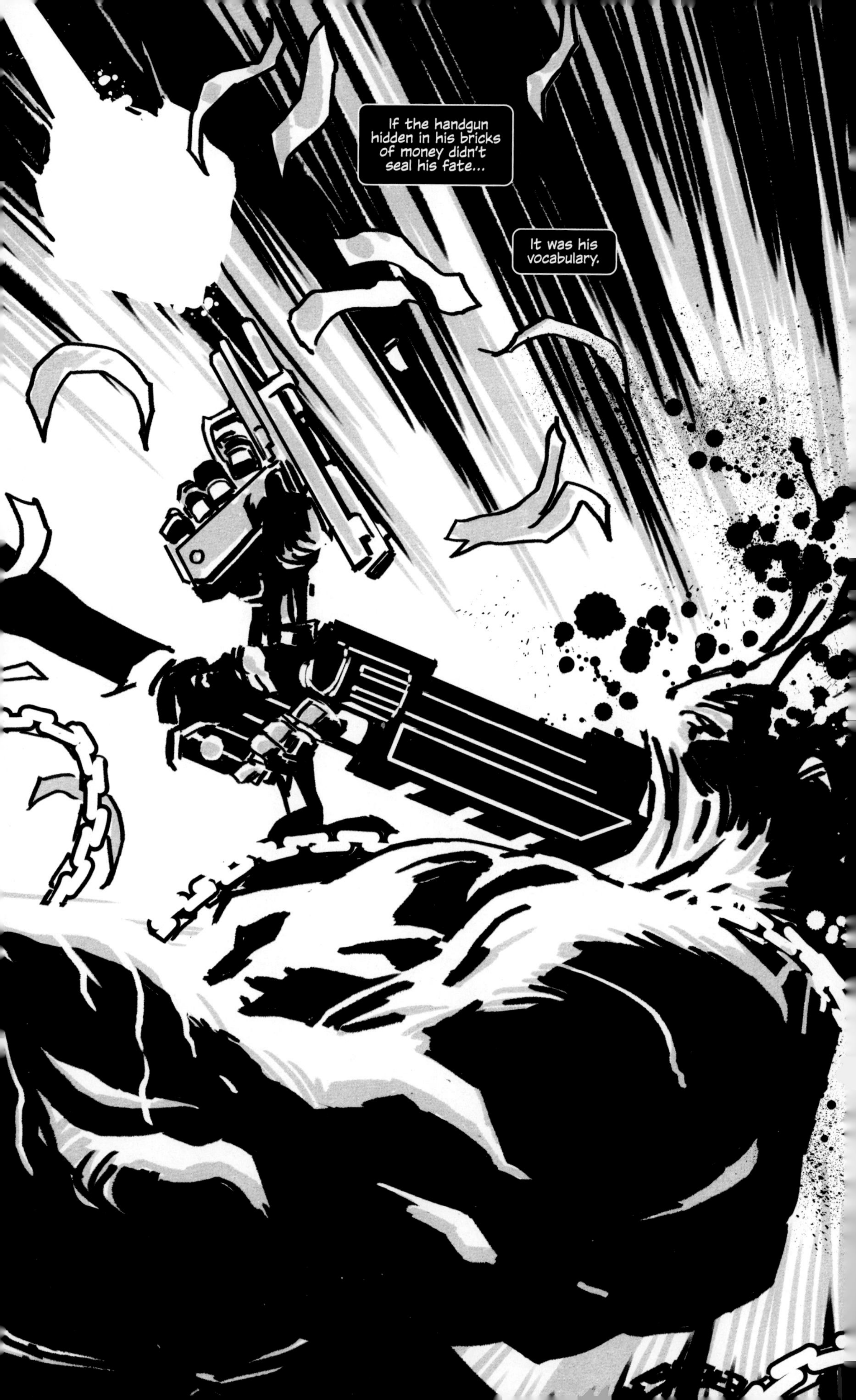
If the handgun hidden in his bricks of money didn't seal his fate...
It was his vocabulary.

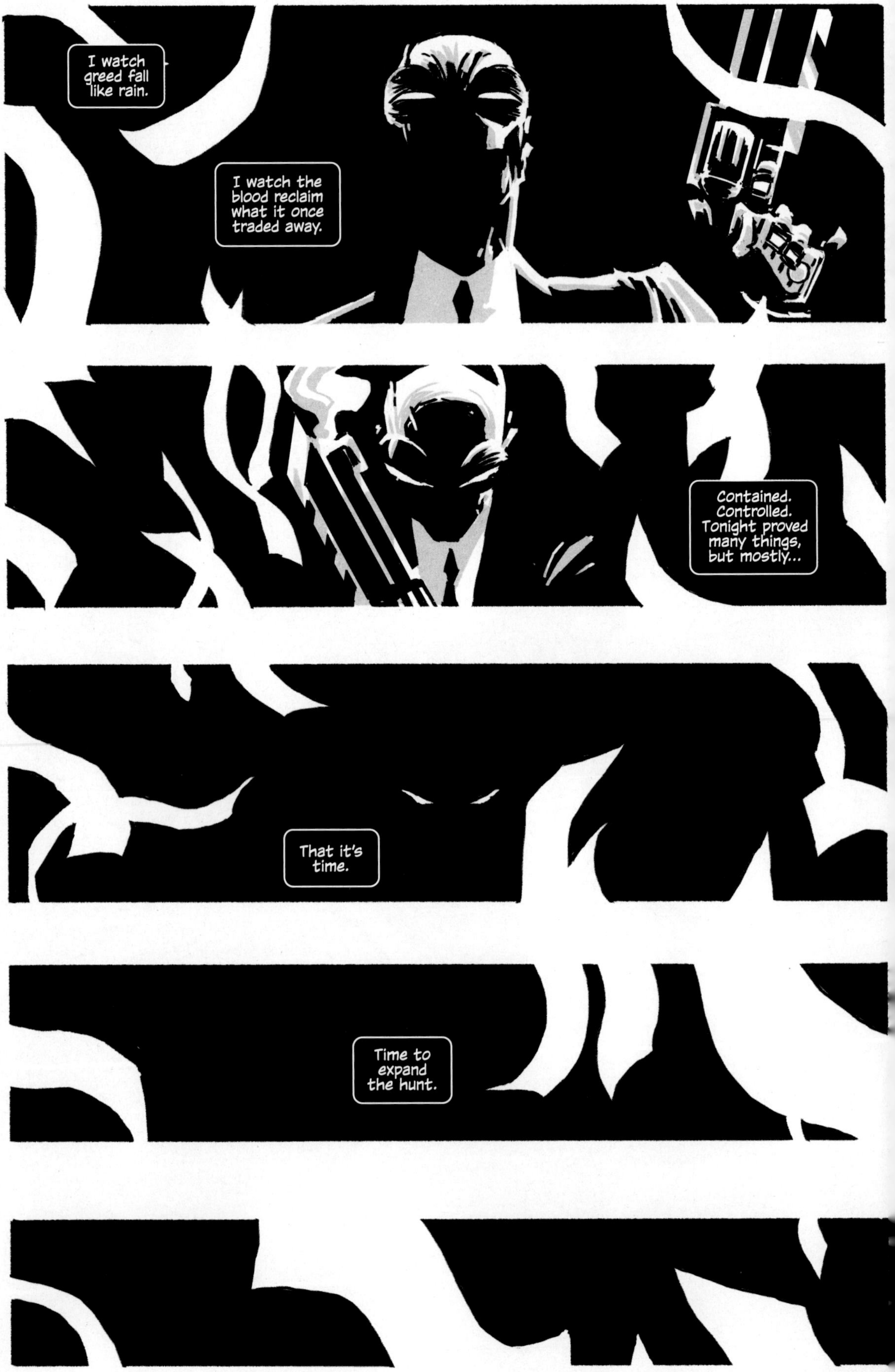
I watch greed fall like rain.
I watch the blood reclaim what it once traded away.
Contained. Controlled. Tonight proved many things, but mostly...
That it's time.
Time to expand the hunt.

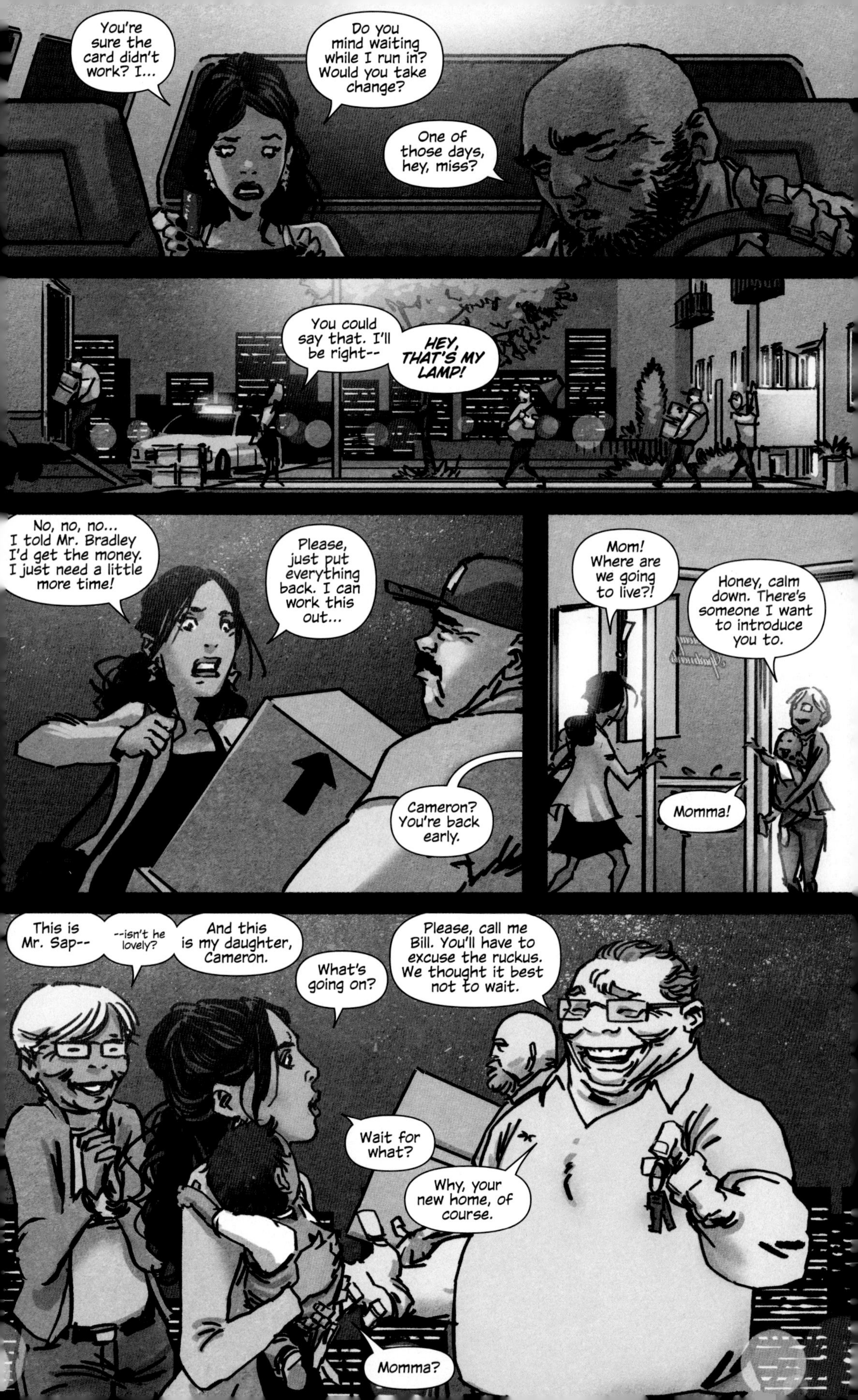
You're sure the card didn't work? I...
Do you mind waiting while I run in? Would you take change?
One of those days, hey, miss?
You could say that. I'll be right--
HEY, THAT'S MY LAMP!
No, no, no... I told Mr. Bradley I'd get the money. I just need a little more time!
Please, just put everything back. I can work this out...
Cameron? You're back early.
Mom! Where are we going to live?!
Honey, calm down. There's someone I want to introduce you to.
Momma!
This is Mr. Sap--
--isn't he lovely?
And this is my daughter, Cameron.
What's going on?
Please, call me Bill. You'll have to excuse the ruckus. We thought it best not to wait.
Wait for what?
Why, your new home, of course.
Momma?

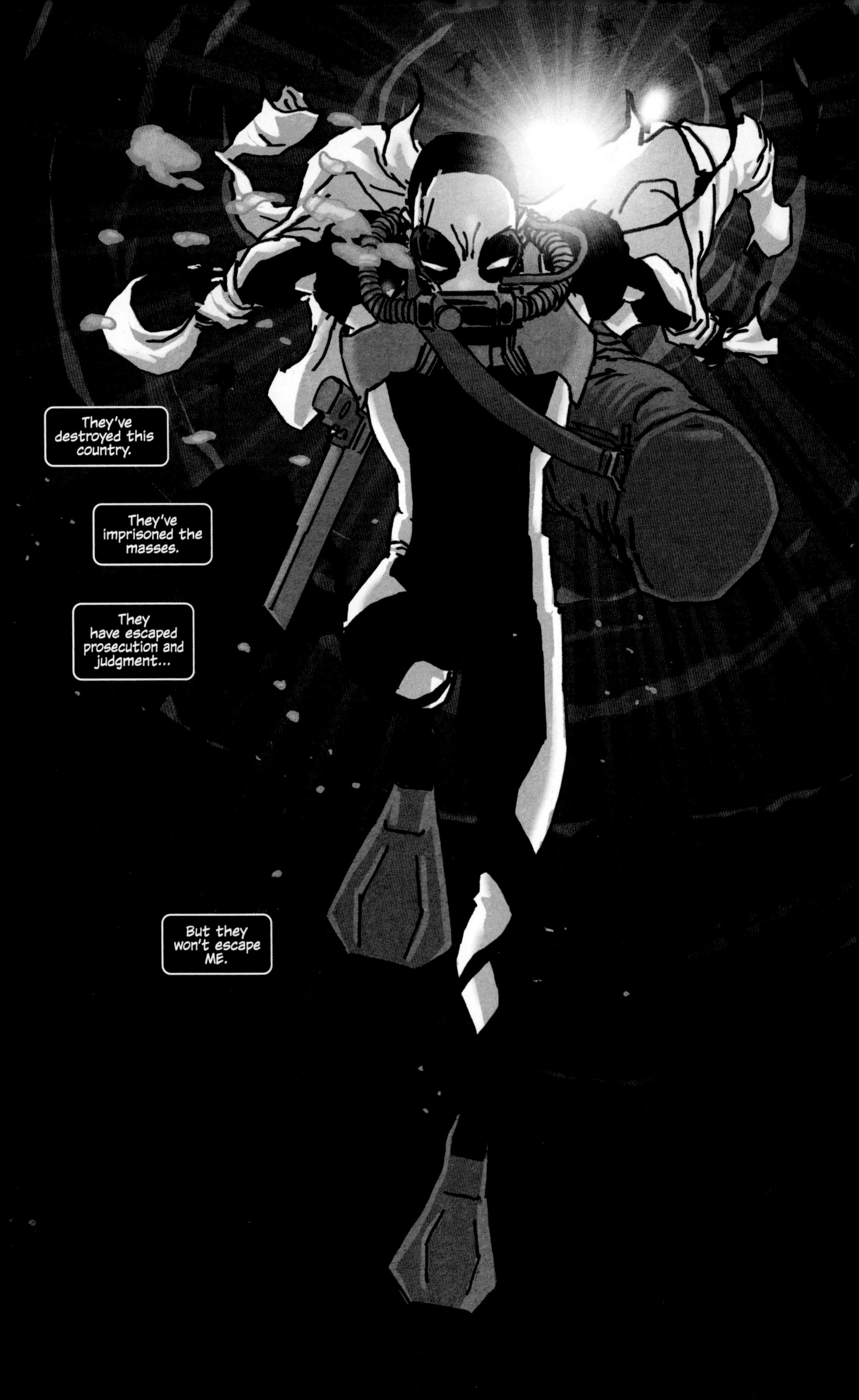
They've destroyed this country.
They've imprisoned the masses.
They have escaped prosecution and judgment...
But they won't escape ME.

"Thought this dude was a

fairy tale.

Like

government

regulation."

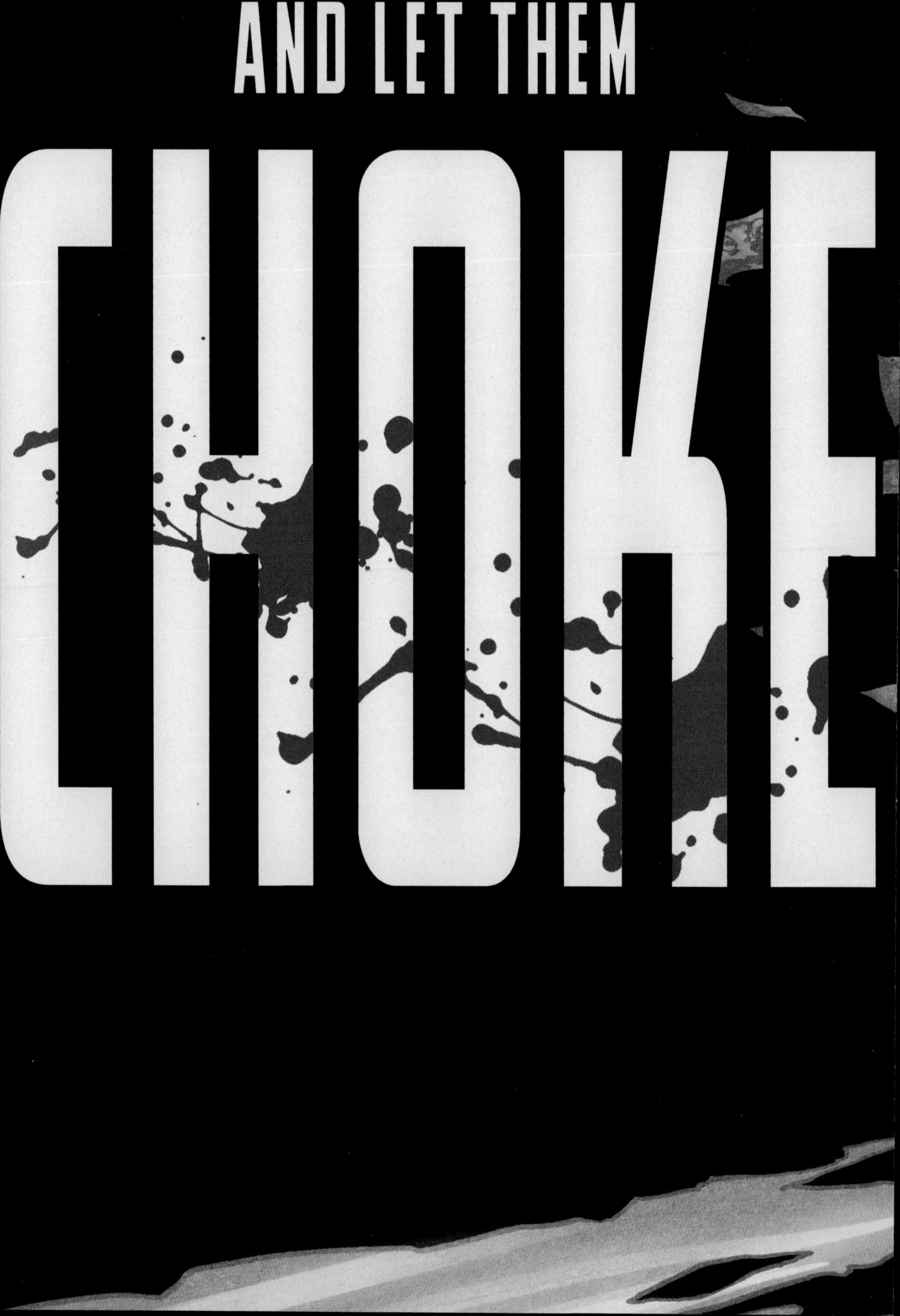
AND LET THEM
CHOKE

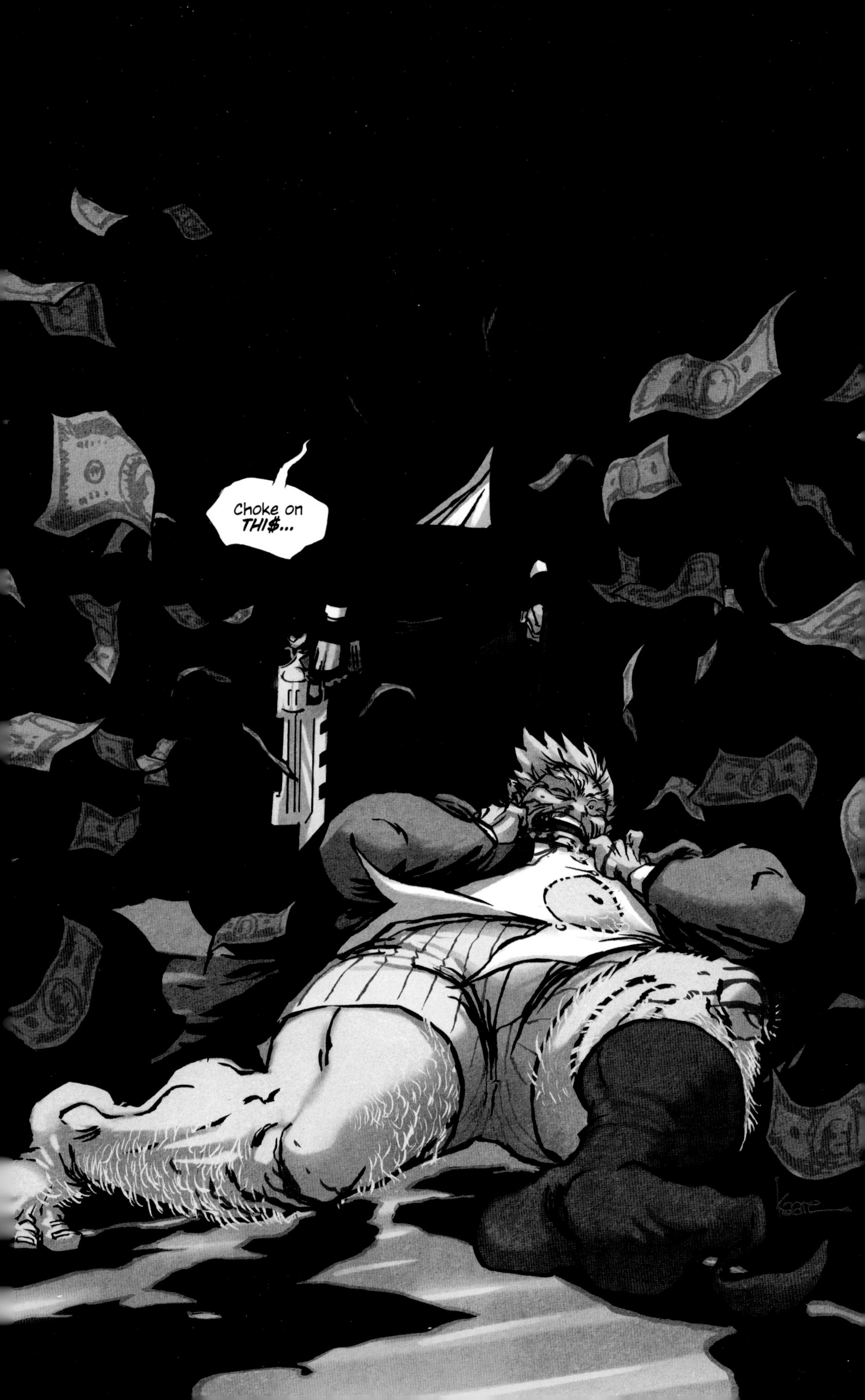
Choke on THI$...

$$\frac{2}{\quad}$$

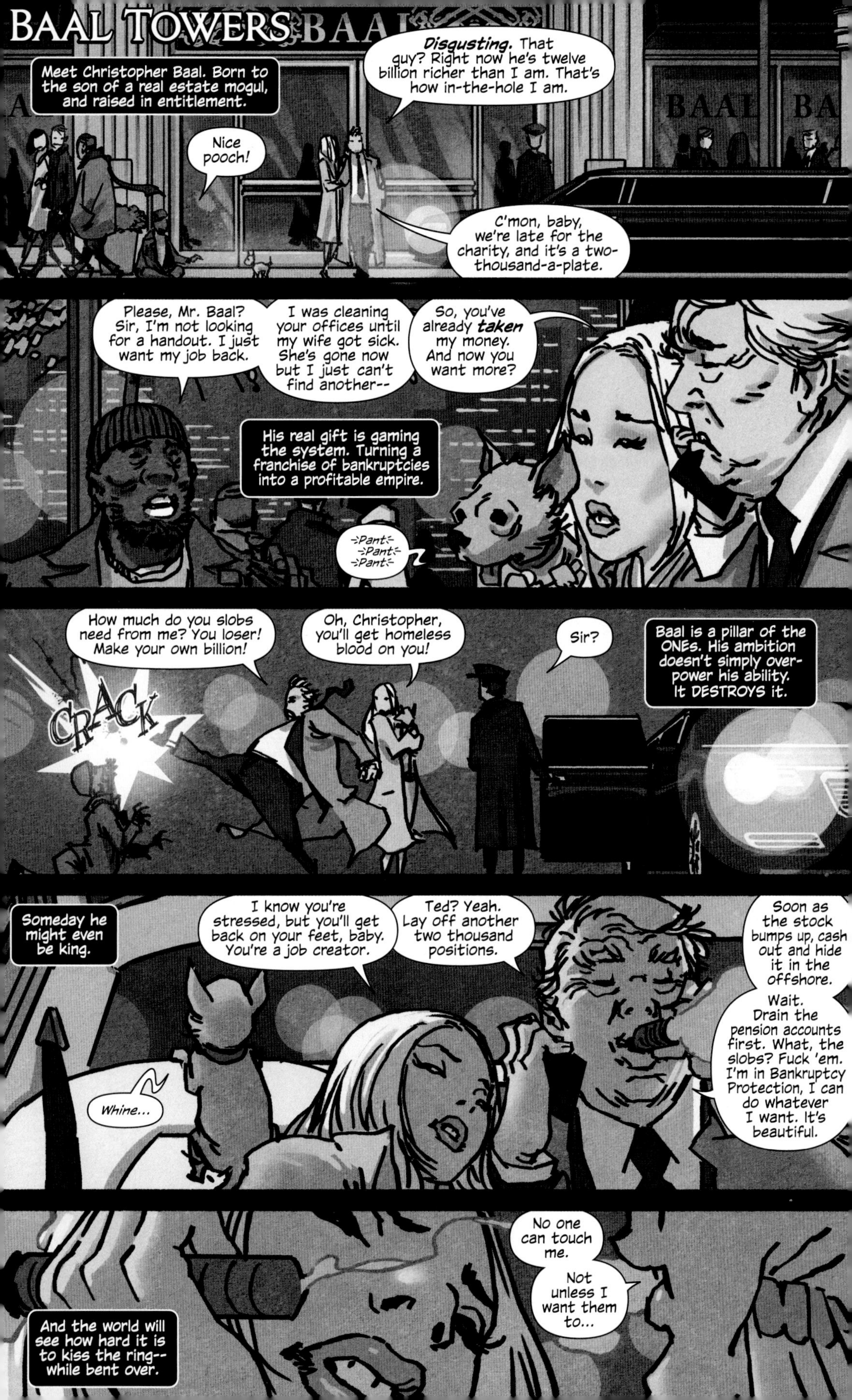
BAAL TOWERS
BAAL
Meet Christopher Baal. Born to the son of a real estate mogul, and raised in entitlement.
Disgusting. That guy? Right now he's twelve billion richer than I am. That's how in-the-hole I am.
Nice pooch!
C'mon, baby, we're late for the charity, and it's a two-thousand-a-plate.
Please, Mr. Baal? Sir, I'm not looking for a handout. I just want my job back.
I was cleaning your offices until my wife got sick. She's gone now but I just can't find another--
So, you've already taken my money. And now you want more?
His real gift is gaming the system. Turning a franchise of bankruptcies into a profitable empire.
Pant Pant Pant
How much do you slobs need from me? You loser! Make your own billion!
Oh, Christopher, you'll get homeless blood on you!
Sir?
Baal is a pillar of the ONEs. His ambition doesn't simply over-power his ability. It DESTROYS it.
CRACK
Someday he might even be king.
I know you're stressed, but you'll get back on your feet, baby. You're a job creator.
Ted? Yeah. Lay off another two thousand positions.
Soon as the stock bumps up, cash out and hide it in the offshore.
Wait. Drain the pension accounts first. What, the slobs? Fuck 'em. I'm in Bankruptcy Protection, I can do whatever I want. It's beautiful.
Whine...
No one can touch me.
Not unless I want them to...
And the world will see how hard it is to kiss the ring--while bent over.

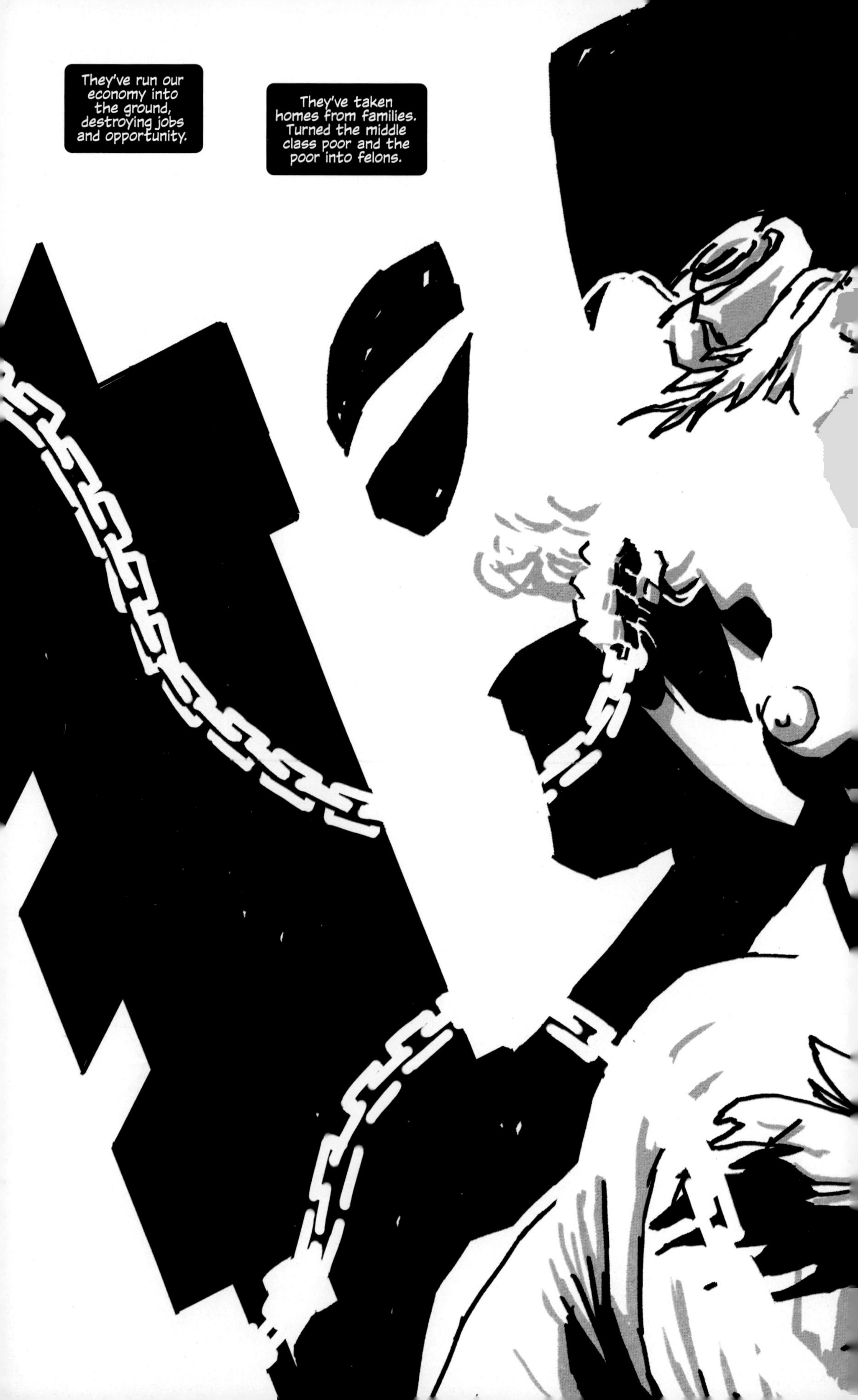
They've run our economy into the ground, destroying jobs and opportunity.
They've taken homes from families. Turned the middle class poor and the poor into felons.

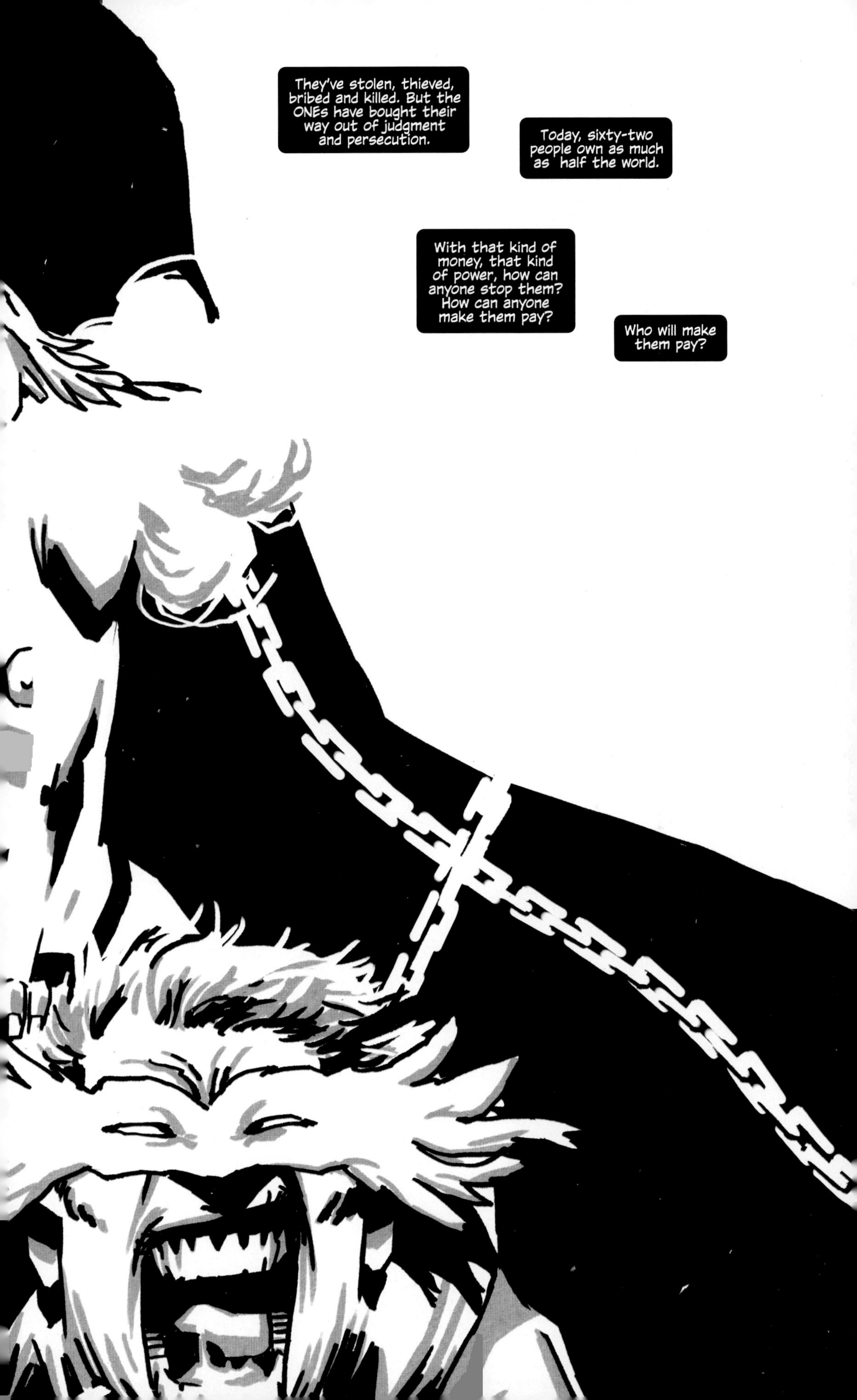
They've stolen, thieved, bribed and killed. But the ONEs have bought their way out of judgment and persecution.
Today, sixty-two people own as much as half the world.
With that kind of money, that kind of power, how can anyone stop them? How can anyone make them pay?
Who will make them pay?

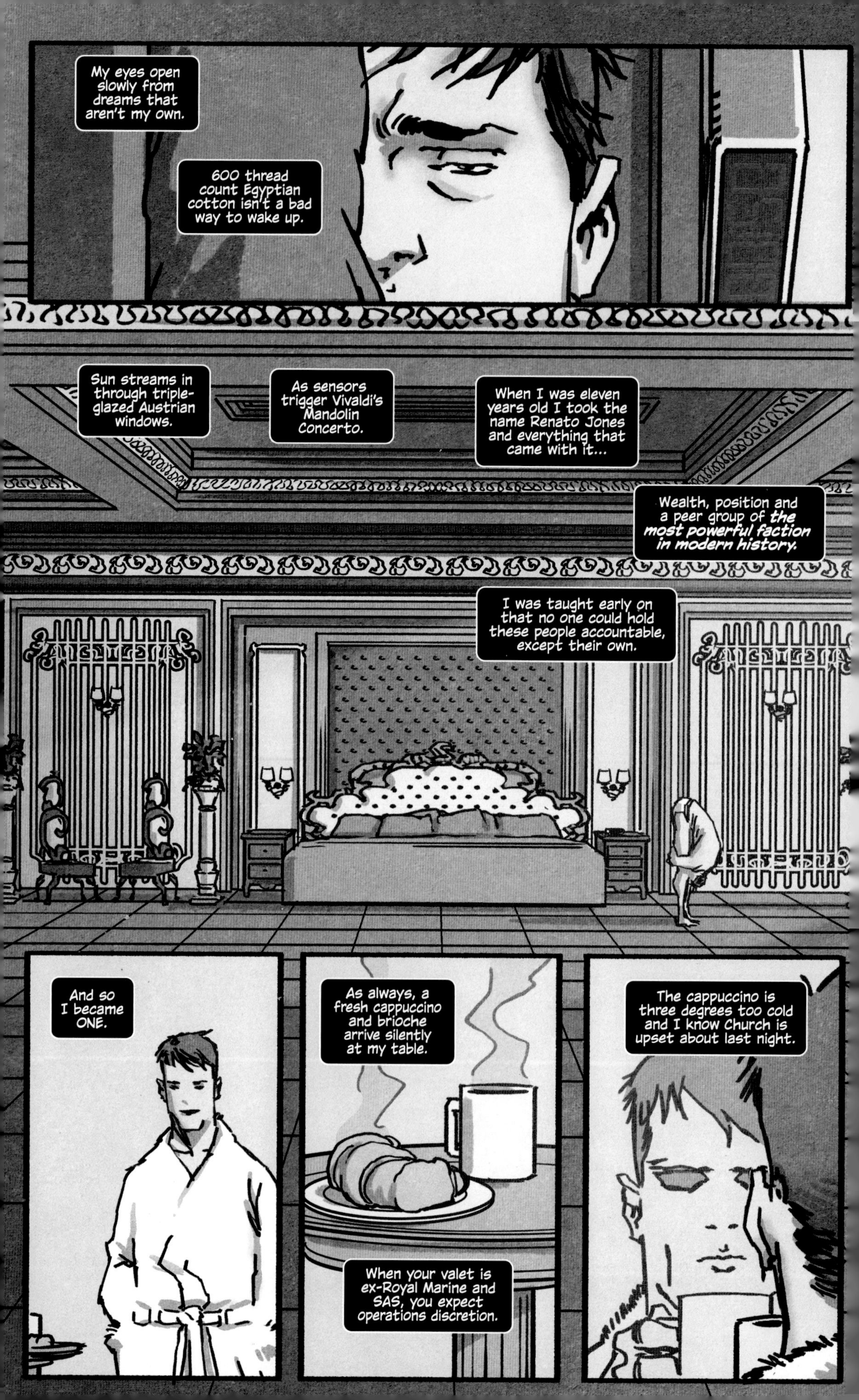

My eyes open slowly from dreams that aren't my own.
600 thread count Egyptian cotton isn't a bad way to wake up.
Sun streams in through triple-glazed Austrian windows.
As sensors trigger Vivaldi's Mandolin Concerto.
When I was eleven years old I took the name Renato Jones and everything that came with it...
Wealth, position and a peer group of ***the most powerful faction in modern history.***
I was taught early on that no one could hold these people accountable, except their own.
And so I became ONE.
As always, a fresh cappuccino and brioche arrive silently at my table.
When your valet is ex-Royal Marine and SAS, you expect operations discretion.
The cappuccino is three degrees too cold and I know Church is upset about last night.

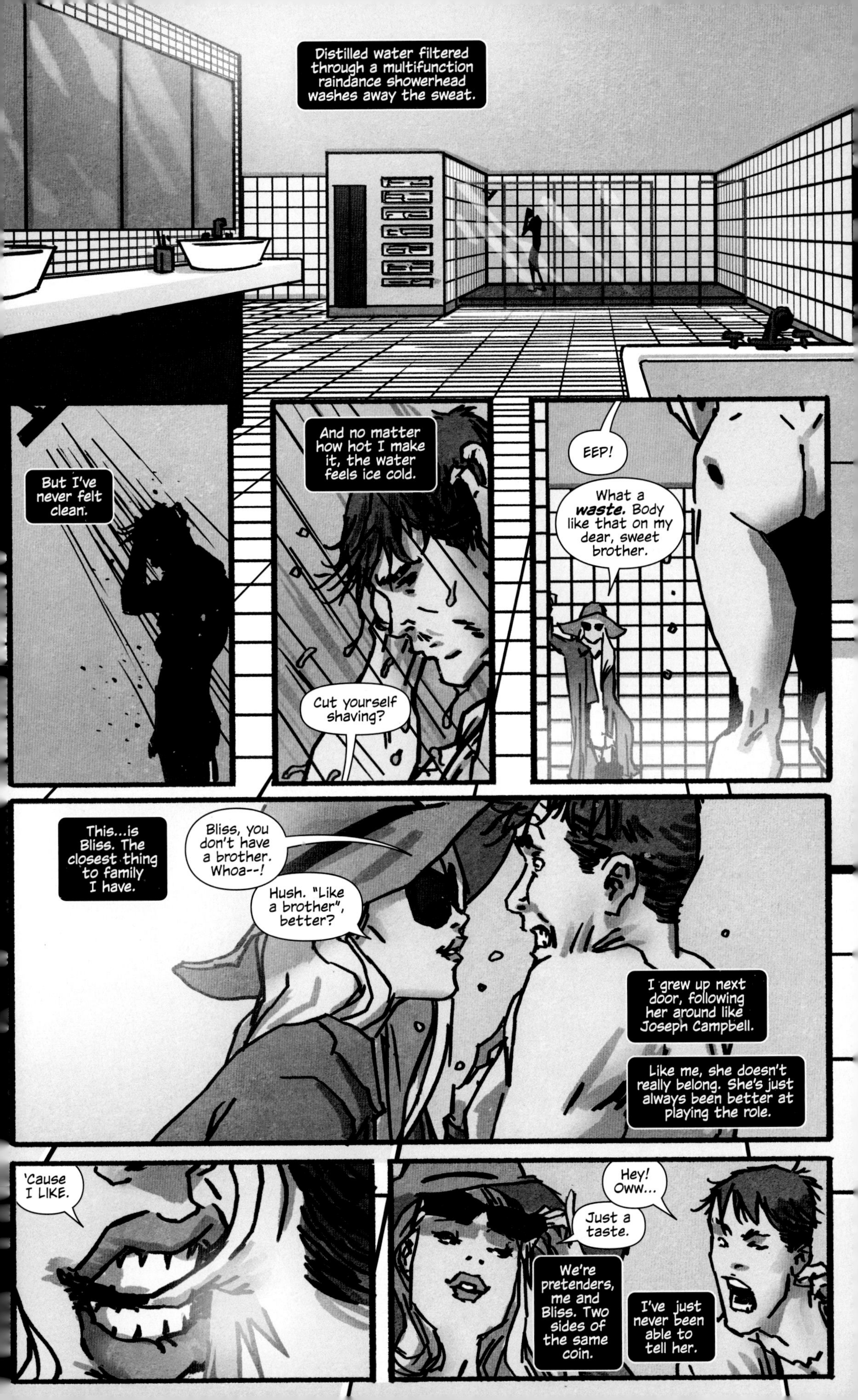
Distilled water filtered through a multifunction raindance showerhead washes away the sweat.
But I've never felt clean.
And no matter how hot I make it, the water feels ice cold.
Cut yourself shaving?
EEP!
What a waste. Body like that on my dear, sweet brother.
This...is Bliss. The closest thing to family I have.
Bliss, you don't have a brother. Whoa--!
Hush. "Like a brother", better?
I grew up next door, following her around like Joseph Campbell.
Like me, she doesn't really belong. She's just always been better at playing the role.
'Cause I LIKE.
Hey! Oww...
Just a taste.
We're pretenders, me and Bliss. Two sides of the same coin.
I've just never been able to tell her.

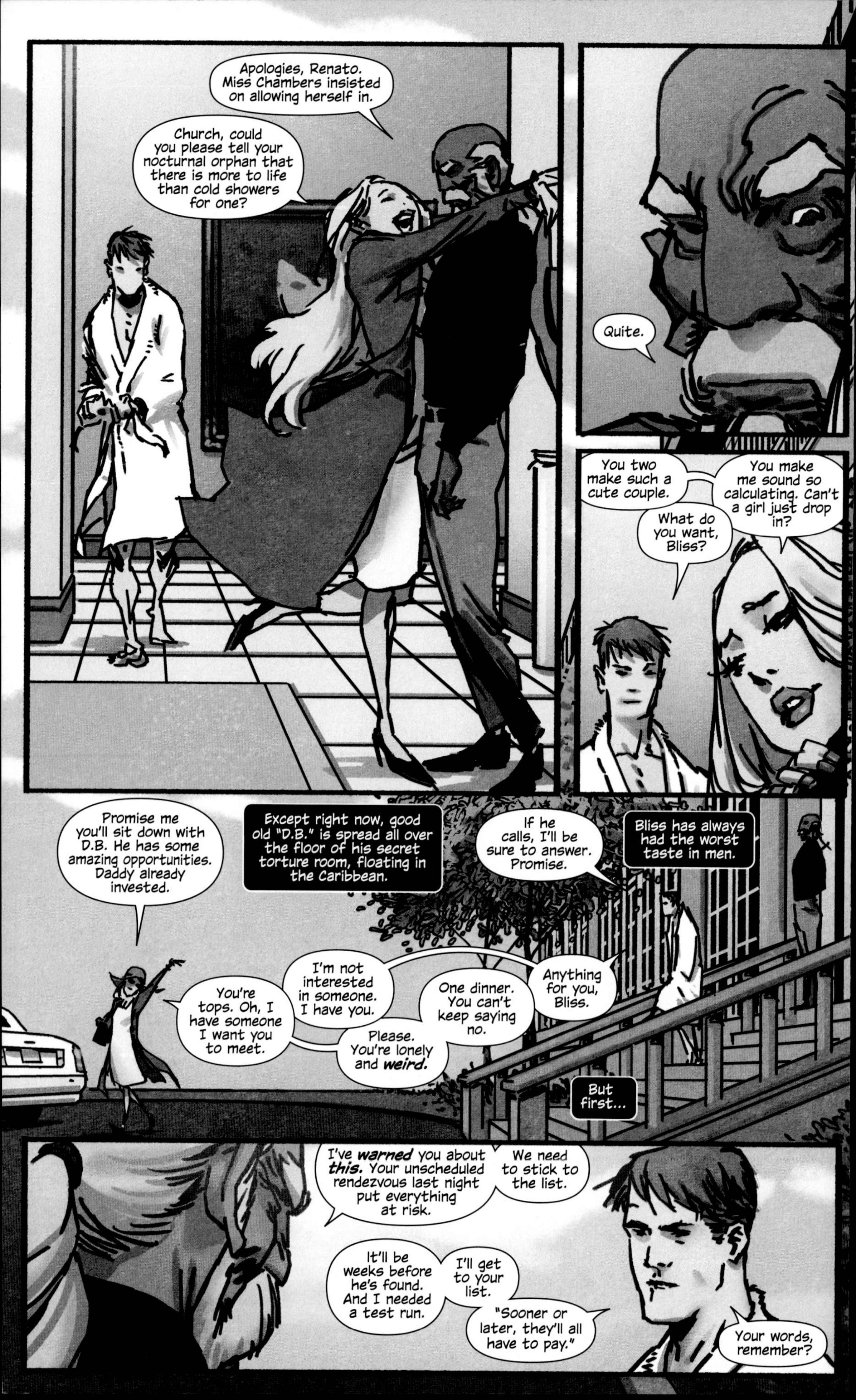

Apologies, Renato. Miss Chambers insisted on allowing herself in.
Church, could you please tell your nocturnal orphan that there is more to life than cold showers for one?
Quite.
You two make such a cute couple.
You make me sound so calculating. Can't a girl just drop in?
What do you want, Bliss?
Promise me you'll sit down with D.B. He has some amazing opportunities. Daddy already invested.
Except right now, good old "D.B." is spread all over the floor of his secret torture room, floating in the Caribbean.
If he calls, I'll be sure to answer. Promise.
Bliss has always had the worst taste in men.
You're tops. Oh, I have someone I want you to meet.
I'm not interested in someone. I have you.
Please. You're lonely and *weird.*
One dinner. You can't keep saying no.
Anything for you, Bliss.
But first...
I've ***warned*** you about ***this.*** Your unscheduled rendezvous last night put everything at risk.
We need to stick to the list.
It'll be weeks before he's found. And I needed a test run.
I'll get to your list.
"Sooner or later, they'll all have to pay."
Your words, remember?

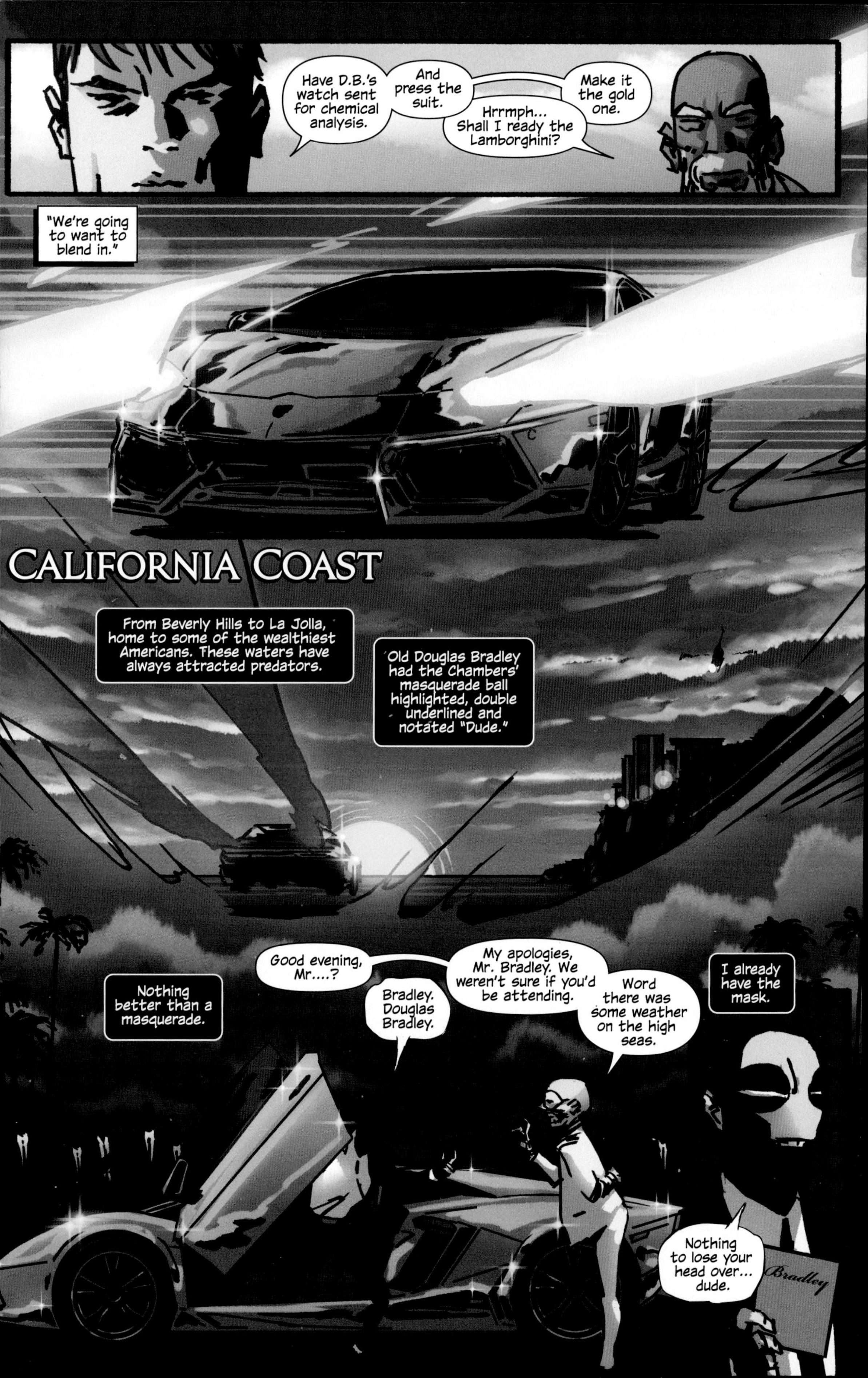
Have D.B.'s watch sent for chemical analysis.
And press the suit.
Make it the gold one.
Hrrmph... Shall I ready the Lamborghini?
"We're going to want to blend in."
CALIFORNIA COAST
From Beverly Hills to La Jolla, home to some of the wealthiest Americans. These waters have always attracted predators.
Old Douglas Bradley had the Chambers' masquerade ball highlighted, double underlined and notated "Dude."
Nothing better than a masquerade.
Good evening, Mr....?
Bradley. Douglas Bradley.
My apologies, Mr. Bradley. We weren't sure if you'd be attending.
Word there was some weather on the high seas.
I already have the mask.
Nothing to lose your head over... dude.
Bradley

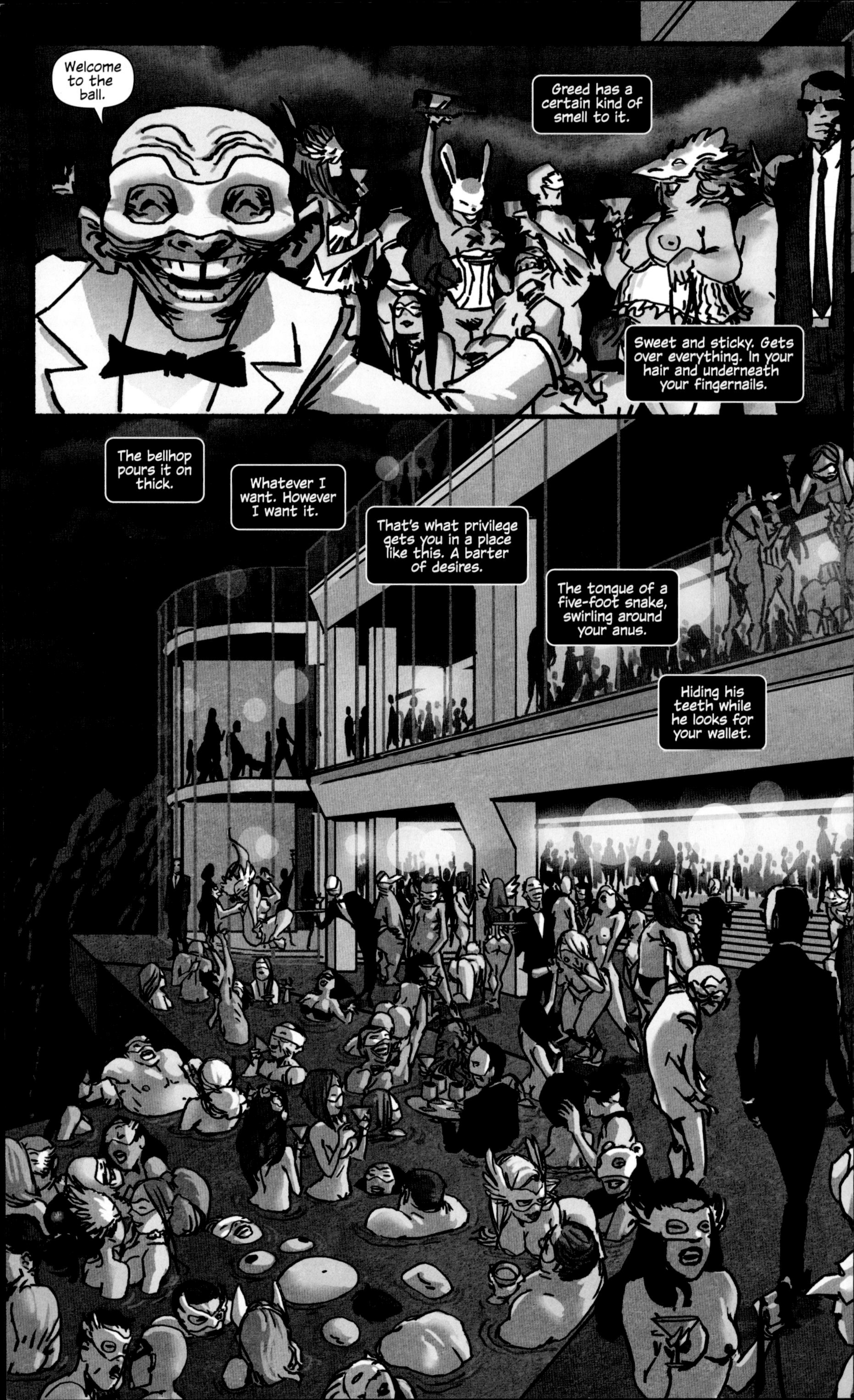
Welcome to the ball.
Greed has a certain kind of smell to it.
Sweet and sticky. Gets over everything. In your hair and underneath your fingernails.
The bellhop pours it on thick.
Whatever I want. However I want it.
That's what privilege gets you in a place like this. A barter of desires.
The tongue of a five-foot snake, swirling around your anus.
Hiding his teeth while he looks for your wallet.

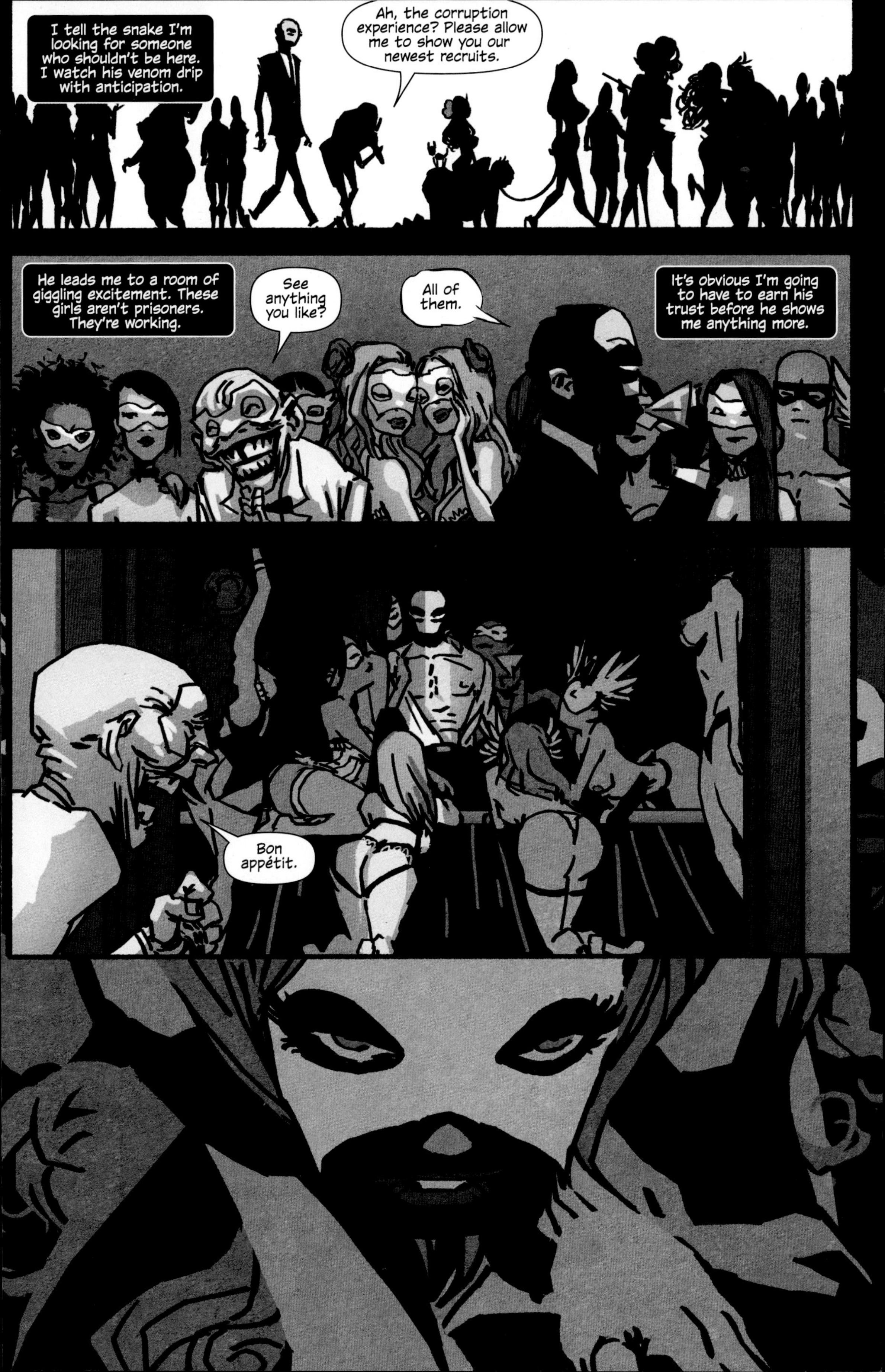
I tell the snake I'm looking for someone who shouldn't be here. I watch his venom drip with anticipation.
Ah, the corruption experience? Please allow me to show you our newest recruits.
He leads me to a room of giggling excitement. These girls aren't prisoners. They're working.
See anything you like?
All of them.
It's obvious I'm going to have to earn his trust before he shows me anything more.
Bon appétit.

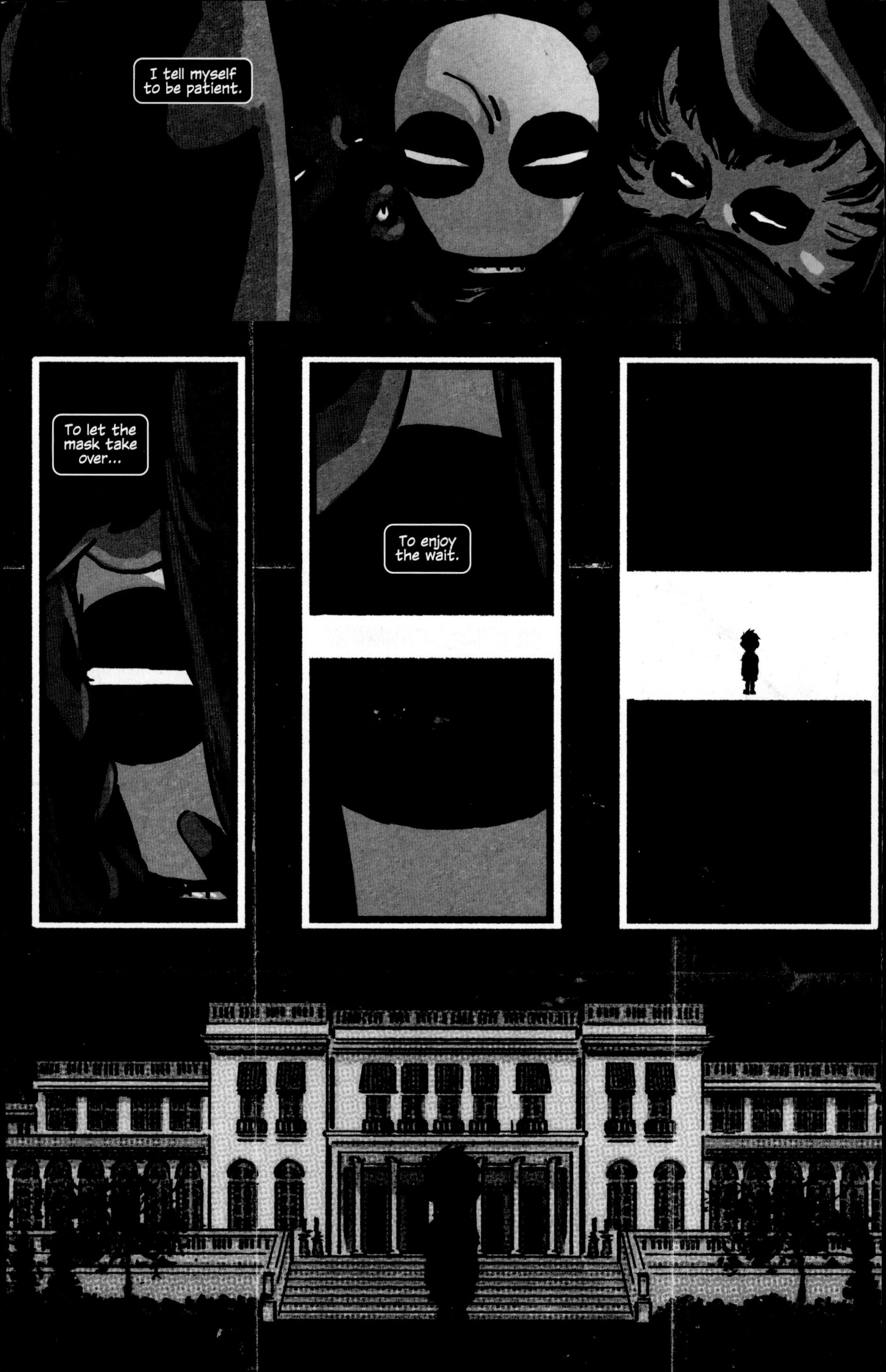
I tell myself to be patient.
To let the mask take over...
To enjoy the wait.

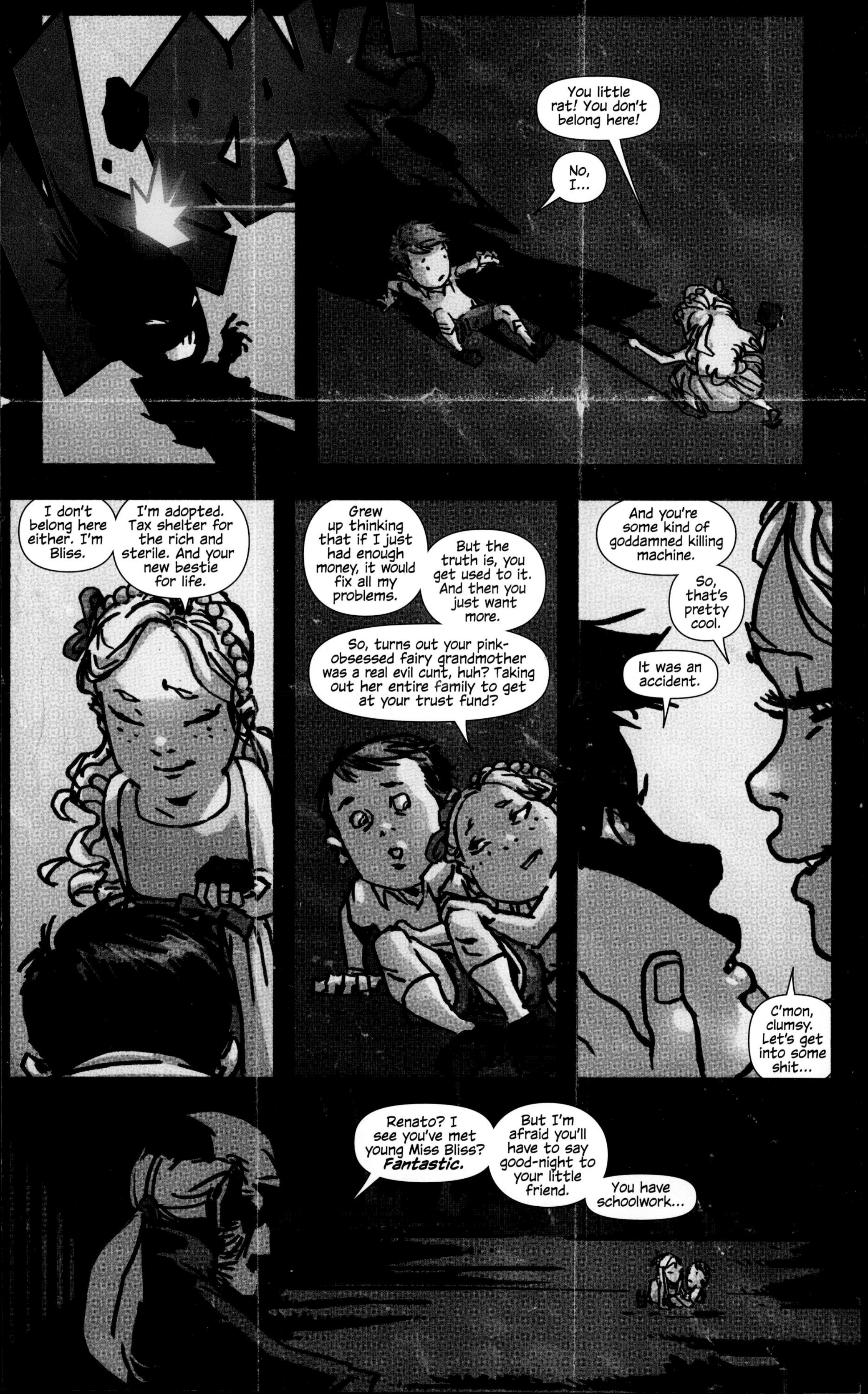
You little rat! You don't belong here!
No, I...
I don't belong here either. I'm Bliss.
I'm adopted. Tax shelter for the rich and sterile. And your new bestie for life.
Grew up thinking that if I just had enough money, it would fix all my problems.
But the truth is, you get used to it. And then you just want more.
So, turns out your pink-obsessed fairy grandmother was a real evil cunt, huh? Taking out her entire family to get at your trust fund?
And you're some kind of goddamned killing machine.
So, that's pretty cool.
It was an accident.
C'mon, clumsy. Let's get into some shit...
Renato? I see you've met young Miss Bliss? *Fantastic.*
But I'm afraid you'll have to say good-night to your little friend.
You have schoolwork...

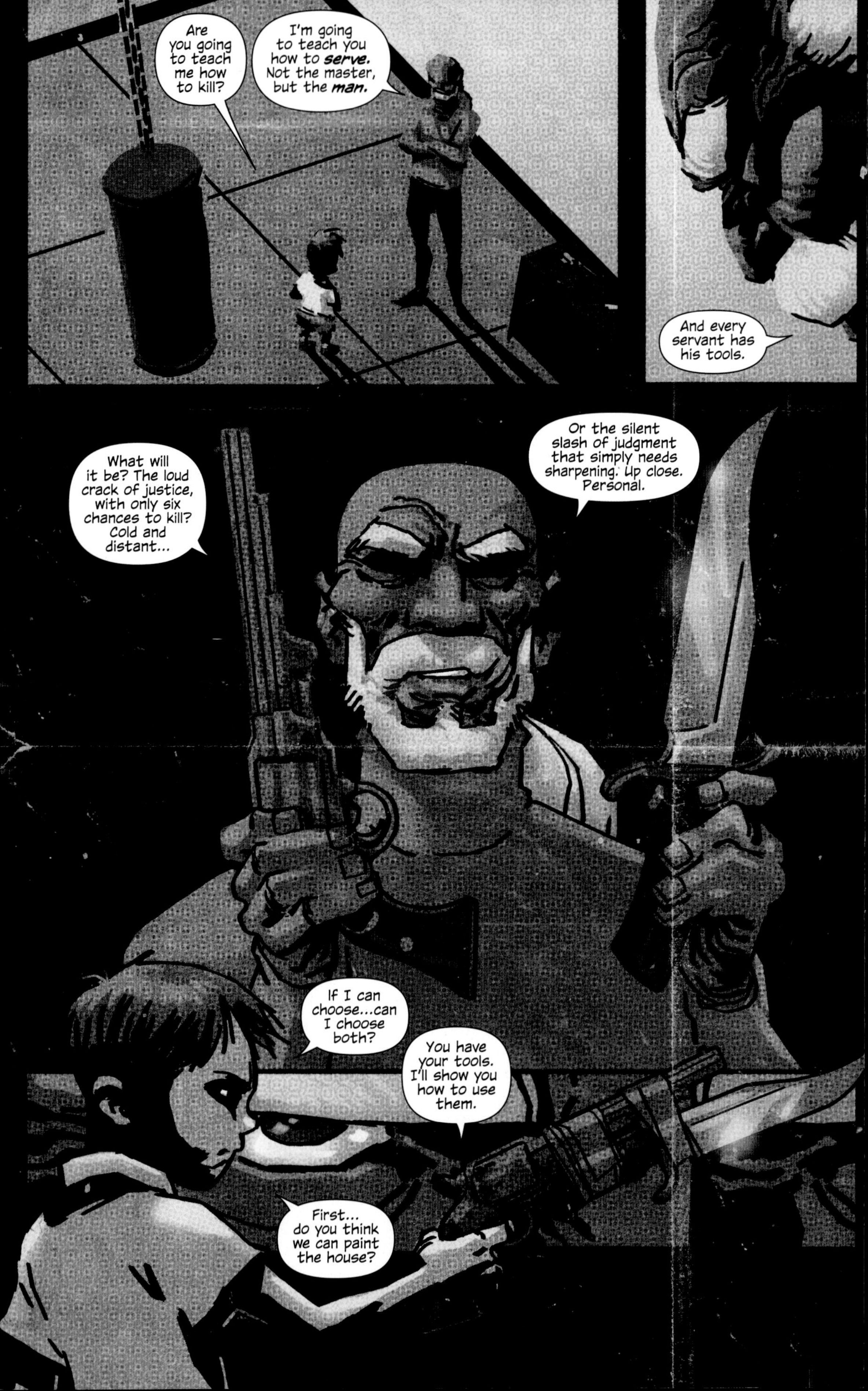

Are you going to teach me how to kill?
I'm going to teach you how to *serve.* Not the master, but the *man.*
And every servant has his tools.
What will it be? The loud crack of justice, with only six chances to kill? Cold and distant...
Or the silent slash of judgment that simply needs sharpening. Up close. Personal.
If I can choose...can I choose both?
You have your tools. I'll show you how to use them.
First... do you think we can paint the house?

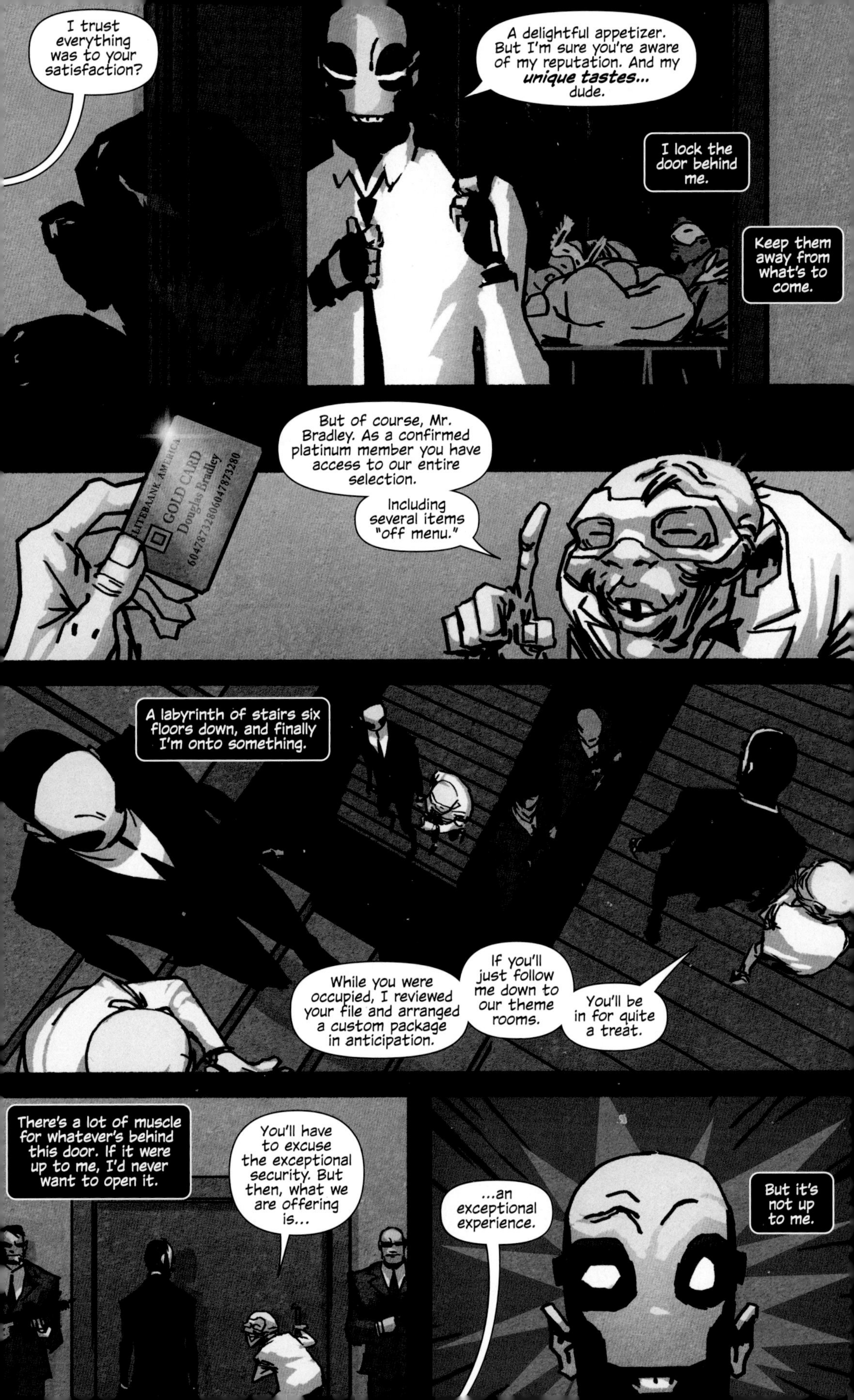
I trust everything was to your satisfaction?
A delightful appetizer. But I'm sure you're aware of my reputation. And my *unique tastes...* dude.
I lock the door behind me.
Keep them away from what's to come.
GOLD CARD
Douglas Bradley
But of course, Mr. Bradley. As a confirmed platinum member you have access to our entire selection.
Including several items "off menu."
A labyrinth of stairs six floors down, and finally I'm onto something.
While you were occupied, I reviewed your file and arranged a custom package in anticipation.
If you'll just follow me down to our theme rooms.
You'll be in for quite a treat.
There's a lot of muscle for whatever's behind this door. If it were up to me, I'd never want to open it.
You'll have to excuse the exceptional security. But then, what we are offering is...
...an exceptional experience.
But it's not up to me.

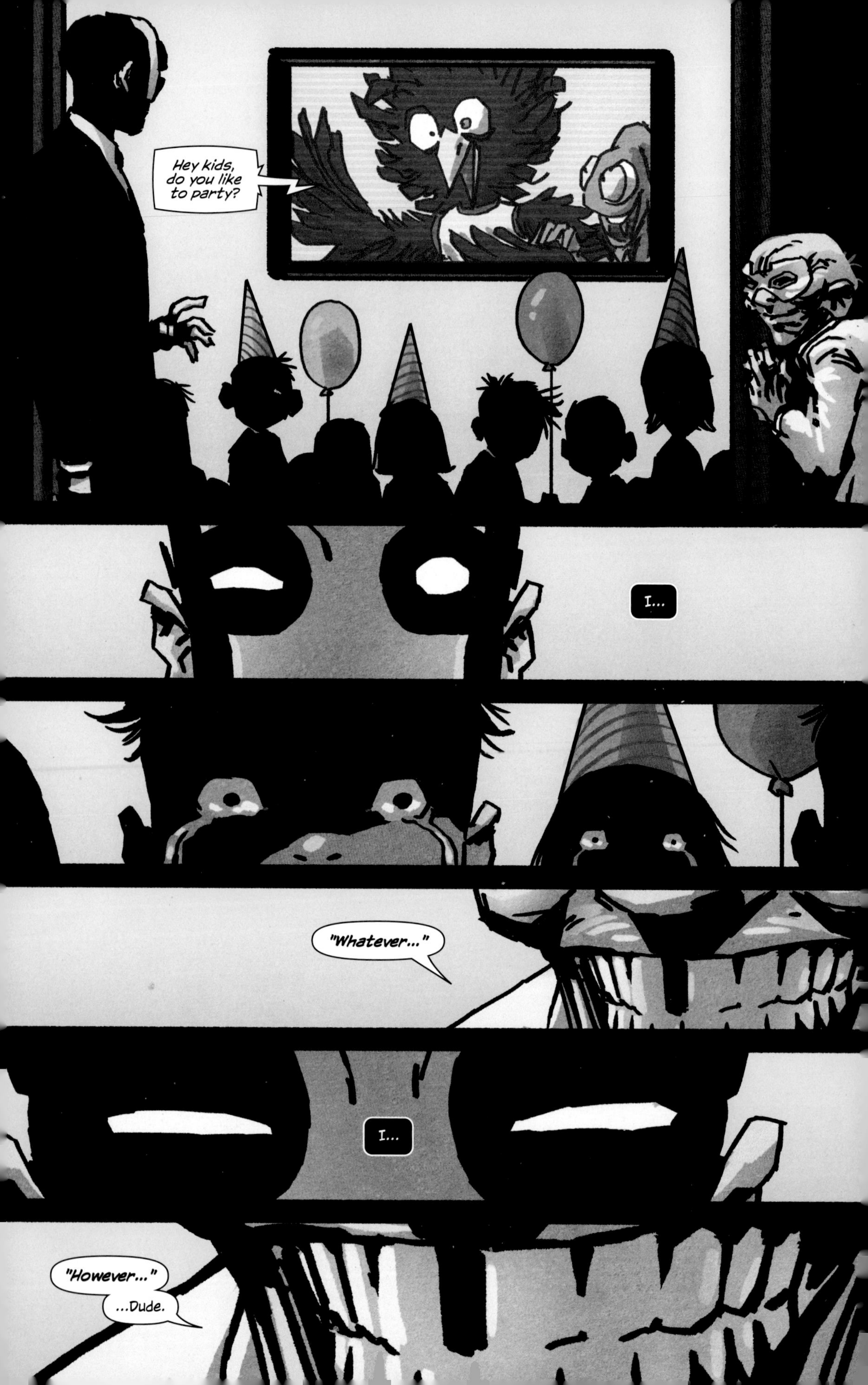
Hey kids, do you like to party?
I...
"Whatever..."
I...
"However..."
...Dude.

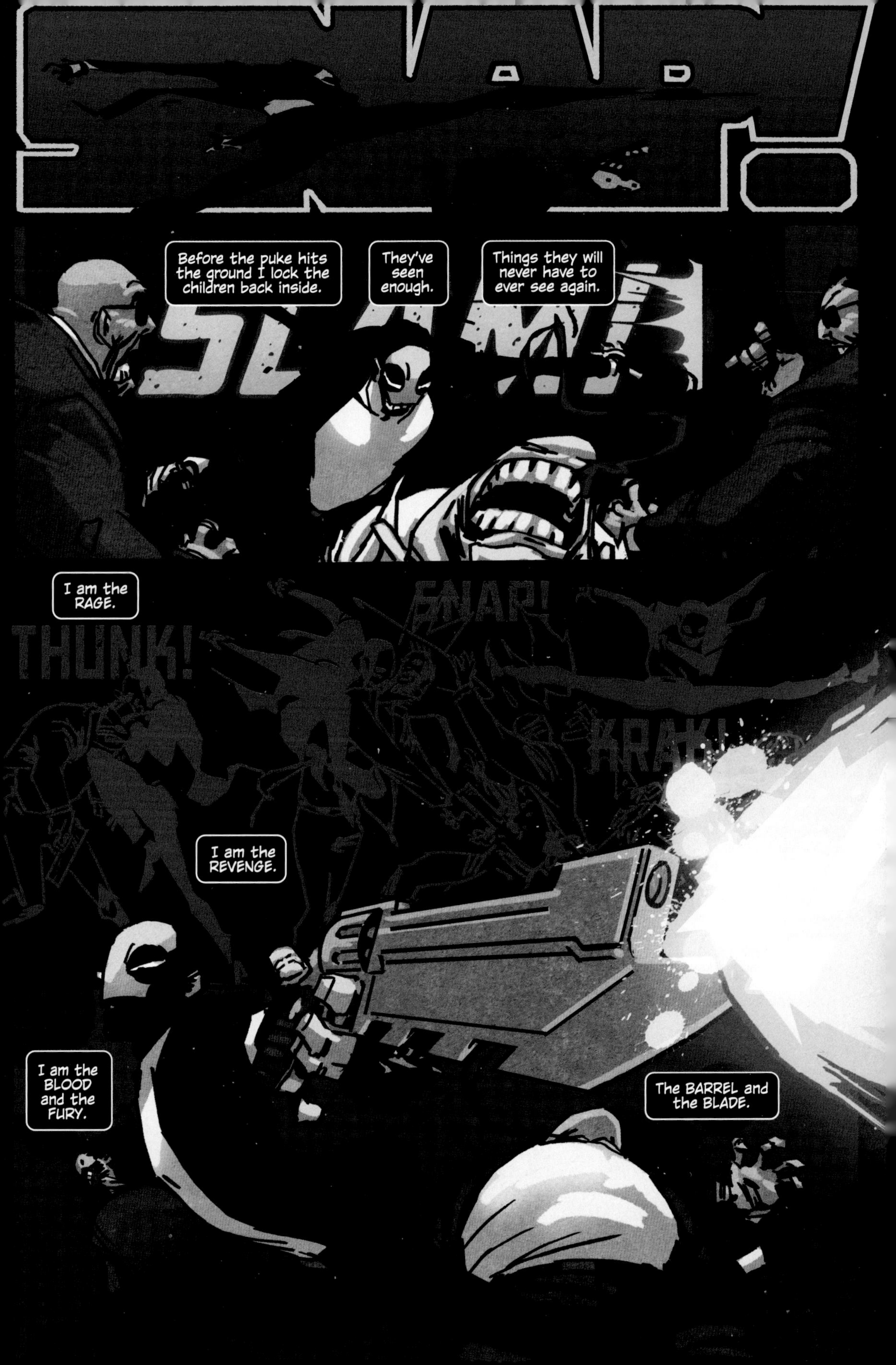
Before the puke hits the ground I lock the children back inside.
They've seen enough.
Things they will never have to ever see again.
I am the RAGE.
THUNK!
SNAP!
KRAK!
I am the REVENGE.
I am the BLOOD and the FURY.
The BARREL and the BLADE.

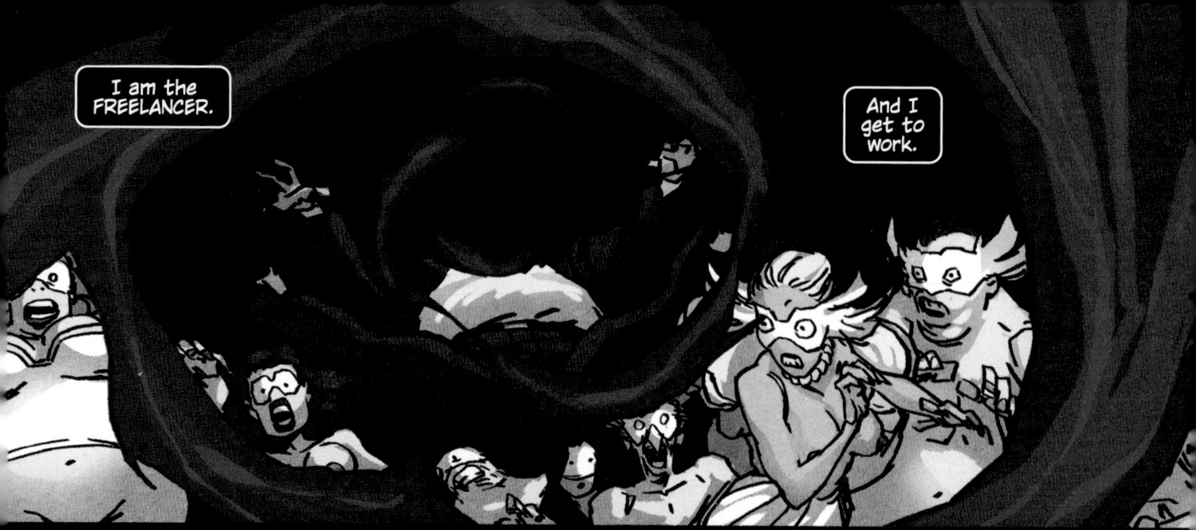
I am the FREELANCER.
And I get to work.
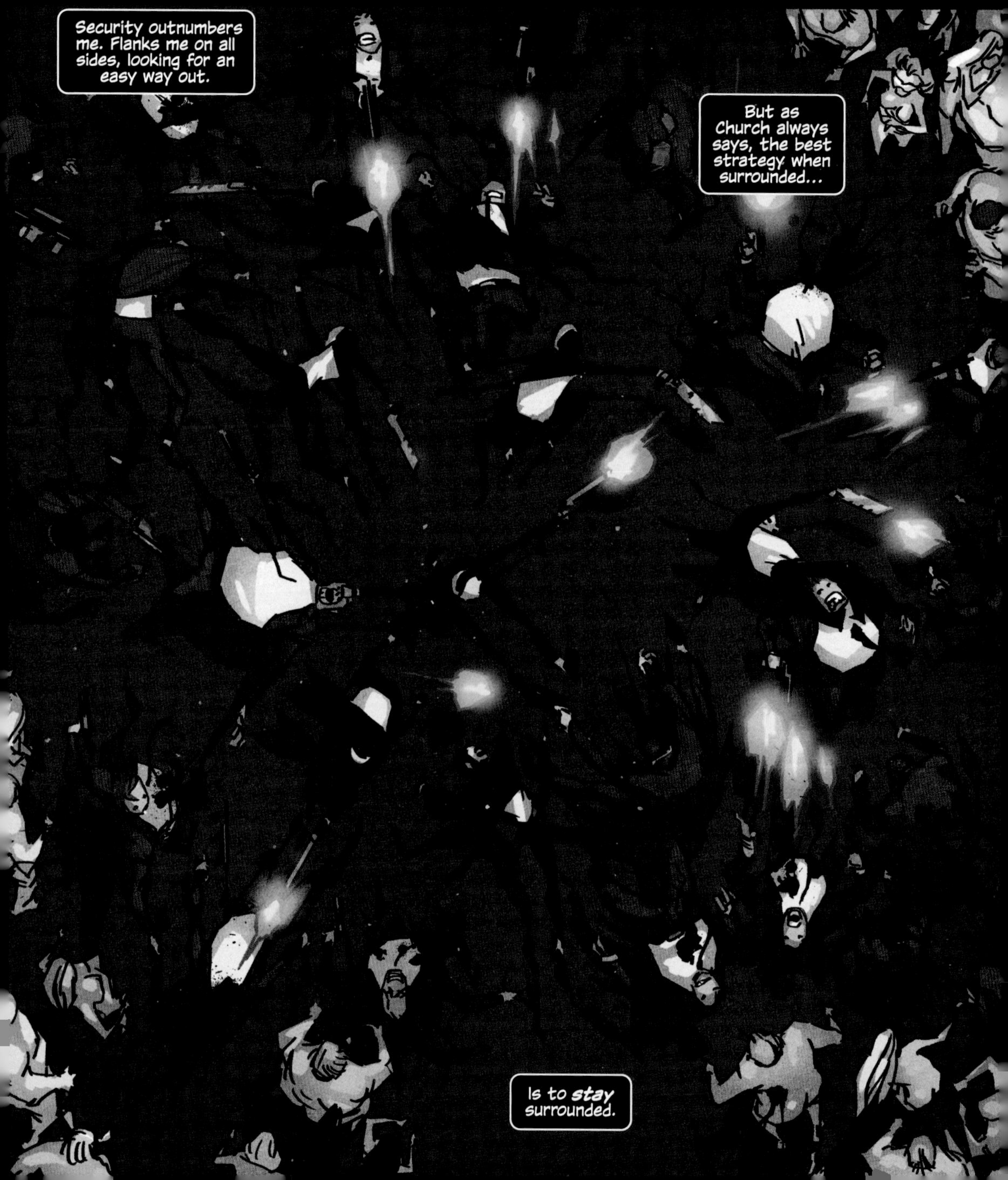
Security outnumbers me. Flanks me on all sides, looking for an easy way out.
But as Church always says, the best strategy when surrounded...
Is to *stay* surrounded.

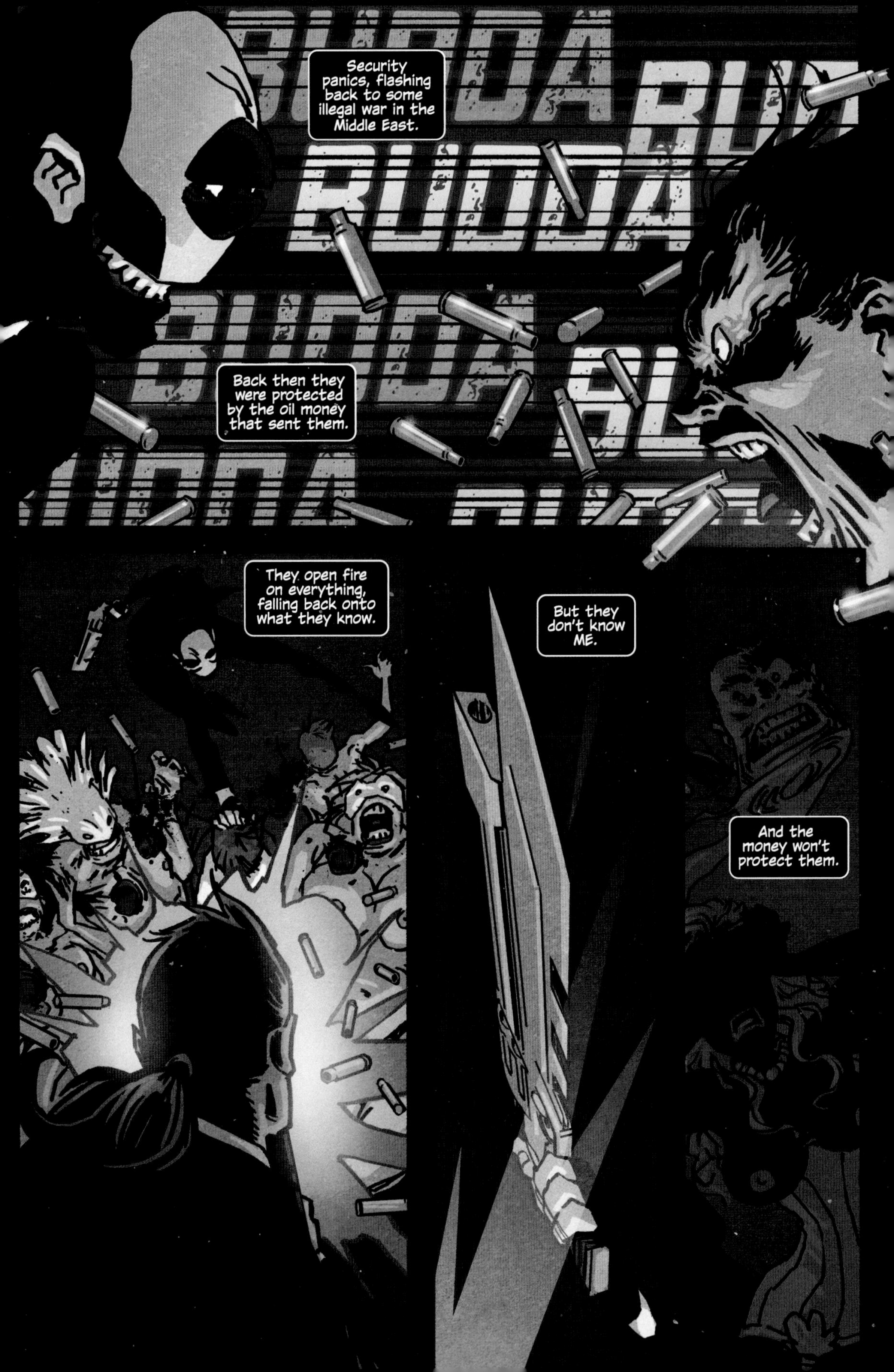
Security panics, flashing back to some illegal war in the Middle East.
Back then they were protected by the oil money that sent them.
They open fire on everything, falling back onto what they know.
But they don't know ME.
And the money won't protect them.

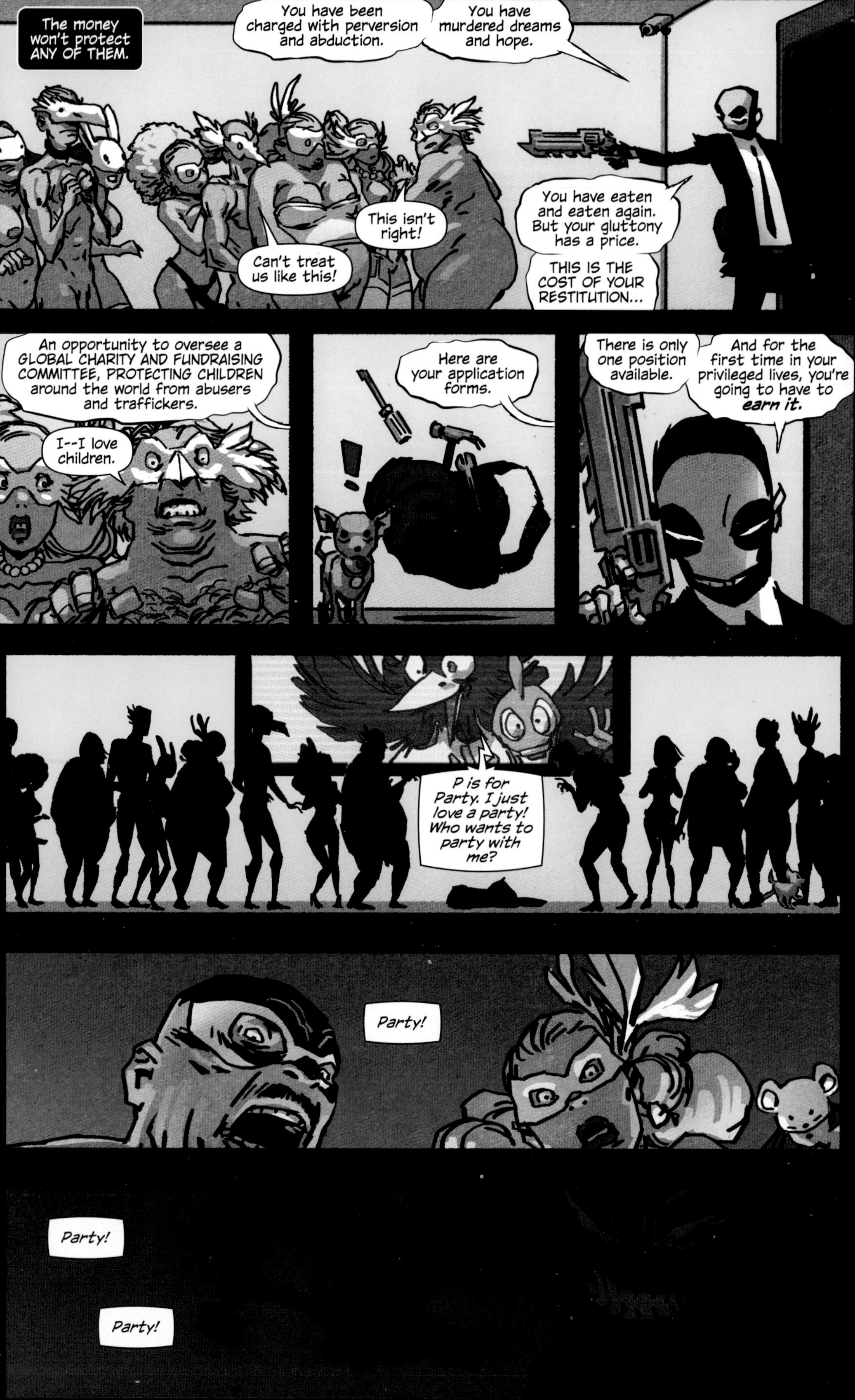
The money won't protect ANY OF THEM.
You have been charged with perversion and abduction.
You have murdered dreams and hope.
This isn't right!
Can't treat us like this!
You have eaten and eaten again. But your gluttony has a price.
THIS IS THE COST OF YOUR RESTITUTION...
An opportunity to oversee a GLOBAL CHARITY AND FUNDRAISING COMMITTEE, PROTECTING CHILDREN around the world from abusers and traffickers.
I--I love children.
Here are your application forms.
!
There is only one position available.
And for the first time in your privileged lives, you're going to have to *earn it.*
P is for Party. I just love a party! Who wants to party with me?
Party!
Party!
Party!

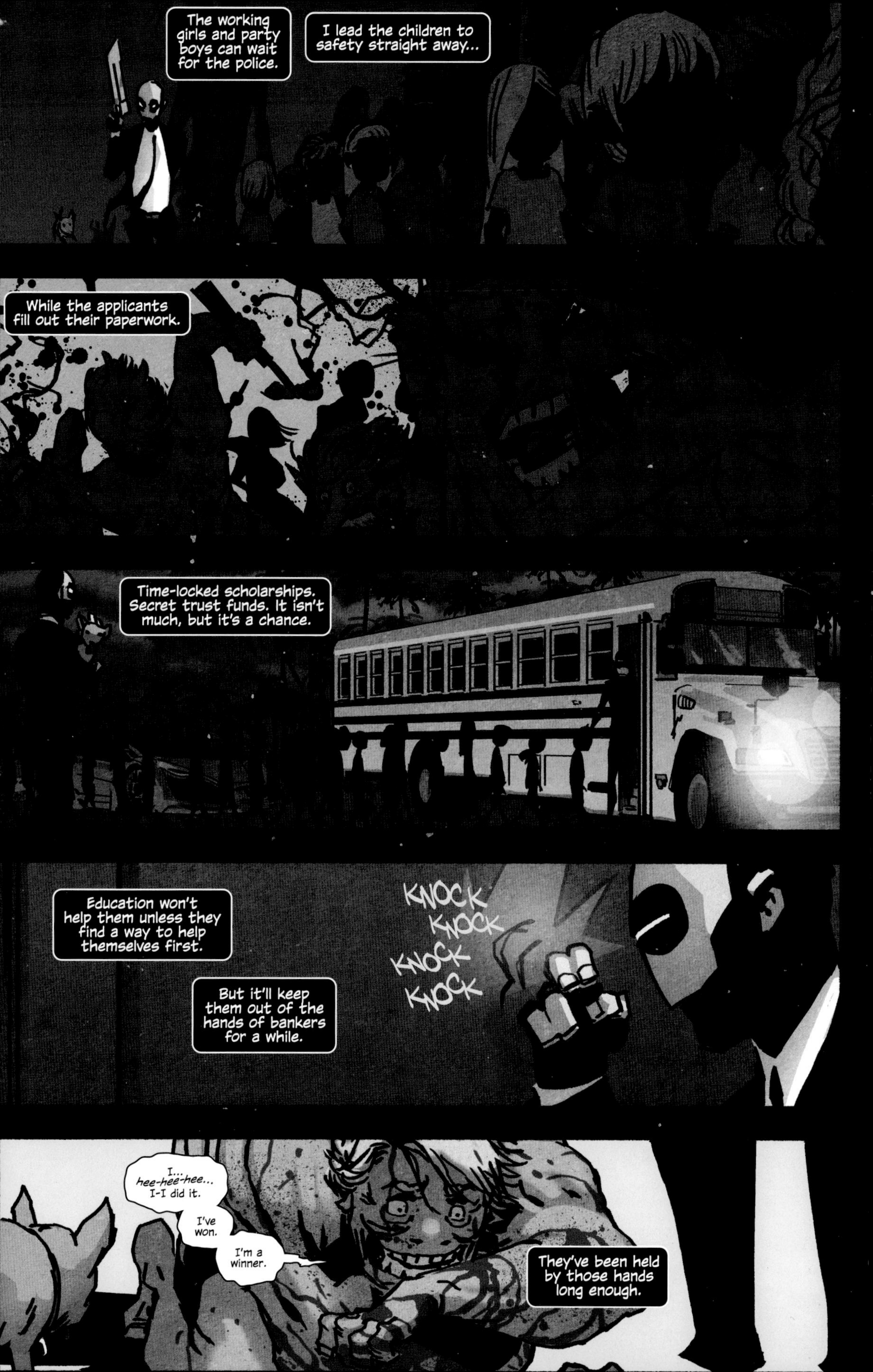

The working girls and party boys can wait for the police.
I lead the children to safety straight away...
While the applicants fill out their paperwork.
Time-locked scholarships. Secret trust funds. It isn't much, but it's a chance.
Education won't help them unless they find a way to help themselves first.
But it'll keep them out of the hands of bankers for a while.
KNOCK KNOCK KNOCK KNOCK
I... *hee-hee-hee*... I-I did it.
I've won.
I'm a winner.
They've been held by those hands long enough.

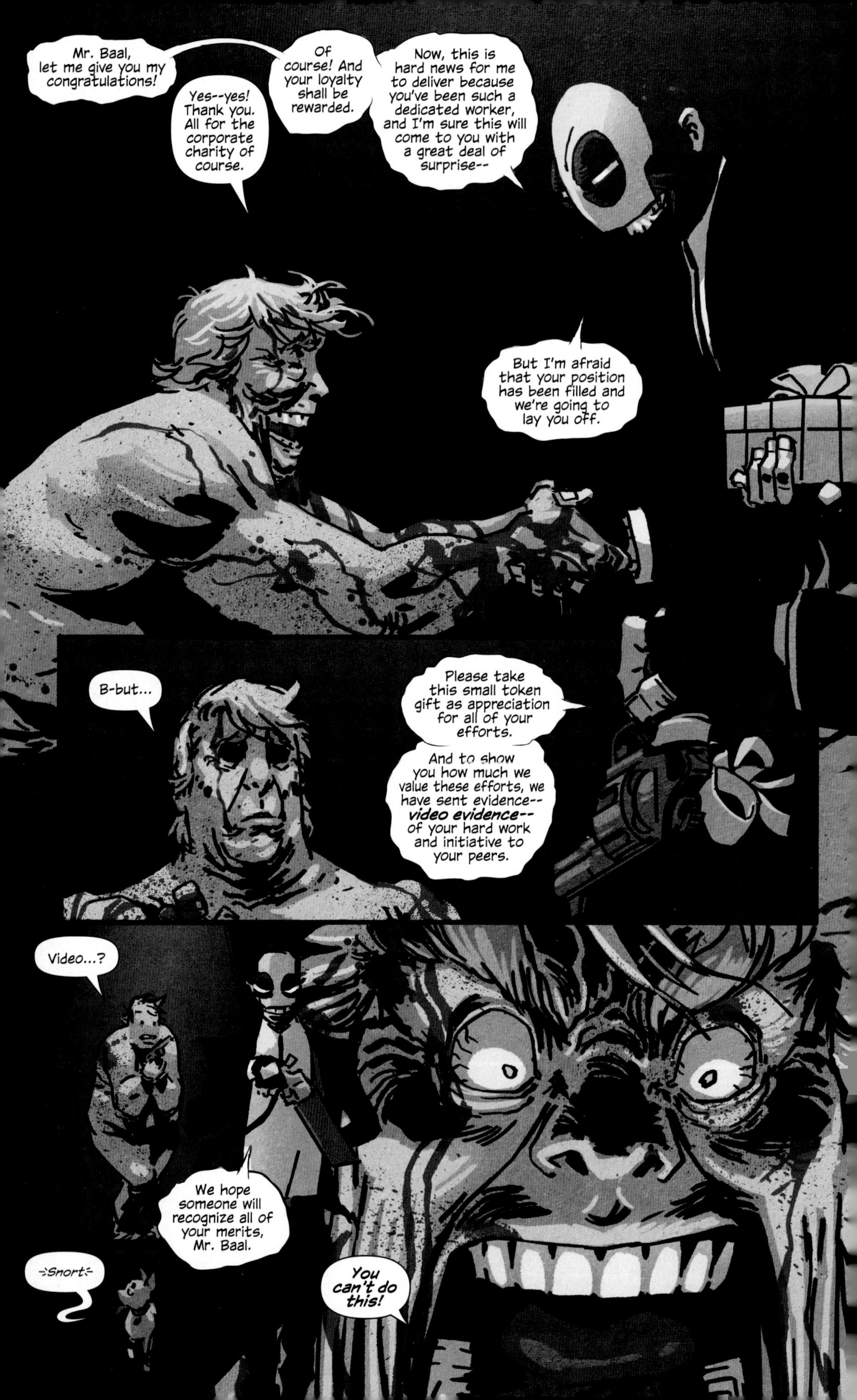

Mr. Baal, let me give you my congratulations!
Yes--yes! Thank you. All for the corporate charity of course.
Of course! And your loyalty shall be rewarded.
Now, this is hard news for me to deliver because you've been such a dedicated worker, and I'm sure this will come to you with a great deal of surprise--
But I'm afraid that your position has been filled and we're going to lay you off.
B-but...
Please take this small token gift as appreciation for all of your efforts.
And to show you how much we value these efforts, we have sent evidence-- *video evidence--* of your hard work and initiative to your peers.
Video...?
We hope someone will recognize all of your merits, Mr. Baal.
Snort
You can't do this!

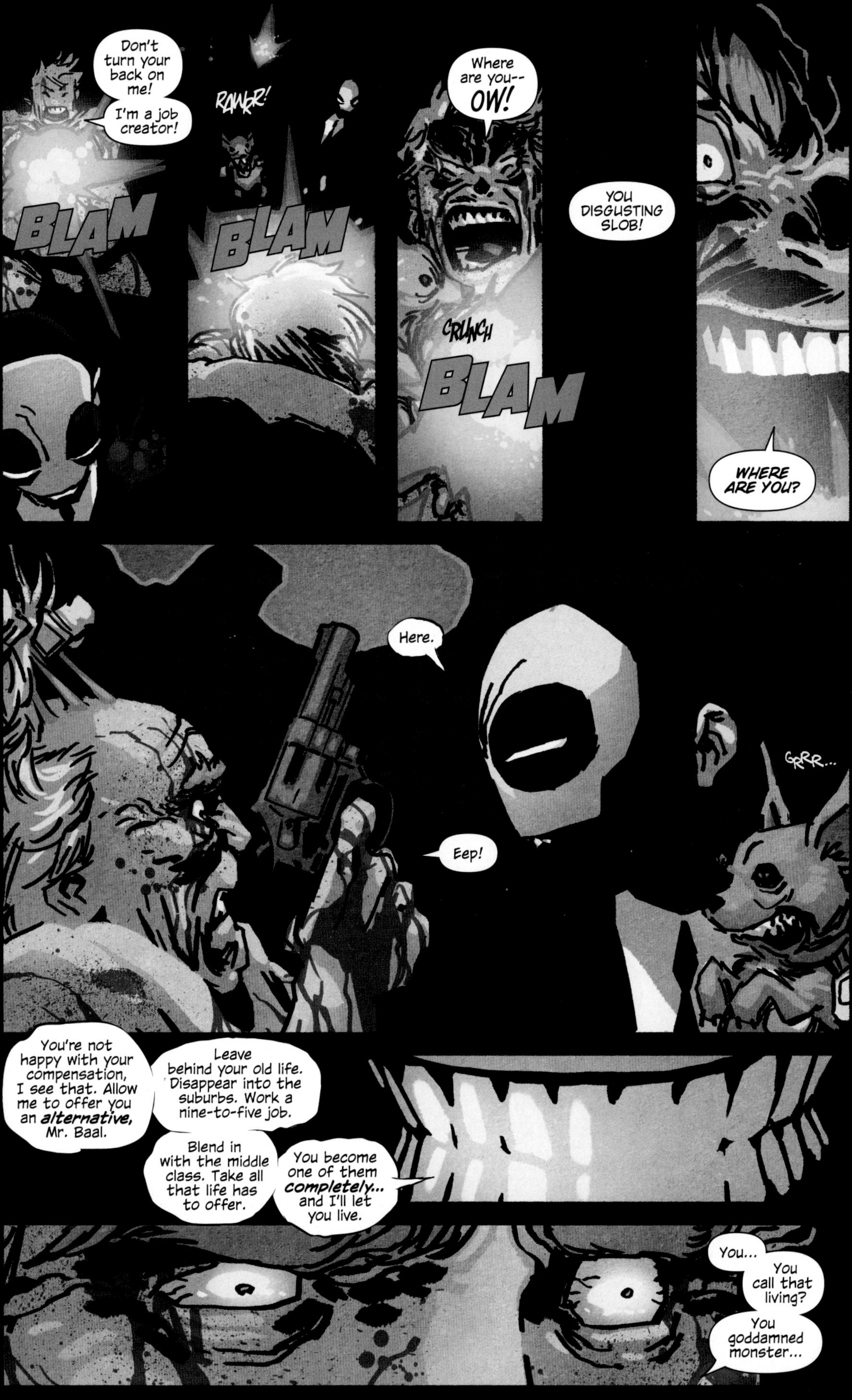
Don't turn your back on me!
I'm a job creator!
BLAM
RAWR!
BLAM
Where are you-- OW!
CRUNCH
BLAM
YOU DISGUSTING SLOB!
WHERE ARE YOU?
Here.
Eep!
GRRR...
You're not happy with your compensation, I see that. Allow me to offer you an *alternative,* Mr. Baal.
Leave behind your old life. Disappear into the suburbs. Work a nine-to-five job.
Blend in with the middle class. Take all that life has to offer.
You become one of them *completely...* and I'll let you live.
You...
You call that living?
You goddamned monster...

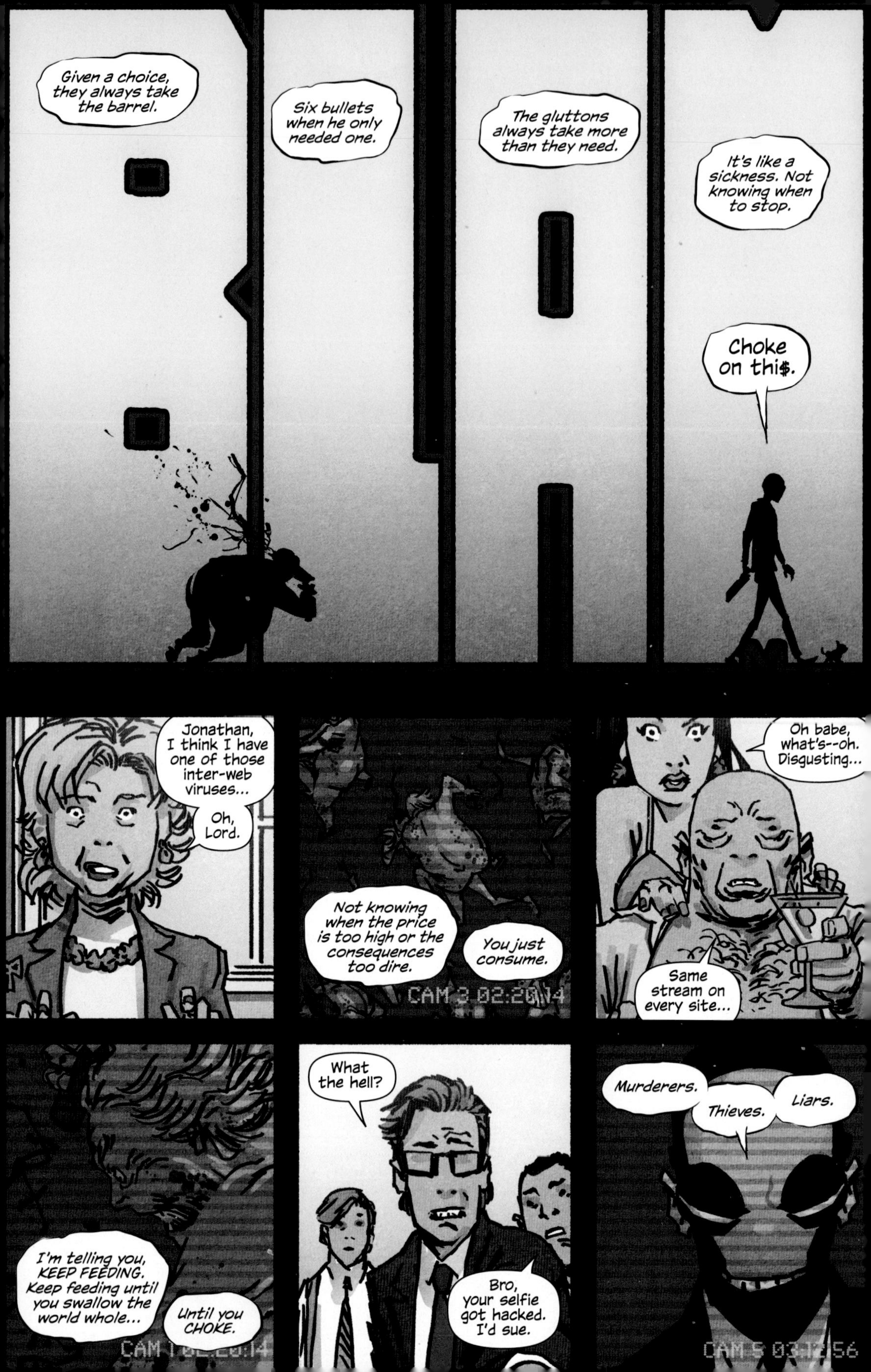
Given a choice, they always take the barrel.
Six bullets when he only needed one.
The gluttons always take more than they need.
It's like a sickness. Not knowing when to stop.
Choke on thi$.
Jonathan, I think I have one of those inter-web viruses...
Oh, Lord.
Not knowing when the price is too high or the consequences too dire.
You just consume.
CAM 3 02:20:14
Oh babe, what's--oh. Disgusting...
Same stream on every site...
I'm telling you, KEEP FEEDING. Keep feeding until you swallow the world whole...
Until you CHOKE.
CAM 1 02:20:14
What the hell?
Bro, your selfie got hacked. I'd sue.
Murderers.
Thieves.
Liars.
CAM 5 03:12:56

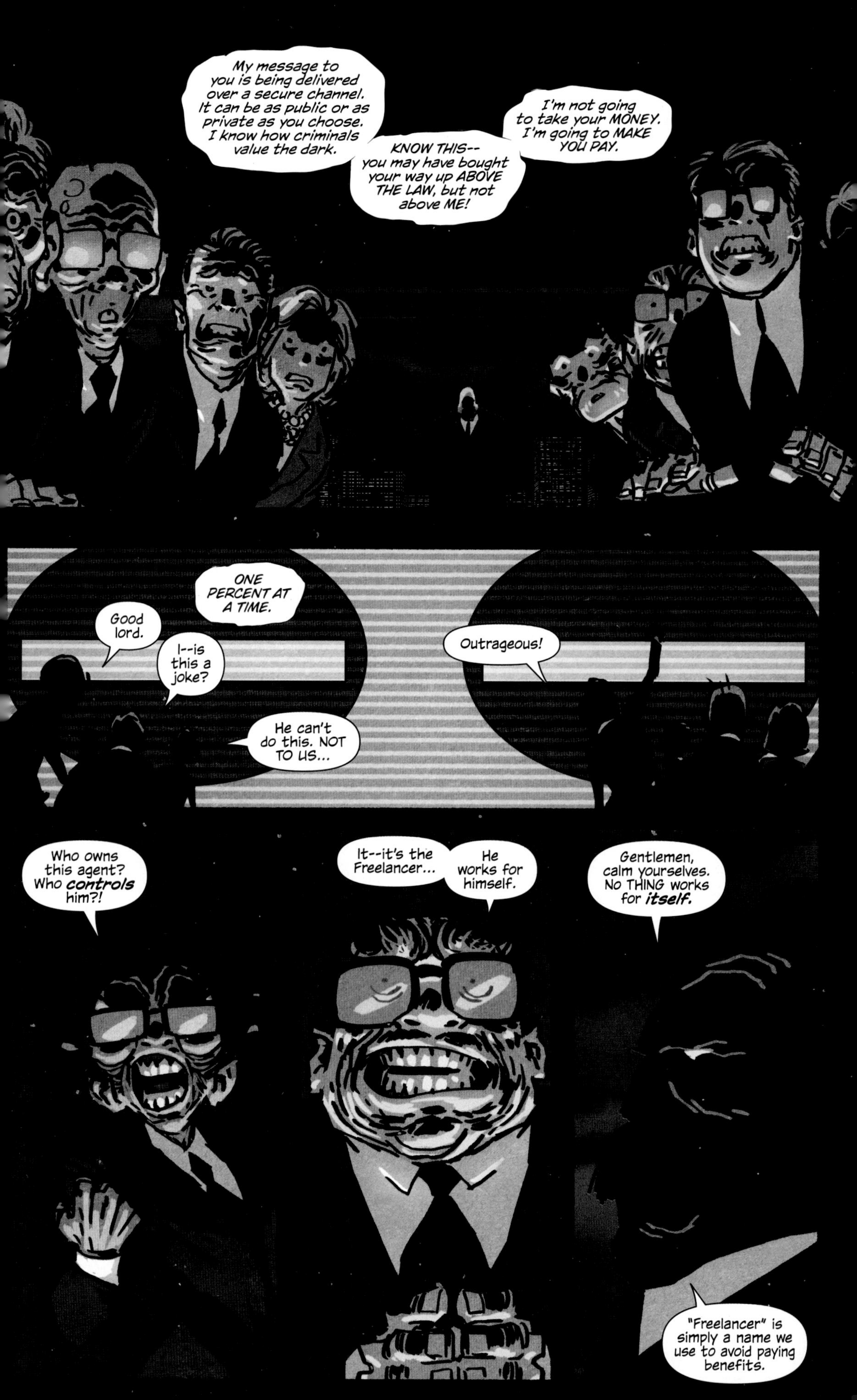
My message to you is being delivered over a secure channel. It can be as public or as private as you choose. I know how criminals value the dark.
KNOW THIS-- you may have bought your way up ABOVE THE LAW, but not above ME!
I'm not going to take your MONEY. I'm going to MAKE YOU PAY.
ONE PERCENT AT A TIME.
Good lord.
I--is this a joke?
He can't do this. NOT TO US...
Outrageous!
Who owns this agent? Who ***controls*** him?!
It--it's the Freelancer...
He works for himself.
Gentlemen, calm yourselves. No THING works for ***itself.***
"Freelancer" is simply a name we use to avoid paying benefits.

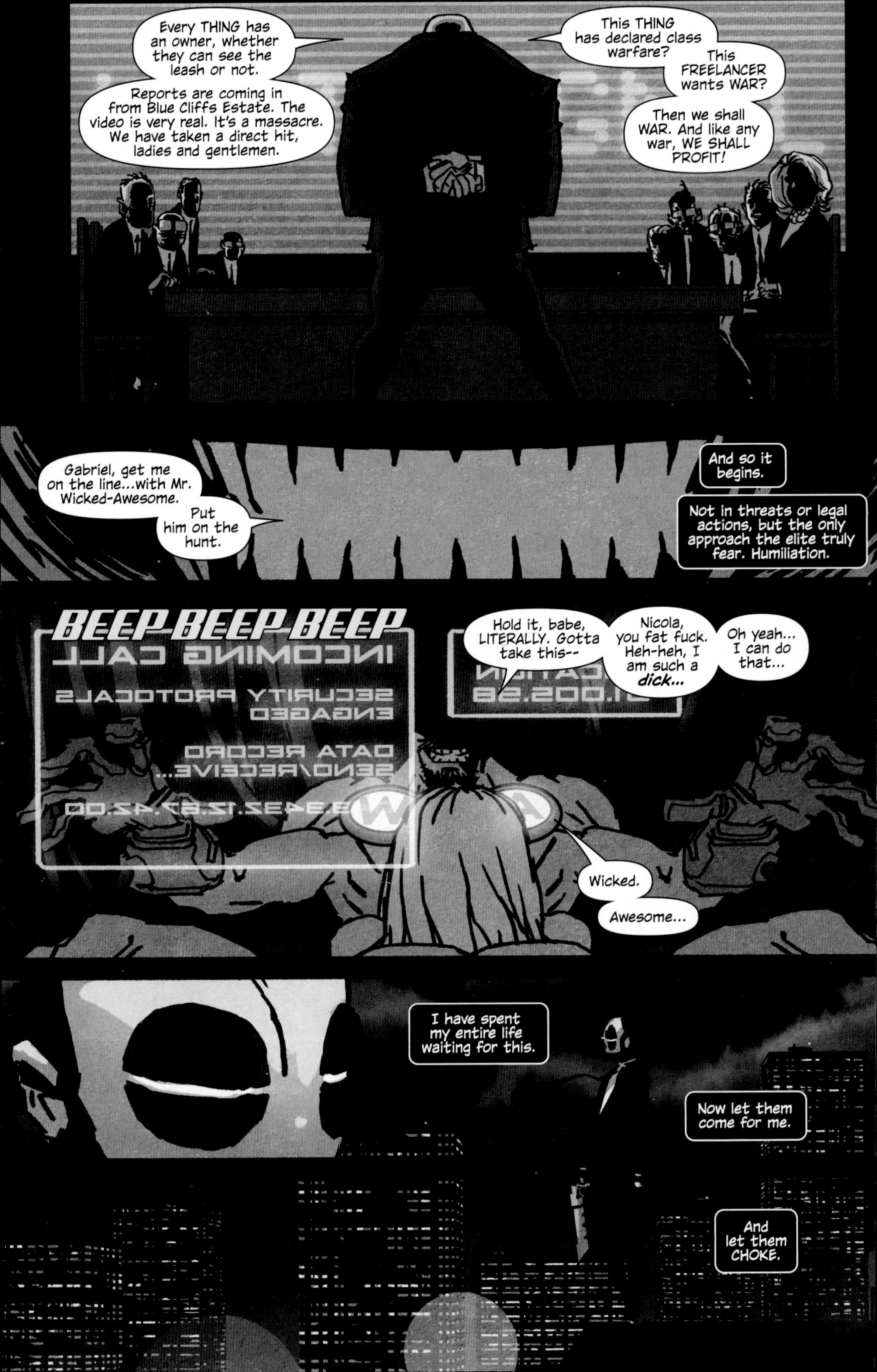
Every THING has an owner, whether they can see the leash or not.
Reports are coming in from Blue Cliffs Estate. The video is very real. It's a massacre. We have taken a direct hit, ladies and gentlemen.
This THING has declared class warfare?
This FREELANCER wants WAR?
Then we shall WAR. And like any war, WE SHALL PROFIT!
Gabriel, get me on the line...with Mr. Wicked-Awesome.
Put him on the hunt.
And so it begins.
Not in threats or legal actions, but the only approach the elite truly fear. Humiliation.
BEEP BEEP BEEP
Hold it, babe, LITERALLY. Gotta take this--
Nicola, you fat fuck. Heh-heh, I am such a dick...
Oh yeah... I can do that...
Wicked.
Awesome...
I have spent my entire life waiting for this.
Now let them come for me.
And let them CHOKE.

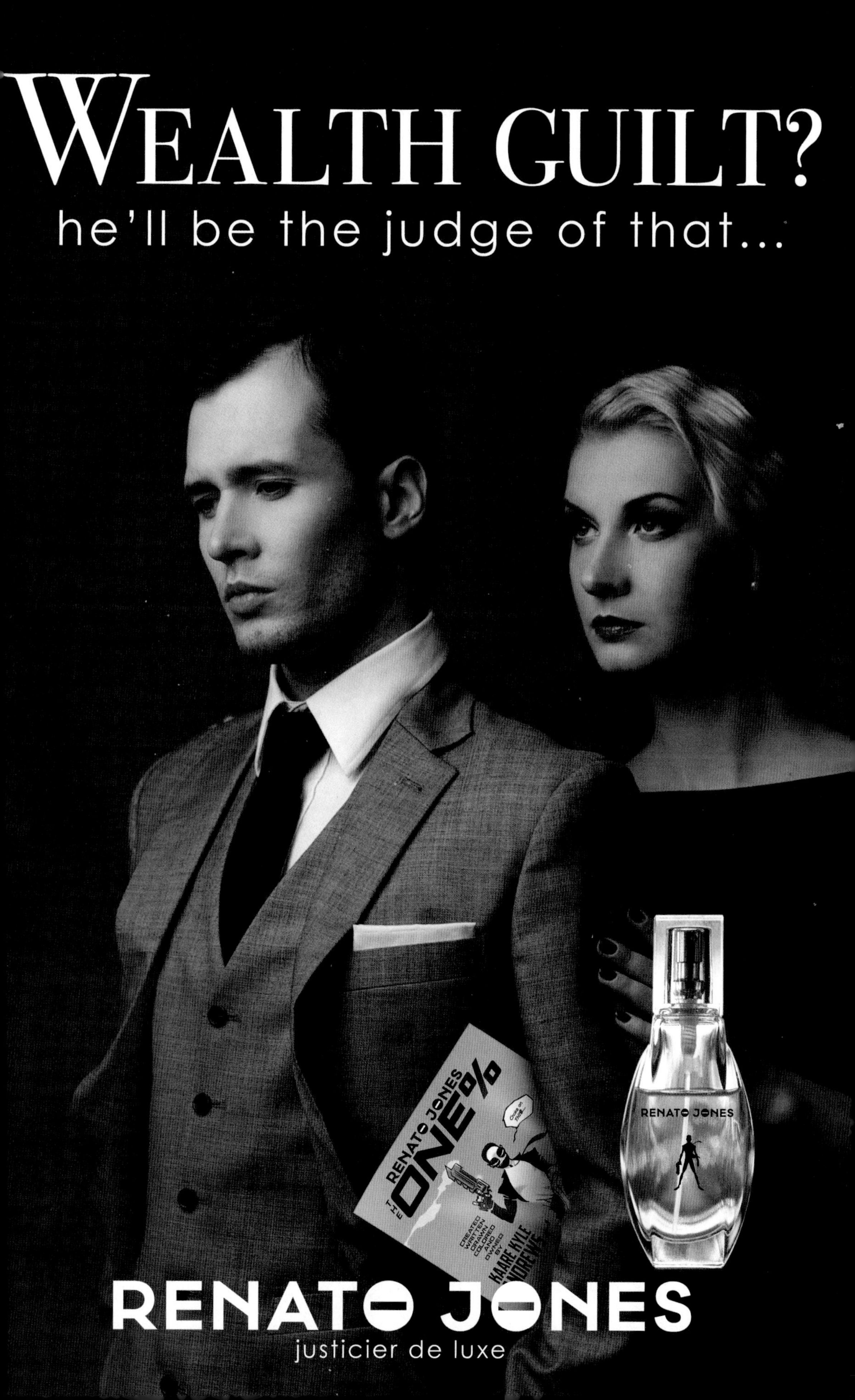
WEALTH GUILT?
he'll be the judge of that...
RENATO JONES
THE ONE%
Choke on THIS...
CREATED WRITTEN DRAWN COLORED AND OWNED BY
KAARE KYLE
RENATO JONES
RENATO JONES
justicier de luxe

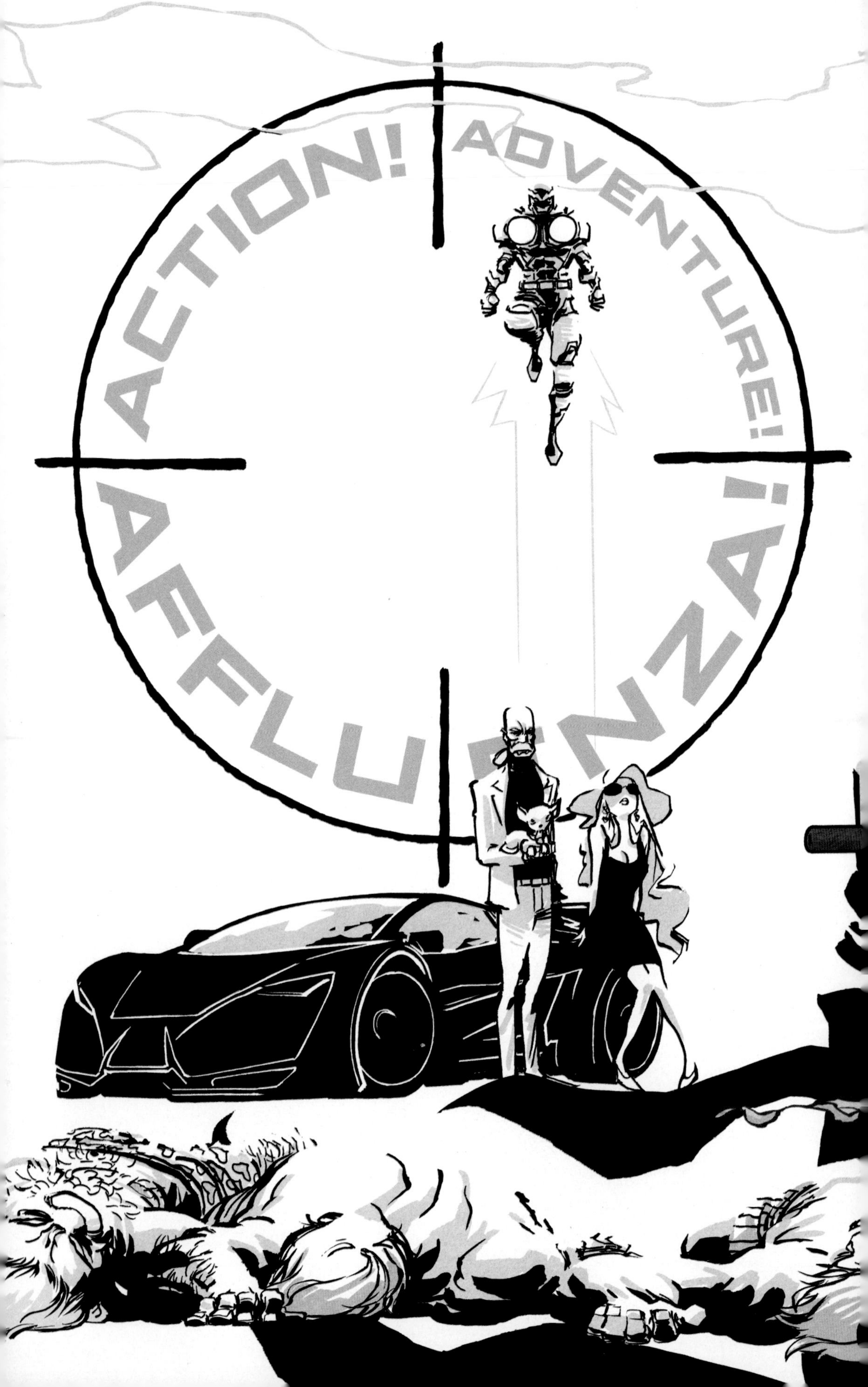
ACTION! ADVENTURE!
AFFLUENZA!

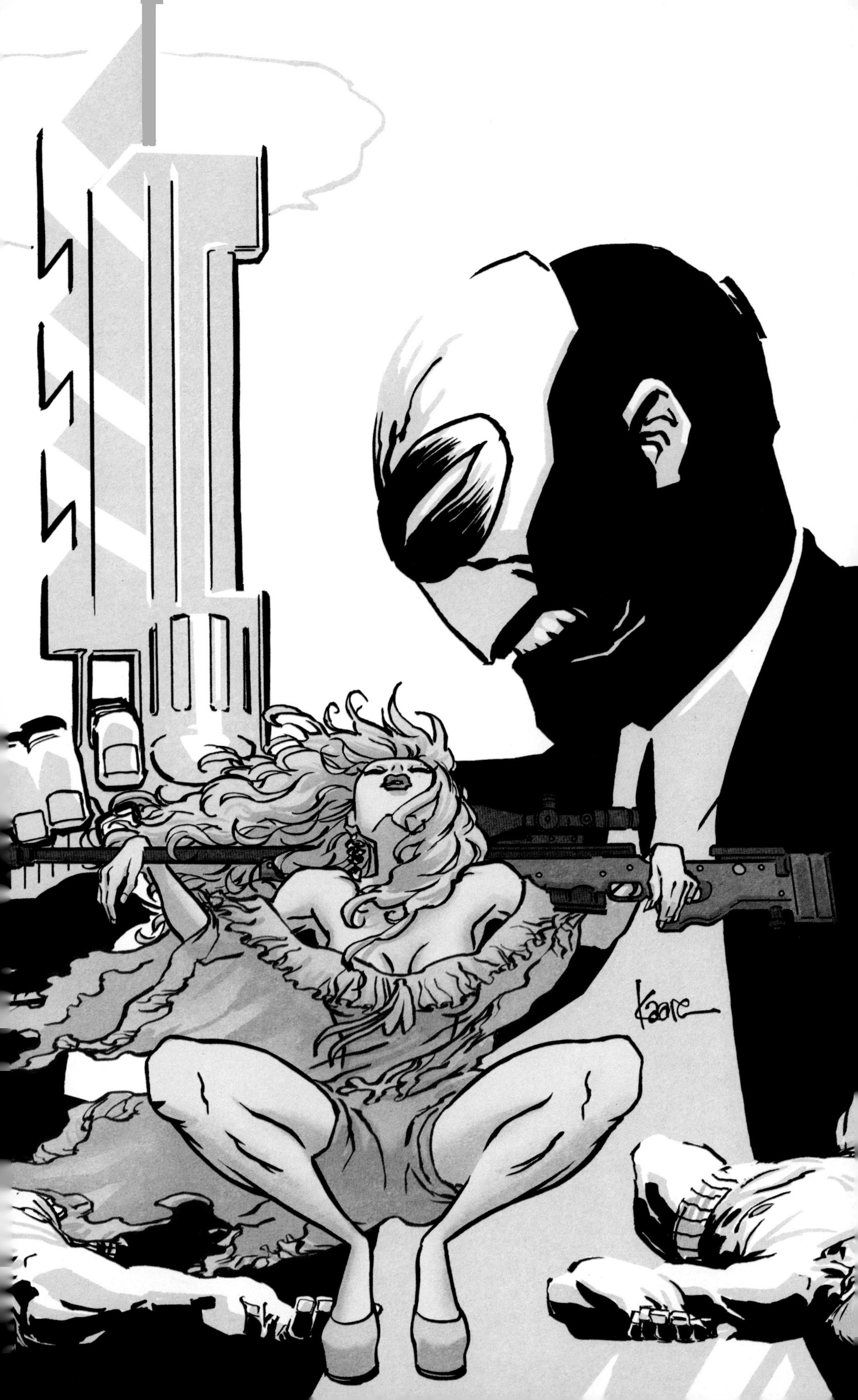

3

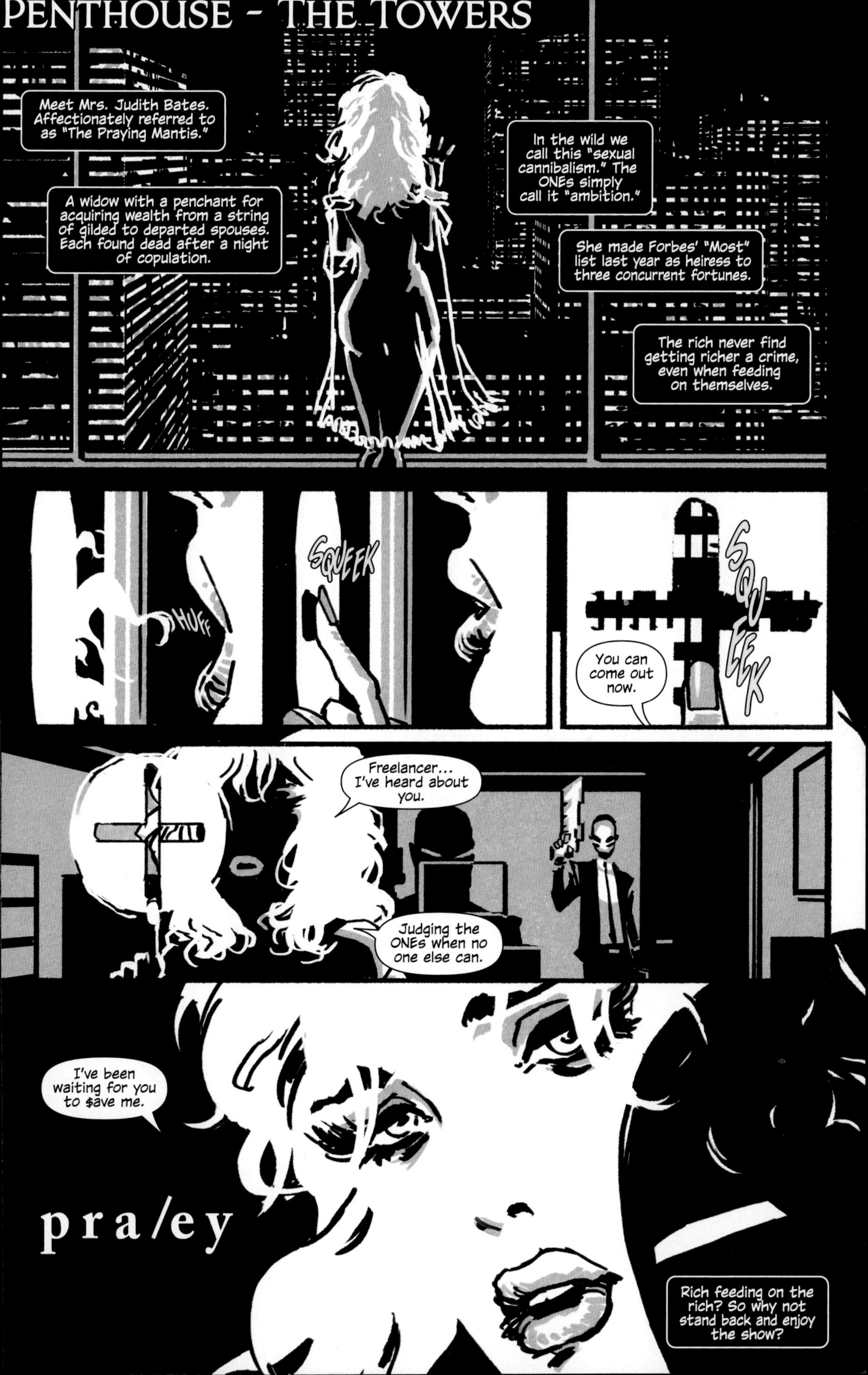
PENTHOUSE - THE TOWERS
Meet Mrs. Judith Bates. Affectionately referred to as "The Praying Mantis."
A widow with a penchant for acquiring wealth from a string of gilded to departed spouses. Each found dead after a night of copulation.
In the wild we call this "sexual cannibalism." The ONEs simply call it "ambition."
She made Forbes' "Most" list last year as heiress to three concurrent fortunes.
The rich never find getting richer a crime, even when feeding on themselves.
HUFF
SQUEEK
SQUEEK
You can come out now.
Freelancer... I've heard about you.
Judging the ONEs when no one else can.
I've been waiting for you to $ave me.
pra/ey
Rich feeding on the rich? So why not stand back and enjoy the show?

For the rest of society, a crime demands an investigation. And so the entitled smirk and play along, thanking the little people for their help.

While civil servants go missing, witnesses gunned down in broad daylight...detectives murdered.

Mrs. Bates didn't scare away the consequences so much as eliminate them.

I put her headcount at sixty-eight that I can directly trace back to her.

Who knows how many others along the way...

It's like some kind of sickness. All of this privilege... this power.

You just can't stop taking.

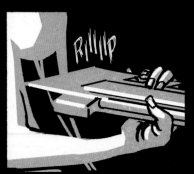

RIIIIP

Do you know what that's like?

Pushing fifty, and Mrs. Bates lures me to her web with the body of a jackhammer.

Eyes like rain.

To lose control?

Teeth like fangs.

I'll show you.

Come.

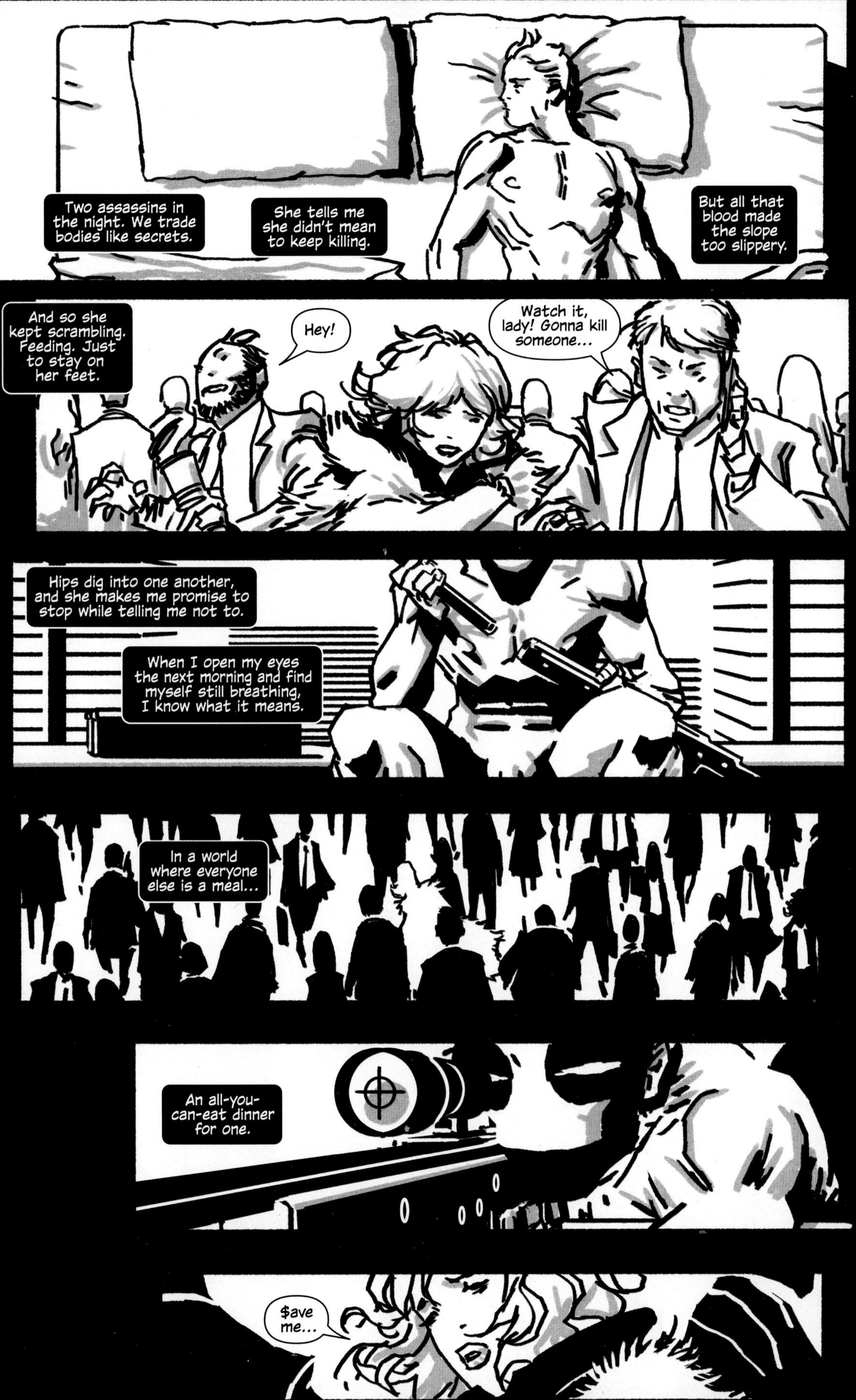
Two assassins in the night. We trade bodies like secrets.
She tells me she didn't mean to keep killing.
But all that blood made the slope too slippery.
And so she kept scrambling. Feeding. Just to stay on her feet.
Hey!
Watch it, lady! Gonna kill someone...
Hips dig into one another, and she makes me promise to stop while telling me not to.
When I open my eyes the next morning and find myself still breathing, I know what it means.
In a world where everyone else is a meal...
An all-you-can-eat dinner for one.
$ave me...

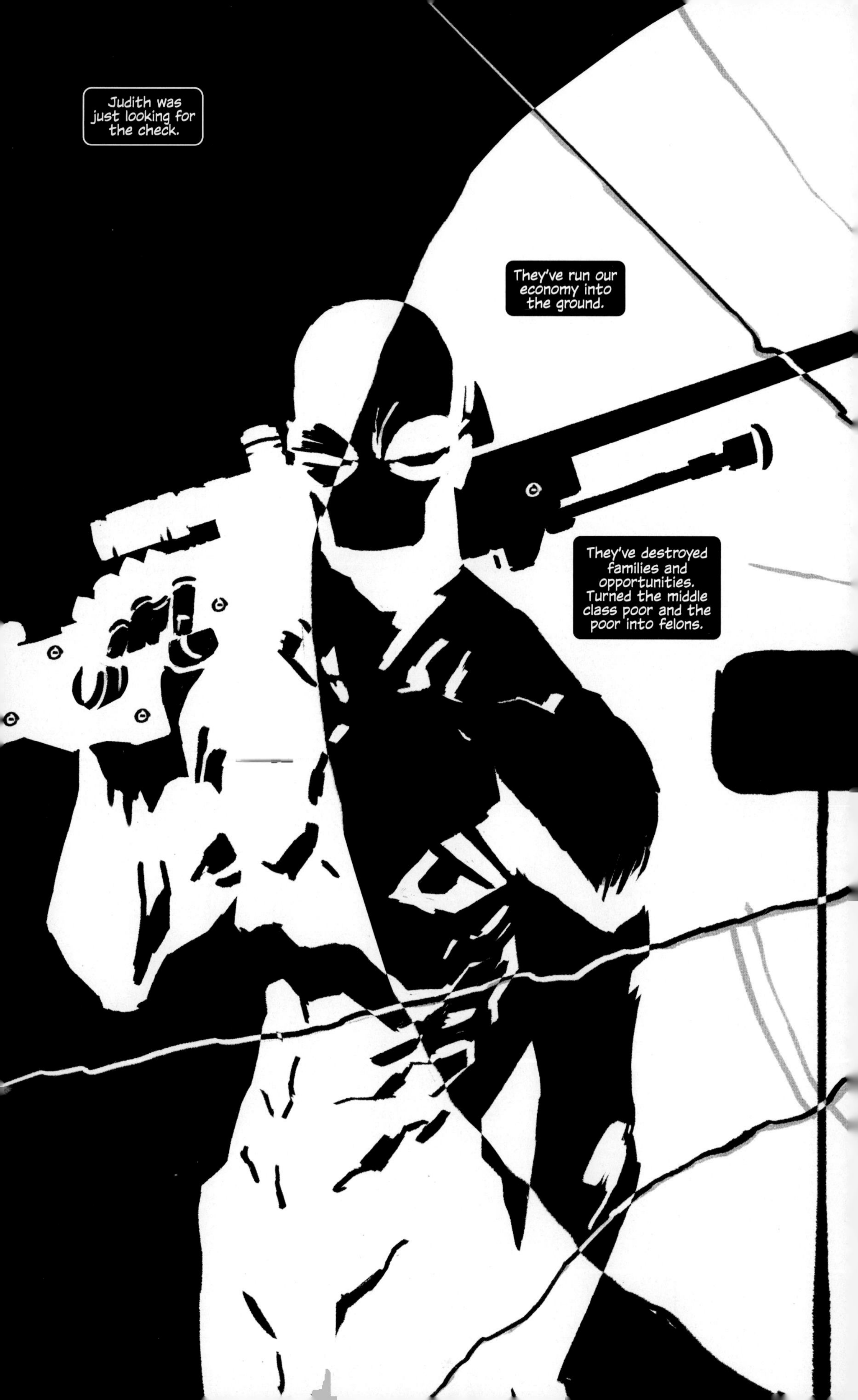
Judith was just looking for the check.
They've run our economy into the ground.
They've destroyed families and opportunities. Turned the middle class poor and the poor into felons.

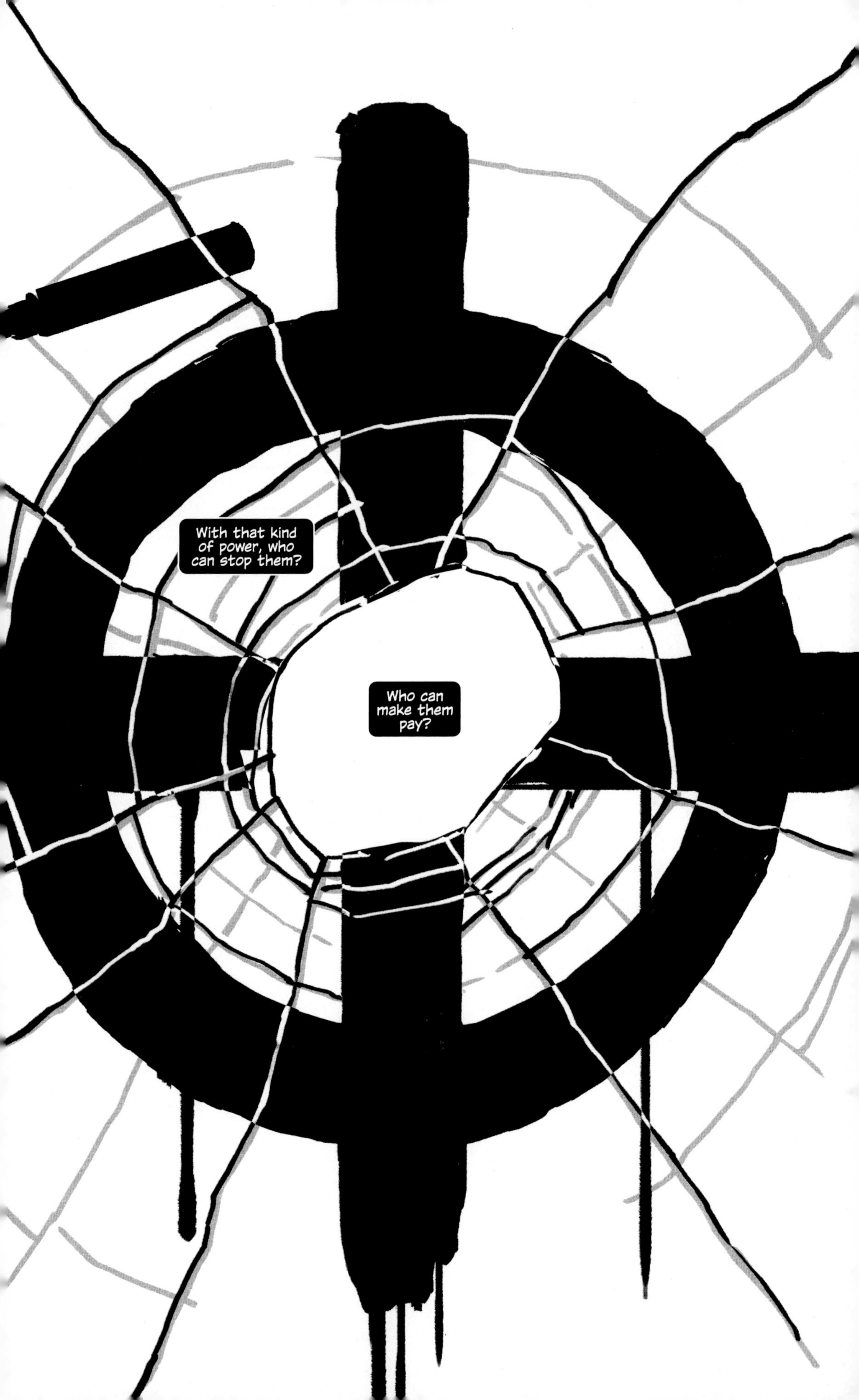
With that kind of power, who can stop them?
Who can make them pay?

SUBURBIA

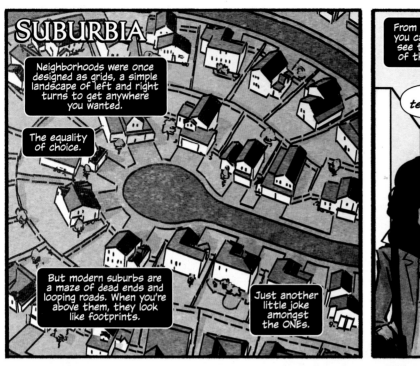

Neighborhoods were once designed as grids, a simple landscape of left and right turns to get anywhere you wanted.

The equality of choice.

But modern suburbs are a maze of dead ends and looping roads. When you're above them, they look like footprints.

Just another little joke amongst the ONEs.

From the dirt, you can't even see the bars of the cage.

"Home." It feels good doesn't it?

It feels *temporary.*

Oh, hush. Is it so hard to believe we've finally had something good come our way?

What do you think, Bean?

You believe a fifth cousin I've never heard of wrote me into a will for a fully furnished home and then slipped in the shower?

Just when we were two months behind rent?

Cameron this isn't luck, it's opportunity.

Well, I'm off to find an opportunity to put food on the table of our poor, departed "Cousin Elda."

#@$*!

Morning, Bill. Trouble?

This darned hose is broken!

Have you tried turning the water on?

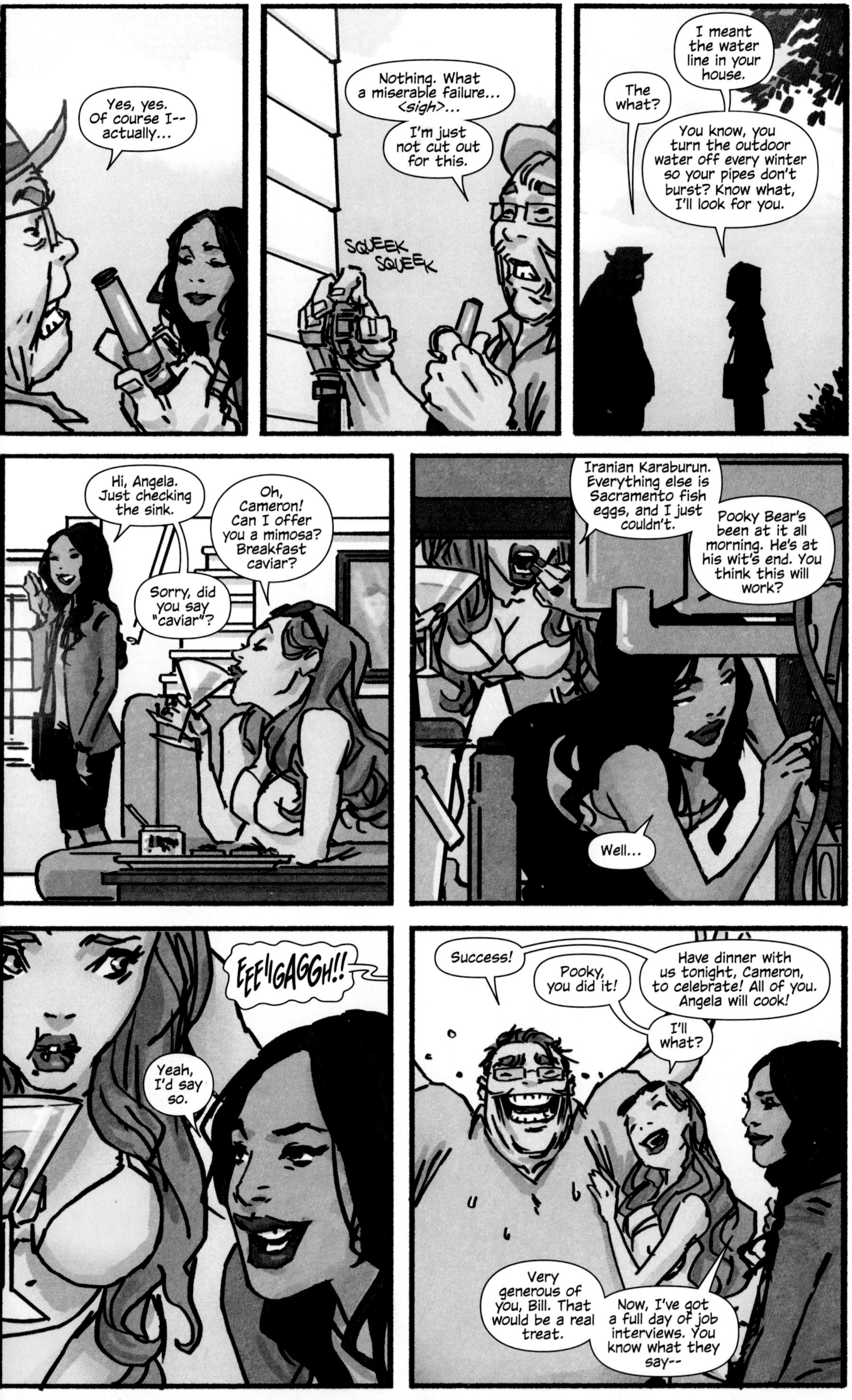
Yes, yes. Of course I-- actually...
Nothing. What a miserable failure... <sigh>...
I'm just not cut out for this.
SQUEEK SQUEEK
The what?
I meant the water line in your house.
You know, you turn the outdoor water off every winter so your pipes don't burst? Know what, I'll look for you.
Hi, Angela. Just checking the sink.
Oh, Cameron! Can I offer you a mimosa? Breakfast caviar?
Sorry, did you say "caviar"?
Iranian Karaburun. Everything else is Sacramento fish eggs, and I just couldn't.
Pooky Bear's been at it all morning. He's at his wit's end. You think this will work?
Well...
EEE!!GAGGH!!
Yeah, I'd say so.
Success!
Pooky, you did it!
Have dinner with us tonight, Cameron, to celebrate! All of you. Angela will cook!
I'll what?
Very generous of you, Bill. That would be a real treat.
Now, I've got a full day of job interviews. You know what they say--

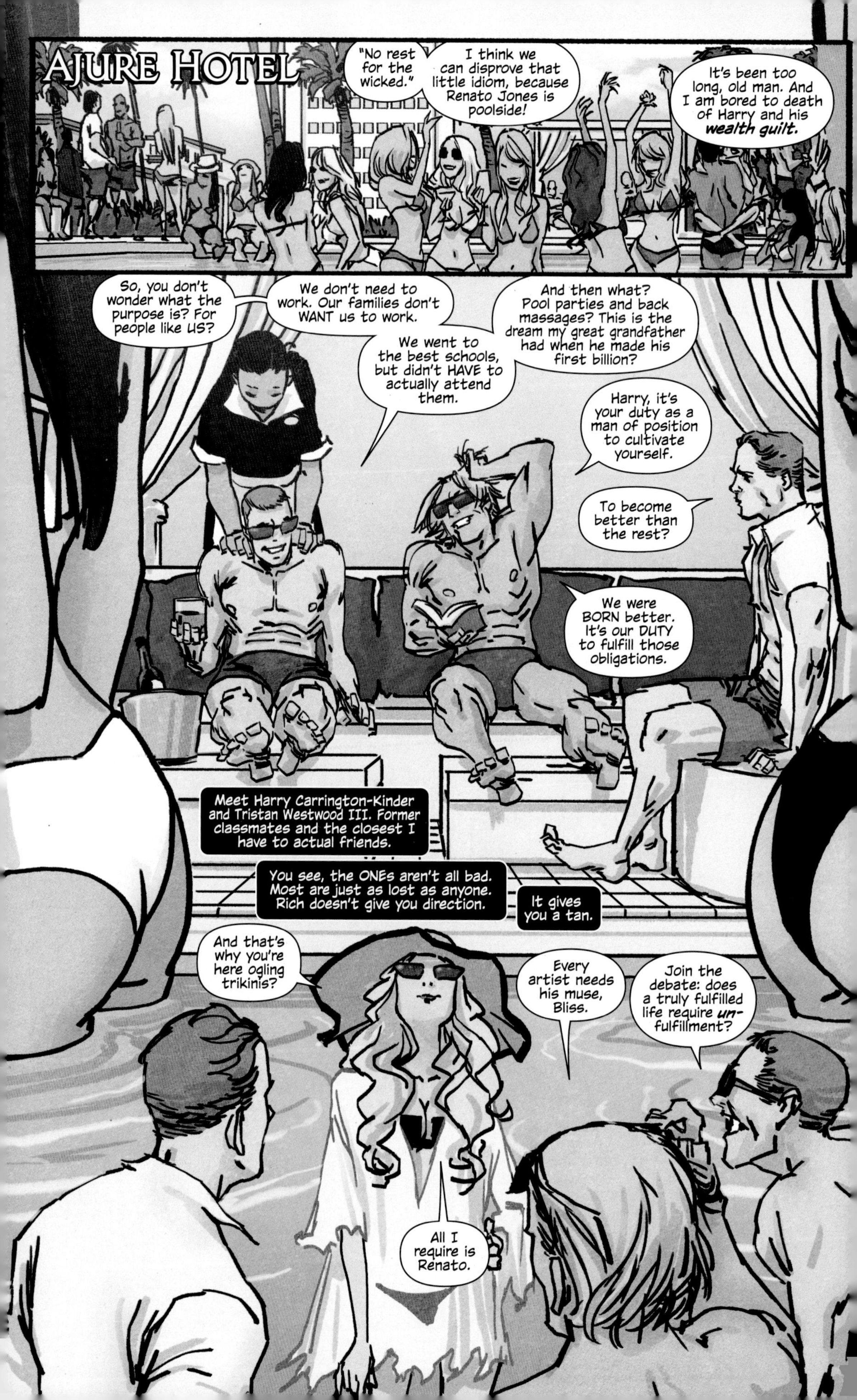
AJURE HOTEL
"No rest for the wicked."
I think we can disprove that little idiom, because Renato Jones is poolside!
It's been too long, old man. And I am bored to death of Harry and his *wealth guilt.*
So, you don't wonder what the purpose is? For people like US?
We don't need to work. Our families don't WANT us to work.
We went to the best schools, but didn't HAVE to actually attend them.
And then what? Pool parties and back massages? This is the dream my great grandfather had when he made his first billion?
Harry, it's your duty as a man of position to cultivate yourself.
To become better than the rest?
We were BORN better. It's our DUTY to fulfill those obligations.
Meet Harry Carrington-Kinder and Tristan Westwood III. Former classmates and the closest I have to actual friends.
You see, the ONEs aren't all bad. Most are just as lost as anyone. Rich doesn't give you direction.
It gives you a tan.
And that's why you're here ogling trikinis?
Every artist needs his muse, Bliss.
Join the debate: does a truly fulfilled life require *un*-fulfillment?
All I require is Renato.

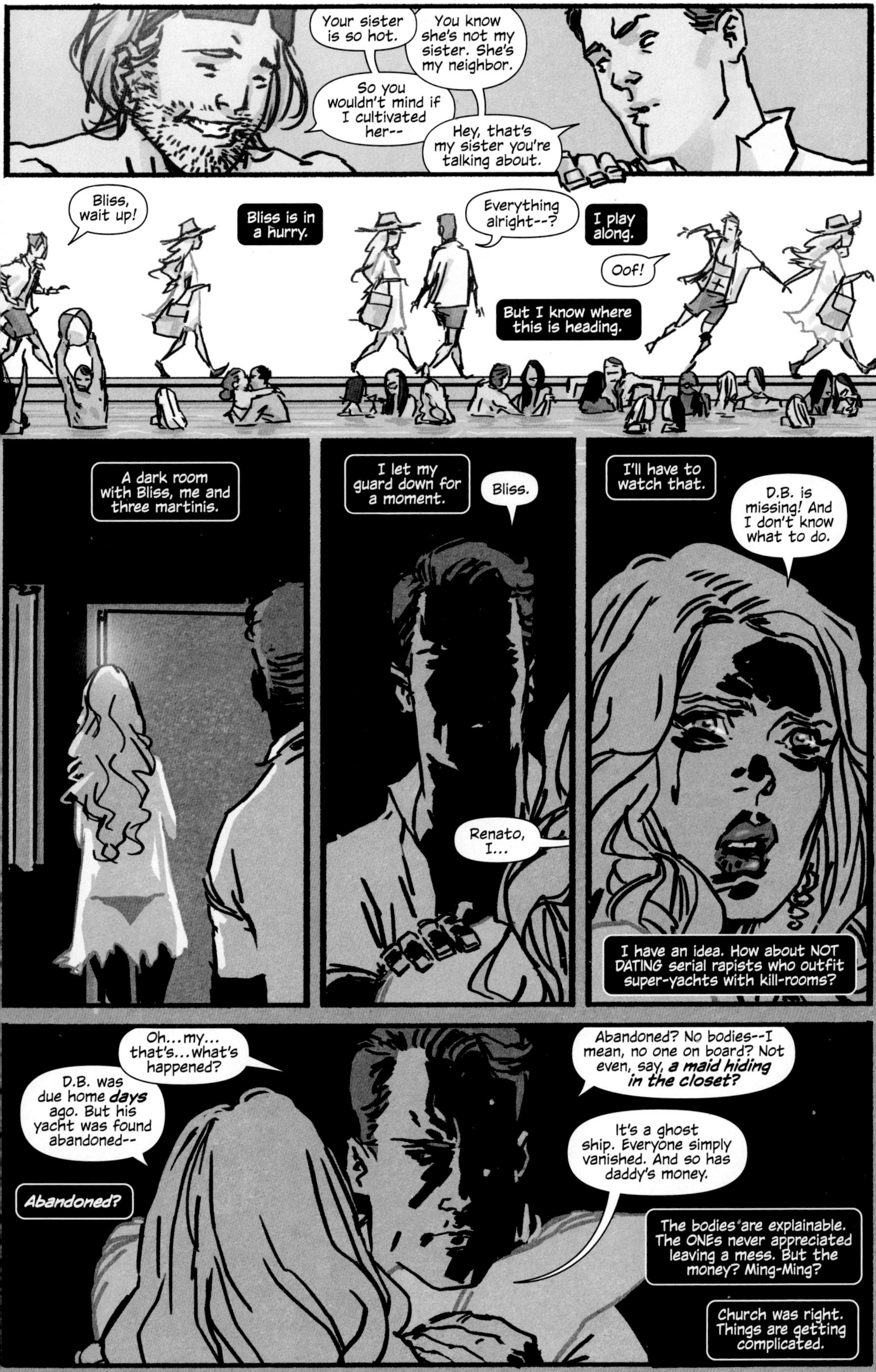
Your sister is so hot.
You know she's not my sister. She's my neighbor.
So you wouldn't mind if I cultivated her--
Hey, that's my sister you're talking about.
Bliss, wait up!
Bliss is in a hurry.
Everything alright--?
I play along.
Oof!
But I know where this is heading.
A dark room with Bliss, me and three martinis.
I let my guard down for a moment.
Bliss.
Renato, I...
I'll have to watch that.
D.B. is missing! And I don't know what to do.
I have an idea. How about NOT DATING serial rapists who outfit super-yachts with kill-rooms?
Oh...my... that's...what's happened?
D.B. was due home *days* ago. But his yacht was found abandoned--
Abandoned?
Abandoned? No bodies--I mean, no one on board? Not even, say, *a maid hiding in the closet?*
It's a ghost ship. Everyone simply vanished. And so has daddy's money.
The bodies are explainable. The ONEs never appreciated leaving a mess. But the money? Ming-Ming?
Church was right. Things are getting complicated.

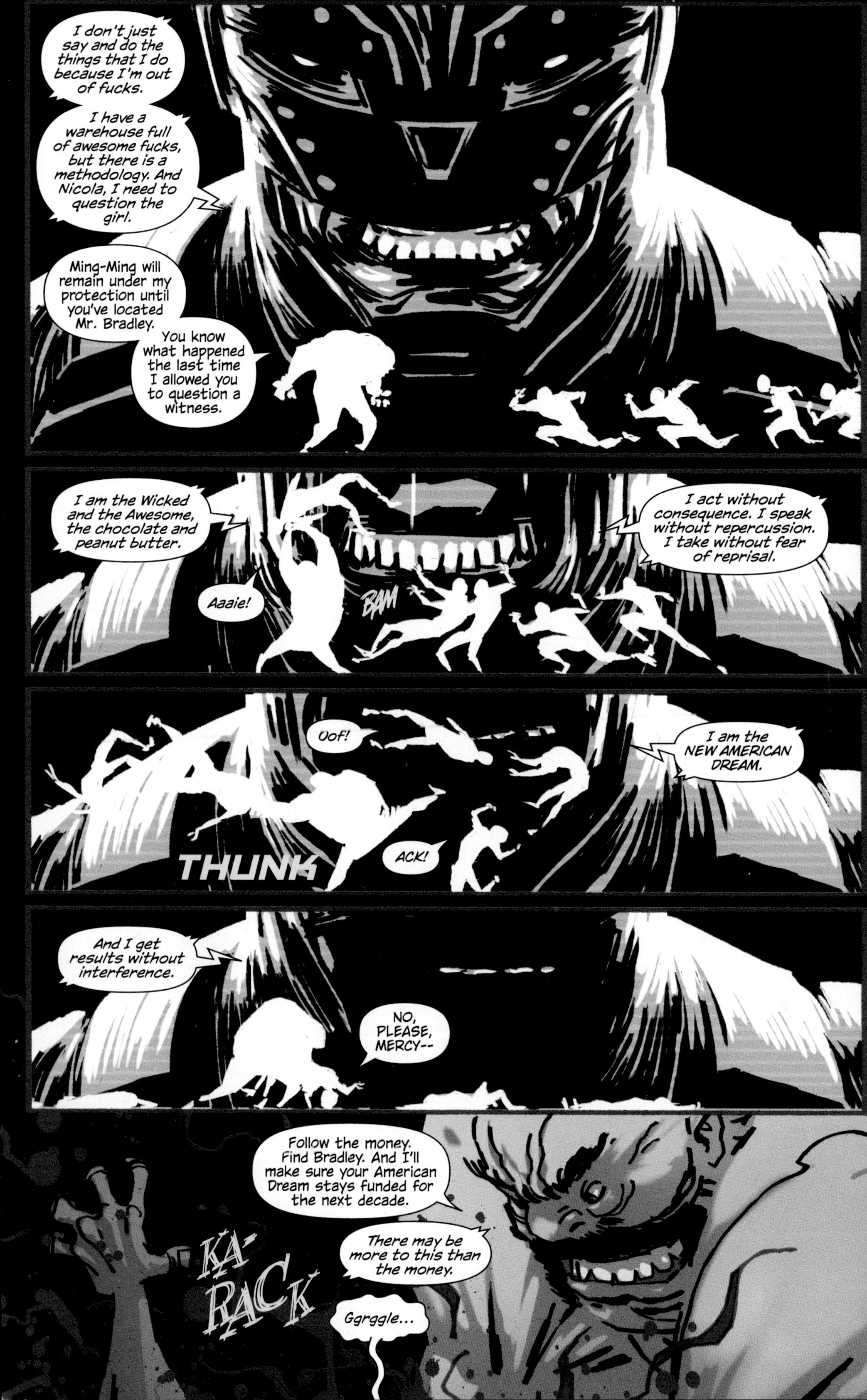
I don't just say and do the things that I do because I'm out of fucks.
I have a warehouse full of awesome fucks, but there is a methodology. And Nicola, I need to question the girl.
Ming-Ming will remain under my protection until you've located Mr. Bradley.
You know what happened the last time I allowed you to question a witness.
I am the Wicked and the Awesome, the chocolate and peanut butter.
I act without consequence. I speak without repercussion. I take without fear of reprisal.
Aaaie!
BAM
Uof!
I am the NEW AMERICAN DREAM.
THUNK
ACK!
And I get results without interference.
NO, PLEASE, MERCY--
Follow the money. Find Bradley. And I'll make sure your American Dream stays funded for the next decade.
KA-RACK
There may be more to this than the money.
Ggrggle...

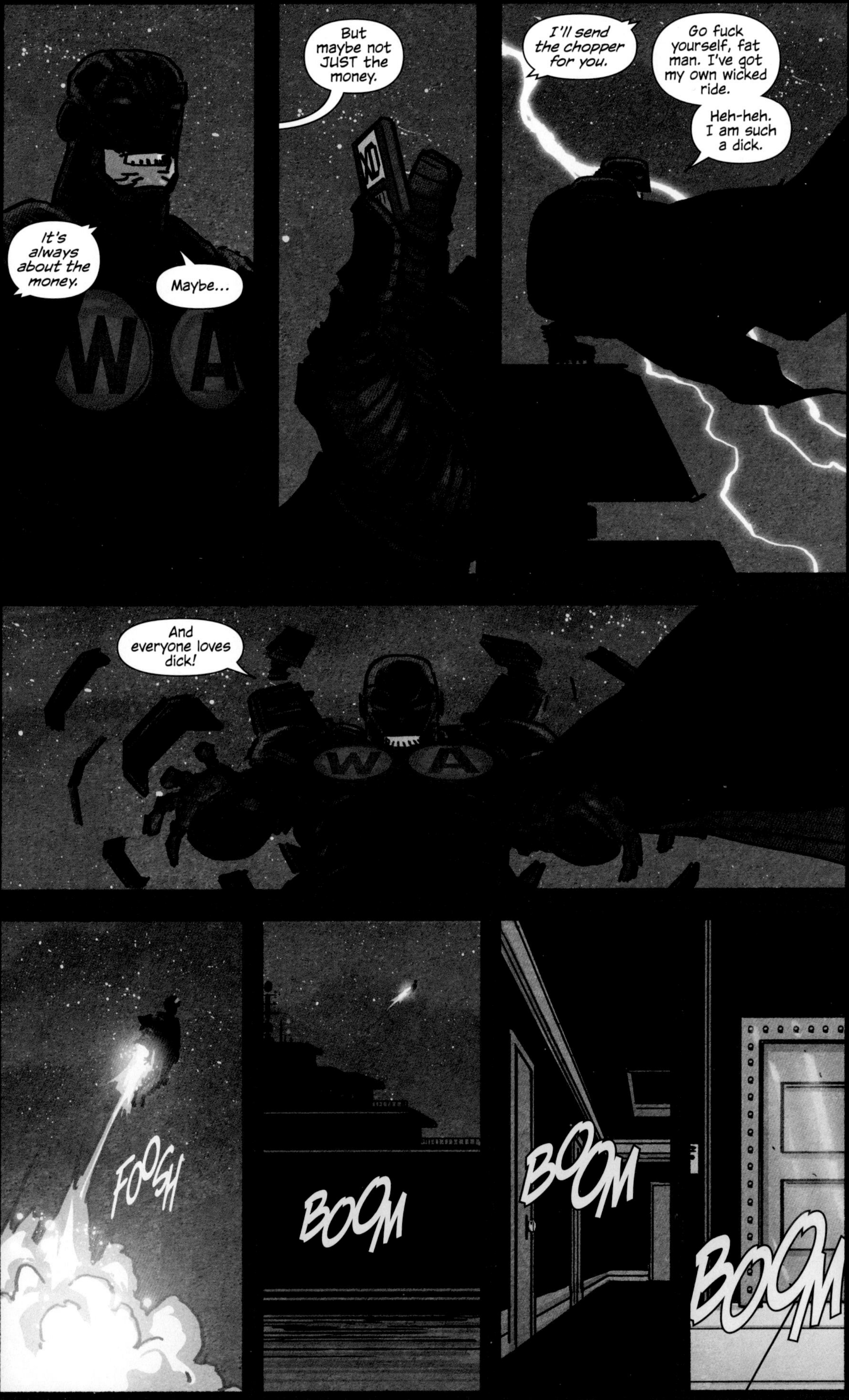

It's always about the money.
Maybe...
But maybe not JUST the money.
I'll send the chopper for you.
Go fuck yourself, fat man. I've got my own wicked ride.
Heh-heh. I am such a dick.
And everyone loves dick!
FOOSH
BOOM
BOOM
BOOM

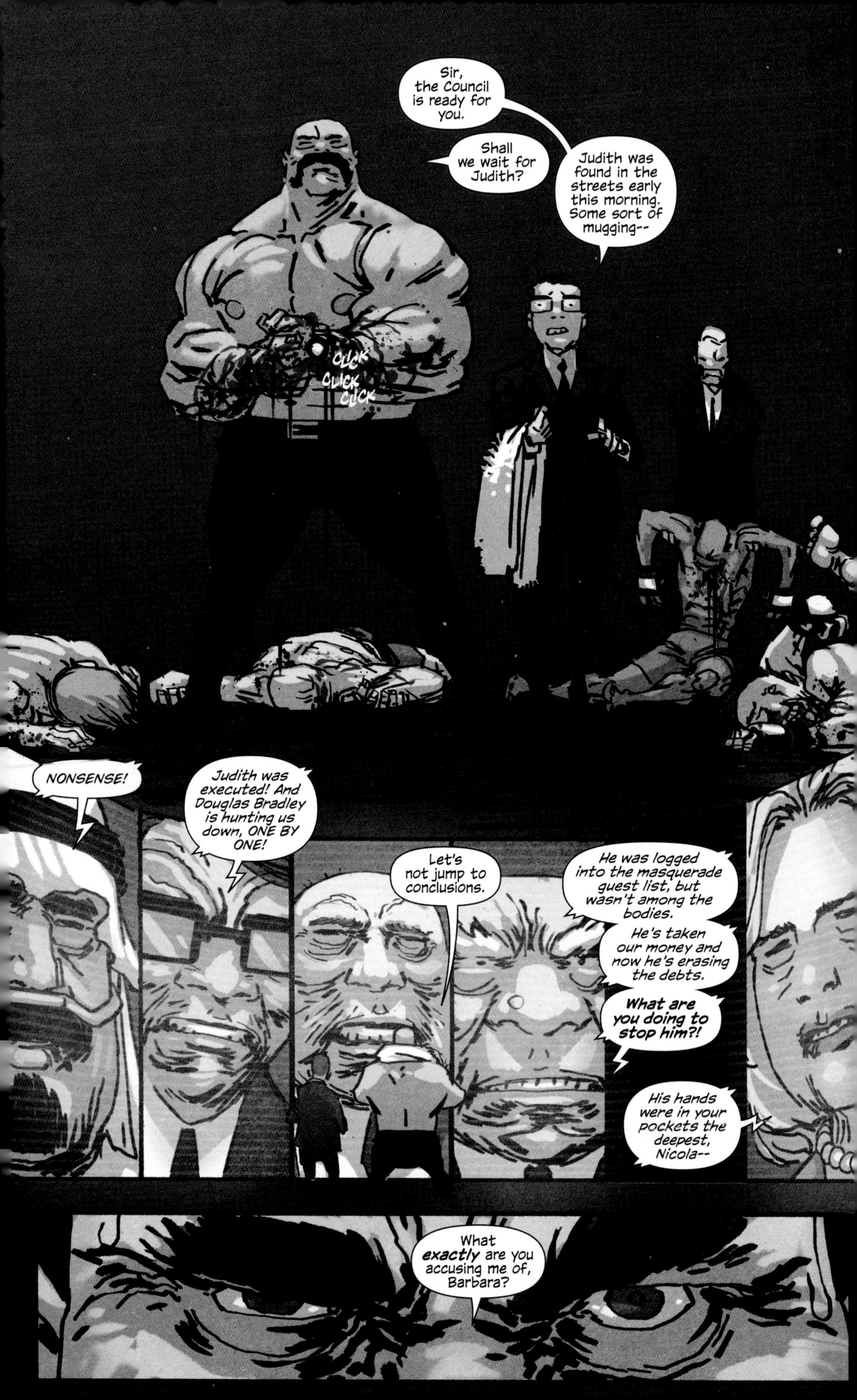
Sir, the Council is ready for you.
Shall we wait for Judith?
Judith was found in the streets early this morning. Some sort of mugging--
CLICK CLICK CLICK
NONSENSE!
Judith was executed! And Douglas Bradley is hunting us down, ONE BY ONE!
Let's not jump to conclusions.
He was logged into the masquerade guest list, but wasn't among the bodies.
He's taken our money and now he's erasing the debts.
What are you doing to stop him?!
His hands were in your pockets the deepest, Nicola--
What exactly are you accusing me of, Barbara?

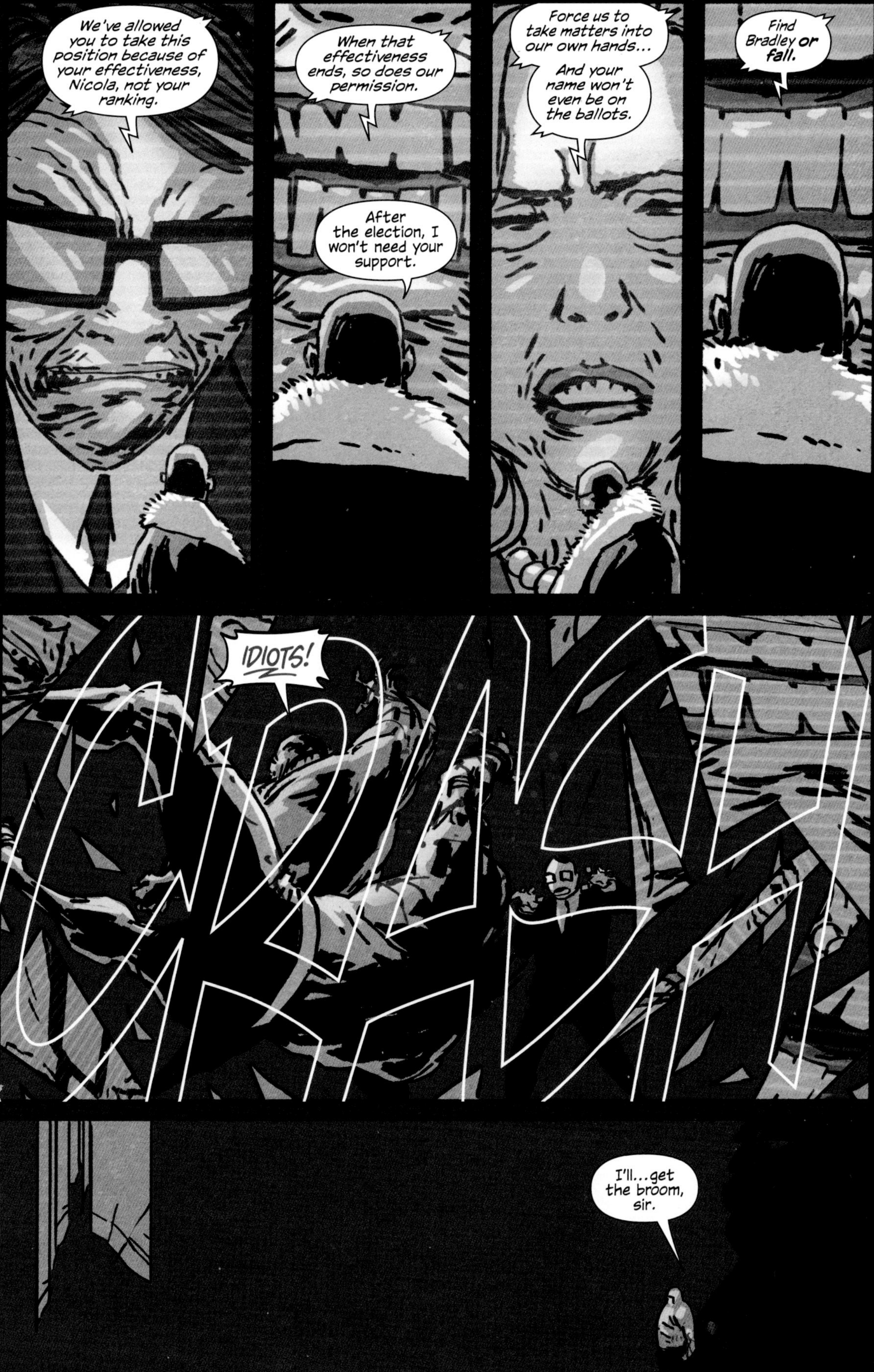

We've allowed you to take this position because of your effectiveness, Nicola, not your ranking.
When that effectiveness ends, so does our permission.
After the election, I won't need your support.
Force us to take matters into our own hands...
And your name won't even be on the ballots.
Find Bradley or fall.
IDIOTS!
CRASH!
I'll...get the broom, sir.

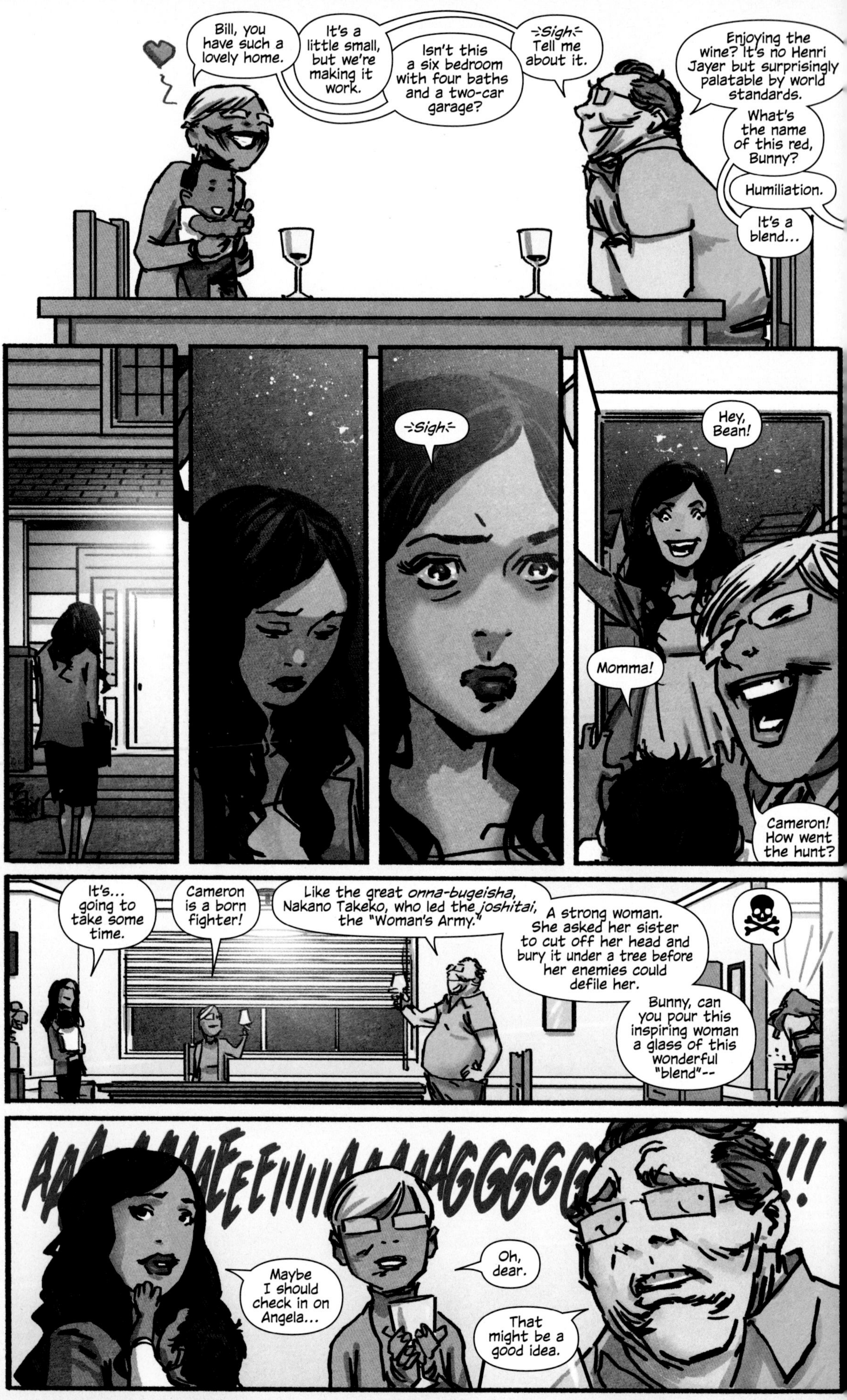
Bill, you have such a lovely home.
It's a little small, but we're making it work.
Isn't this a six bedroom with four baths and a two-car garage?
-Sigh- Tell me about it.
Enjoying the wine? It's no Henri Jayer but surprisingly palatable by world standards.
What's the name of this red, Bunny?
Humiliation.
It's a blend...
-Sigh-
Hey, Bean!
Momma!
Cameron! How went the hunt?
It's... going to take some time.
Cameron is a born fighter!
Like the great onna-bugeisha, Nakano Takeko, who led the joshitai, the "Woman's Army."
A strong woman. She asked her sister to cut off her head and bury it under a tree before her enemies could defile her.
Bunny, can you pour this inspiring woman a glass of this wonderful "blend"--
Maybe I should check in on Angela...
Oh, dear.
That might be a good idea.

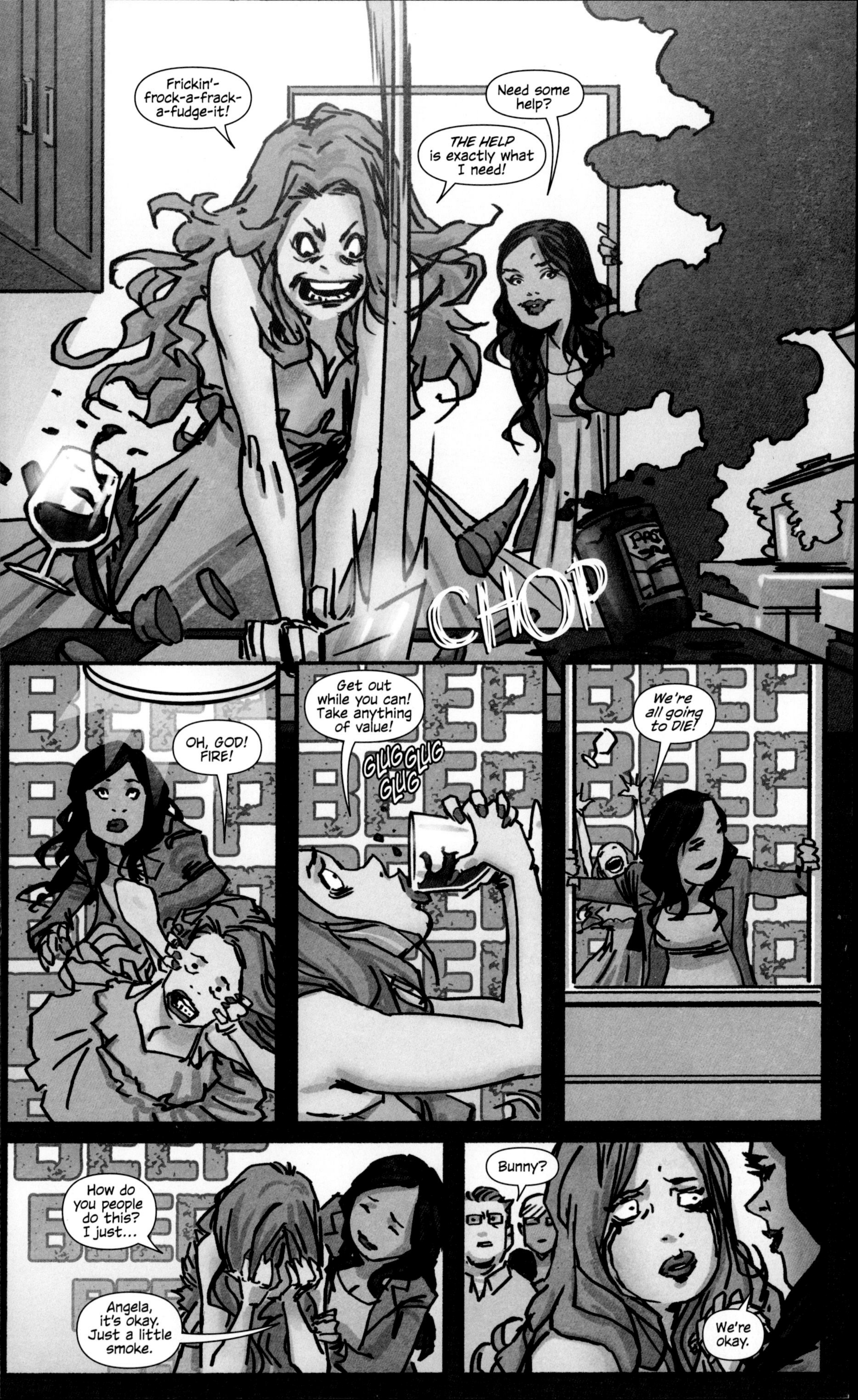
Frickin'-frock-a-frack-a-fudge-it!
Need some help?
THE HELP is exactly what I need!
CHOP
OH, GOD! FIRE!
Get out while you can! Take anything of value!
GLUG GLUG GLUG
We're all going to DIE!
How do you people do this? I just...
Angela, it's okay. Just a little smoke.
Bunny?
We're okay.

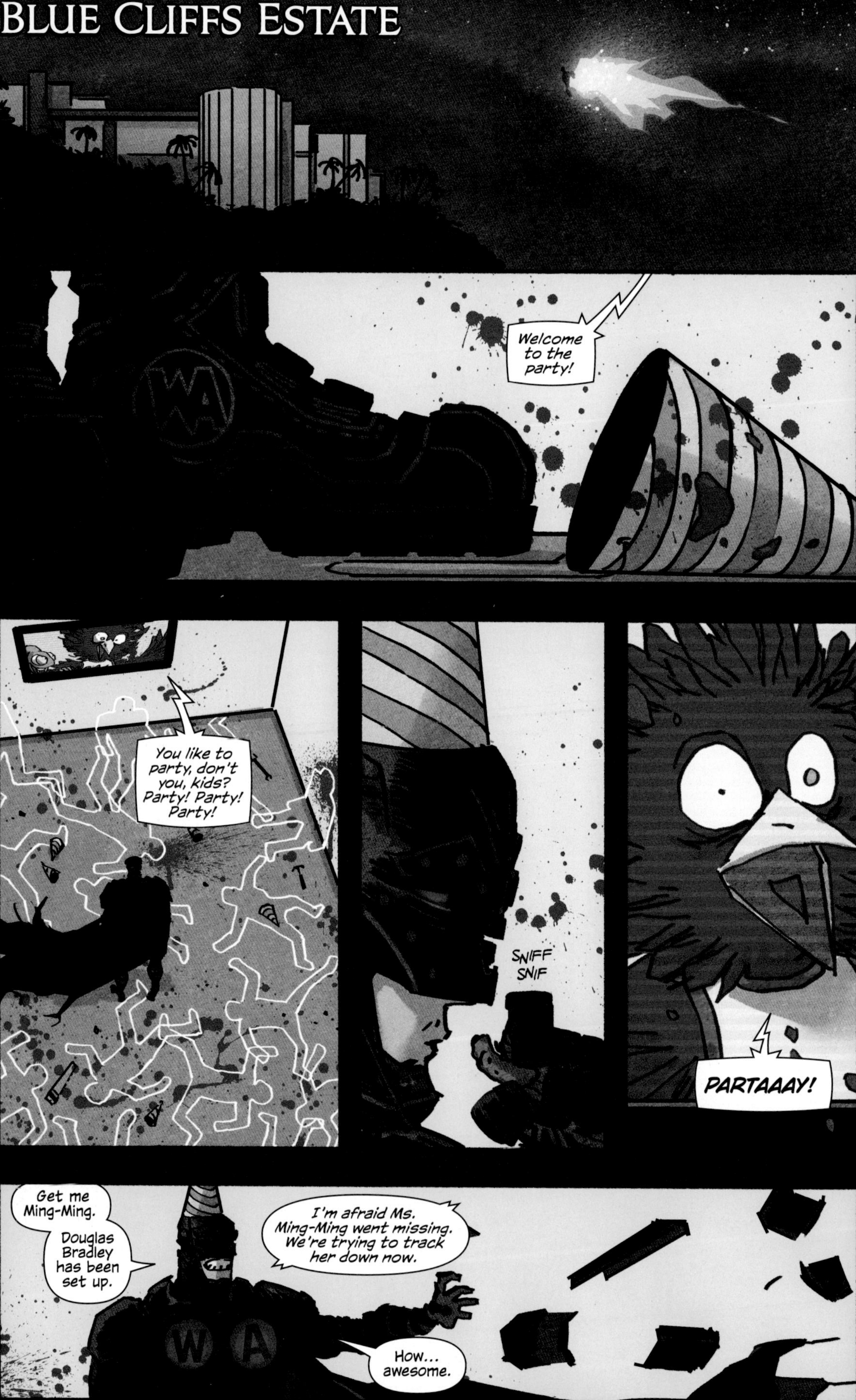
BLUE CLIFFS ESTATE
Welcome to the party!
You like to party, don't you, kids? Party! Party! Party!
SNIFF SNIF
PARTAAAY!
Get me Ming-Ming.
Douglas Bradley has been set up.
I'm afraid Ms. Ming-Ming went missing. We're trying to track her down now.
How... awesome.

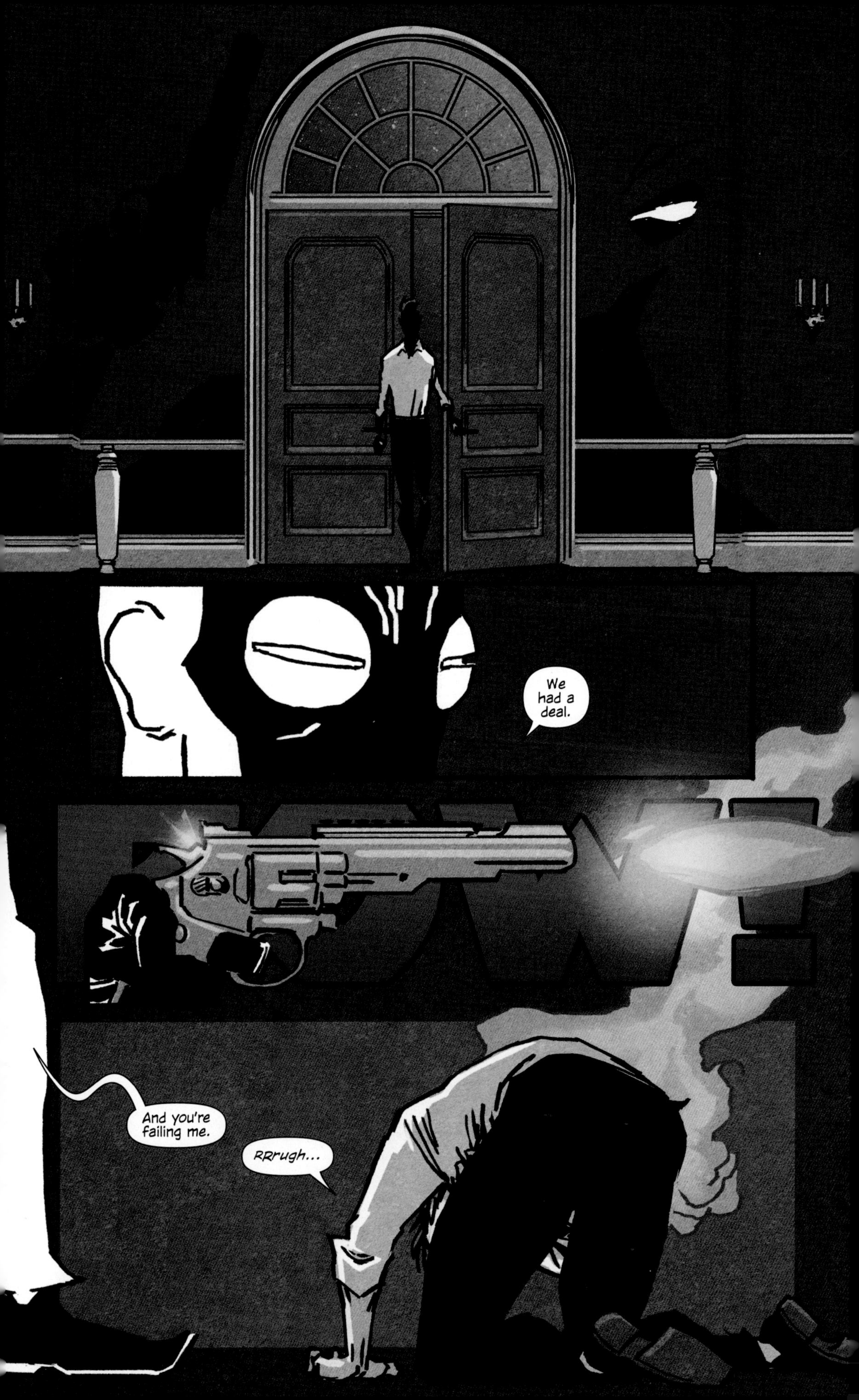
We had a deal.
And you're failing me.
RRrugh...

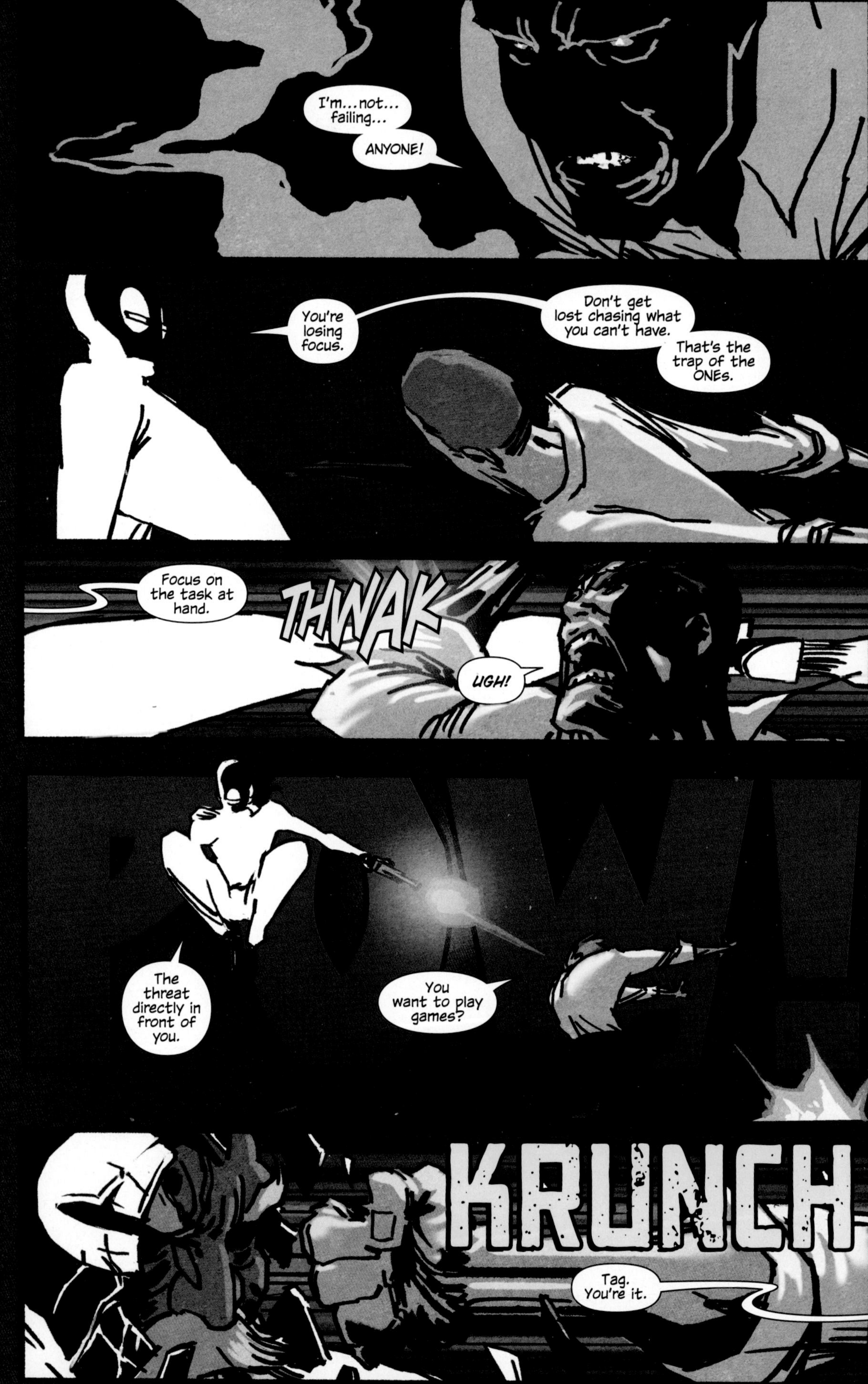
I'm...not... failing...
ANYONE!
You're losing focus.
Don't get lost chasing what you can't have.
That's the trap of the ONEs.
Focus on the task at hand.
THWAK
UGH!
The threat directly in front of you.
You want to play games?
KRUNCH
Tag. You're it.

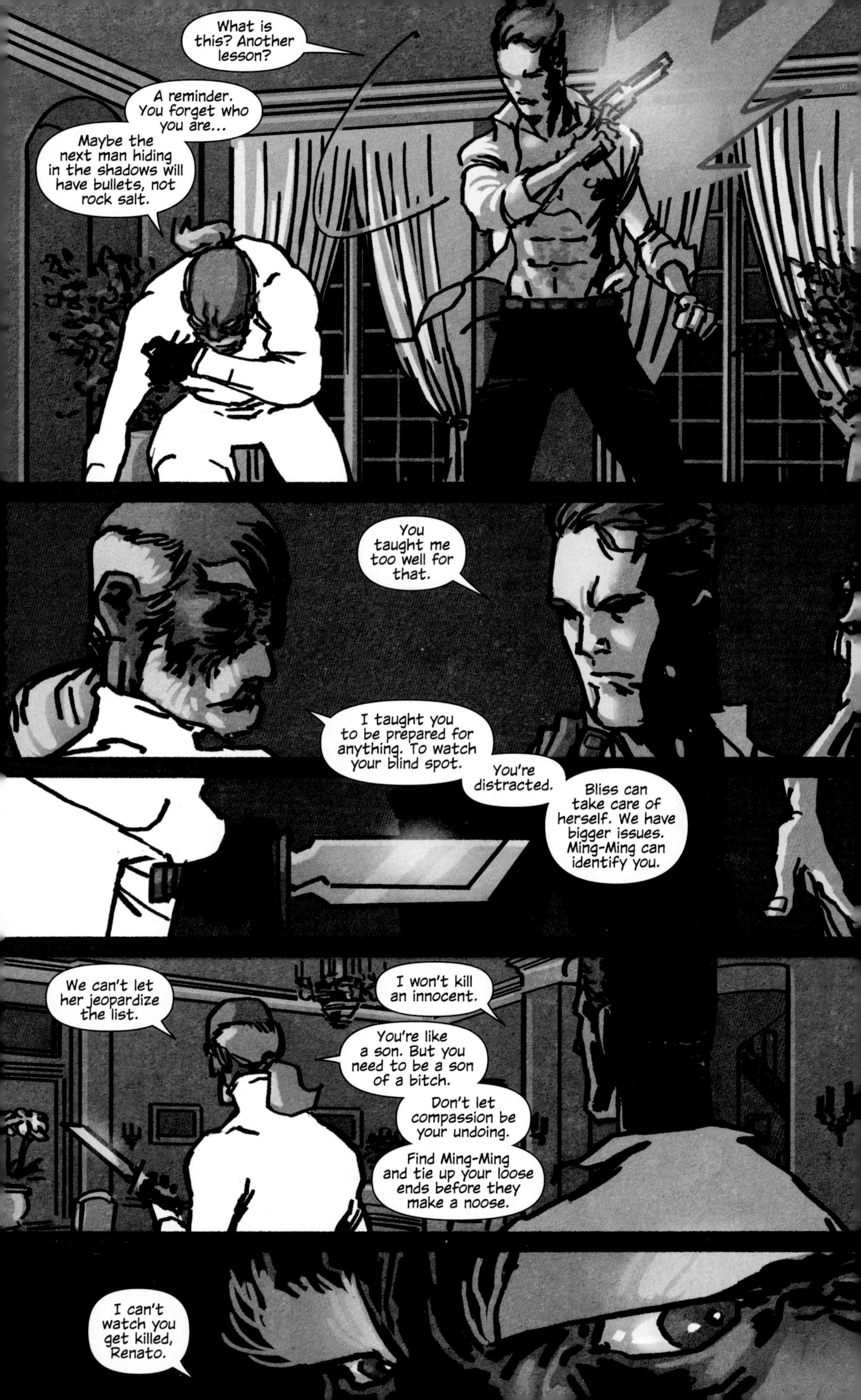
What is this? Another lesson?
A reminder. You forget who you are...
Maybe the next man hiding in the shadows will have bullets, not rock salt.
You taught me too well for that.
I taught you to be prepared for anything. To watch your blind spot.
You're distracted.
Bliss can take care of herself. We have bigger issues. Ming-Ming can identify you.
We can't let her jeopardize the list.
I won't kill an innocent.
You're like a son. But you need to be a son of a bitch.
Don't let compassion be your undoing.
Find Ming-Ming and tie up your loose ends before they make a noose.
I can't watch you get killed, Renato.

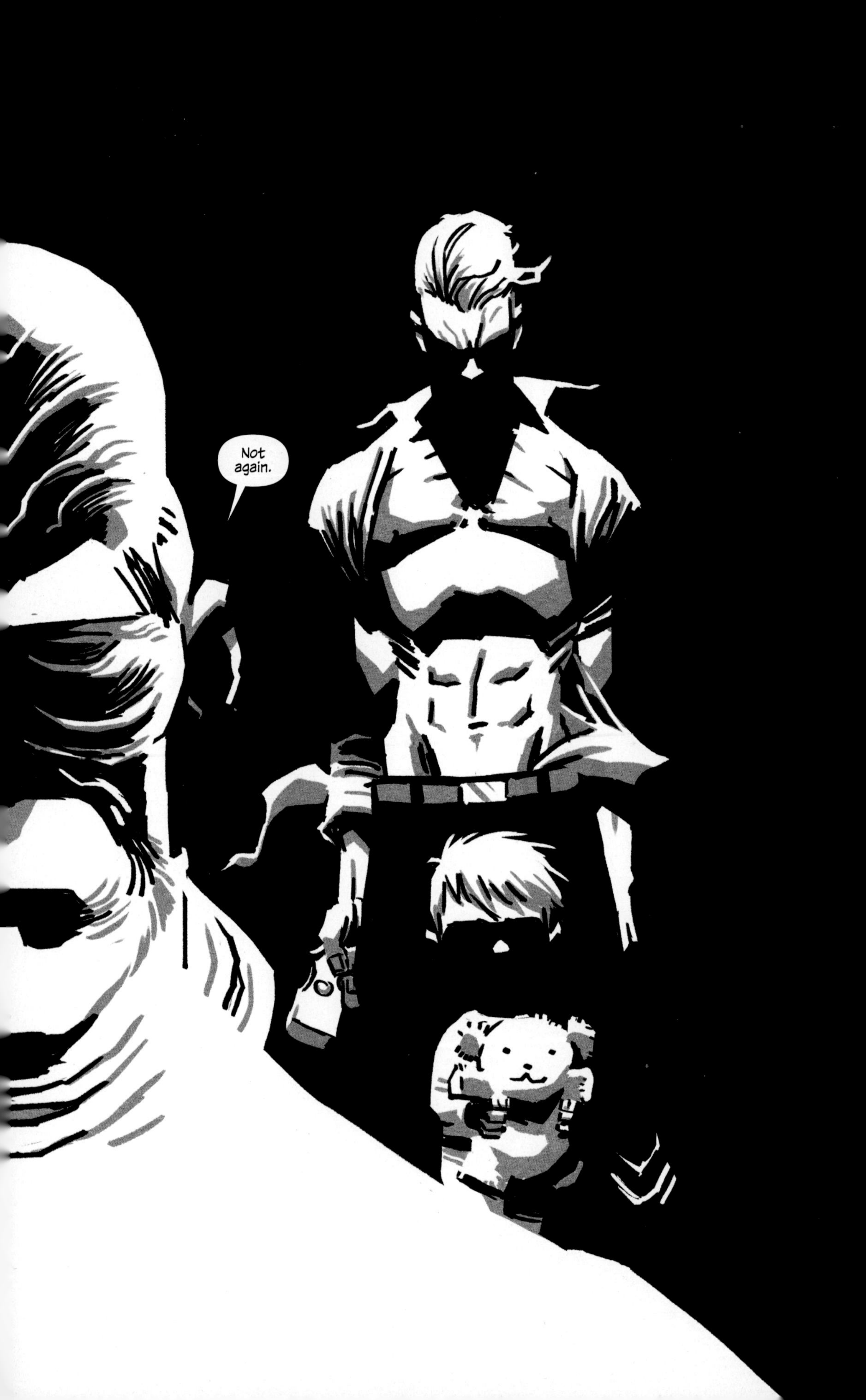
Not again.

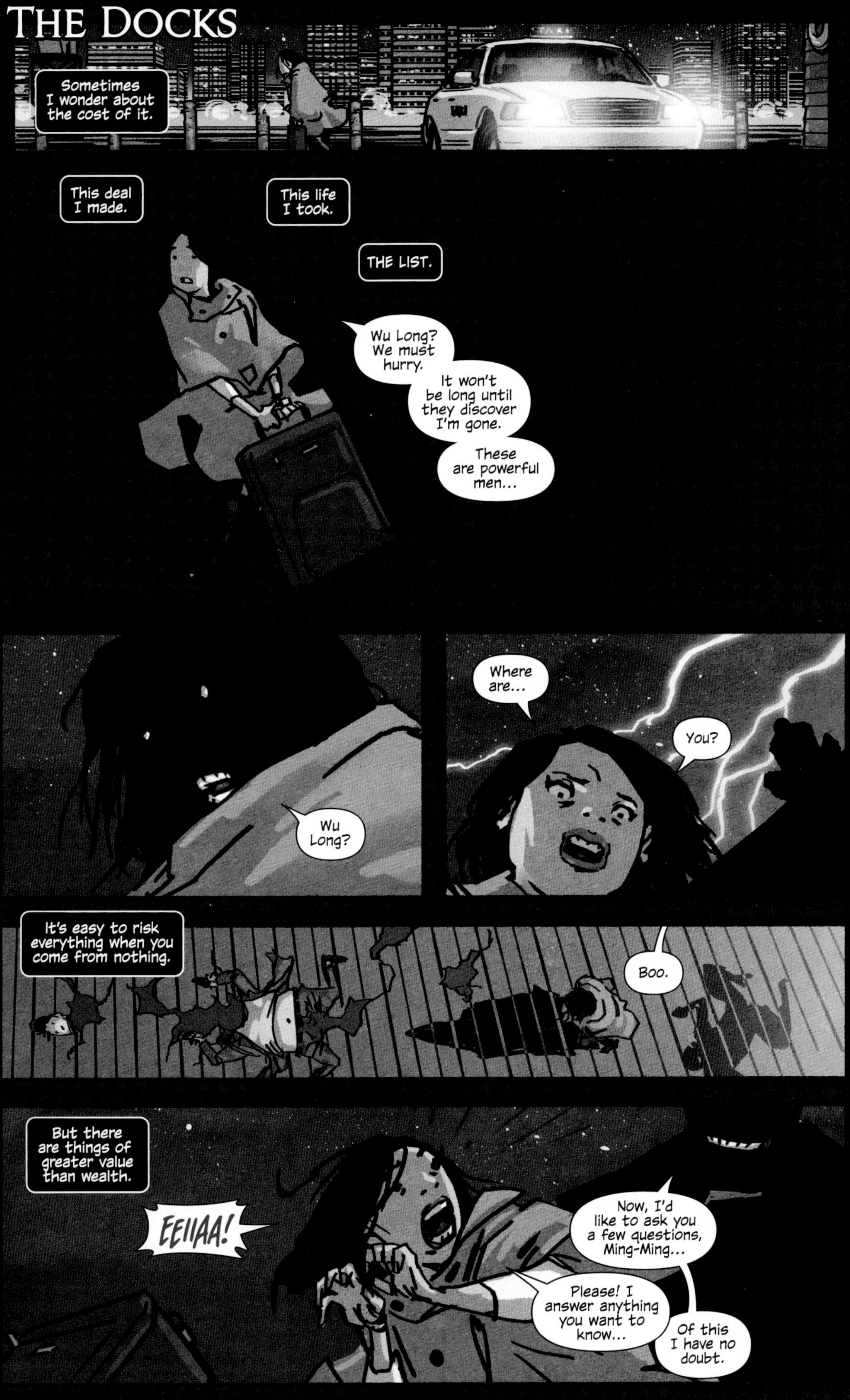
THE DOCKS
Sometimes I wonder about the cost of it.
This deal I made.
This life I took.
THE LIST.
Wu Long? We must hurry.
It won't be long until they discover I'm gone.
These are powerful men...
Wu Long?
Where are...
You?
It's easy to risk everything when you come from nothing.
Boo.
But there are things of greater value than wealth.
EEIIAA!
Now, I'd like to ask you a few questions, Ming-Ming...
Please! I answer anything you want to know...
Of this I have no doubt.

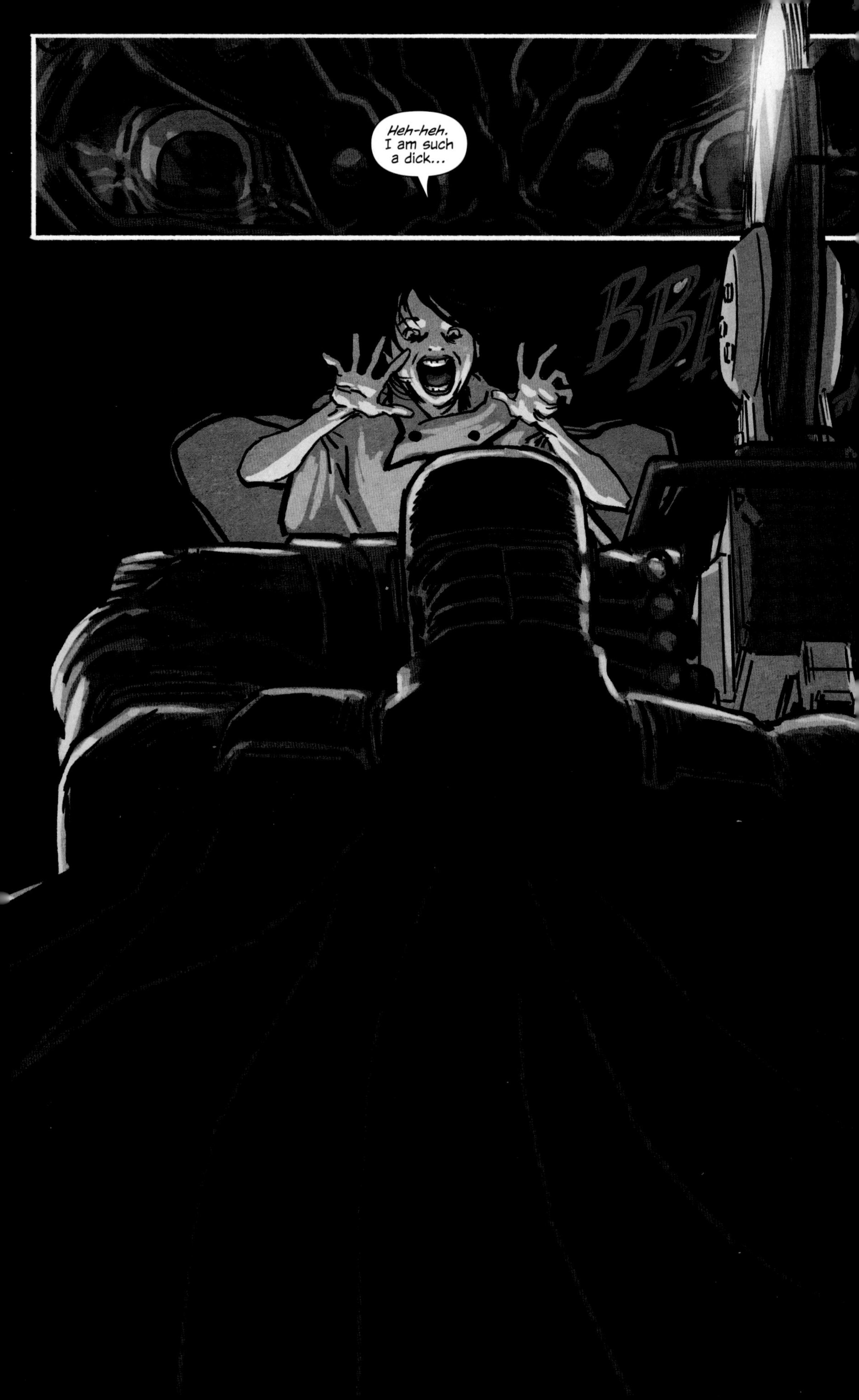
Heh-heh. I am such a dick...

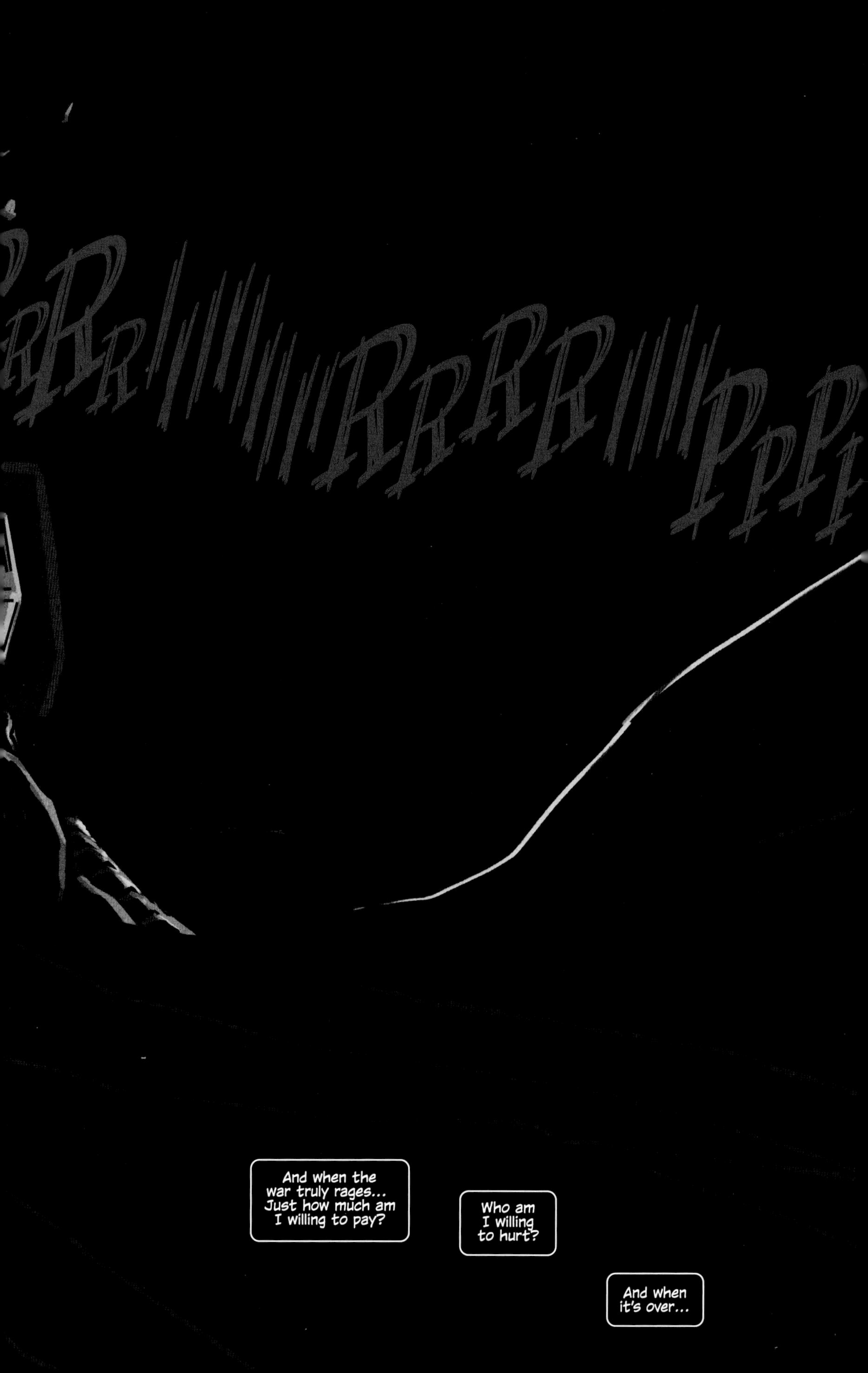
RRRRIIIIIIIIRRRRRIIIIPPP
And when the war truly rages... Just how much am I willing to pay?
Who am I willing to hurt?
And when it's over...

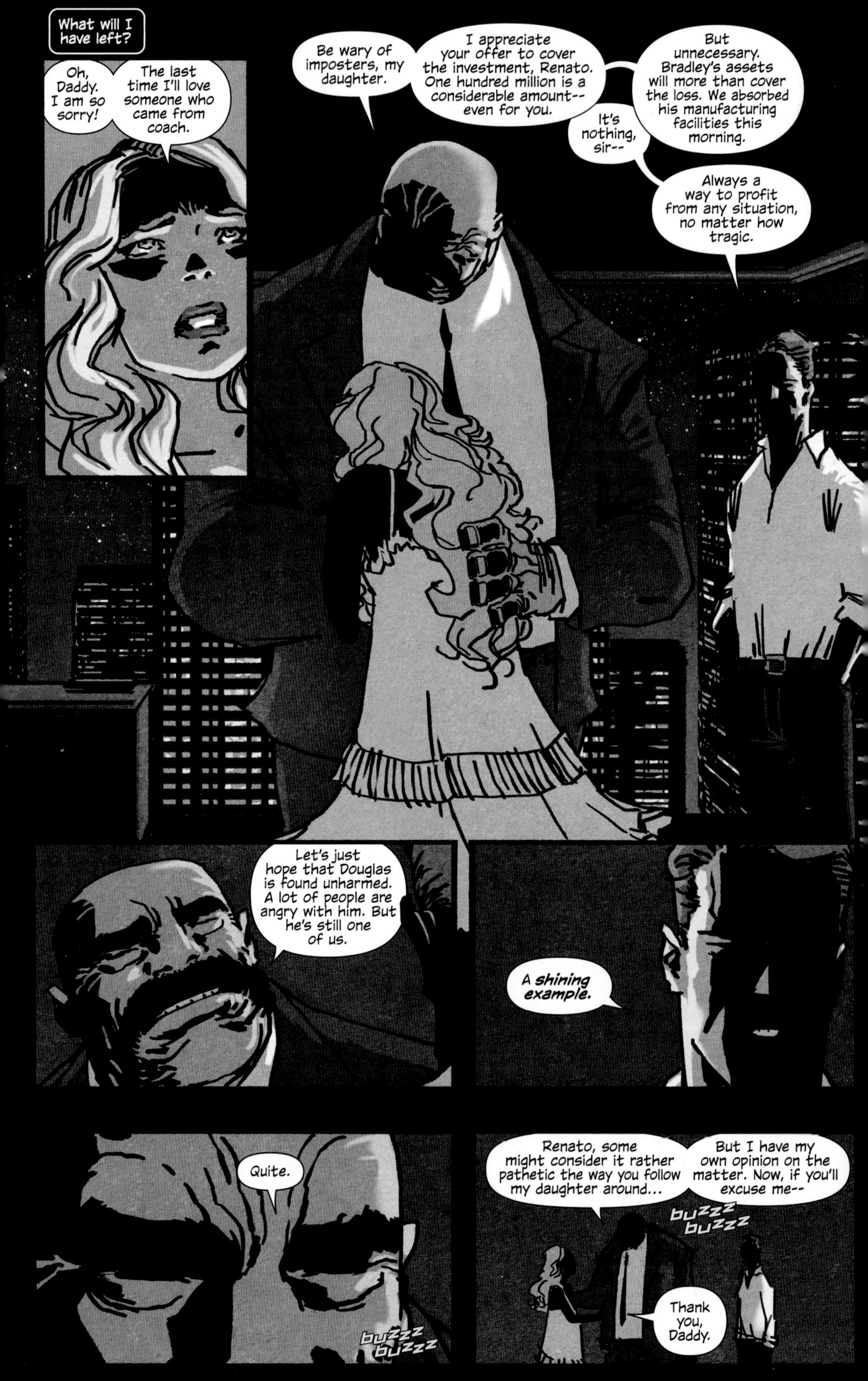
What will I have left?
Oh, Daddy. I am so sorry!
The last time I'll love someone who came from coach.
Be wary of imposters, my daughter.
I appreciate your offer to cover the investment, Renato. One hundred million is a considerable amount-- even for you.
It's nothing, sir--
But unnecessary. Bradley's assets will more than cover the loss. We absorbed his manufacturing facilities this morning.
Always a way to profit from any situation, no matter how tragic.
Let's just hope that Douglas is found unharmed. A lot of people are angry with him. But he's still one of us.
A *shining example.*
Quite.
buzzz buzzz
Renato, some might consider it rather pathetic the way you follow my daughter around...
But I have my own opinion on the matter. Now, if you'll excuse me--
buzzz buzzz
Thank you, Daddy.

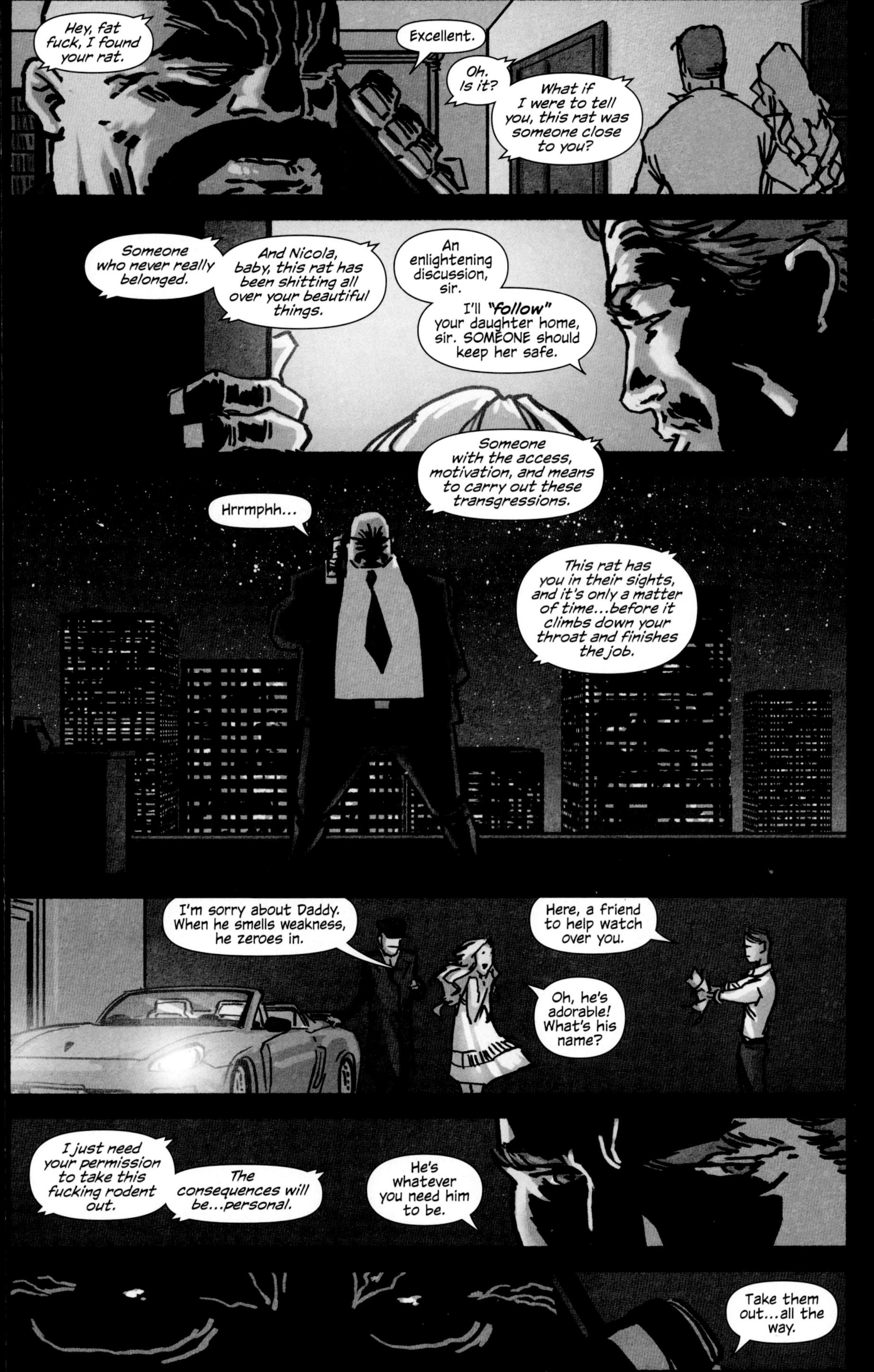

Hey, fat fuck, I found your rat.
Excellent.
Oh. Is it?
What if I were to tell you, this rat was someone close to you?
Someone who never really belonged.
And Nicola, baby, this rat has been shitting all over your beautiful things.
An enlightening discussion, sir.
I'll "follow" your daughter home, sir. SOMEONE should keep her safe.
Someone with the access, motivation, and means to carry out these transgressions.
Hrrmphh...
This rat has you in their sights, and it's only a matter of time...before it climbs down your throat and finishes the job.
I'm sorry about Daddy. When he smells weakness, he zeroes in.
Here, a friend to help watch over you.
Oh, he's adorable! What's his name?
I just need your permission to take this fucking rodent out.
The consequences will be...personal.
He's whatever you need him to be.
Take them out...all the way.

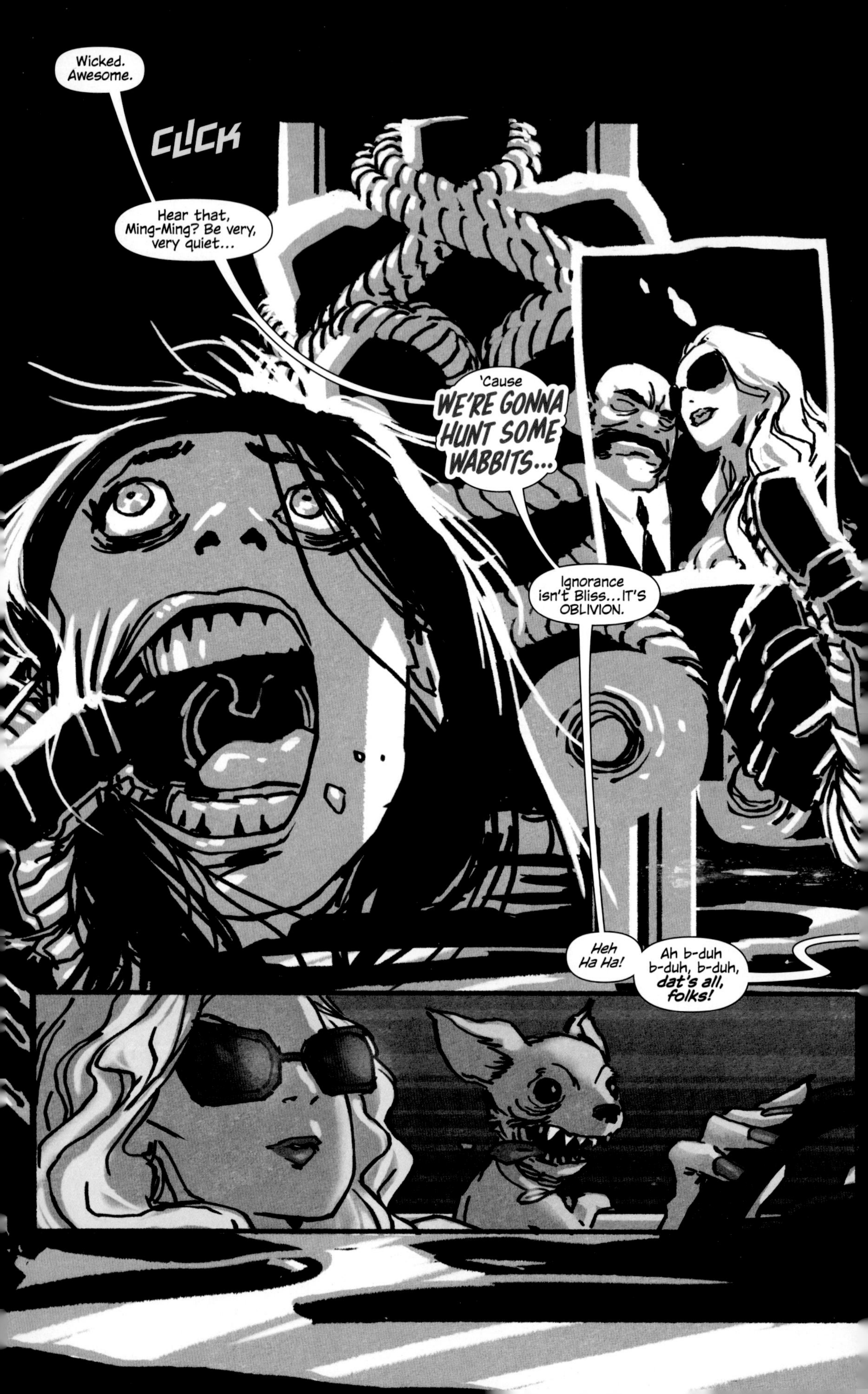
Wicked. Awesome.
CLICK
Hear that, Ming-Ming? Be very, very quiet...
'Cause WE'RE GONNA HUNT SOME WABBITS...
Ignorance isn't Bliss...IT'S OBLIVION.
Heh Ha Ha!
Ah b-duh b-duh, b-duh, dat's all, folks!

"From the dirt, you can't even see the bars of the cage."

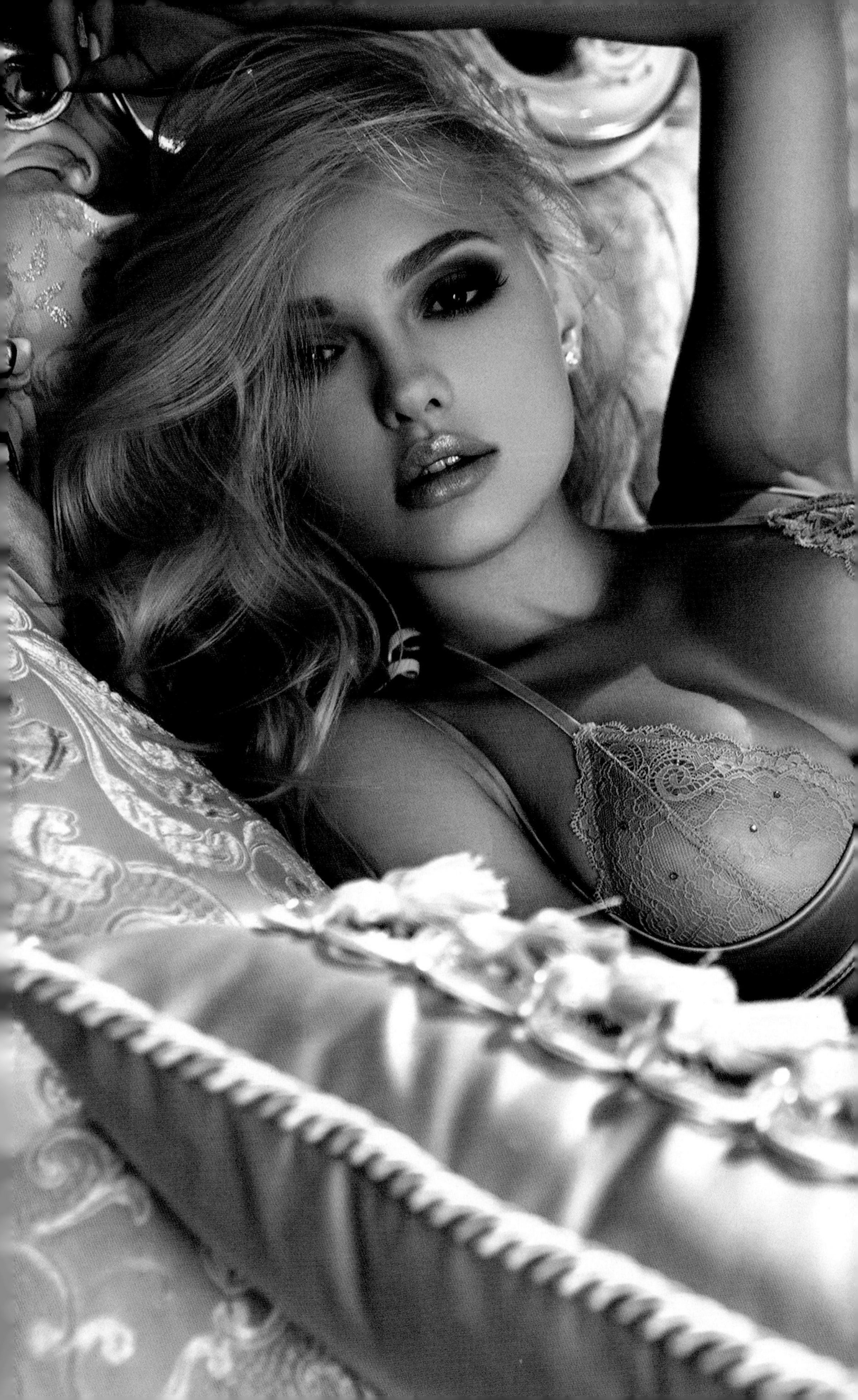

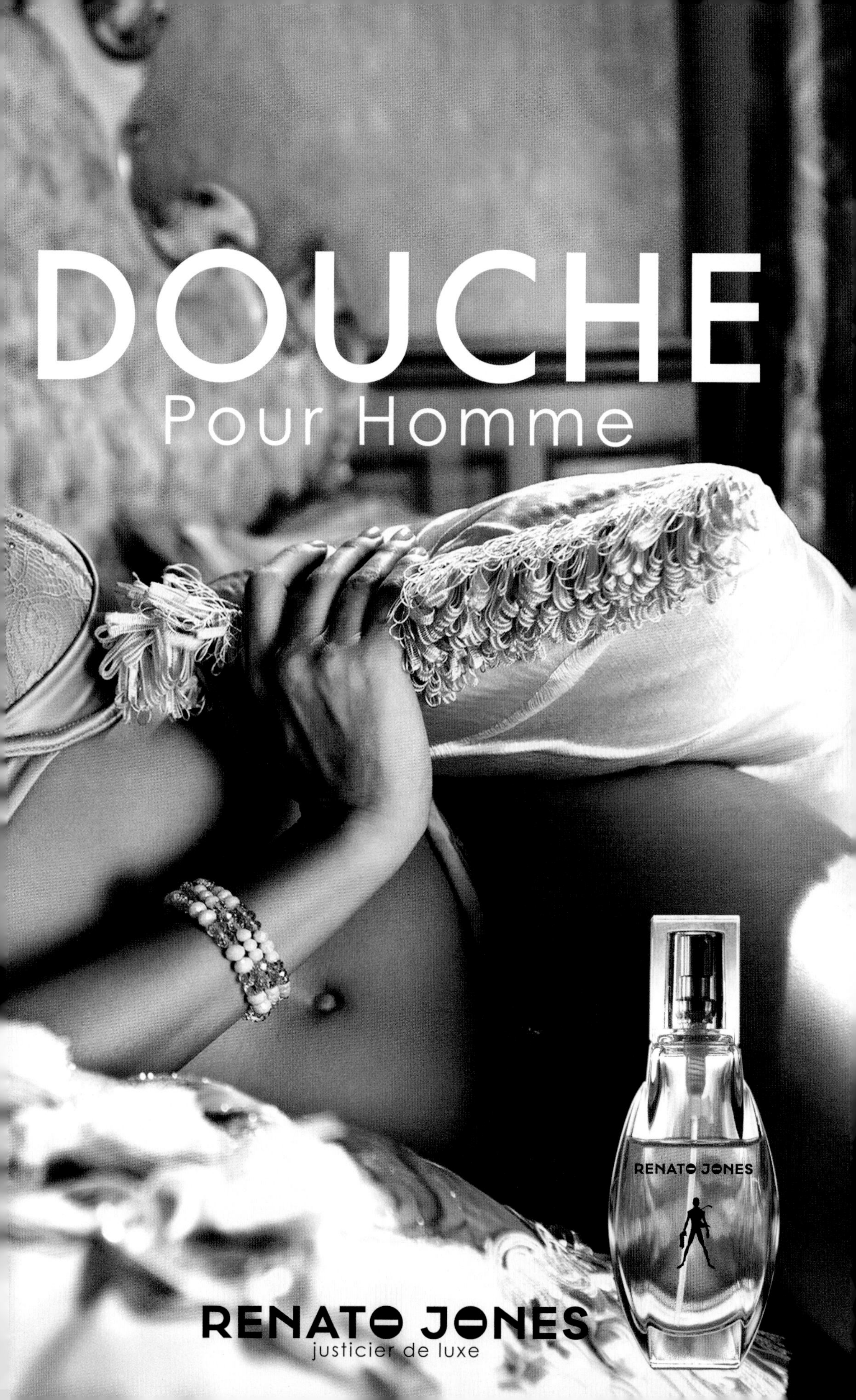

DOUCHE
Pour Homme
RENATO JONES
RENATO JONES
justicier de luxe

"Let me tell you about the very rich. They are different from you and me."
—F. Scott Fitzgerald

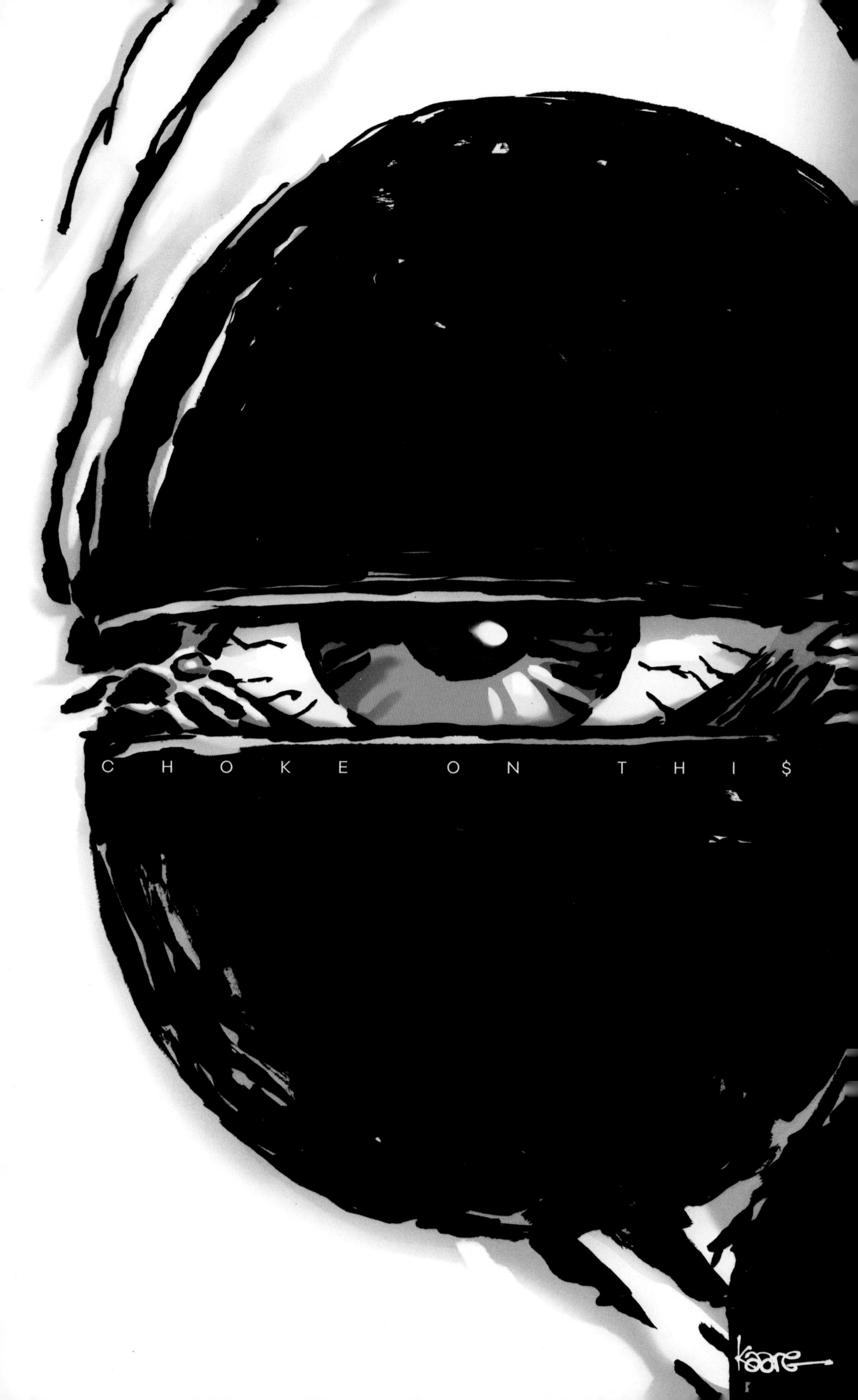
C H O K E O N T H I $
kaare

4

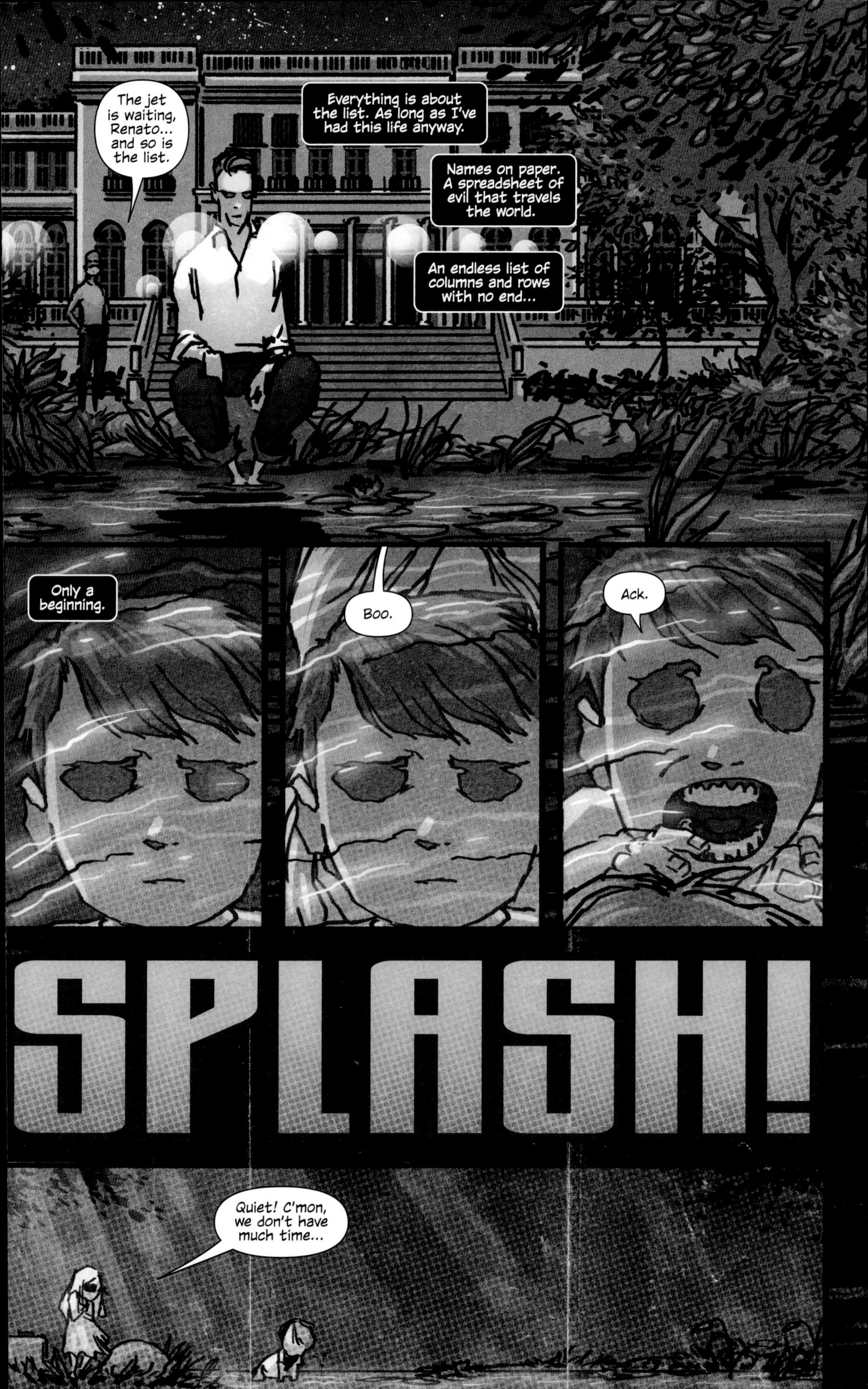
The jet is waiting, Renato... and so is the list.
Everything is about the list. As long as I've had this life anyway.
Names on paper. A spreadsheet of evil that travels the world.
An endless list of columns and rows with no end...
Only a beginning.
Boo.
Ack.
SPLASH!
Quiet! C'mon, we don't have much time...

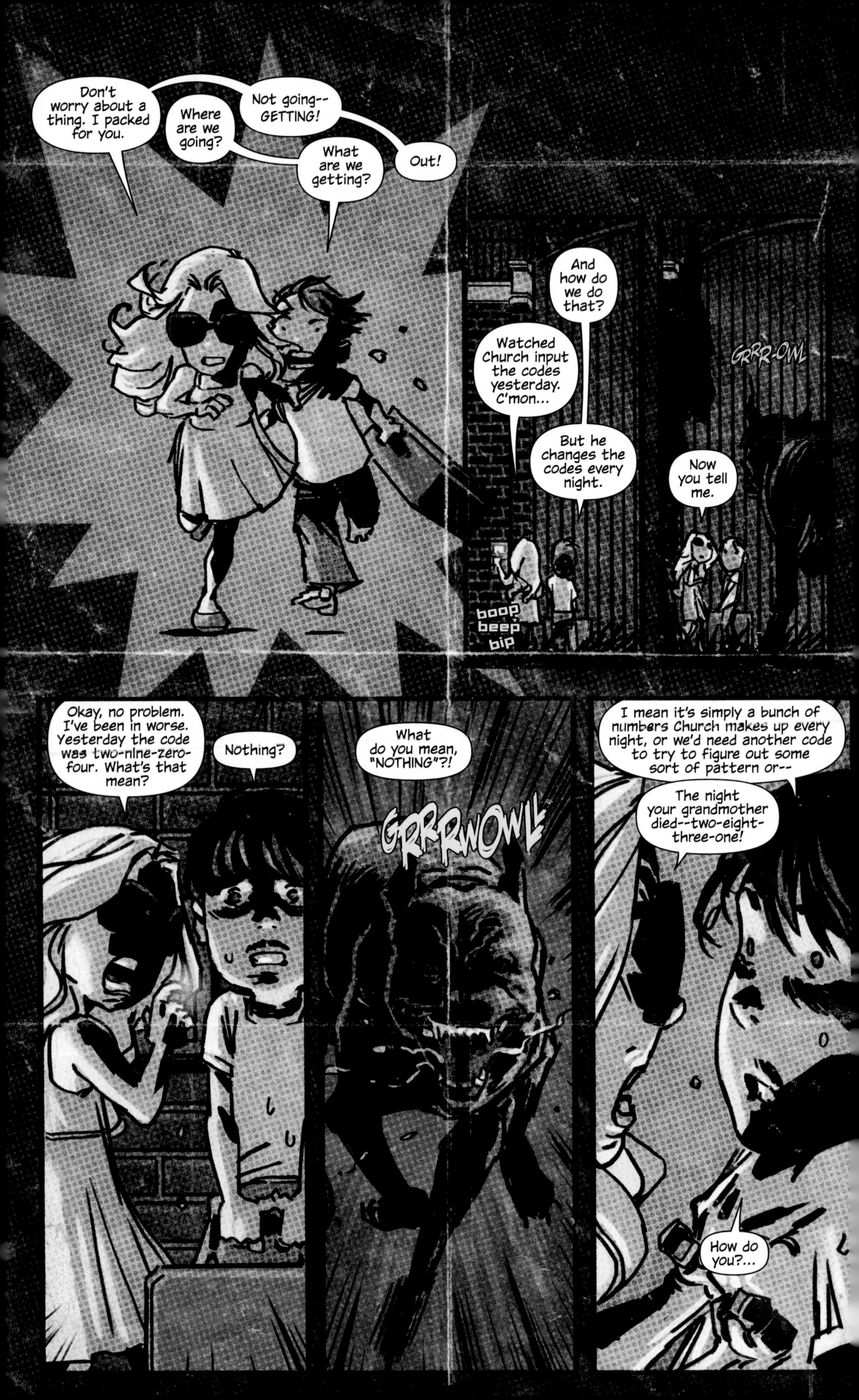
Don't worry about a thing. I packed for you.
Where are we going?
Not going-- GETTING!
What are we getting?
Out!
And how do we do that?
Watched Church input the codes yesterday. C'mon...
But he changes the codes every night.
boop beep bip
GRRR-OWL
Now you tell me.
Okay, no problem. I've been in worse. Yesterday the code was two-nine-zero-four. What's that mean?
Nothing?
What do you mean, "NOTHING"?!
GRRRWOWLL
I mean it's simply a bunch of numbers Church makes up every night, or we'd need another code to try to figure out some sort of pattern or--
The night your grandmother died--two-eight-three-one!
How do you?...

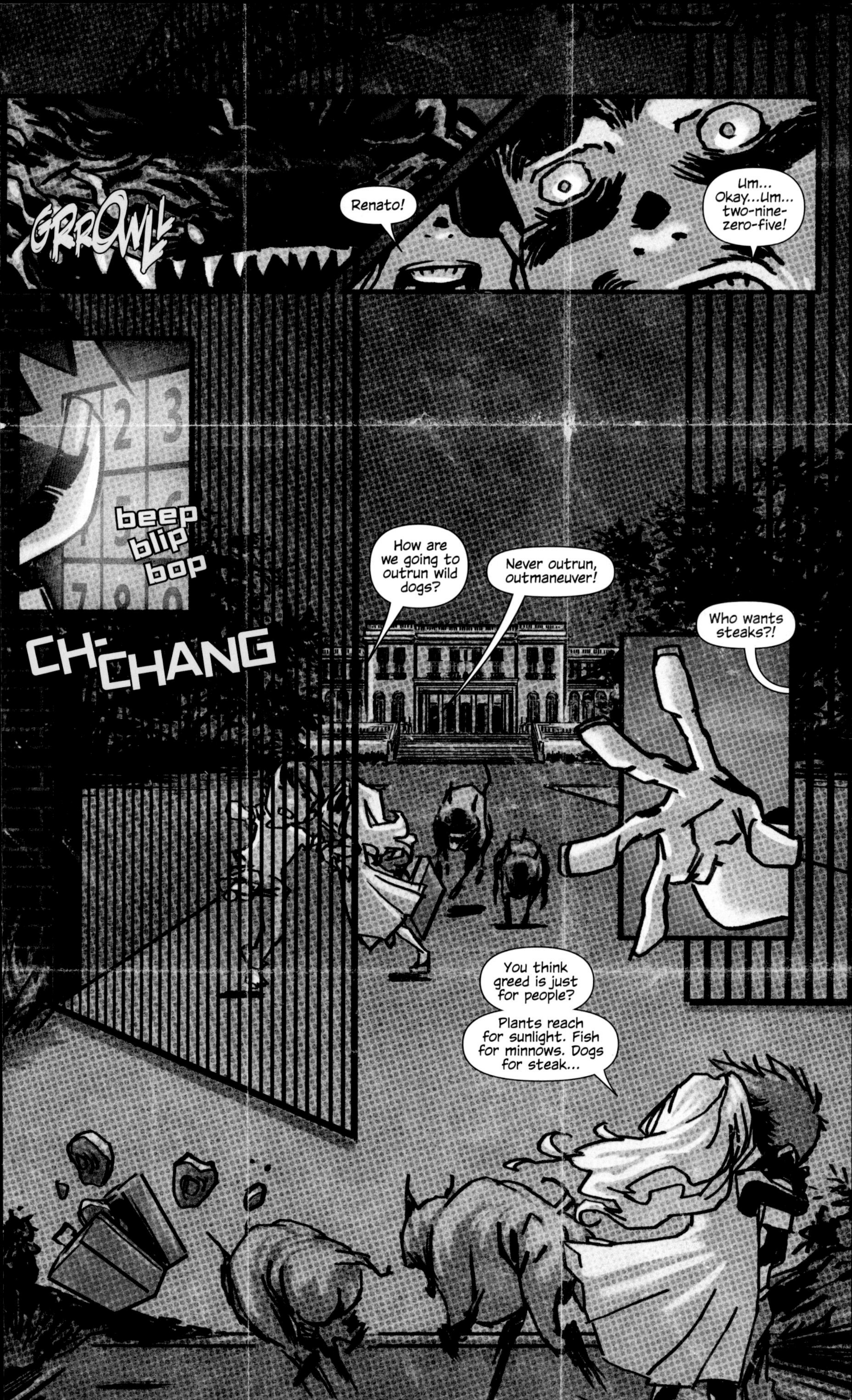
GRROWL!
Renato!
Um... Okay...Um... two-nine-zero-five!
beep blip bop
CH-CHANG
How are we going to outrun wild dogs?
Never outrun, outmaneuver!
Who wants steaks?!
You think greed is just for people?
Plants reach for sunlight. Fish for minnows. Dogs for steak...

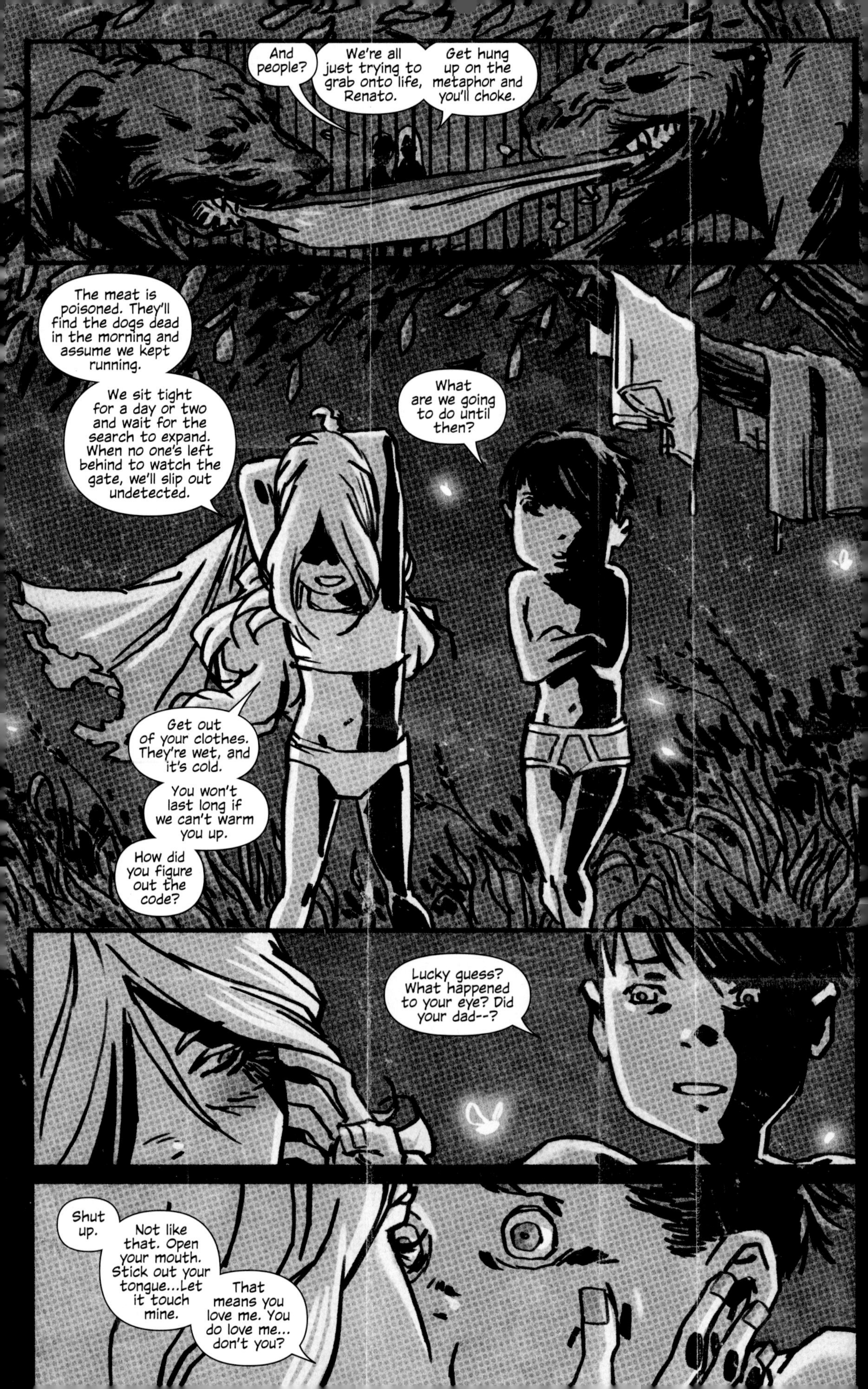
And people?
We're all just trying to grab onto life, Renato.
Get hung up on the metaphor and you'll choke.
The meat is poisoned. They'll find the dogs dead in the morning and assume we kept running.
We sit tight for a day or two and wait for the search to expand. When no one's left behind to watch the gate, we'll slip out undetected.
What are we going to do until then?
Get out of your clothes. They're wet, and it's cold.
You won't last long if we can't warm you up.
How did you figure out the code?
Lucky guess? What happened to your eye? Did your dad--?
Shut up.
Not like that. Open your mouth. Stick out your tongue...Let it touch mine.
That means you love me. You do love me... don't you?

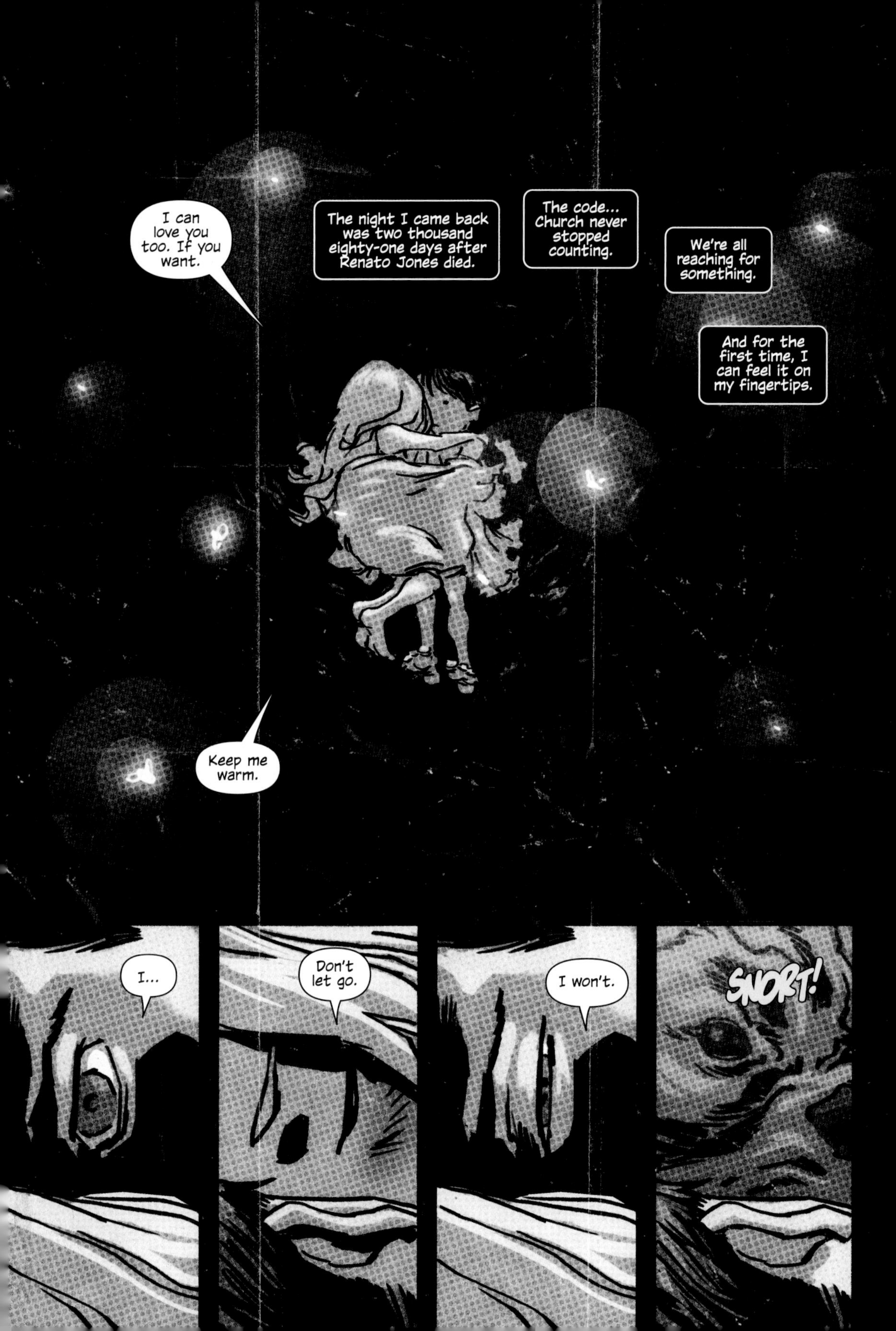
I can love you too. If you want.
The night I came back was two thousand eighty-one days after Renato Jones died.
The code... Church never stopped counting.
We're all reaching for something.
And for the first time, I can feel it on my fingertips.
Keep me warm.
I...
Don't let go.
I won't.
SNORT!

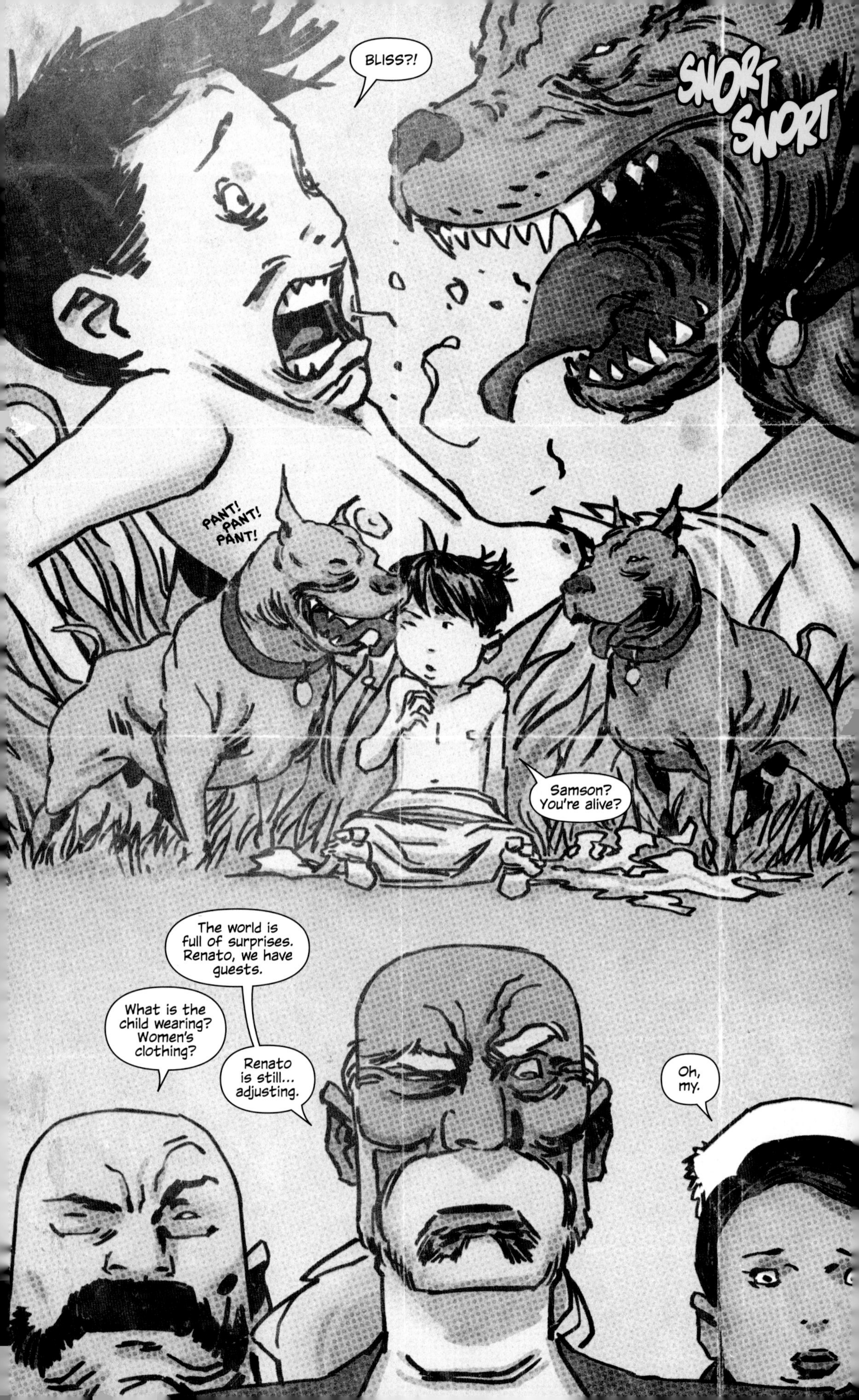
BLISS?!
SNORT SNORT
PANT! PANT! PANT!
Samson? You're alive?
The world is full of surprises. Renato, we have guests.
What is the child wearing? Women's clothing?
Renato is still... adjusting.
Oh, my.

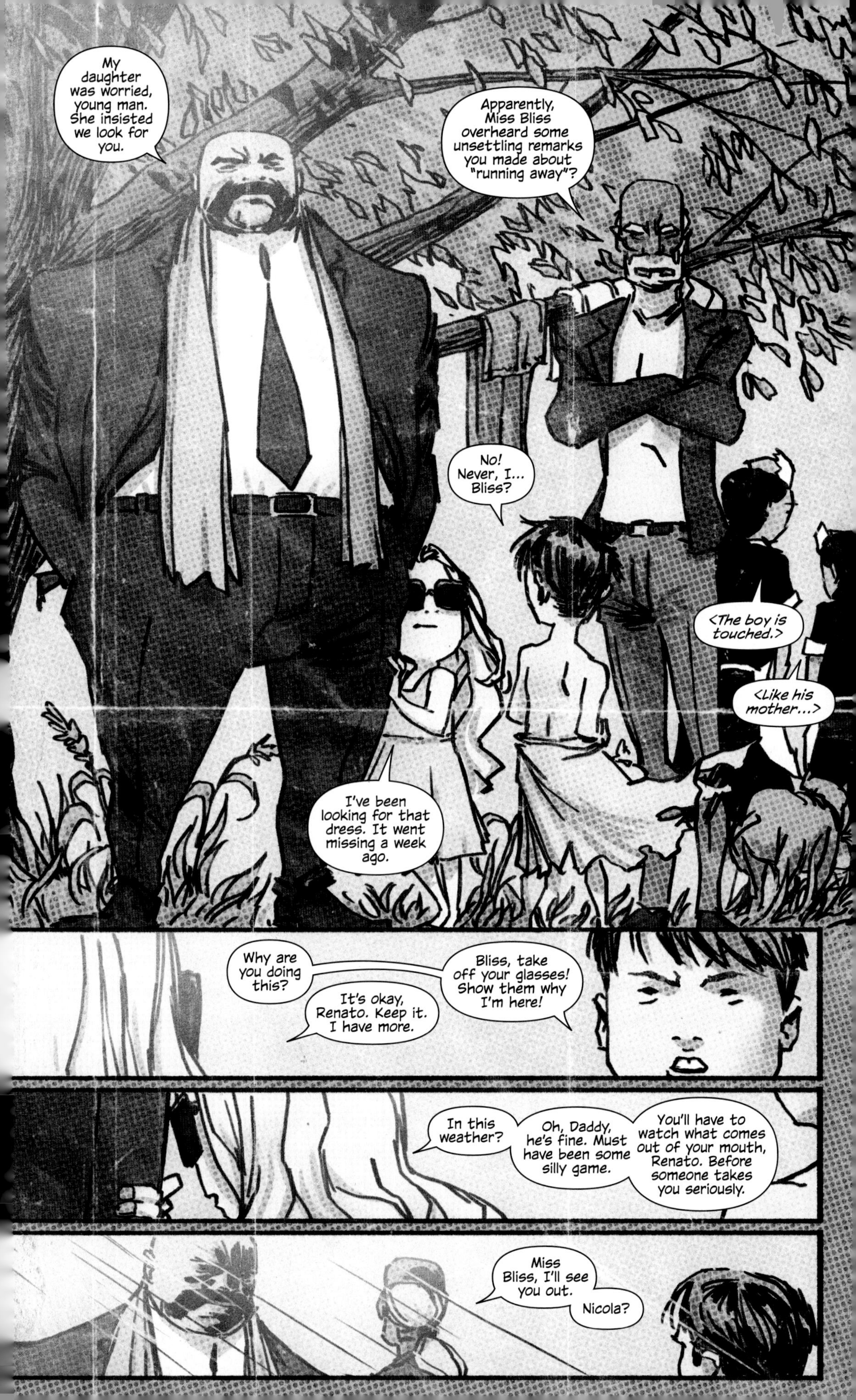
My daughter was worried, young man. She insisted we look for you.
Apparently, Miss Bliss overheard some unsettling remarks you made about "running away"?
No! Never, I... Bliss?
<The boy is touched.>
<Like his mother...>
I've been looking for that dress. It went missing a week ago.
Why are you doing this?
Bliss, take off your glasses! Show them why I'm here!
It's okay, Renato. Keep it. I have more.
In this weather?
Oh, Daddy, he's fine. Must have been some silly game.
You'll have to watch what comes out of your mouth, Renato. Before someone takes you seriously.
Miss Bliss, I'll see you out.
Nicola?

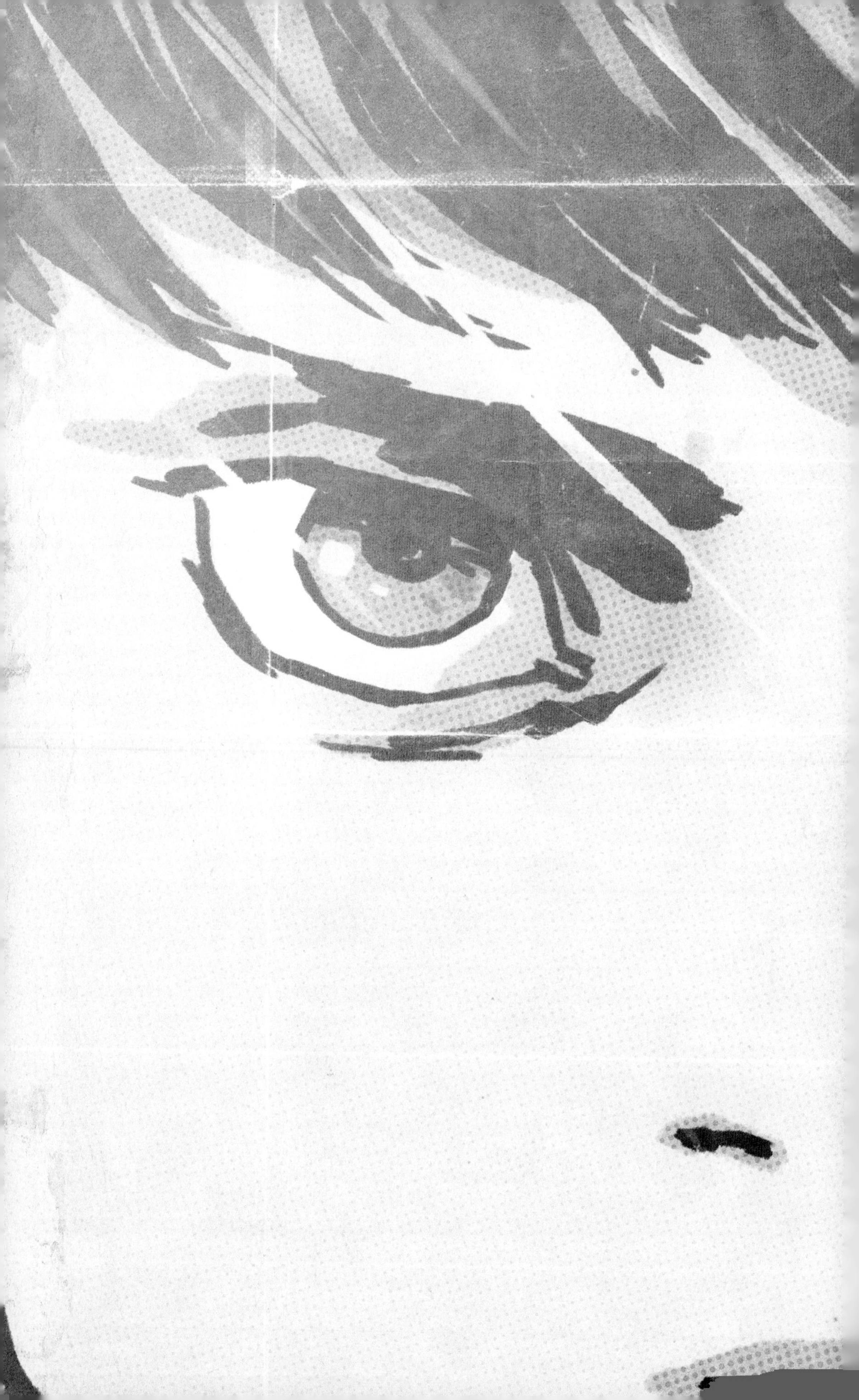

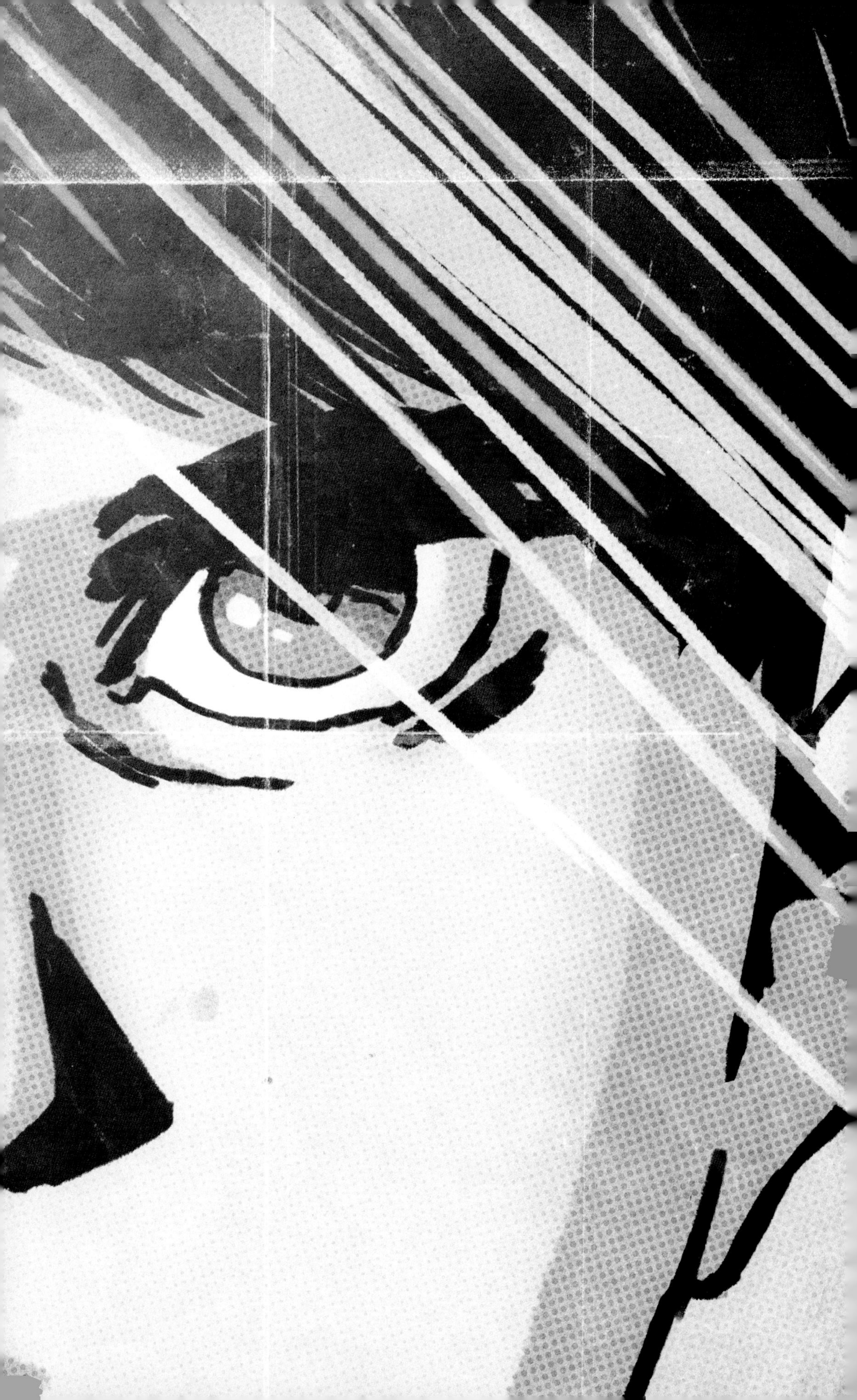

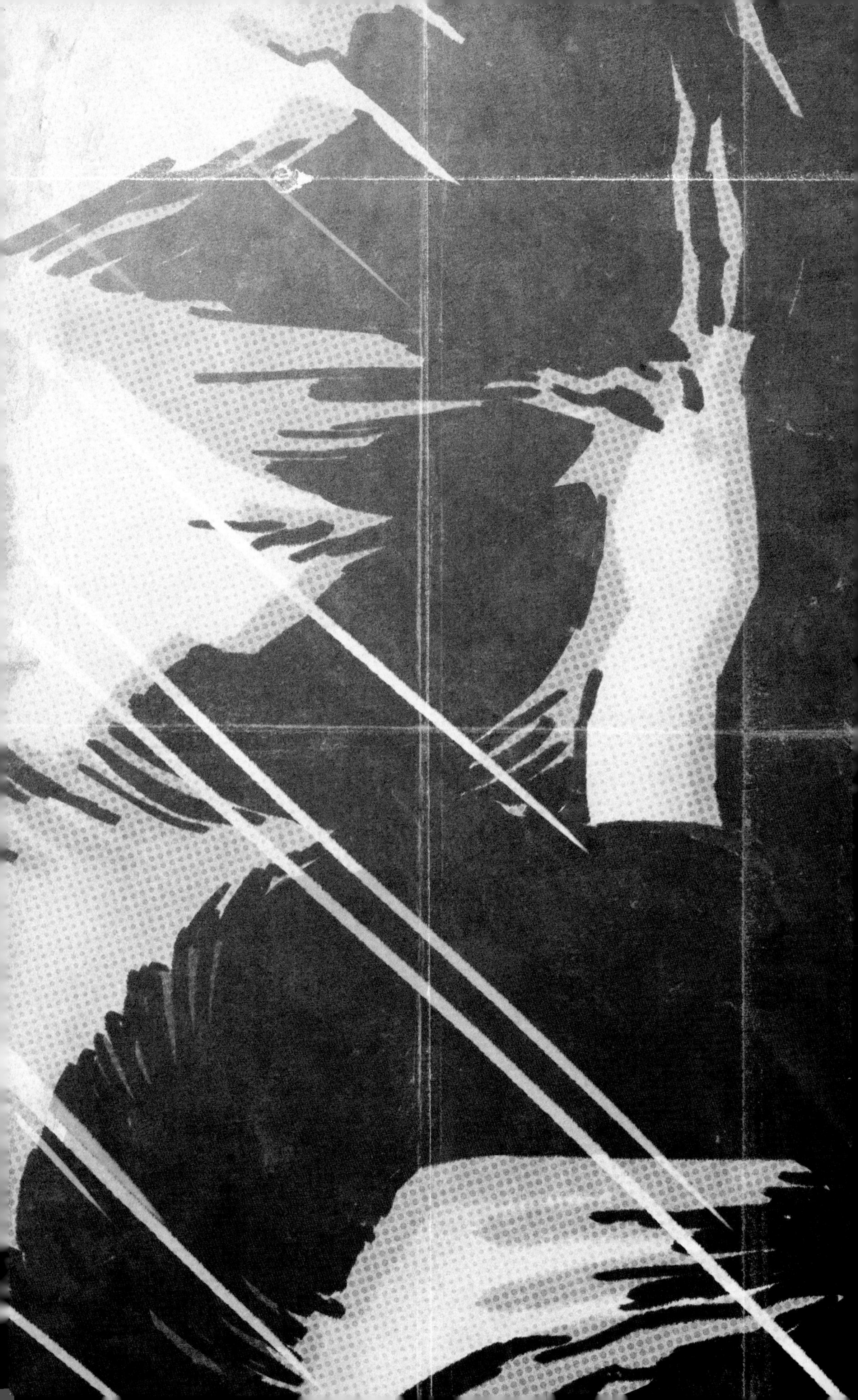

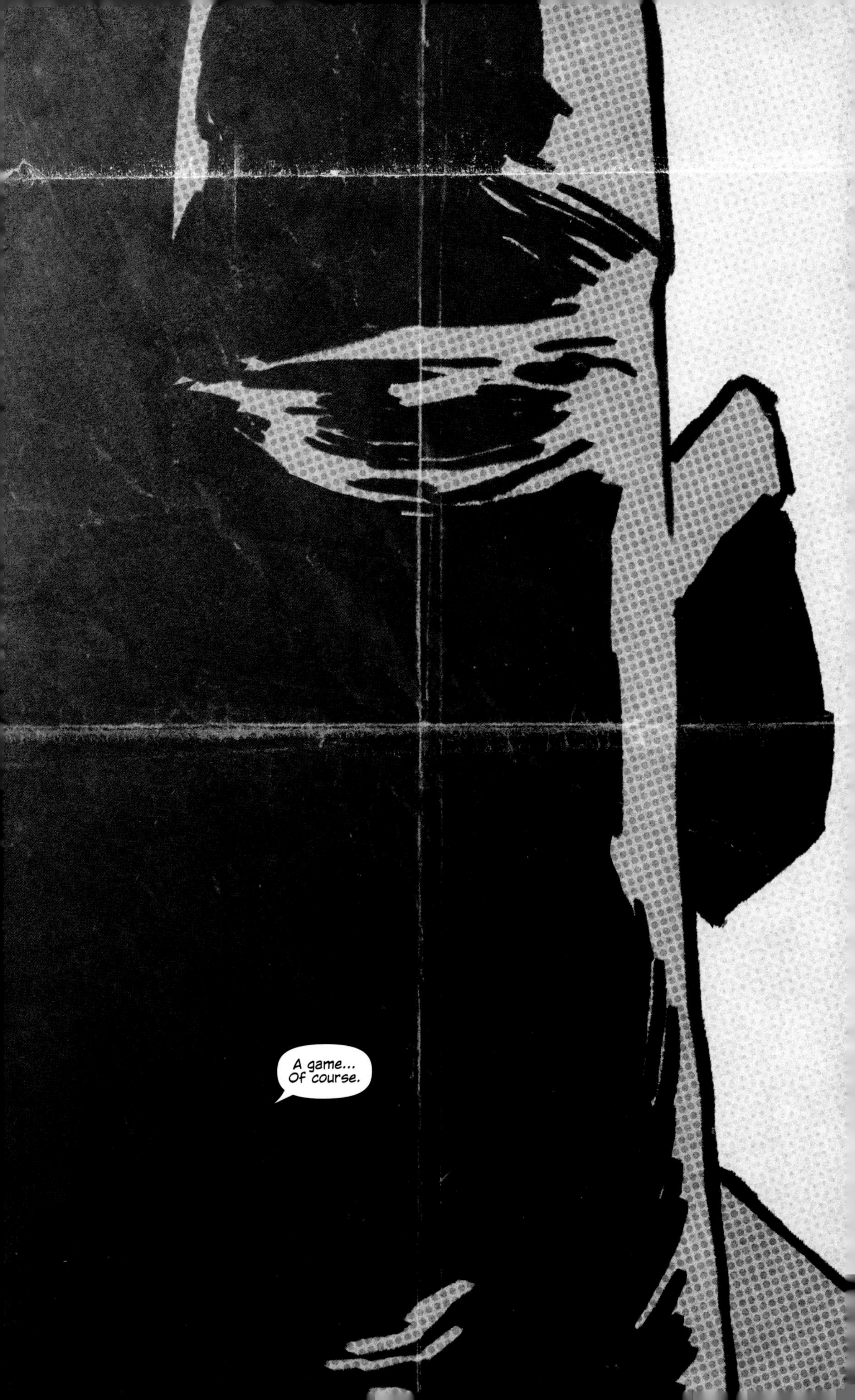
A game... Of course.

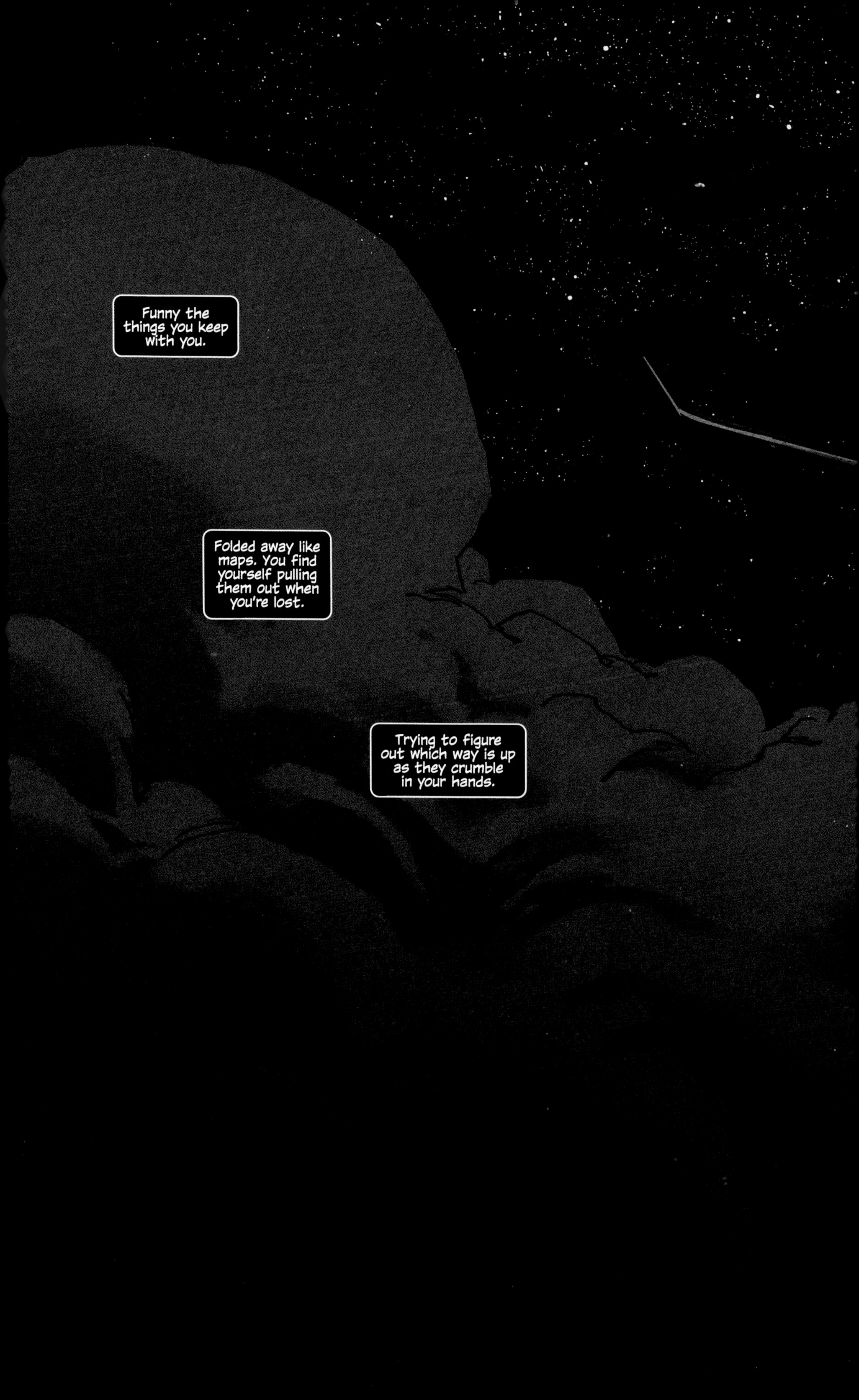
Funny the things you keep with you.
Folded away like maps. You find yourself pulling them out when you're lost.
Trying to figure out which way is up as they crumble in your hands.

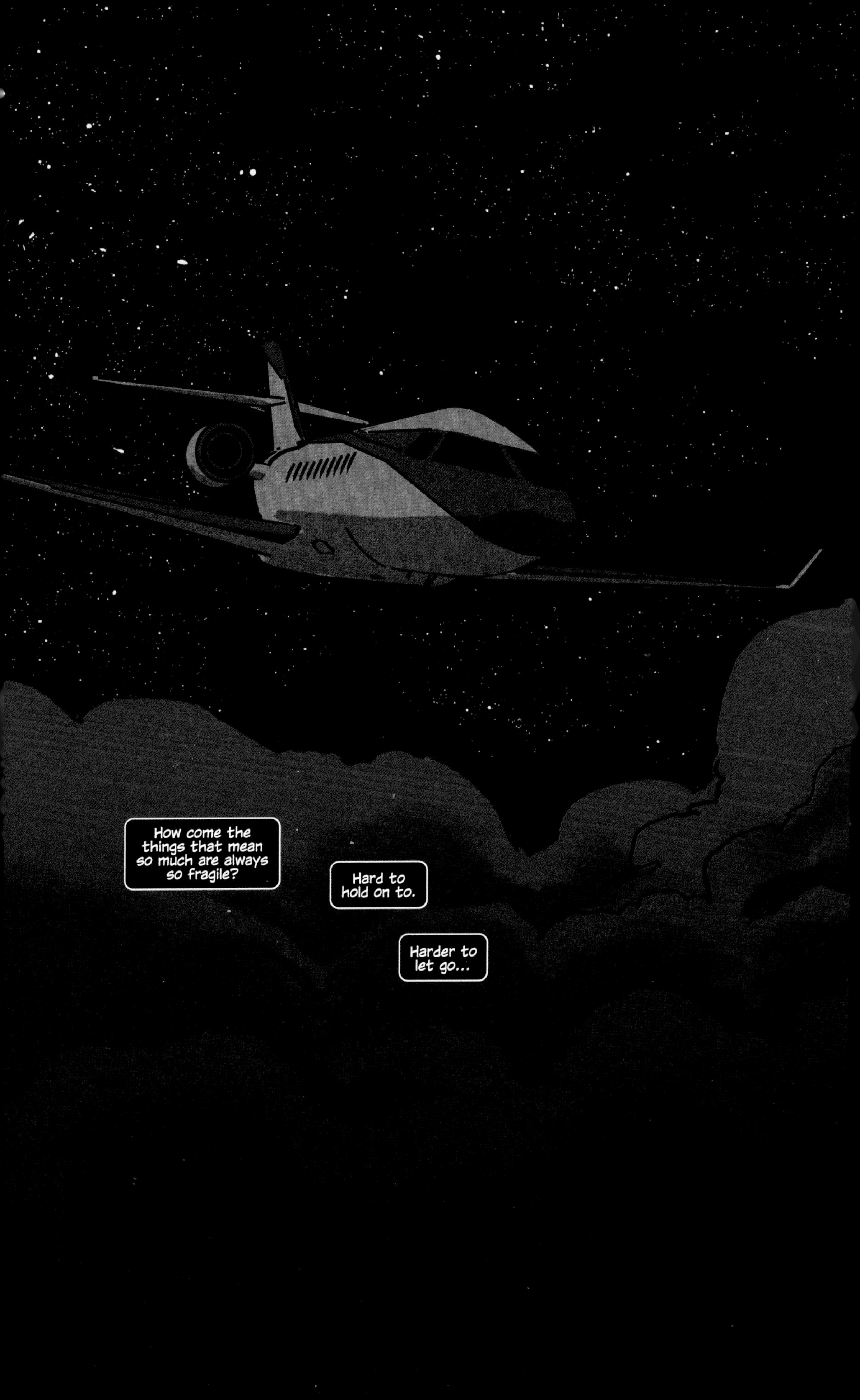
How come the things that mean so much are always so fragile?
Hard to hold on to.
Harder to let go...

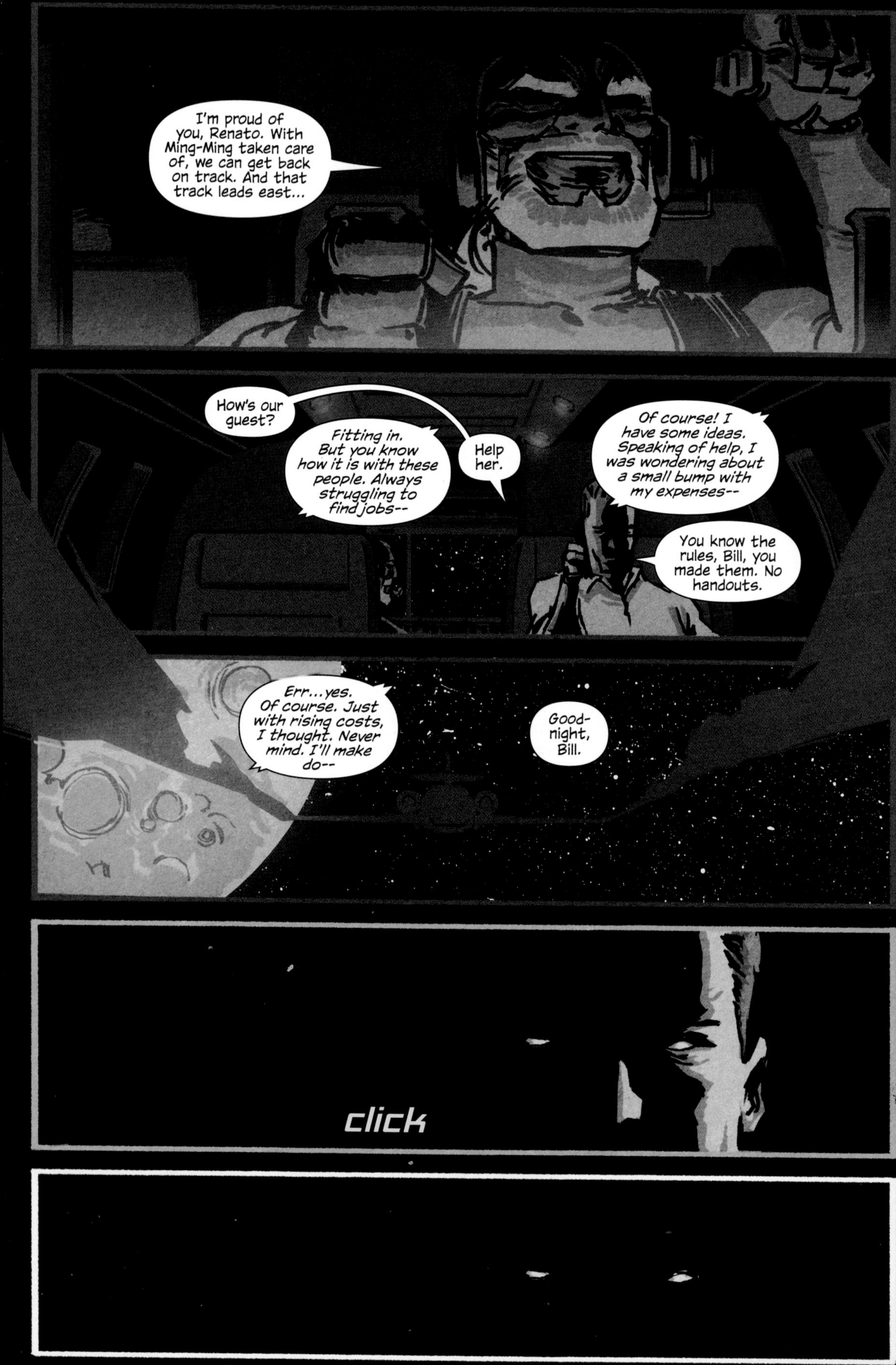

I'm proud of you, Renato. With Ming-Ming taken care of, we can get back on track. And that track leads east...
How's our guest?
Fitting in. But you know how it is with these people. Always struggling to find jobs--
Help her.
Of course! I have some ideas. Speaking of help, I was wondering about a small bump with my expenses--
You know the rules, Bill, you made them. No handouts.
Err...yes. Of course. Just with rising costs, I thought. Never mind. I'll make do--
Good-night, Bill.
click

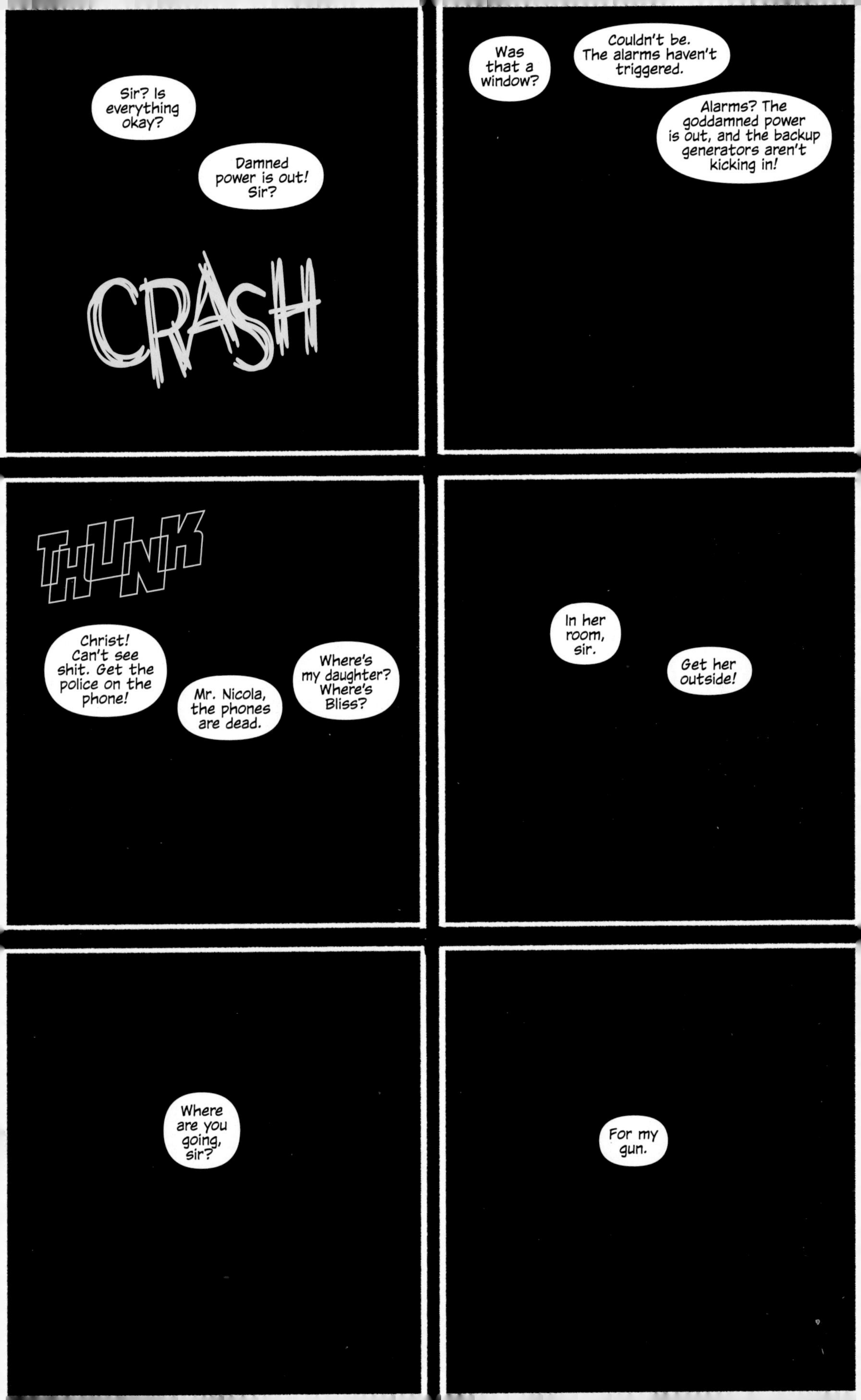
Sir? Is everything okay?
Damned power is out! Sir?
CRASH
Was that a window?
Couldn't be. The alarms haven't triggered.
Alarms? The goddamned power is out, and the backup generators aren't kicking in!
THUNK
Christ! Can't see shit. Get the police on the phone!
Mr. Nicola, the phones are dead.
Where's my daughter? Where's Bliss?
In her room, sir.
Get her outside!
Where are you going, sir?
For my gun.

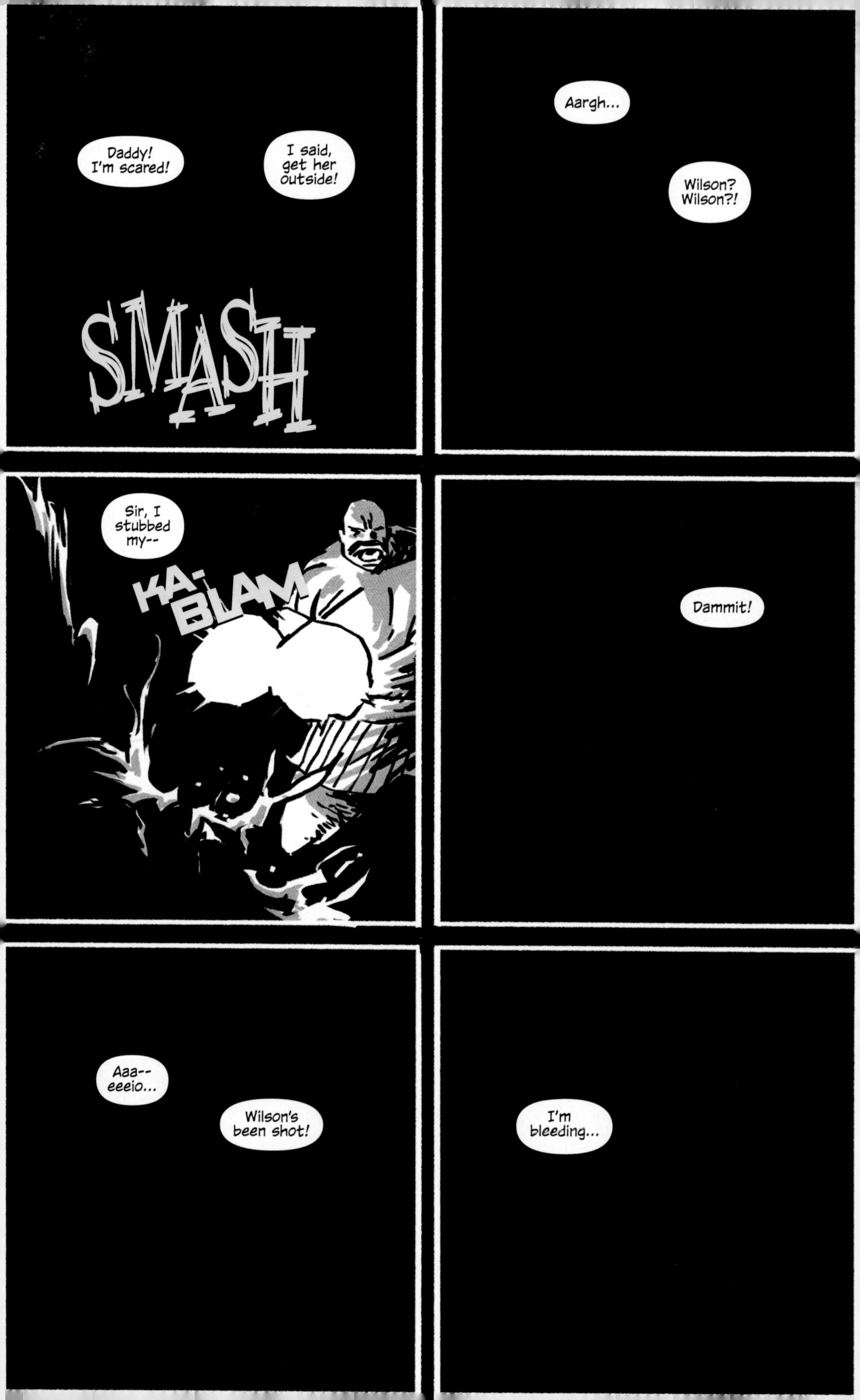
Daddy! I'm scared!
I said, get her outside!
SMASH
Aargh...
Wilson? Wilson?!
Sir, I stubbed my--
KA-BLAM
Dammit!
Aaa-- eeeio...
Wilson's been shot!
I'm bleeding...

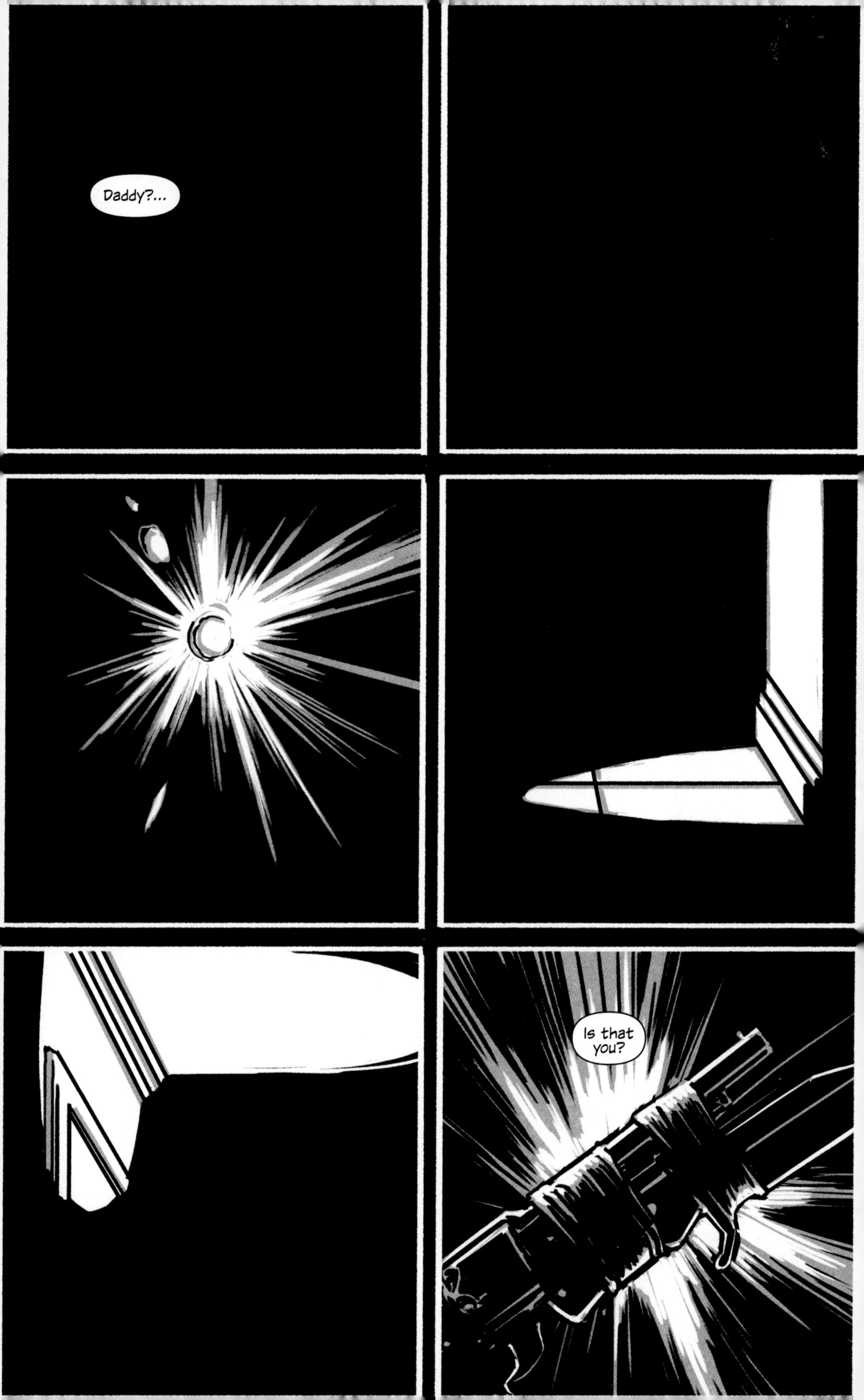
Daddy?...
Is that you?

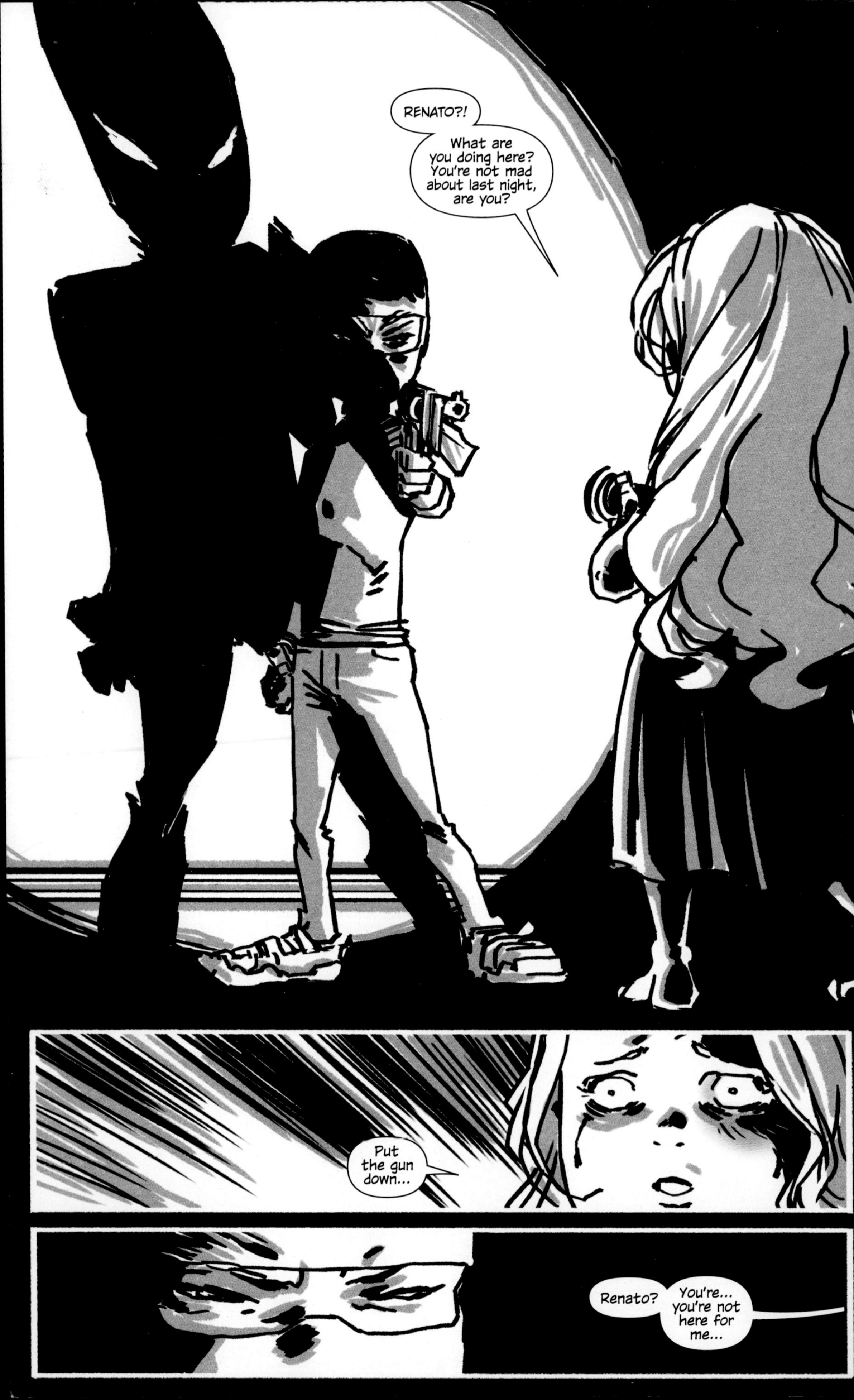
RENATO?!
What are you doing here? You're not mad about last night, are you?
Put the gun down...
Renato?
You're... you're not here for me...

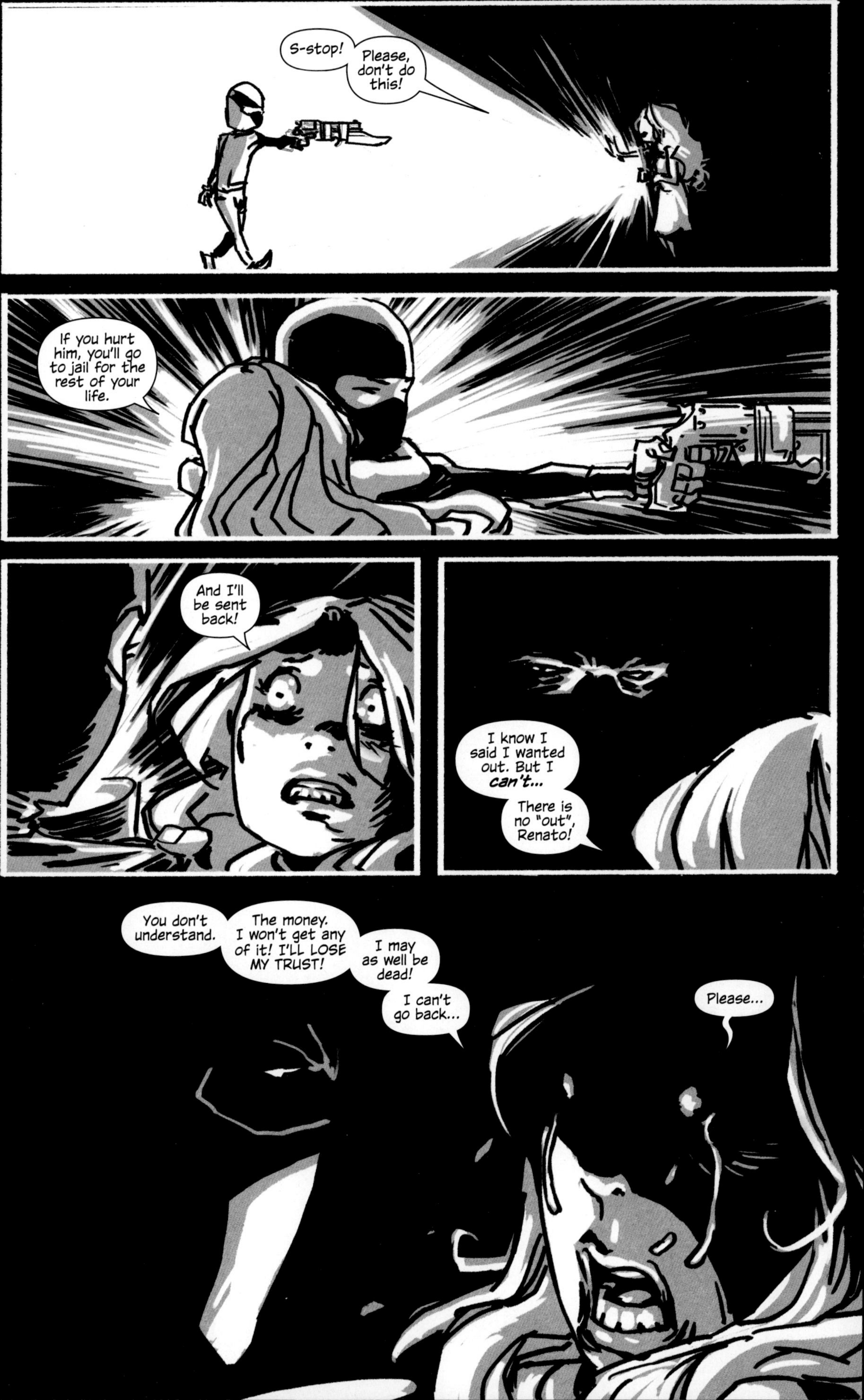
S-stop!
Please, don't do this!
If you hurt him, you'll go to jail for the rest of your life.
And I'll be sent back!
I know I said I wanted out. But I *can't...*
There is no "out", Renato!
You don't understand.
The money. I won't get any of it! I'LL LOSE MY TRUST!
I may as well be dead!
I can't go back...
Please...

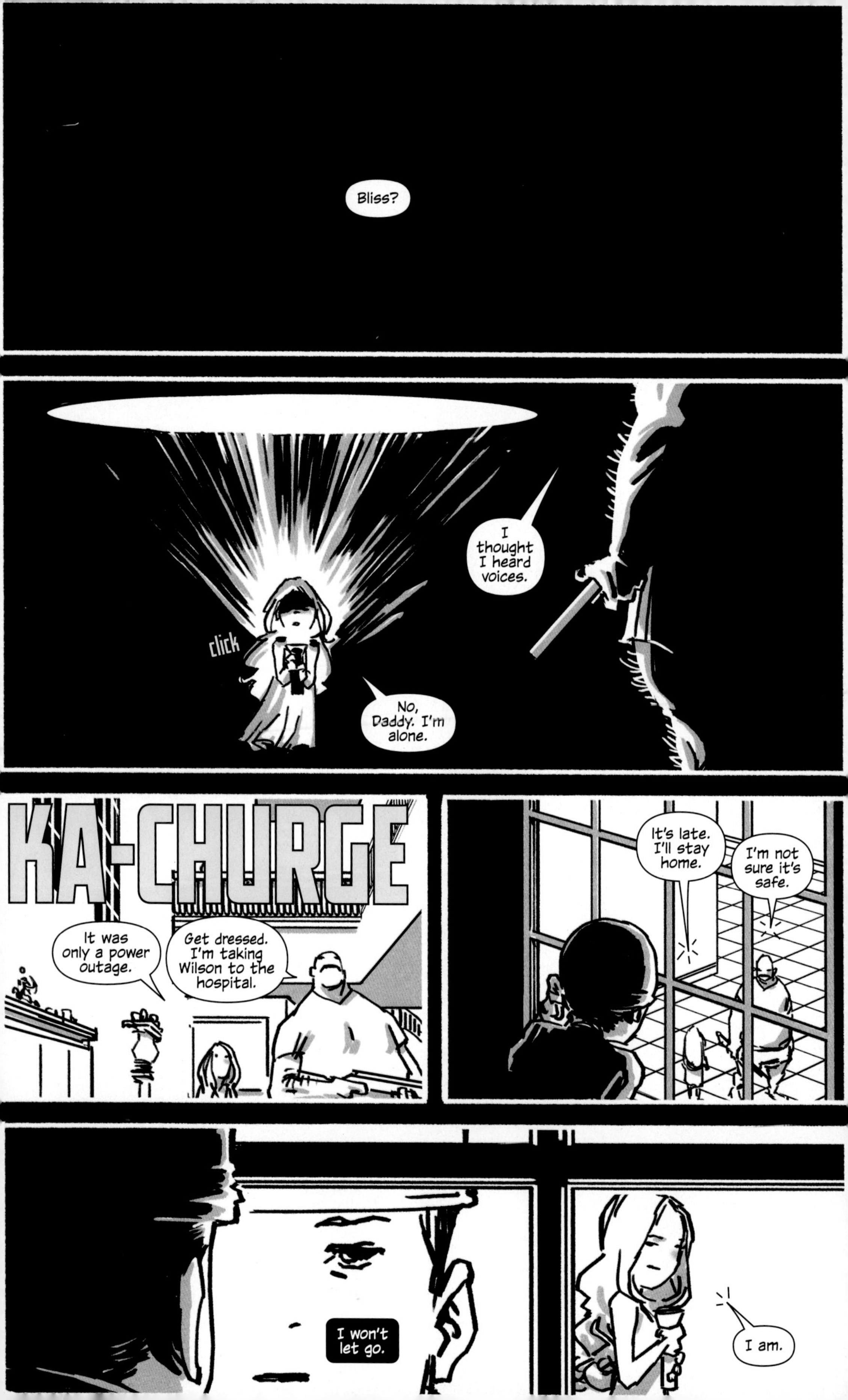
Bliss?
click
I thought I heard voices.
No, Daddy. I'm alone.
KA-CHURGE
It was only a power outage.
Get dressed. I'm taking Wilson to the hospital.
It's late. I'll stay home.
I'm not sure it's safe.
I won't let go.
I am.

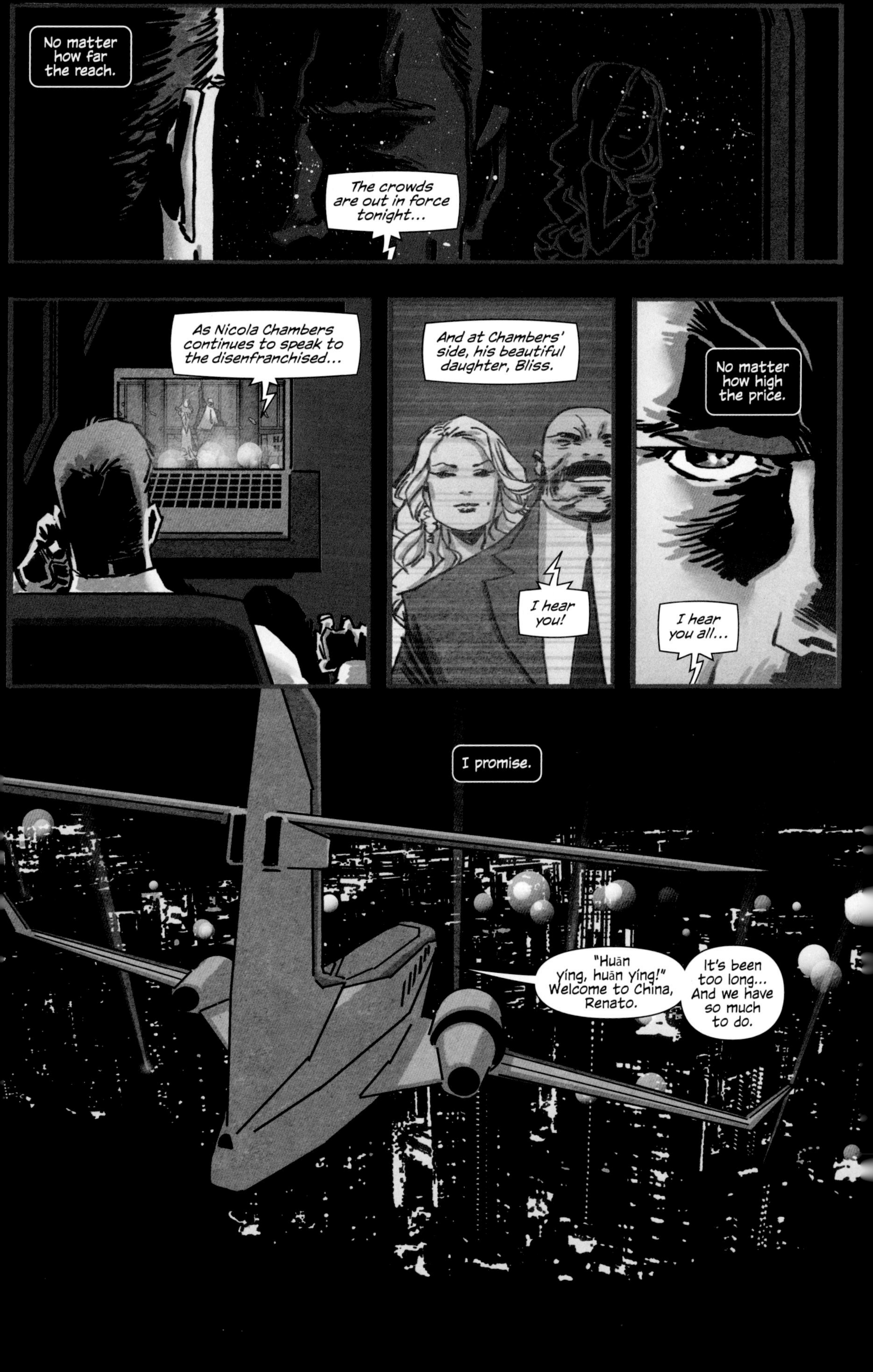
No matter how far the reach.
The crowds are out in force tonight...
As Nicola Chambers continues to speak to the disenfranchised...
And at Chambers' side, his beautiful daughter, Bliss.
No matter how high the price.
I hear you!
I hear you all...
I promise.
"Huān yíng, huān yíng!" Welcome to China, Renato.
It's been too long... And we have so much to do.

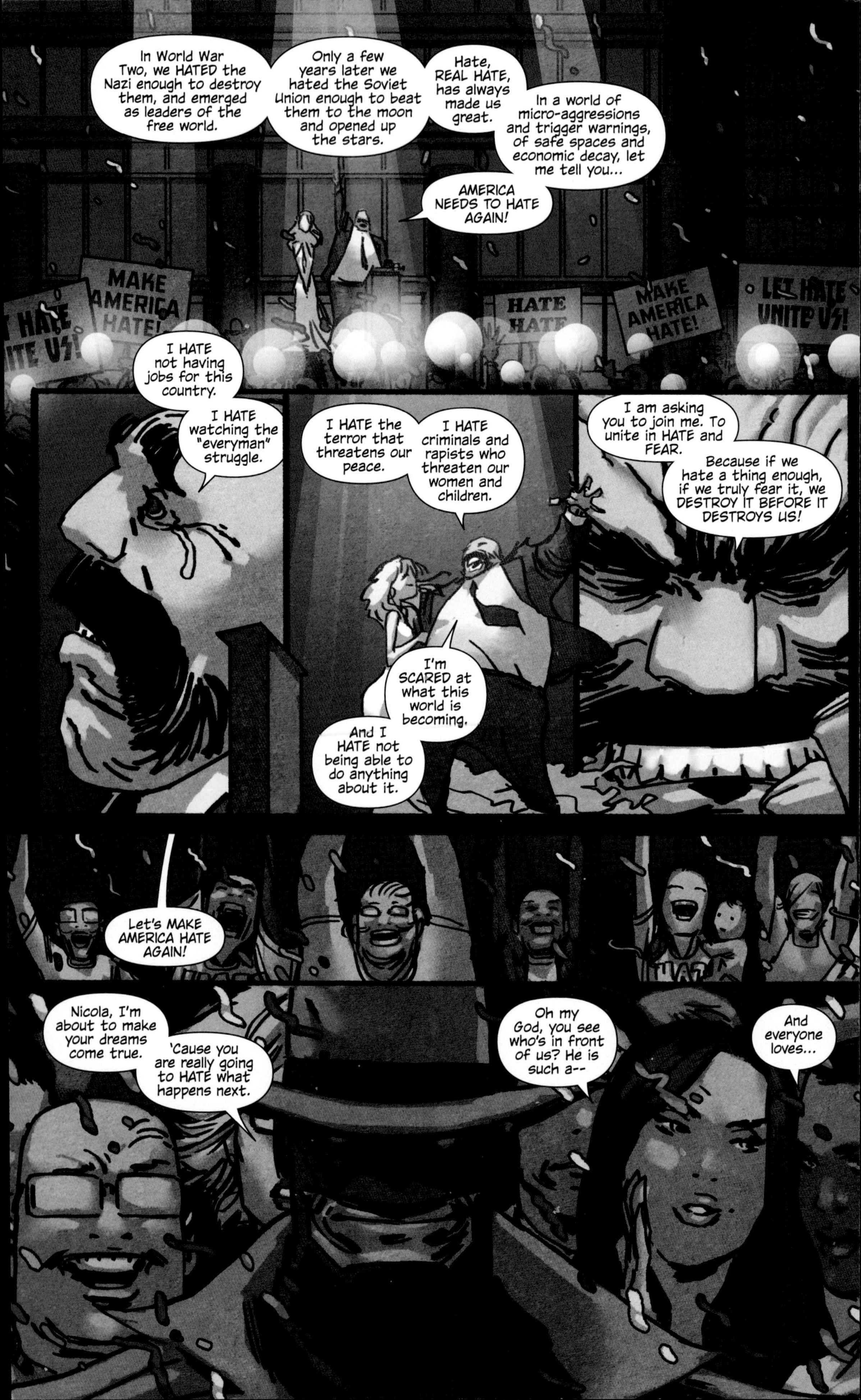
In World War Two, we HATED the Nazi enough to destroy them, and emerged as leaders of the free world.
Only a few years later we hated the Soviet Union enough to beat them to the moon and opened up the stars.
Hate, REAL HATE, has always made us great.
In a world of micro-aggressions and trigger warnings, of safe spaces and economic decay, let me tell you...
AMERICA NEEDS TO HATE AGAIN!
MAKE AMERICA HATE!
HATE HATE
MAKE AMERICA HATE!
LET HATE UNITE US!
I HATE not having jobs for this country.
I HATE watching the "everyman" struggle.
I HATE the terror that threatens our peace.
I HATE criminals and rapists who threaten our women and children.
I'm SCARED at what this world is becoming.
And I HATE not being able to do anything about it.
I am asking you to join me. To unite in HATE and FEAR.
Because if we hate a thing enough, if we truly fear it, we DESTROY IT BEFORE IT DESTROYS US!
Let's MAKE AMERICA HATE AGAIN!
Nicola, I'm about to make your dreams come true.
'Cause you are really going to HATE what happens next.
Oh my God, you see who's in front of us? He is such a--
And everyone loves...

"How come
the things
that mean
so
much
are always
so fragile?"

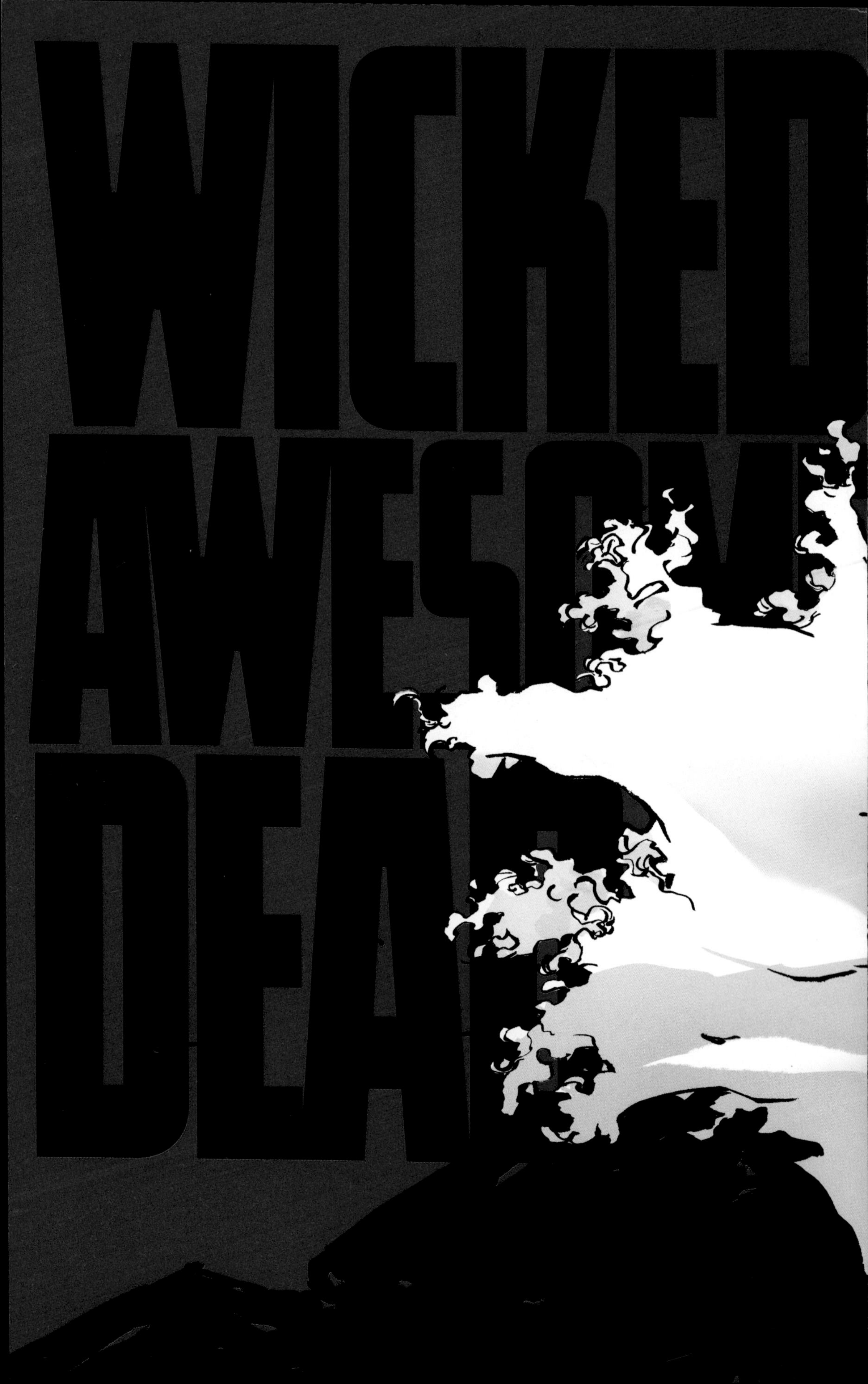
WICKED

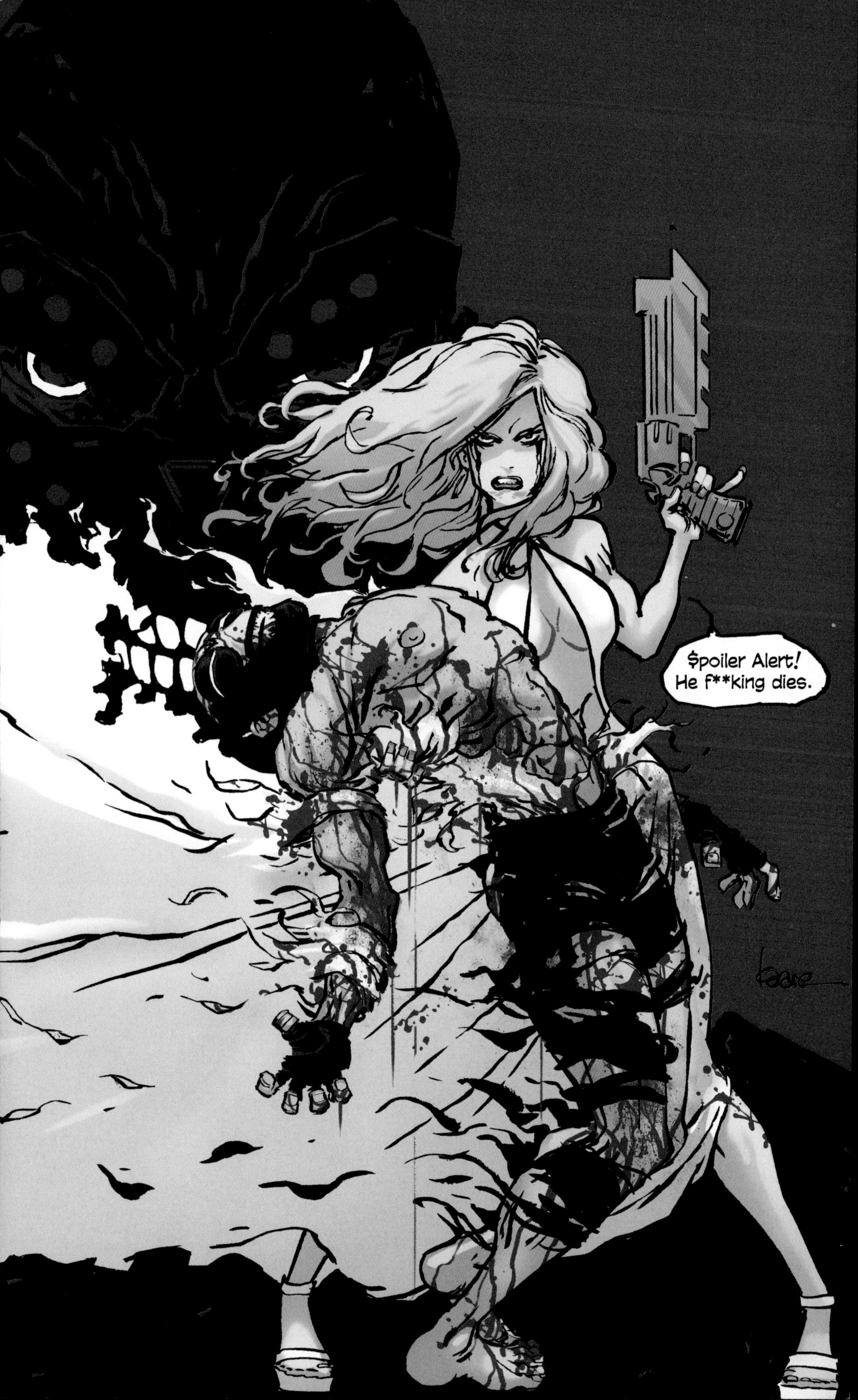
$poiler Alert! He f**king dies.
kaare

5

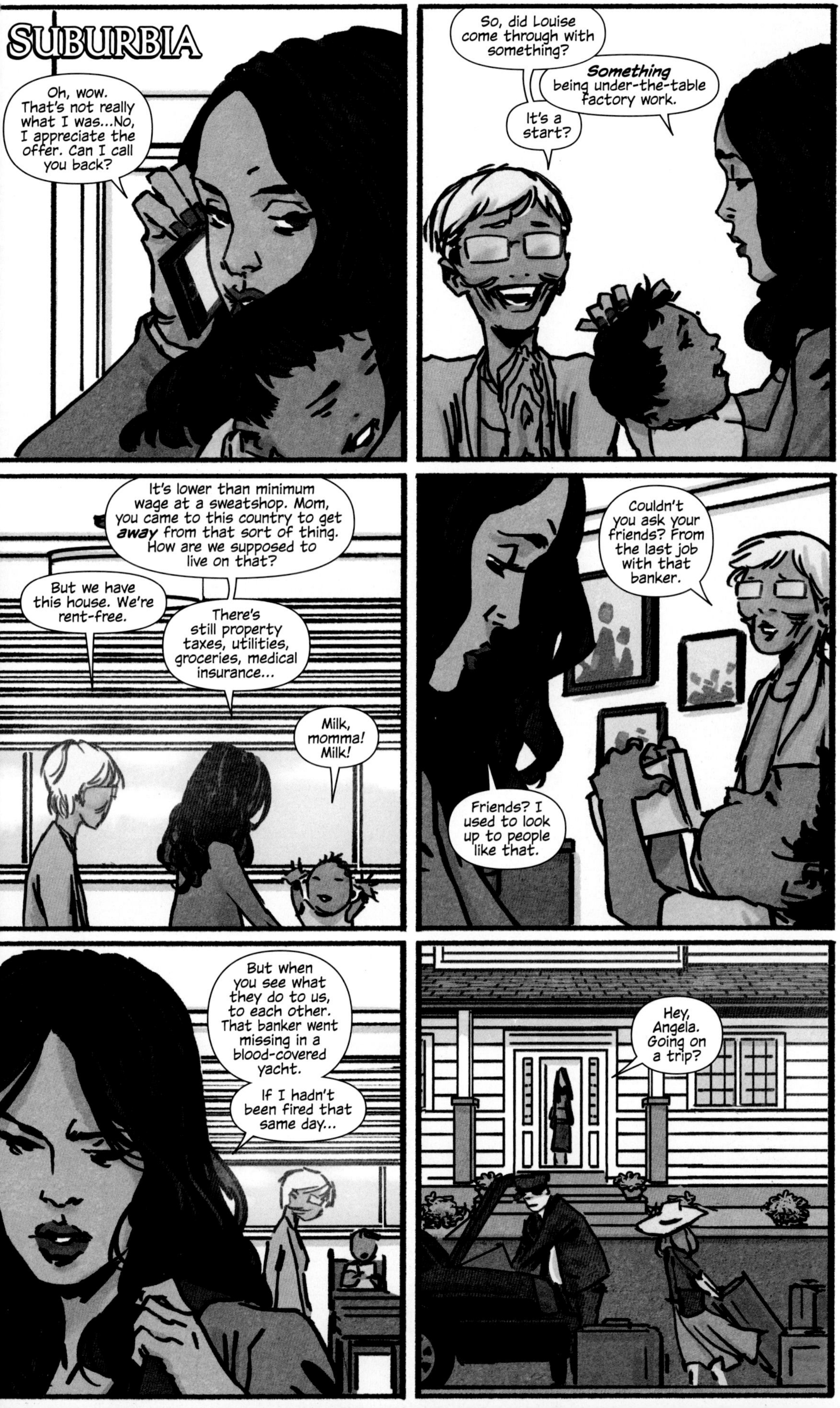
SUBURBIA
Oh, wow. That's not really what I was...No, I appreciate the offer. Can I call you back?
So, did Louise come through with something?
It's a start?
Something being under-the-table factory work.
It's lower than minimum wage at a sweatshop. Mom, you came to this country to get away from that sort of thing. How are we supposed to live on that?
But we have this house. We're rent-free.
There's still property taxes, utilities, groceries, medical insurance...
Milk, momma! Milk!
Couldn't you ask your friends? From the last job with that banker.
Friends? I used to look up to people like that.
But when you see what they do to us, to each other. That banker went missing in a blood-covered yacht.
If I hadn't been fired that same day...
Hey, Angela. Going on a trip?

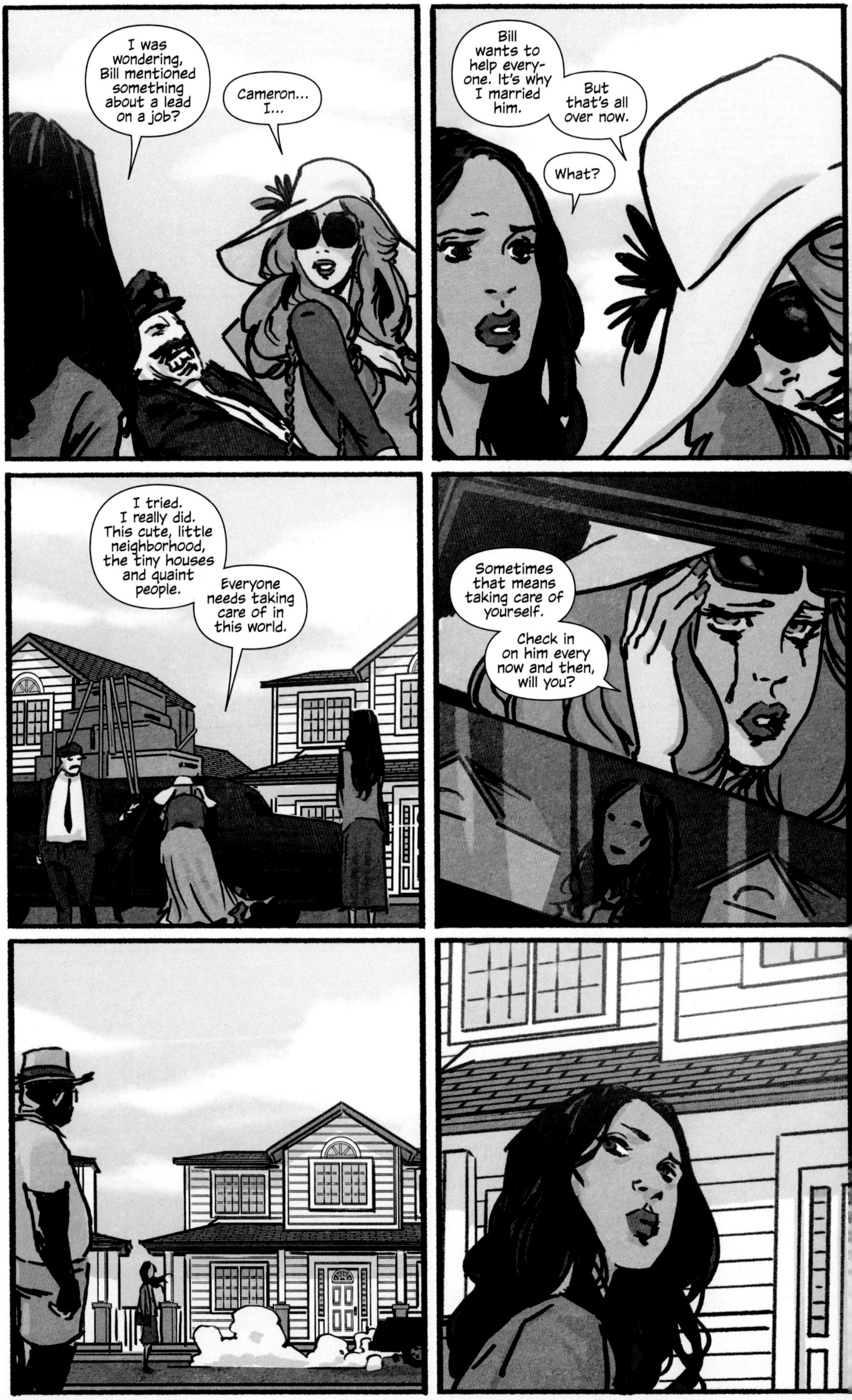
I was wondering, Bill mentioned something about a lead on a job?
Cameron... I...
Bill wants to help every-one. It's why I married him.
But that's all over now.
What?
I tried. I really did. This cute, little neighborhood, the tiny houses and quaint people.
Everyone needs taking care of in this world.
Sometimes that means taking care of yourself.
Check in on him every now and then, will you?

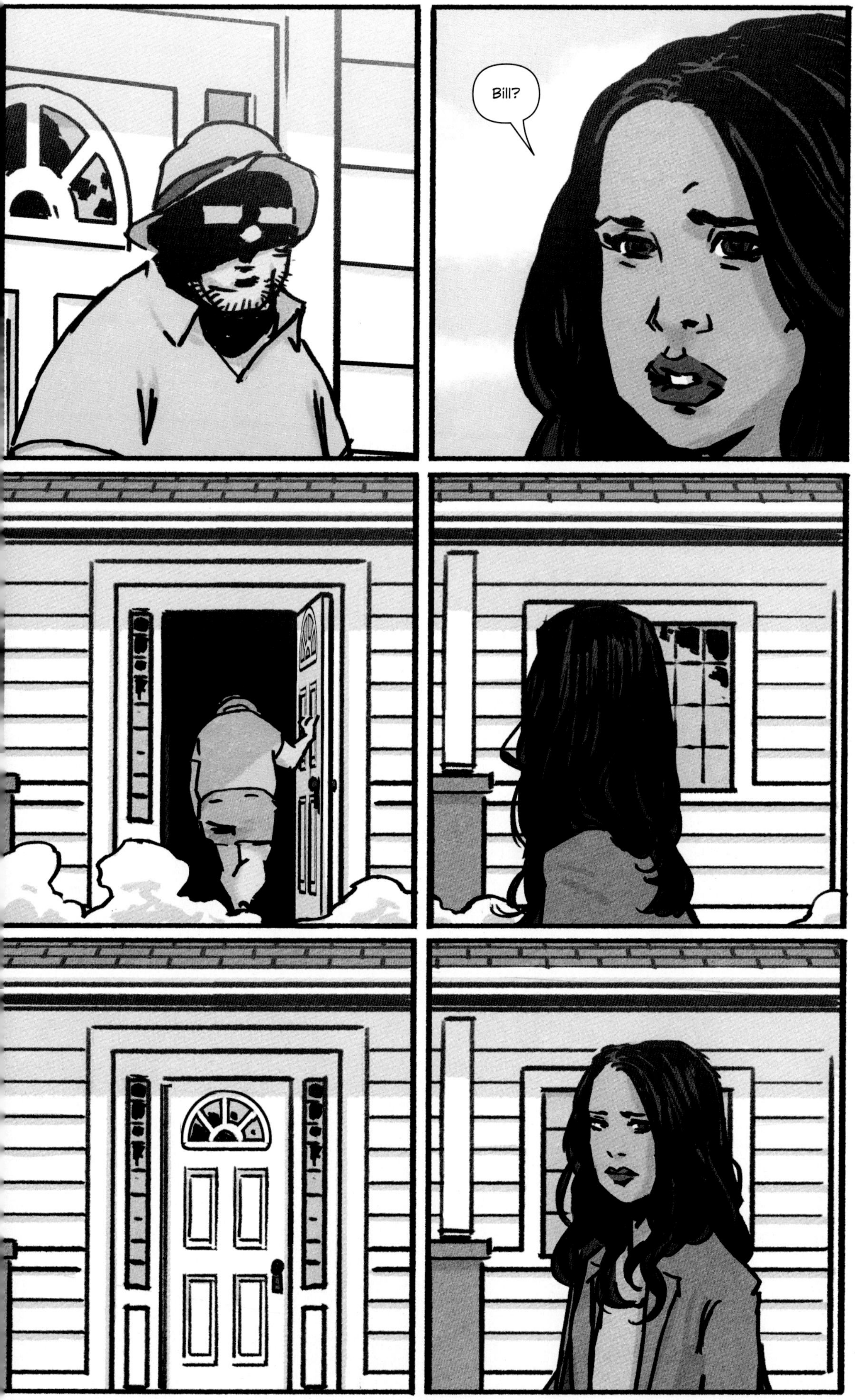
Bill?

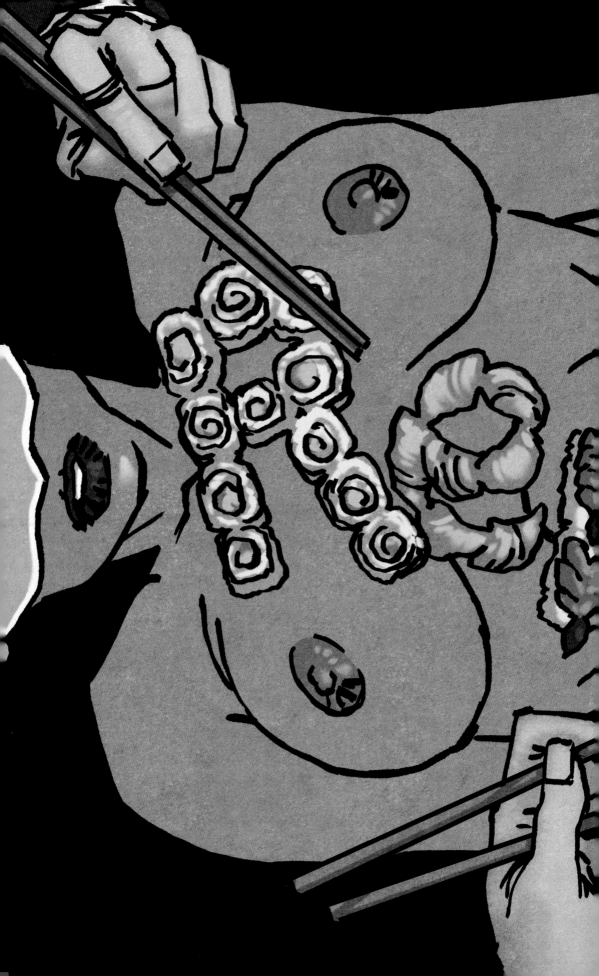

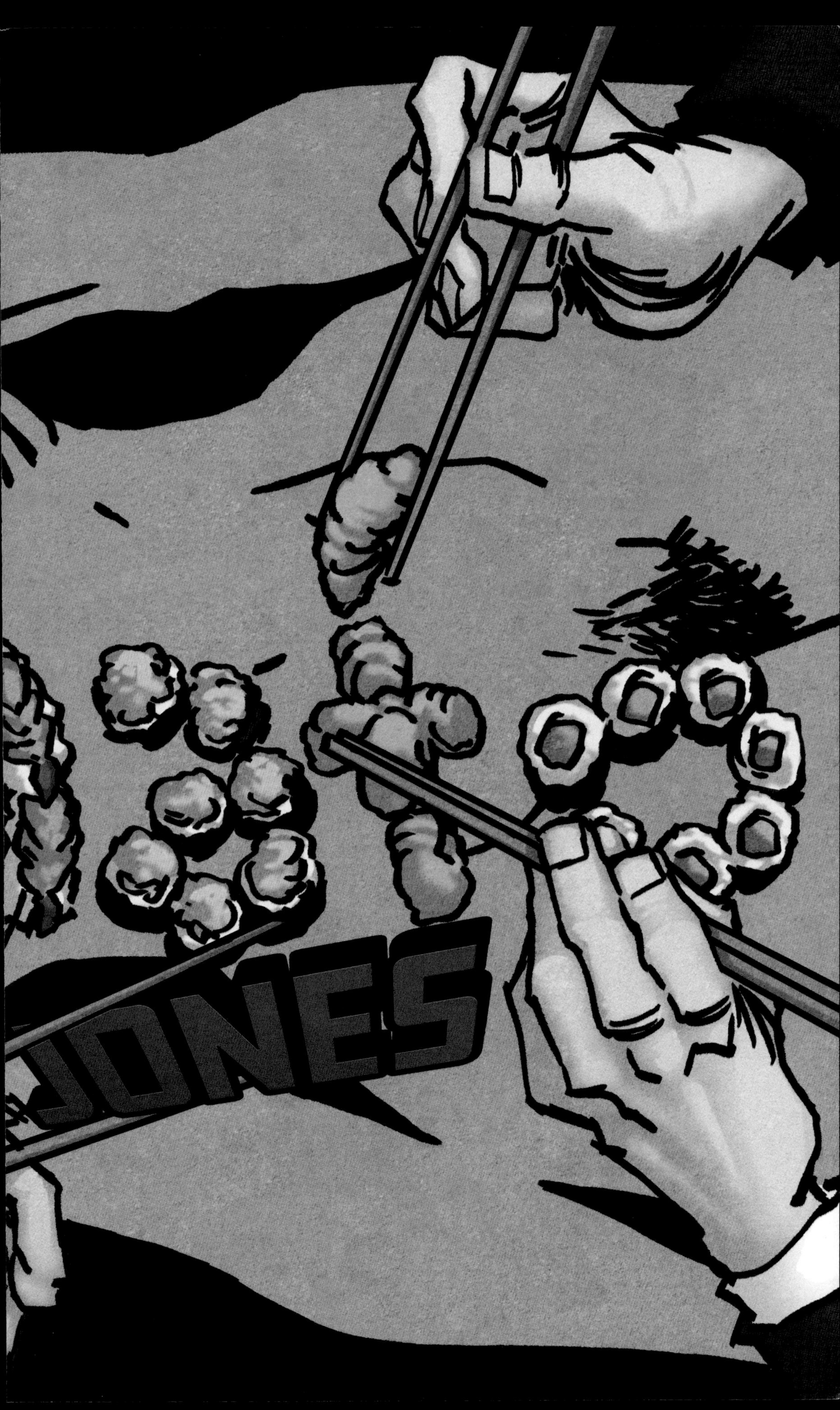
JONES

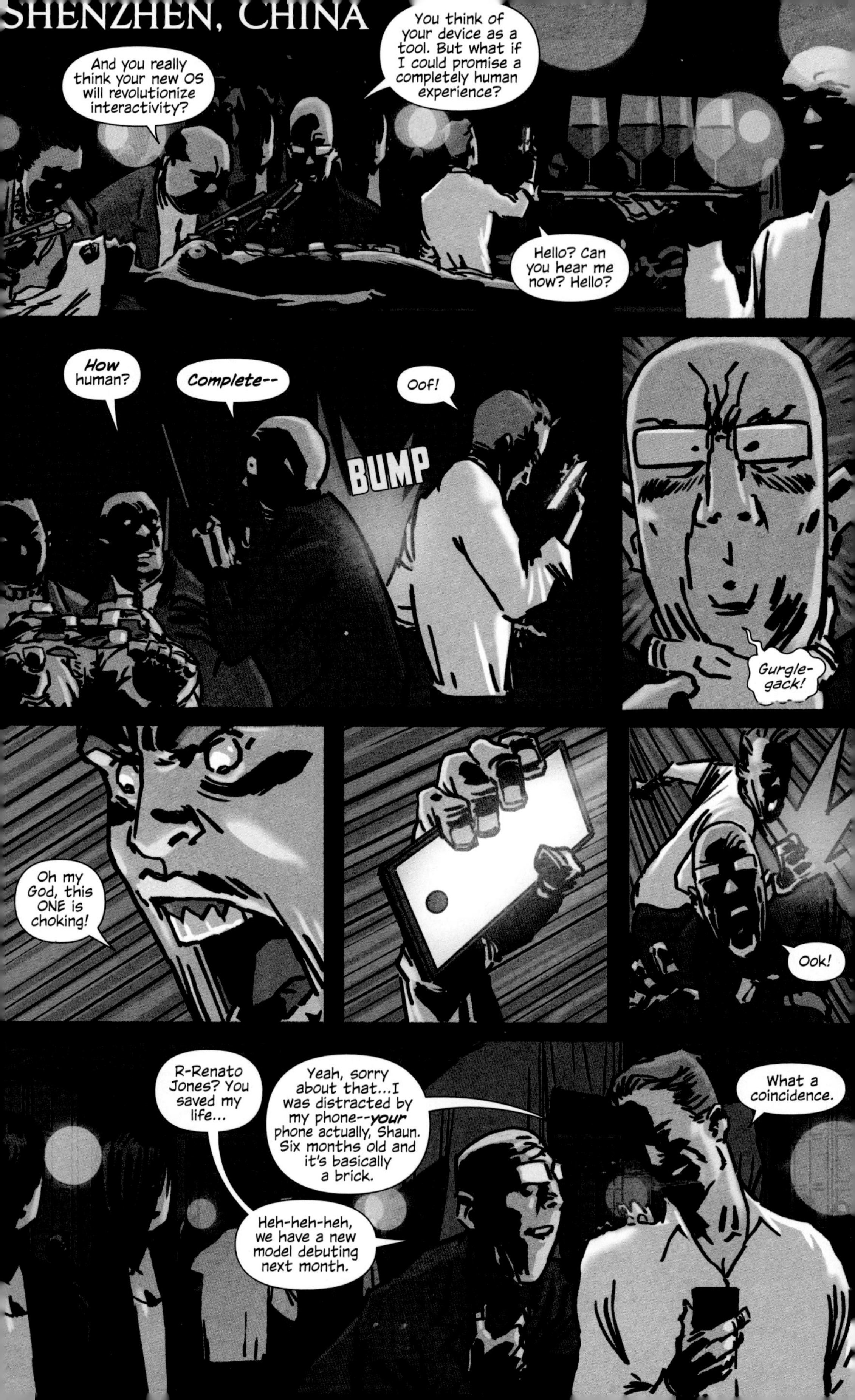
SHENZHEN, CHINA
And you really think your new OS will revolutionize interactivity?
You think of your device as a tool. But what if I could promise a completely human experience?
Hello? Can you hear me now? Hello?
How human?
Complete--
Oof!
BUMP
Gurgle-gack!
Oh my God, this ONE is choking!
Ook!
R-Renato Jones? You saved my life...
Yeah, sorry about that...I was distracted by my phone--your phone actually, Shaun. Six months old and it's basically a brick.
Heh-heh-heh, we have a new model debuting next month.
What a coincidence.

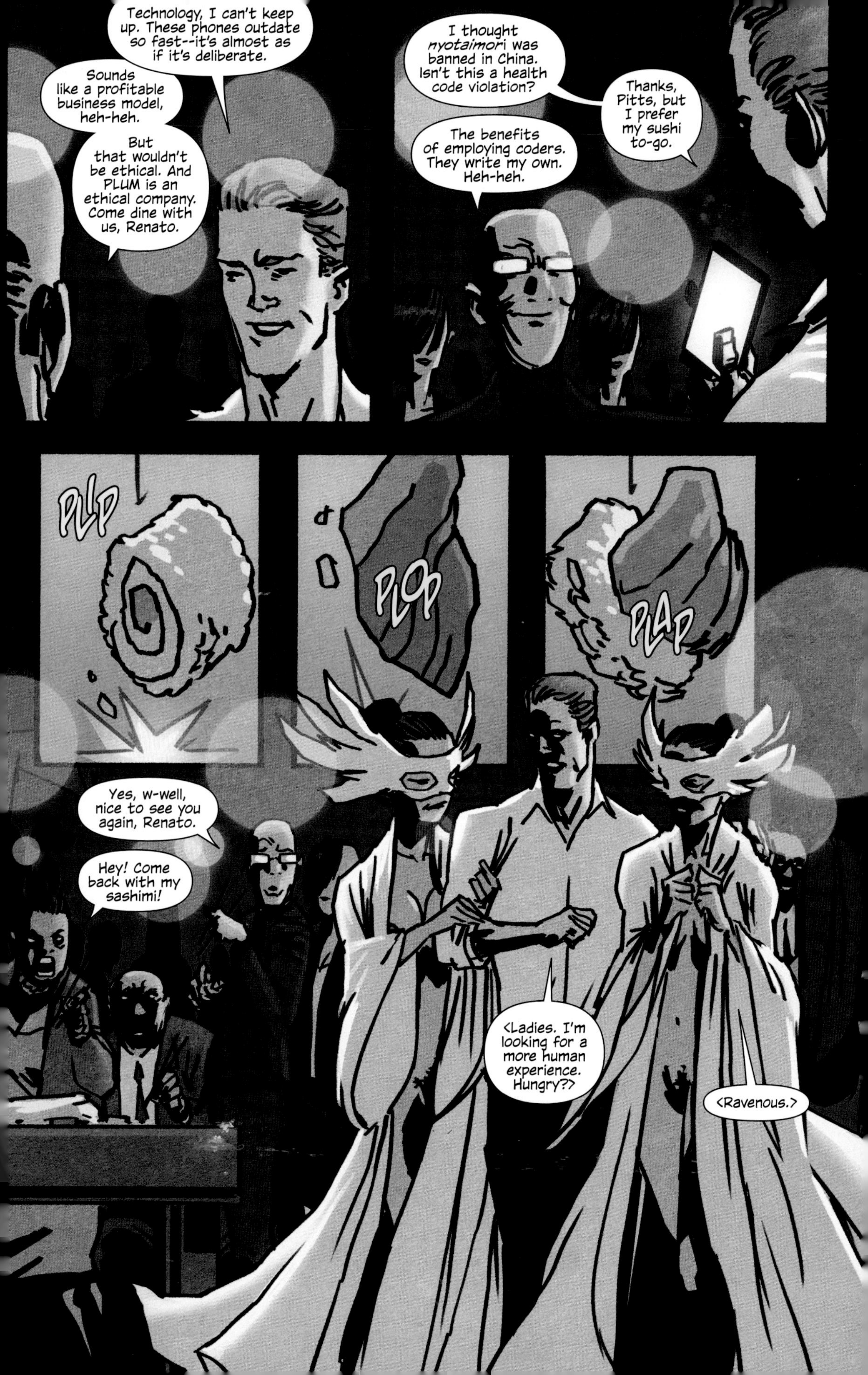
Technology, I can't keep up. These phones outdate so fast--it's almost as if it's deliberate.
Sounds like a profitable business model, heh-heh.
But that wouldn't be ethical. And PLUM is an ethical company. Come dine with us, Renato.
I thought *nyotaimori* was banned in China. Isn't this a health code violation?
The benefits of employing coders. They write my own. Heh-heh.
Thanks, Pitts, but I prefer my sushi to-go.
PLIP
PLOP
PLAP
Yes, w-well, nice to see you again, Renato.
Hey! Come back with my sashimi!
<Ladies. I'm looking for a more human experience. Hungry?>
<Ravenous.>

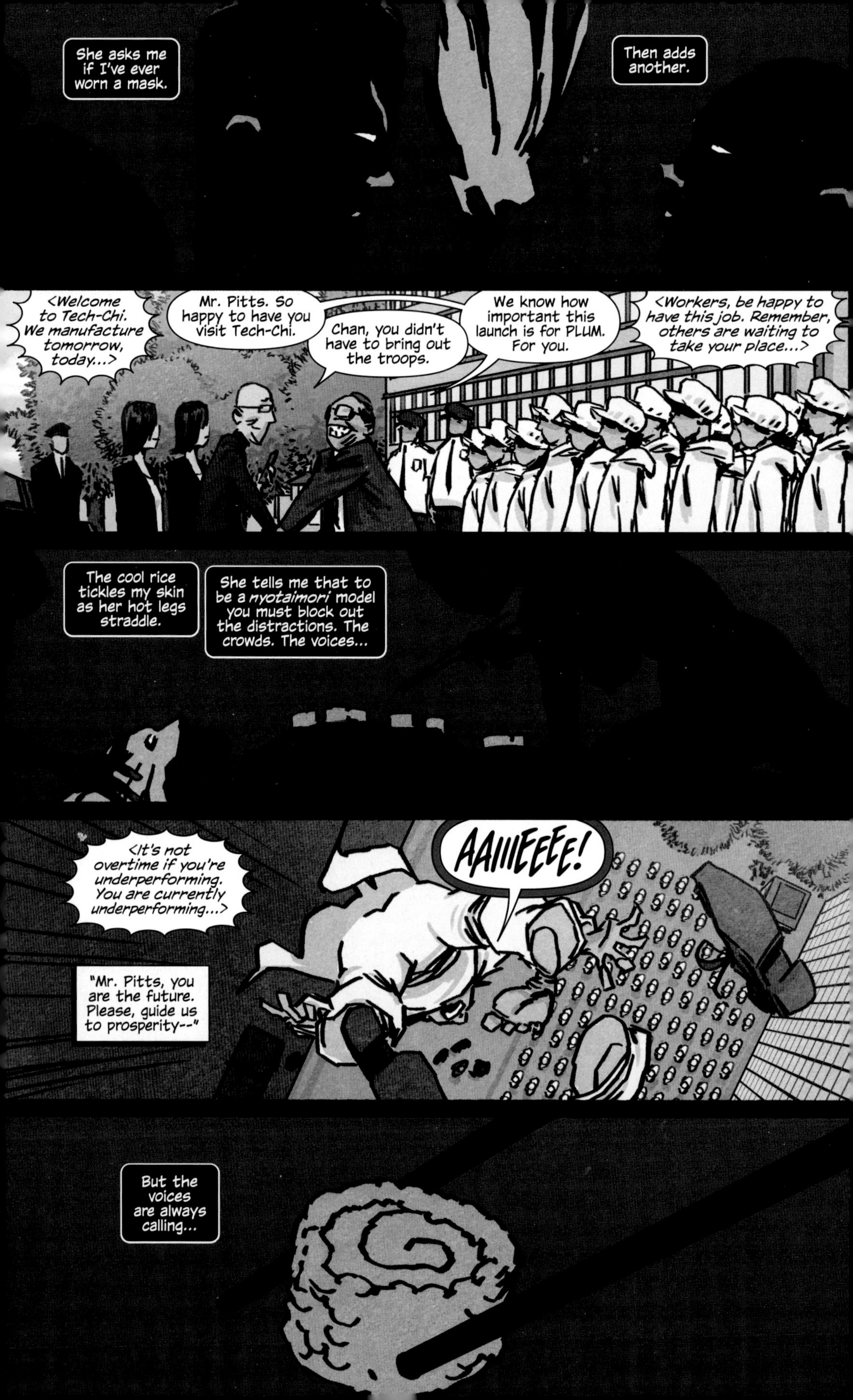

She asks me if I've ever worn a mask.
Then adds another.
<Welcome to Tech-Chi. We manufacture tomorrow, today...>
Mr. Pitts. So happy to have you visit Tech-Chi.
Chan, you didn't have to bring out the troops.
We know how important this launch is for PLUM. For you.
<Workers, be happy to have this job. Remember, others are waiting to take your place...>
The cool rice tickles my skin as her hot legs straddle.
She tells me that to be a *nyotaimori* model you must block out the distractions. The crowds. The voices...
<It's not overtime if you're underperforming. You are currently underperforming...>
AAIIIEEEE!
"Mr. Pitts, you are the future. Please, guide us to prosperity--"
But the voices are always calling...

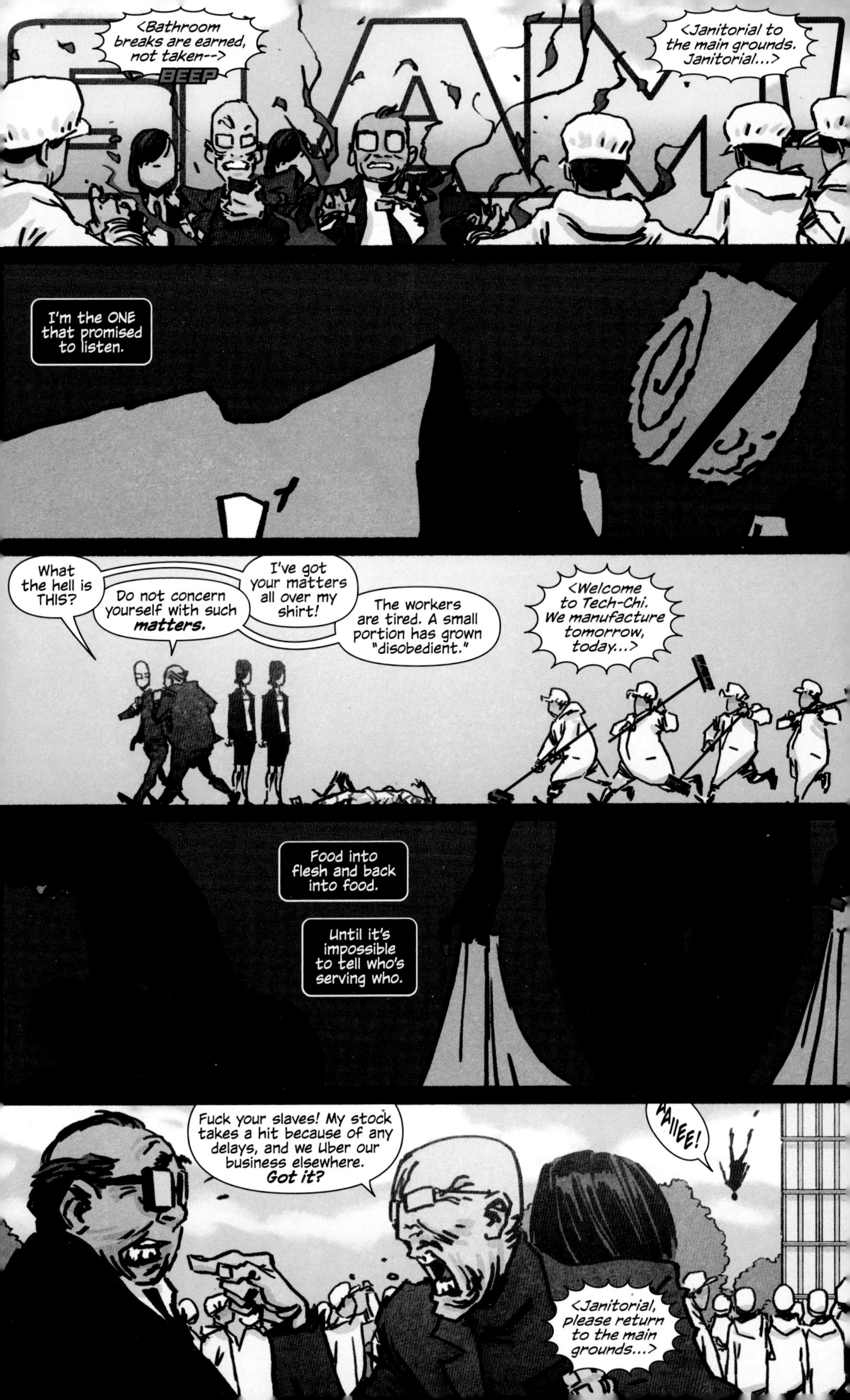
<Bathroom breaks are earned, not taken-->
BEEP
<Janitorial to the main grounds. Janitorial...>
I'm the ONE that promised to listen.
What the hell is THIS?
Do not concern yourself with such **matters.**
I've got your matters all over my shirt!
The workers are tired. A small portion has grown "disobedient."
<Welcome to Tech-Chi. We manufacture tomorrow, today...>
Food into flesh and back into food.
Until it's impossible to tell who's serving who.
Fuck your slaves! My stock takes a hit because of any delays, and we Uber our business elsewhere. **Got it?**
AAIIEE!
<Janitorial, please return to the main grounds...>

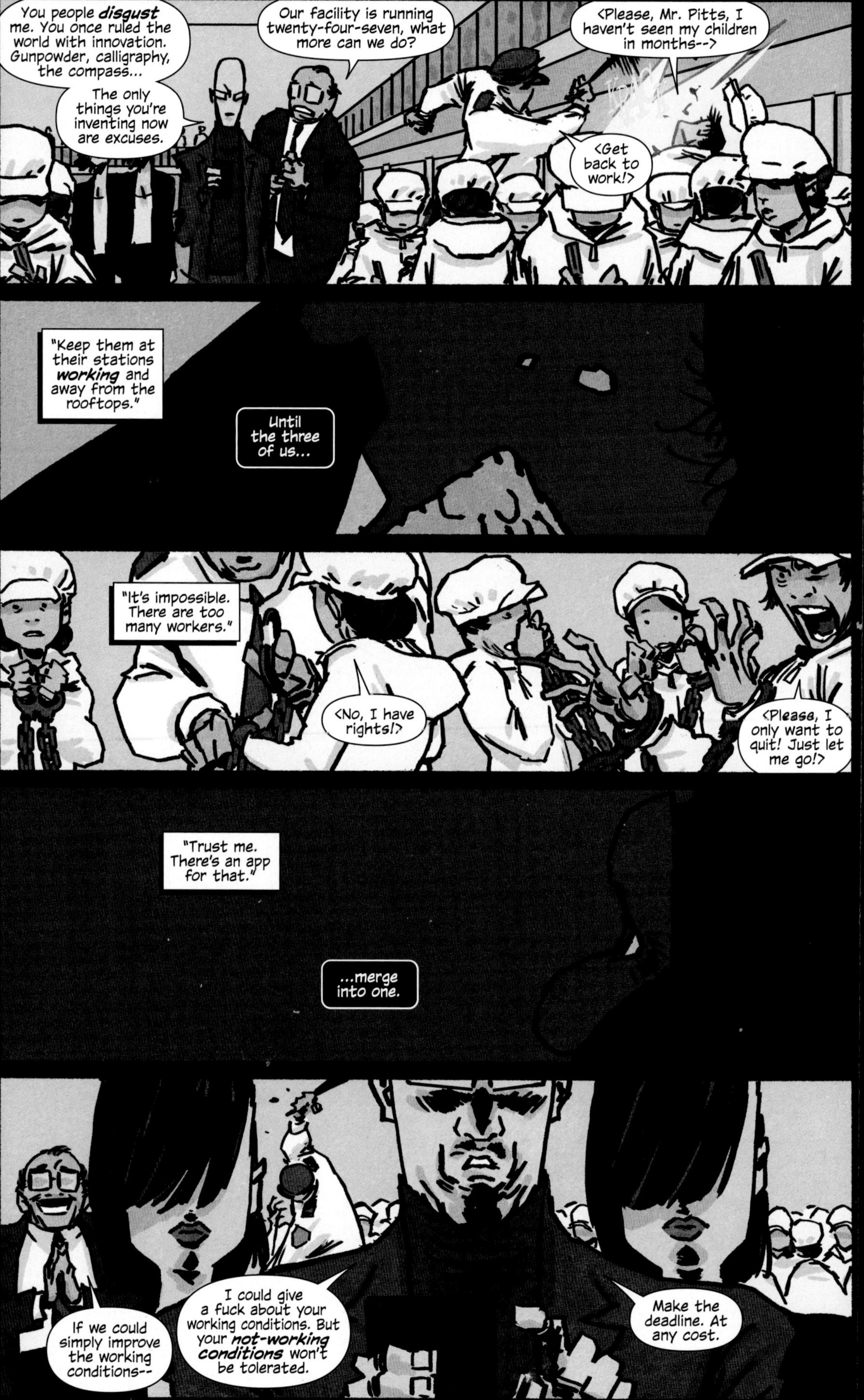
You people *disgust* me. You once ruled the world with innovation. Gunpowder, calligraphy, the compass...
The only things you're inventing now are excuses.
Our facility is running twenty-four-seven, what more can we do?
<Please, Mr. Pitts, I haven't seen my children in months-->
<Get back to work!>
"Keep them at their stations *working* and away from the rooftops."
Until the three of us...
"It's impossible. There are too many workers."
<No, I have rights!>
<Please, I only want to quit! Just let me go!>
"Trust me. There's an app for that."
...merge into one.
If we could simply improve the working conditions--
I could give a fuck about your working conditions. But your *not-working conditions* won't be tolerated.
Make the deadline. At any cost.

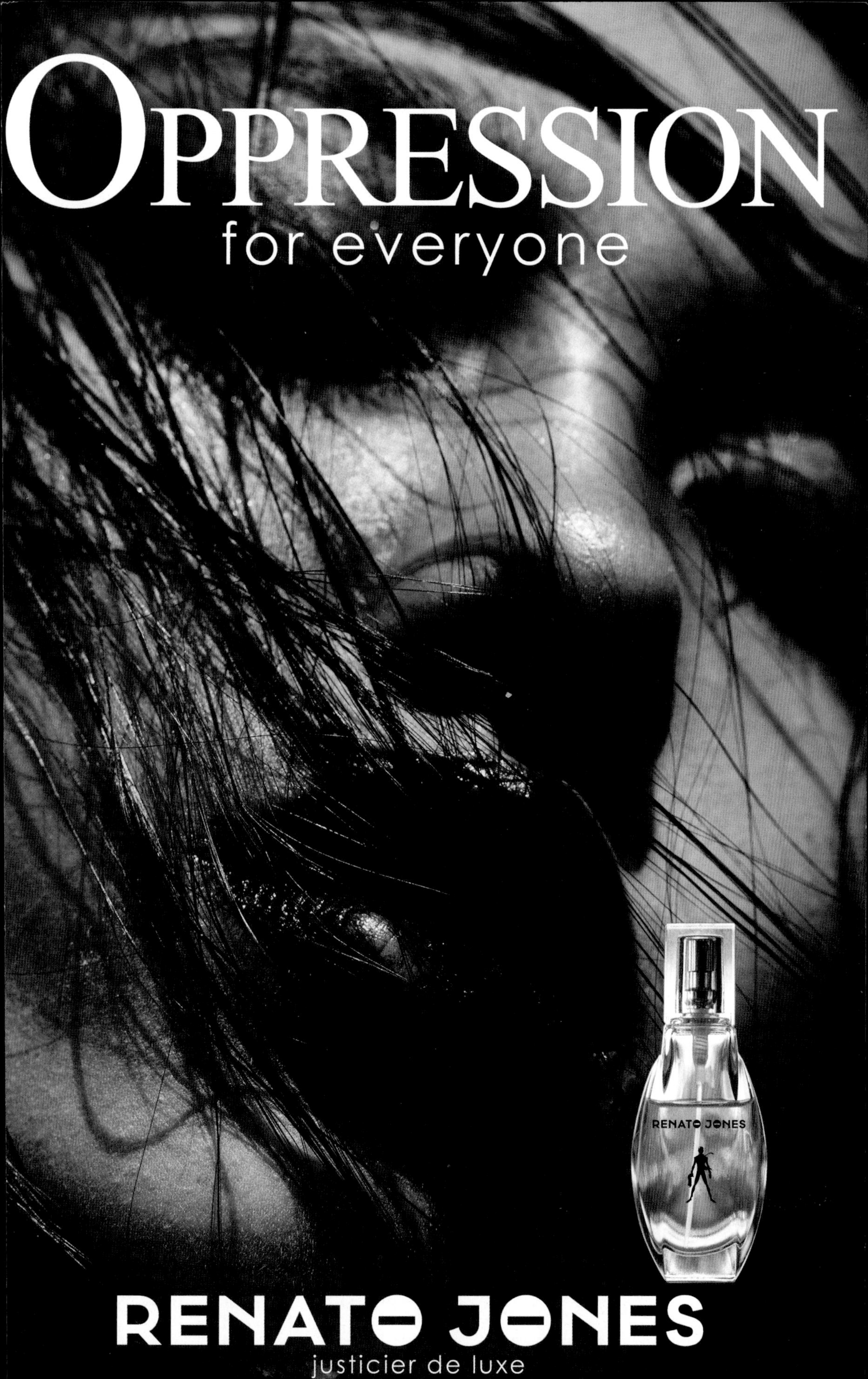
OPPRESSION
for everyone
RENATO JONES
RENATO JONES
justicier de luxe

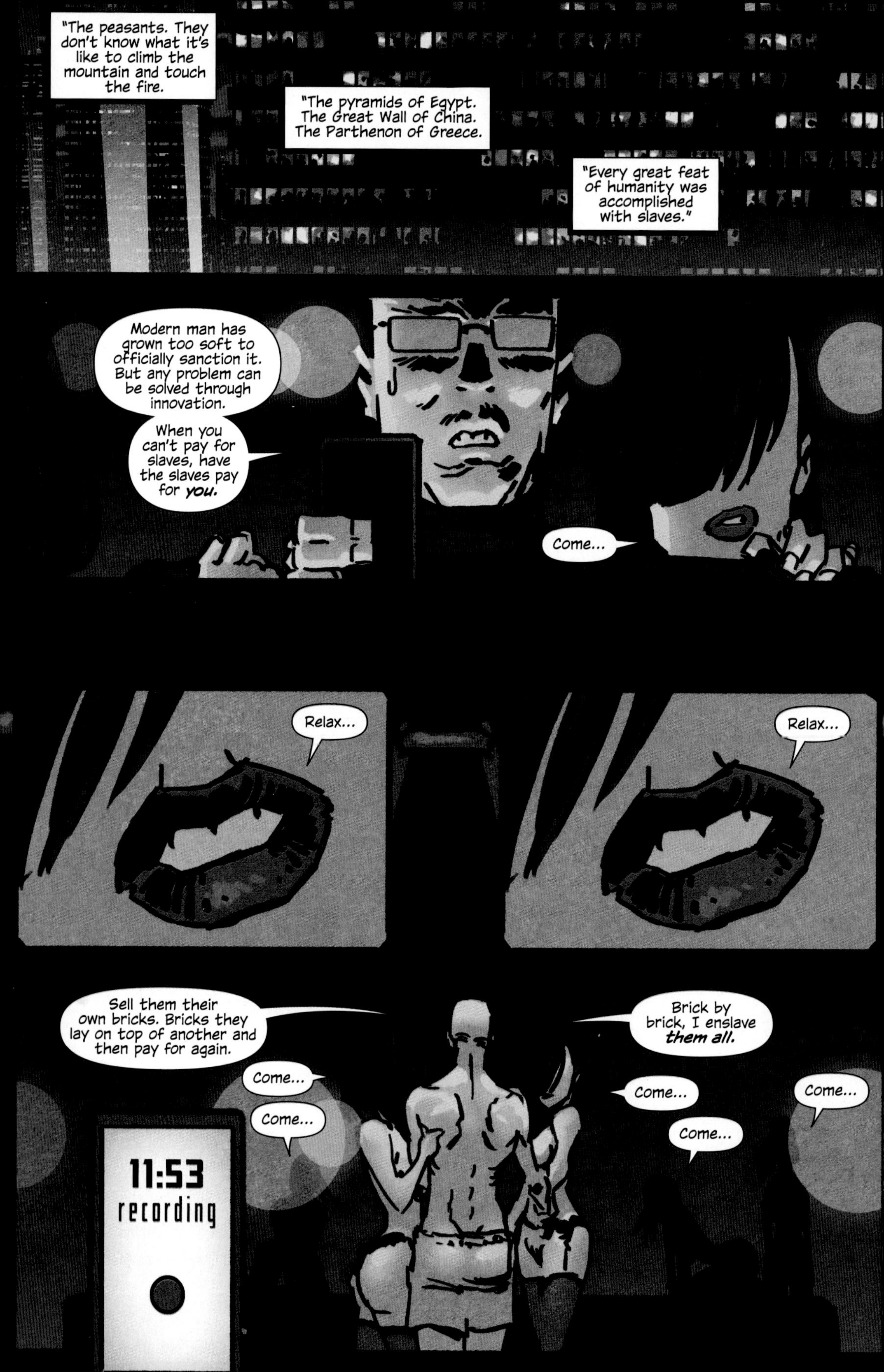
"The peasants. They don't know what it's like to climb the mountain and touch the fire.
"The pyramids of Egypt. The Great Wall of China. The Parthenon of Greece.
"Every great feat of humanity was accomplished with slaves."
Modern man has grown too soft to officially sanction it. But any problem can be solved through innovation.
When you can't pay for slaves, have the slaves pay for *you.*
Come...
Relax...
Relax...
Sell them their own bricks. Bricks they lay on top of another and then pay for again.
Brick by brick, I enslave *them all.*
Come...
Come...
Come...
Come...
Come...
11:53
recording

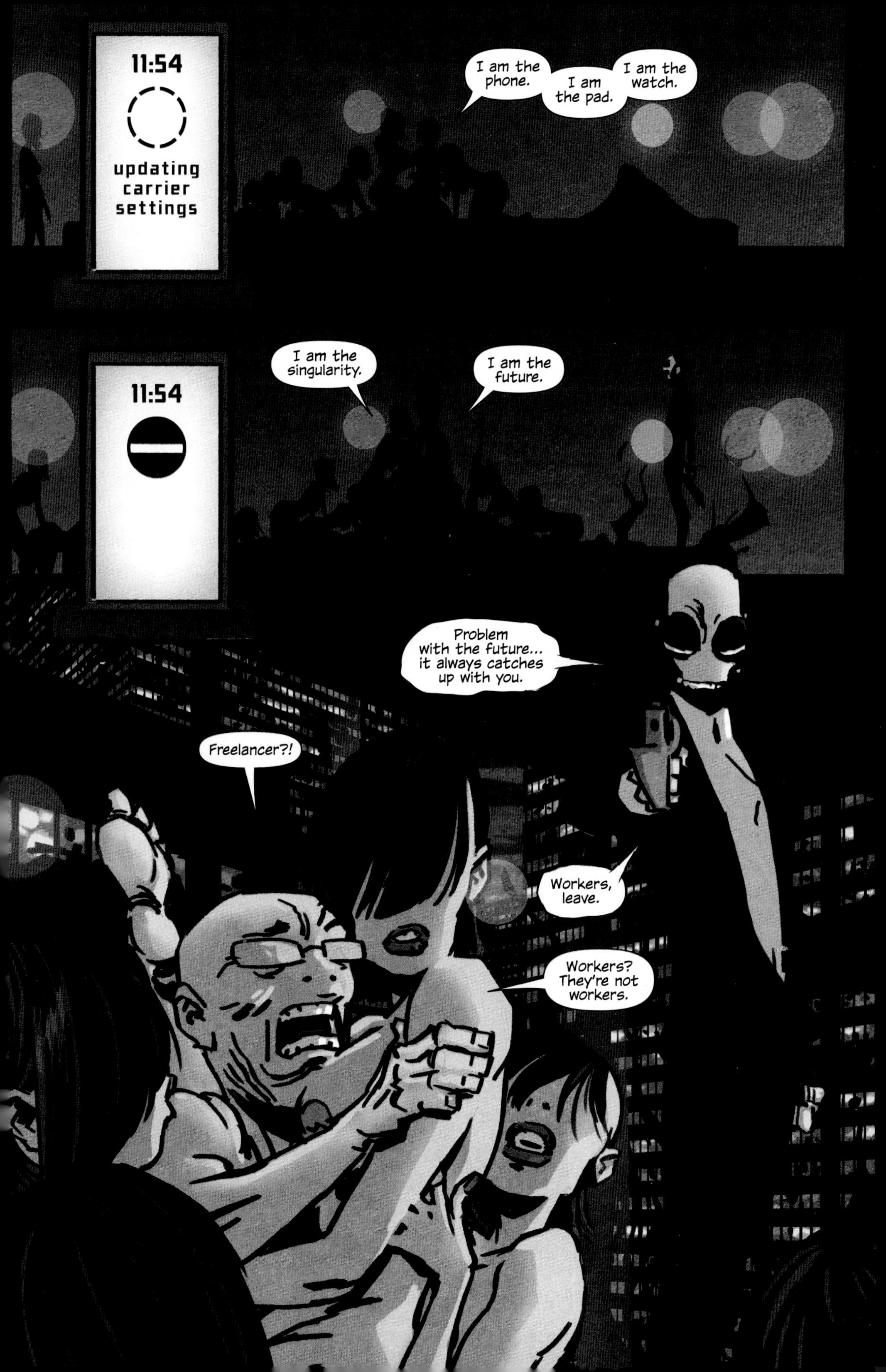
11:54
updating carrier settings
I am the phone.
I am the pad.
I am the watch.
11:54
I am the singularity.
I am the future.
Problem with the future... it always catches up with you.
Freelancer?!
Workers, leave.
Workers? They're not workers.

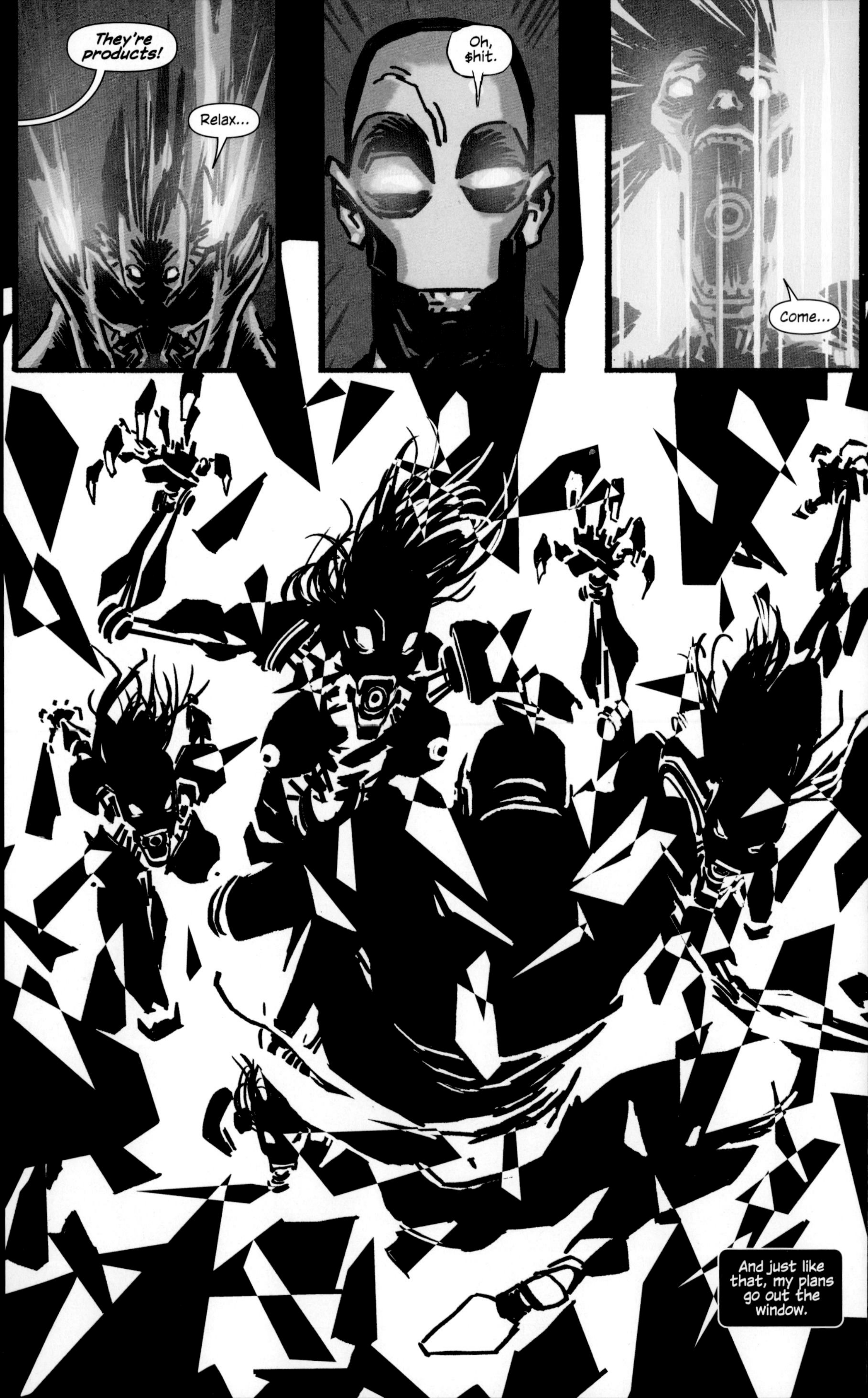
They're products!
Relax...
Oh, $hit.
Come...
And just like that, my plans go out the window.

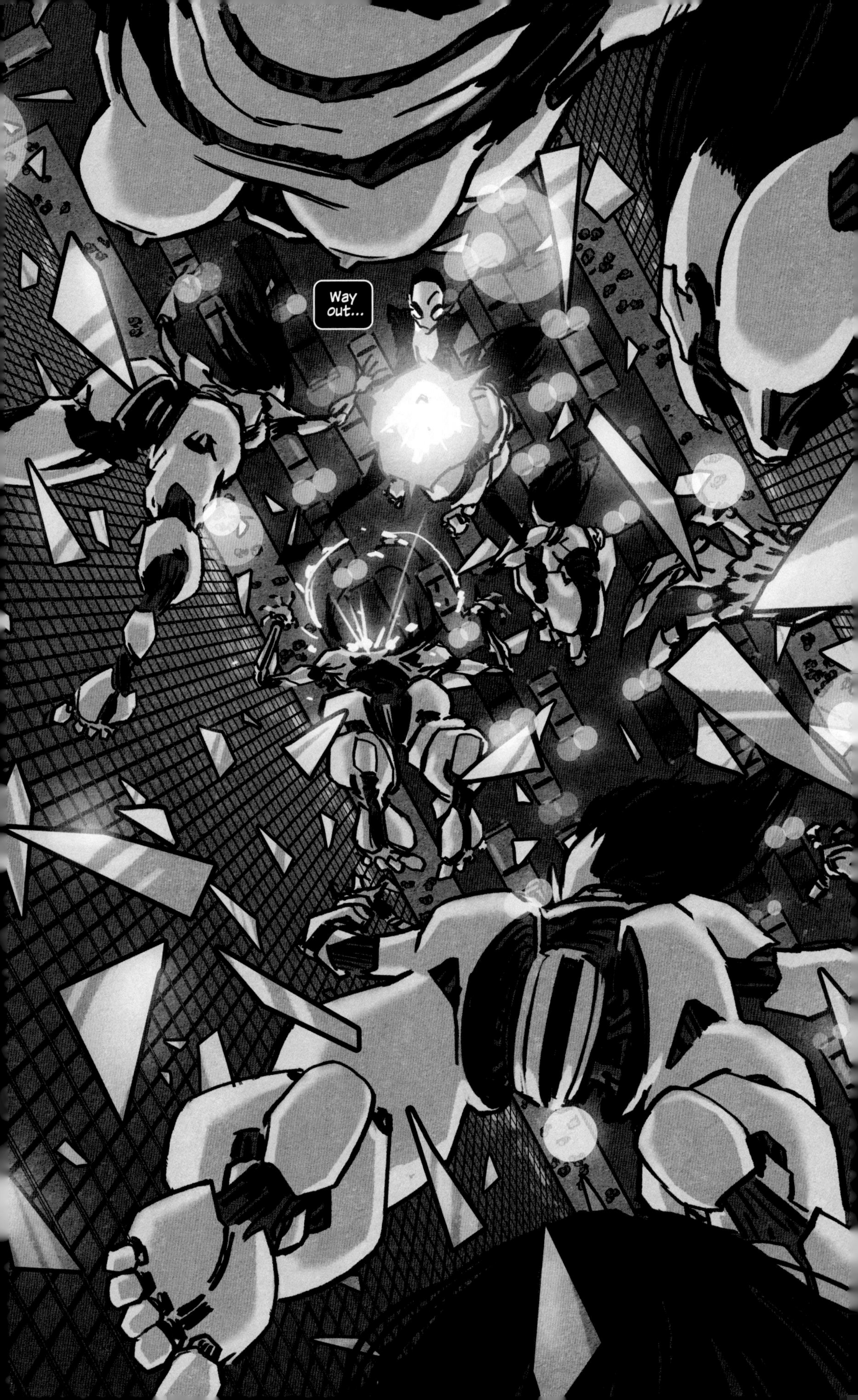
Way out...

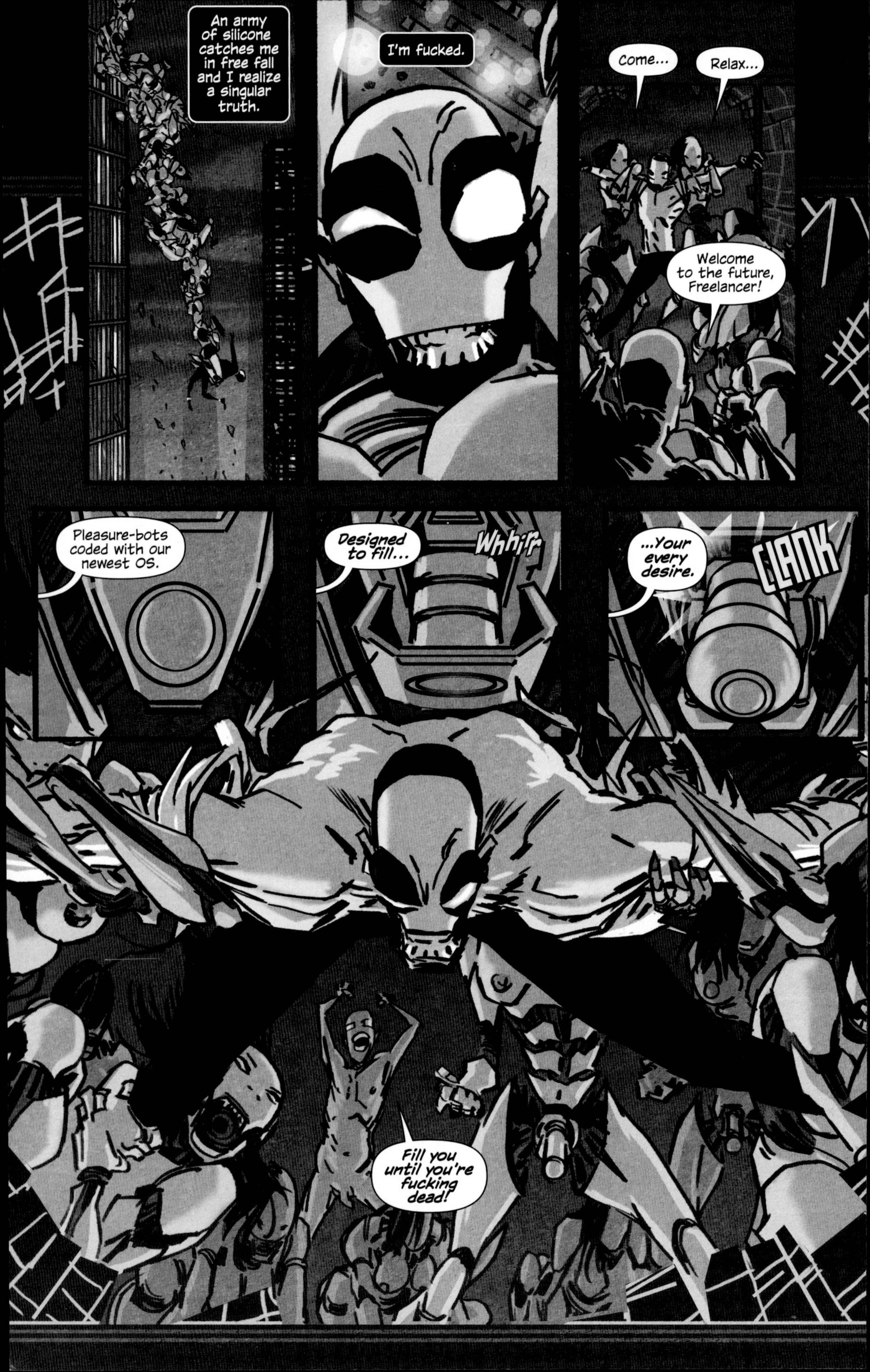

An army of silicone catches me in free fall and I realize a singular truth.
I'm fucked.
Come...
Relax...
Welcome to the future, Freelancer!
Pleasure-bots coded with our newest OS.
Designed to fill...
Whhirr
...Your every desire.
CLANK
Fill you until you're fucking dead!

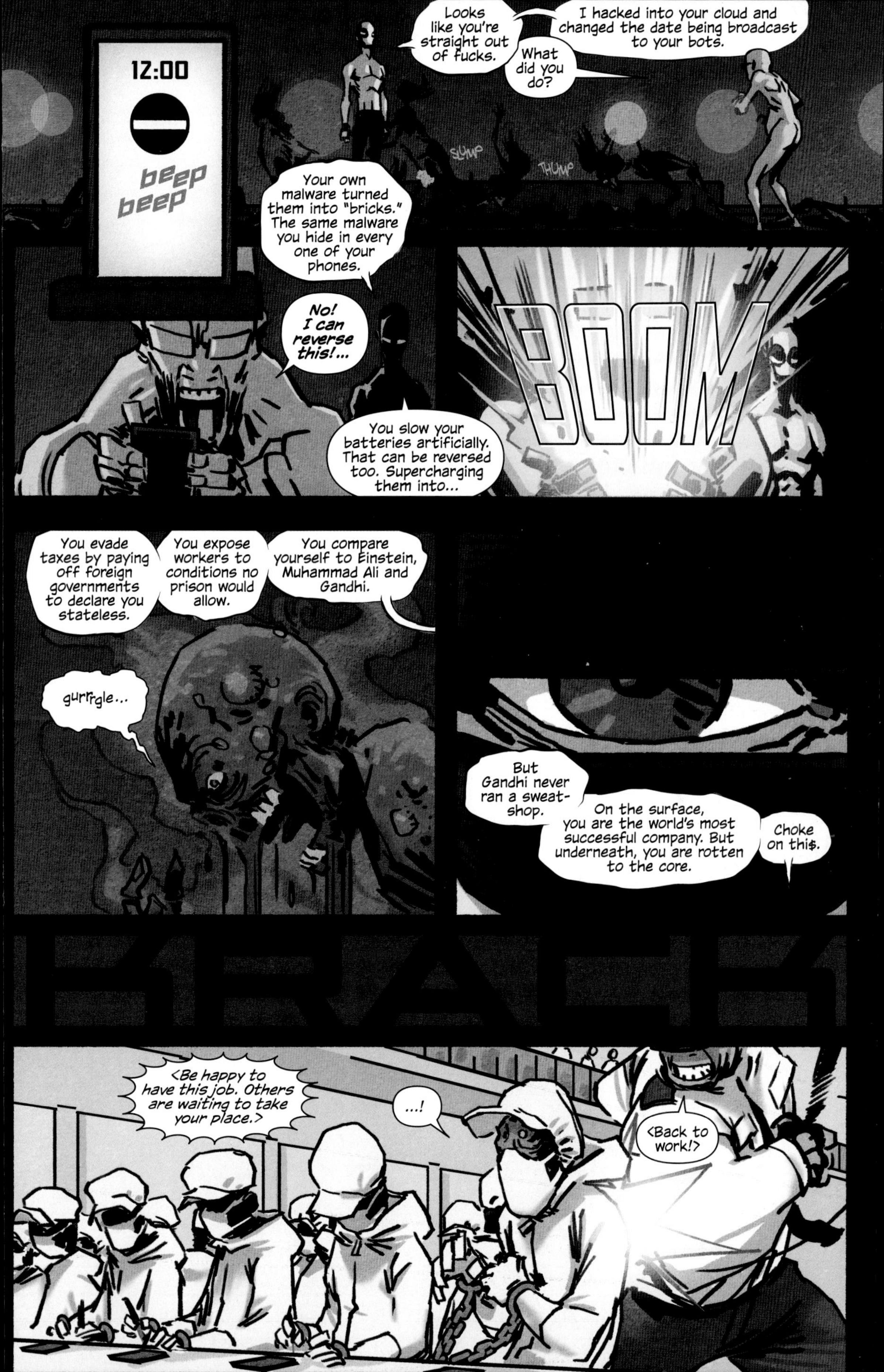

12:00
beep beep
Looks like you're straight out of fucks.
What did you do?
I hacked into your cloud and changed the date being broadcast to your bots.
SLUMP
THUMP
Your own malware turned them into "bricks." The same malware you hide in every one of your phones.
No! I can reverse this!...
You slow your batteries artificially. That can be reversed too. Supercharging them into...
BOOM
You evade taxes by paying off foreign governments to declare you stateless.
You expose workers to conditions no prison would allow.
You compare yourself to Einstein, Muhammad Ali and Gandhi.
gurrrgle...
But Gandhi never ran a sweat-shop.
On the surface, you are the world's most successful company. But underneath, you are rotten to the core.
Choke on thi$.
<Be happy to have this job. Others are waiting to take your place.>
...!
<Back to work!>

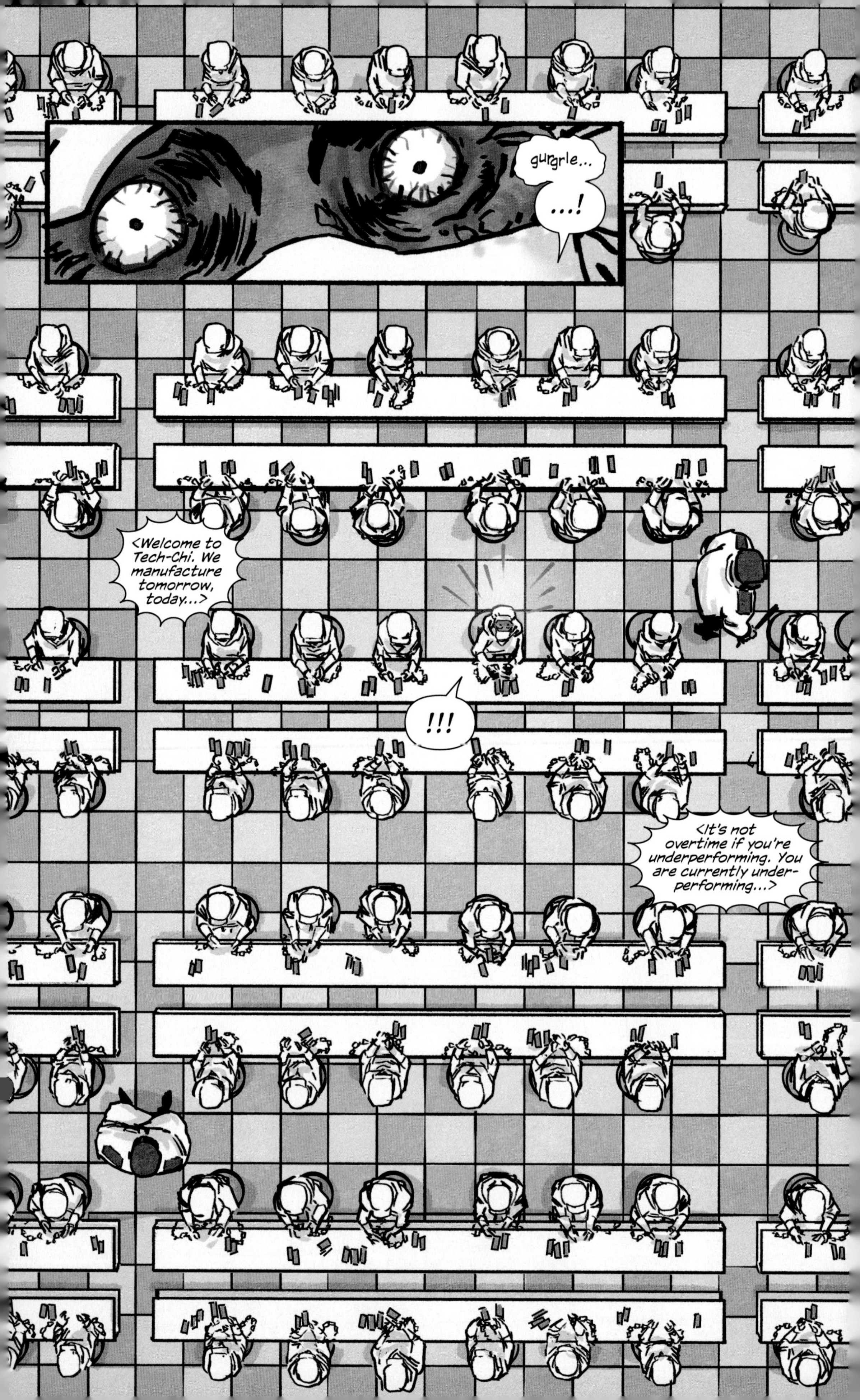
gurgrle...
...!
<Welcome to Tech-Chi. We manufacture tomorrow, today...>
!!!
<It's not overtime if you're underperforming. You are currently under-performing...>

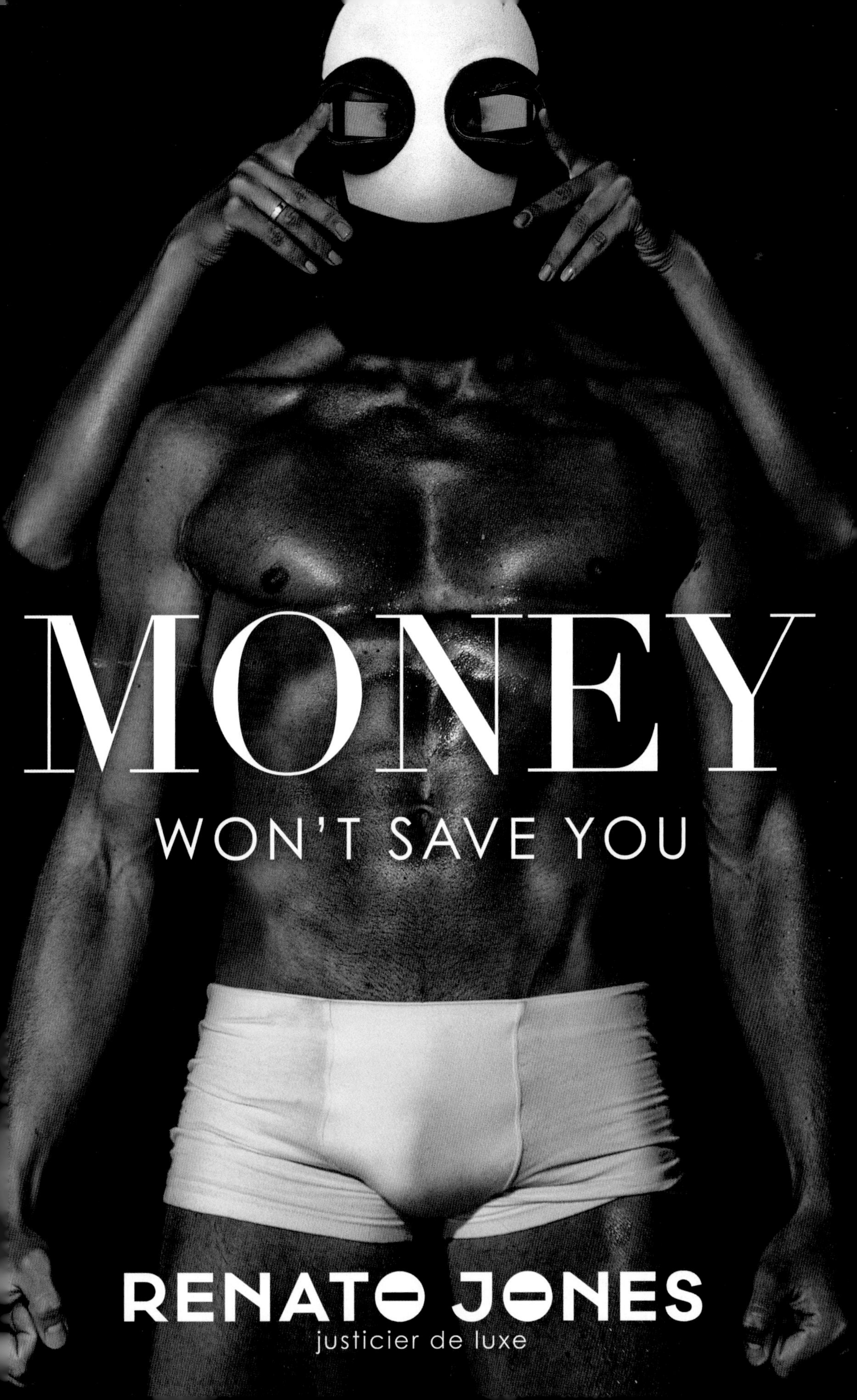
MONEY
WON'T SAVE YOU
RENATO JONES
justicier de luxe

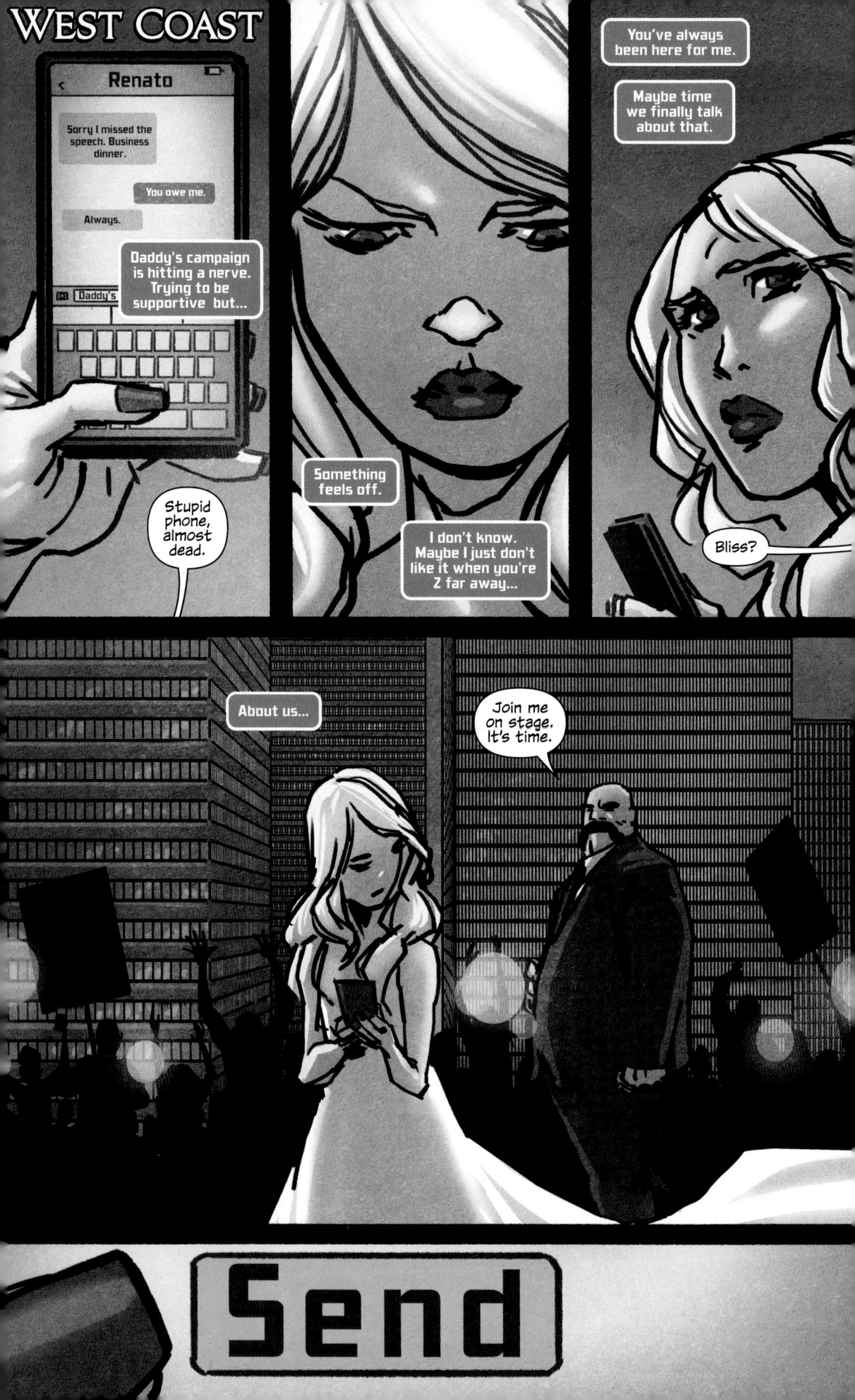

West Coast
Renato
Sorry I missed the speech. Business dinner.
You owe me.
Always.
Daddy's
Daddy's campaign is hitting a nerve. Trying to be supportive but...
Stupid phone, almost dead.
Something feels off.
I don't know. Maybe I just don't like it when you're 2 far away...
You've always been here for me.
Maybe time we finally talk about that.
Bliss?
About us...
Join me on stage. It's time.
Send

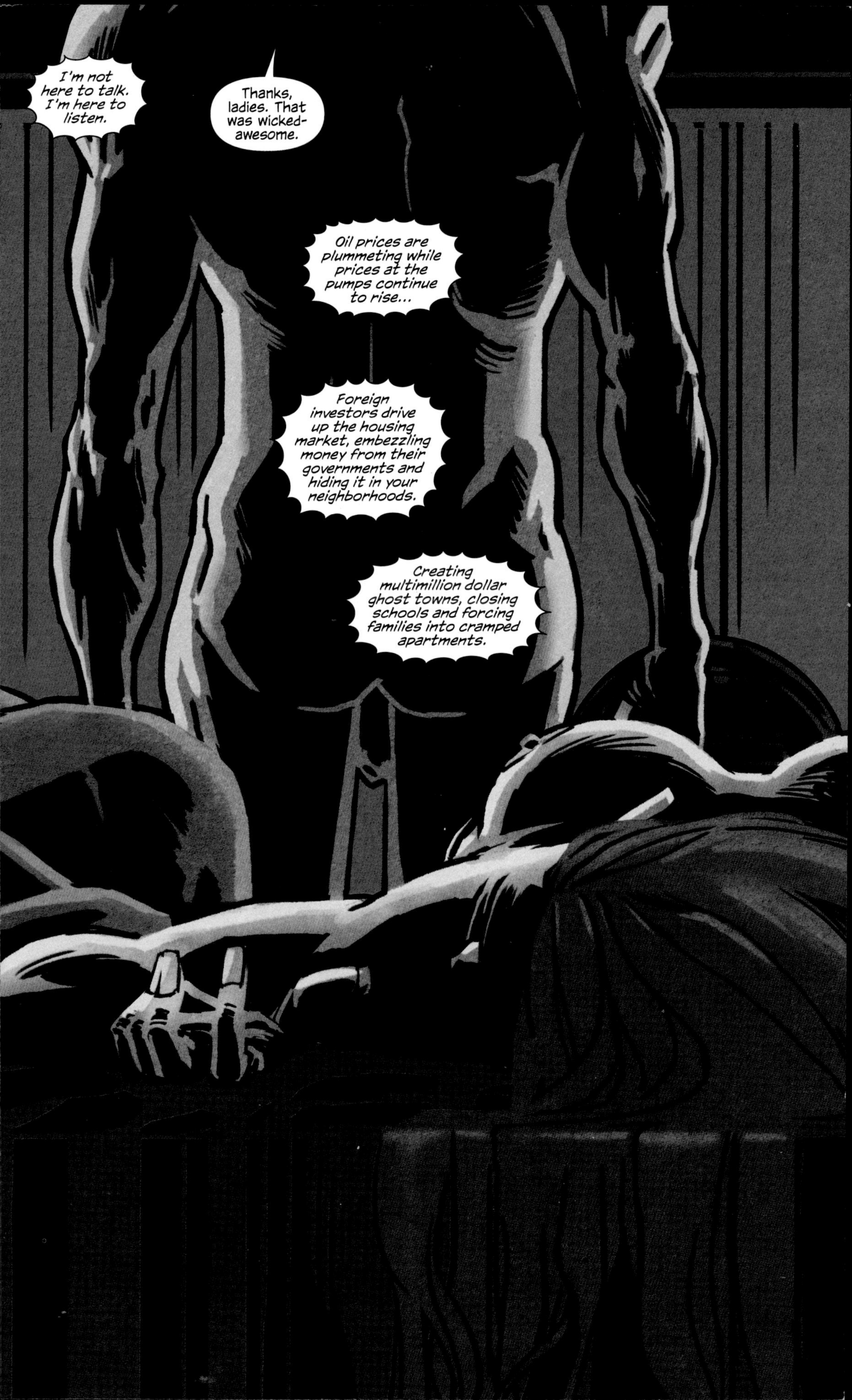
I'm not here to talk. I'm here to listen.
Thanks, ladies. That was wicked-awesome.
Oil prices are plummeting while prices at the pumps continue to rise...
Foreign investors drive up the housing market, embezzling money from their governments and hiding it in your neighborhoods.
Creating multimillion dollar ghost towns, closing schools and forcing families into cramped apartments.

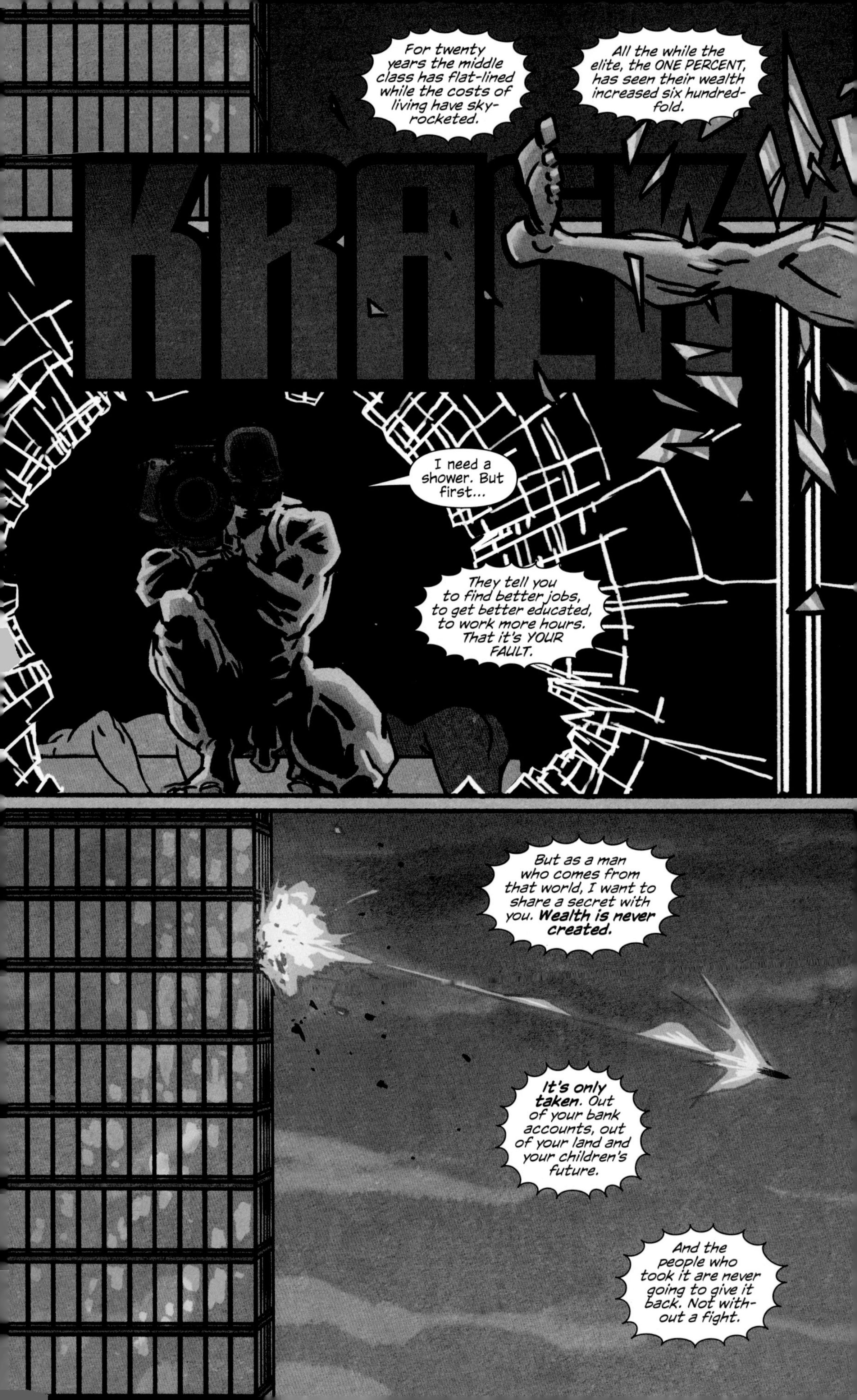
For twenty years the middle class has flat-lined while the costs of living have sky-rocketed.
All the while the elite, the ONE PERCENT, has seen their wealth increased six hundred-fold.
I need a shower. But first...
They tell you to find better jobs, to get better educated, to work more hours. That it's YOUR FAULT.
But as a man who comes from that world, I want to share a secret with you. **Wealth is never created.**
It's only taken. Out of your bank accounts, out of your land and your children's future.
And the people who took it are never going to give it back. Not without a fight.

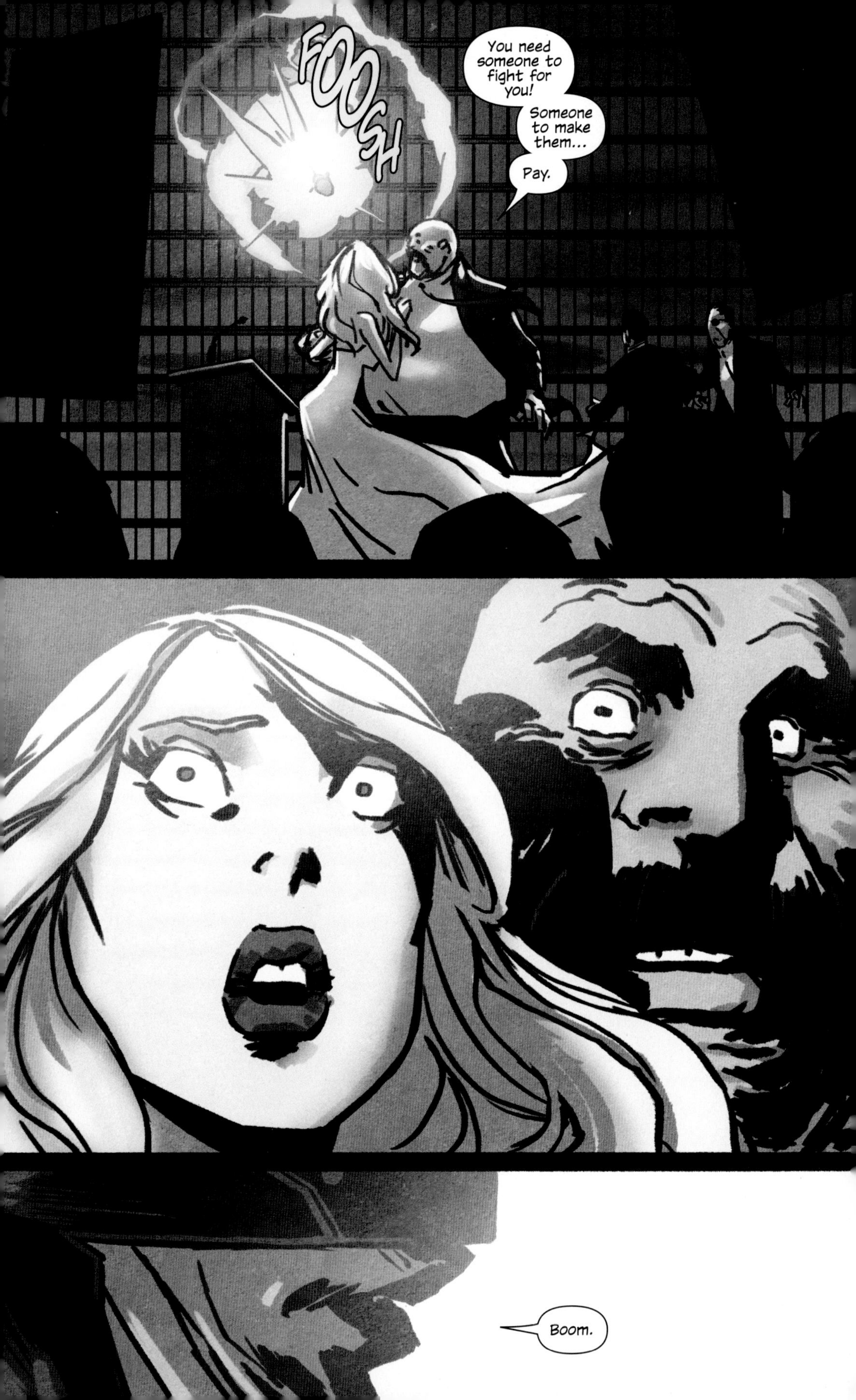
FOOSH
You need someone to fight for you!
Someone to make them...
Pay.
Boom.

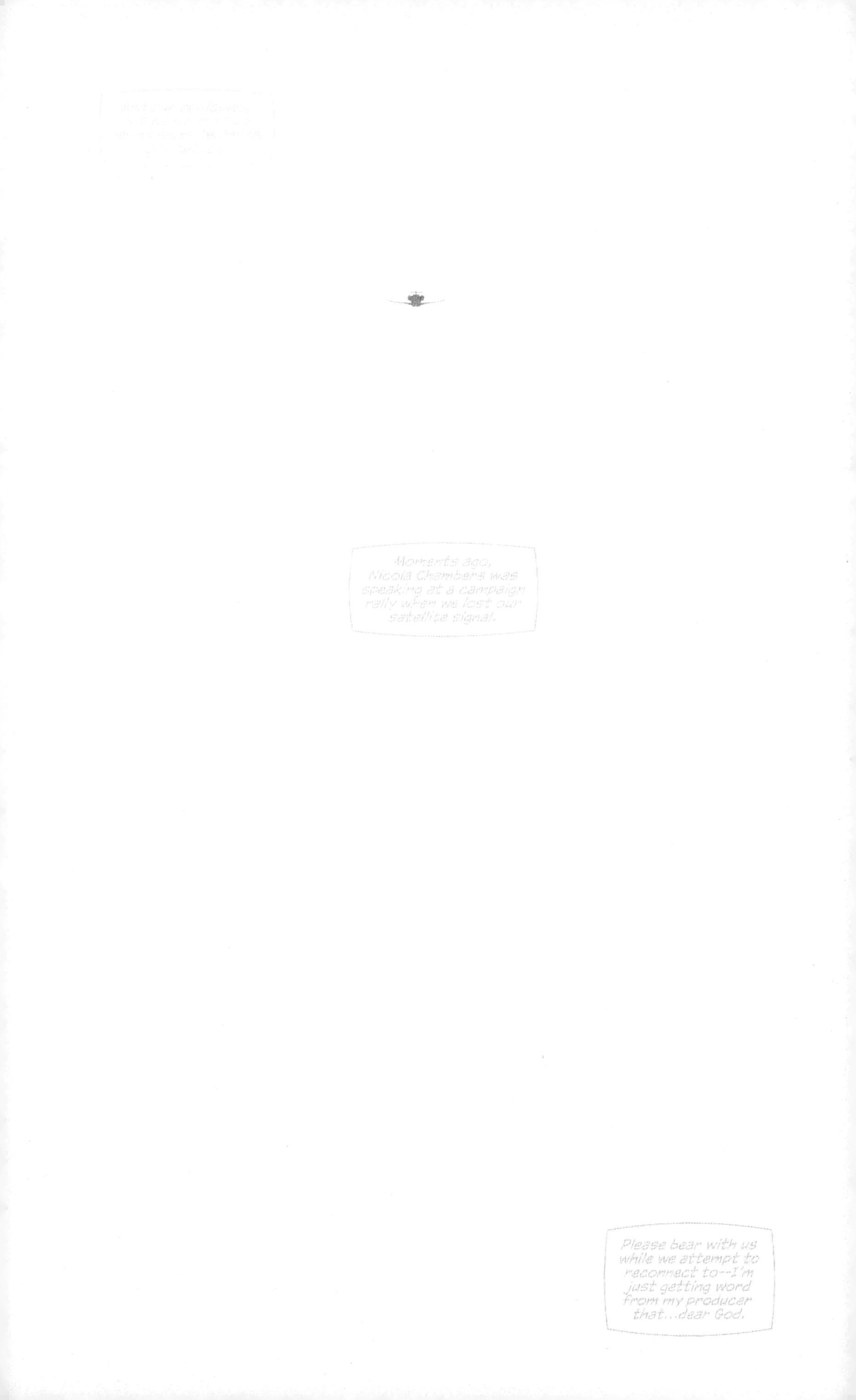
Moments ago, Nicola Chambers was speaking at a campaign rally when we lost our satellite signal.
Please bear with us while we attempt to reconnect to--I'm just getting word from my producer that...dear God.

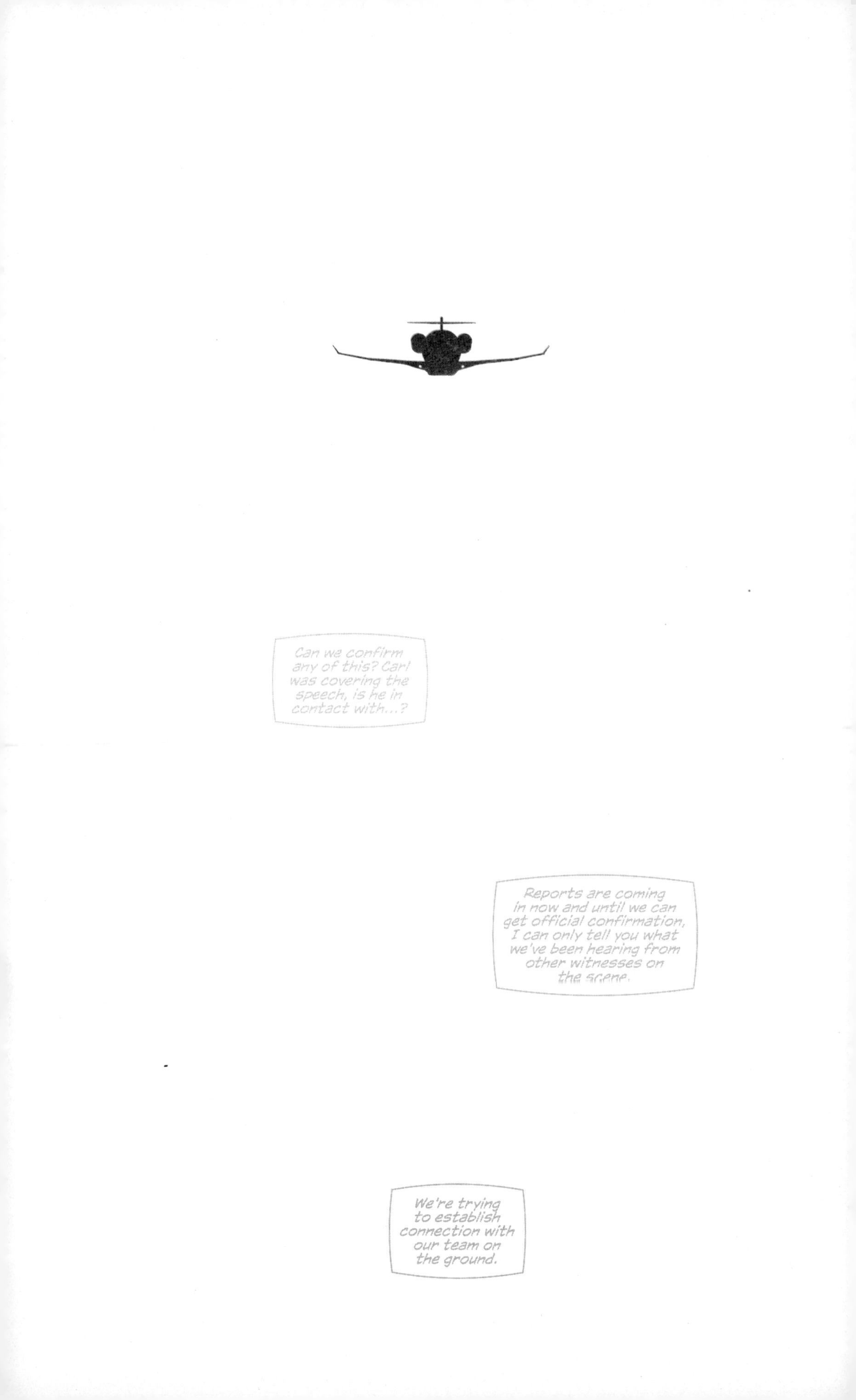
Can we confirm any of this? Carl was covering the speech, is he in contact with...?
Reports are coming in now and until we can get official confirmation, I can only tell you what we've been hearing from other witnesses on the scene.
We're trying to establish connection with our team on the ground.

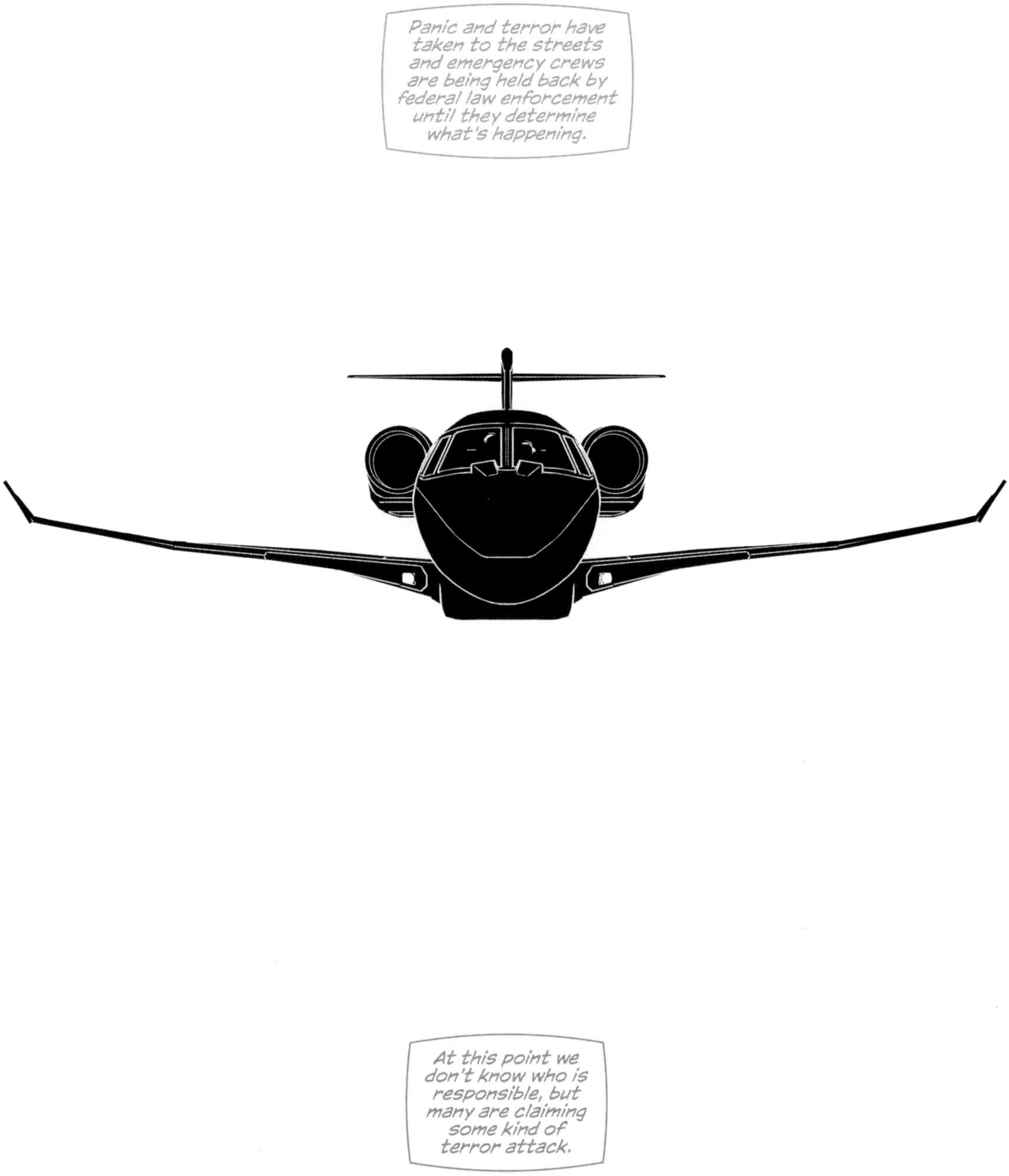
Panic and terror have taken to the streets and emergency crews are being held back by federal law enforcement until they determine what's happening.
At this point we don't know who is responsible, but many are claiming some kind of terror attack.

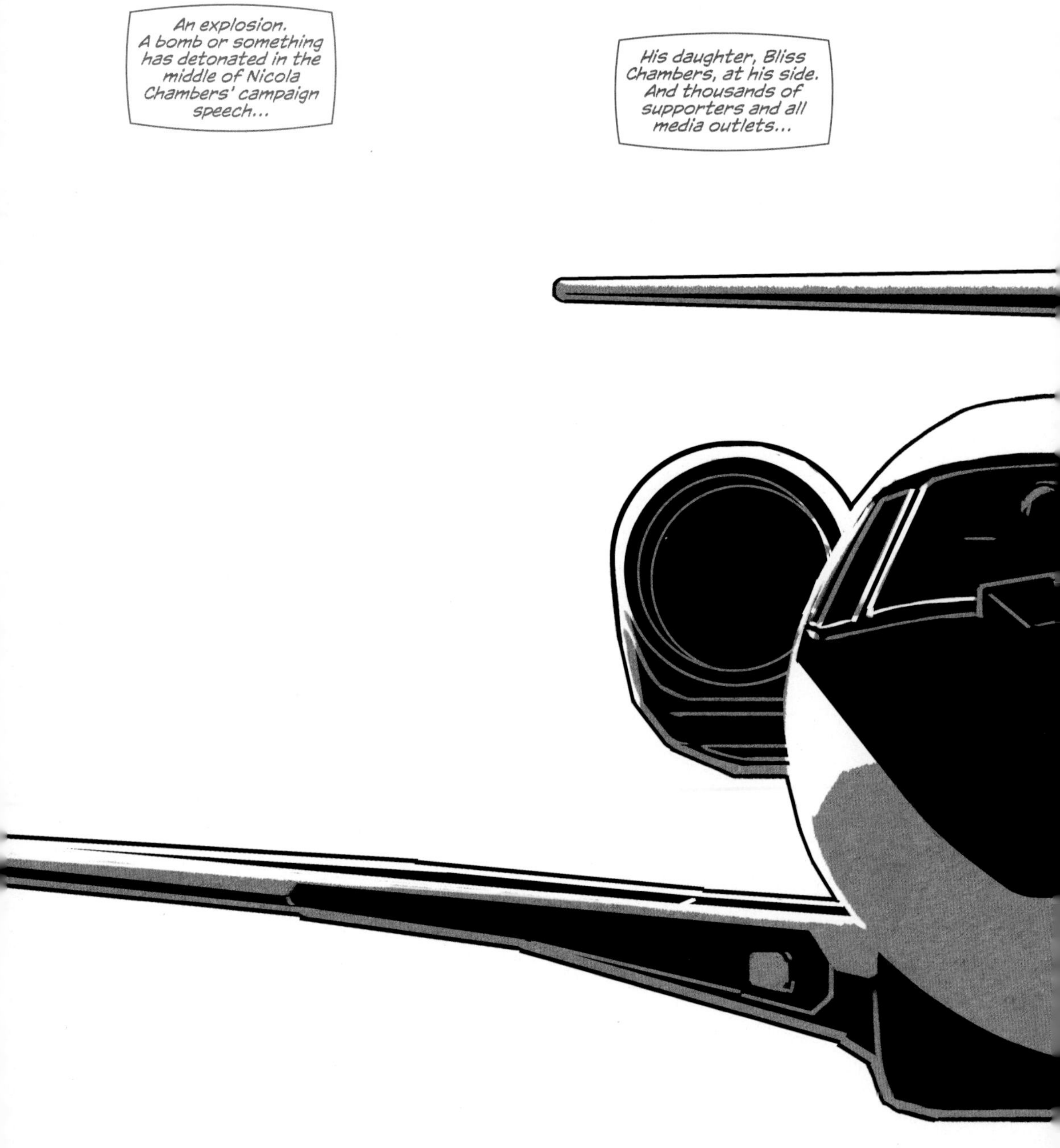
An explosion. A bomb or something has detonated in the middle of Nicola Chambers' campaign speech...
His daughter, Bliss Chambers, at his side. And thousands of supporters and all media outlets...

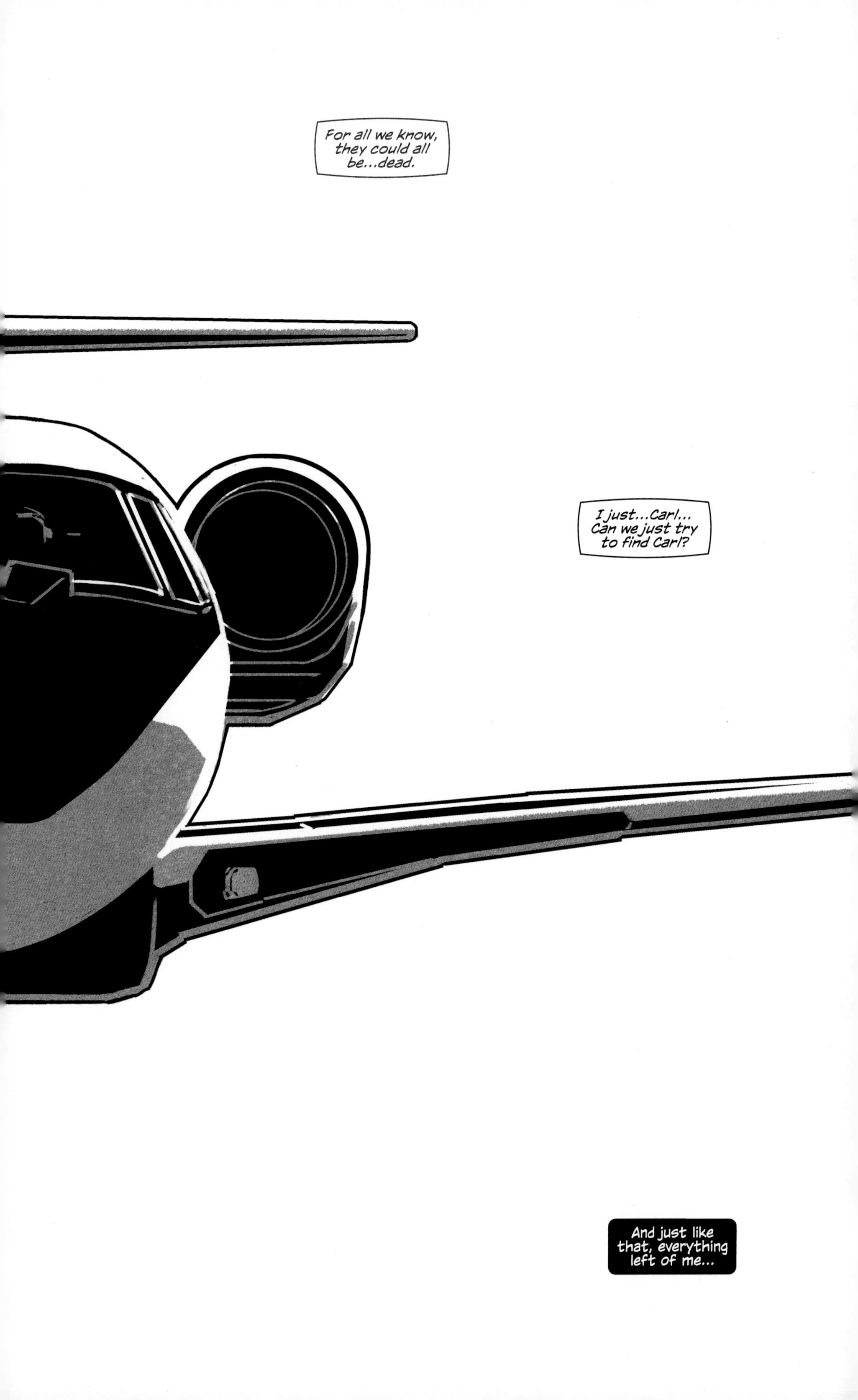
For all we know, they could all be...dead.
I just...Carl... Can we just try to find Carl?
And just like that, everything left of me...

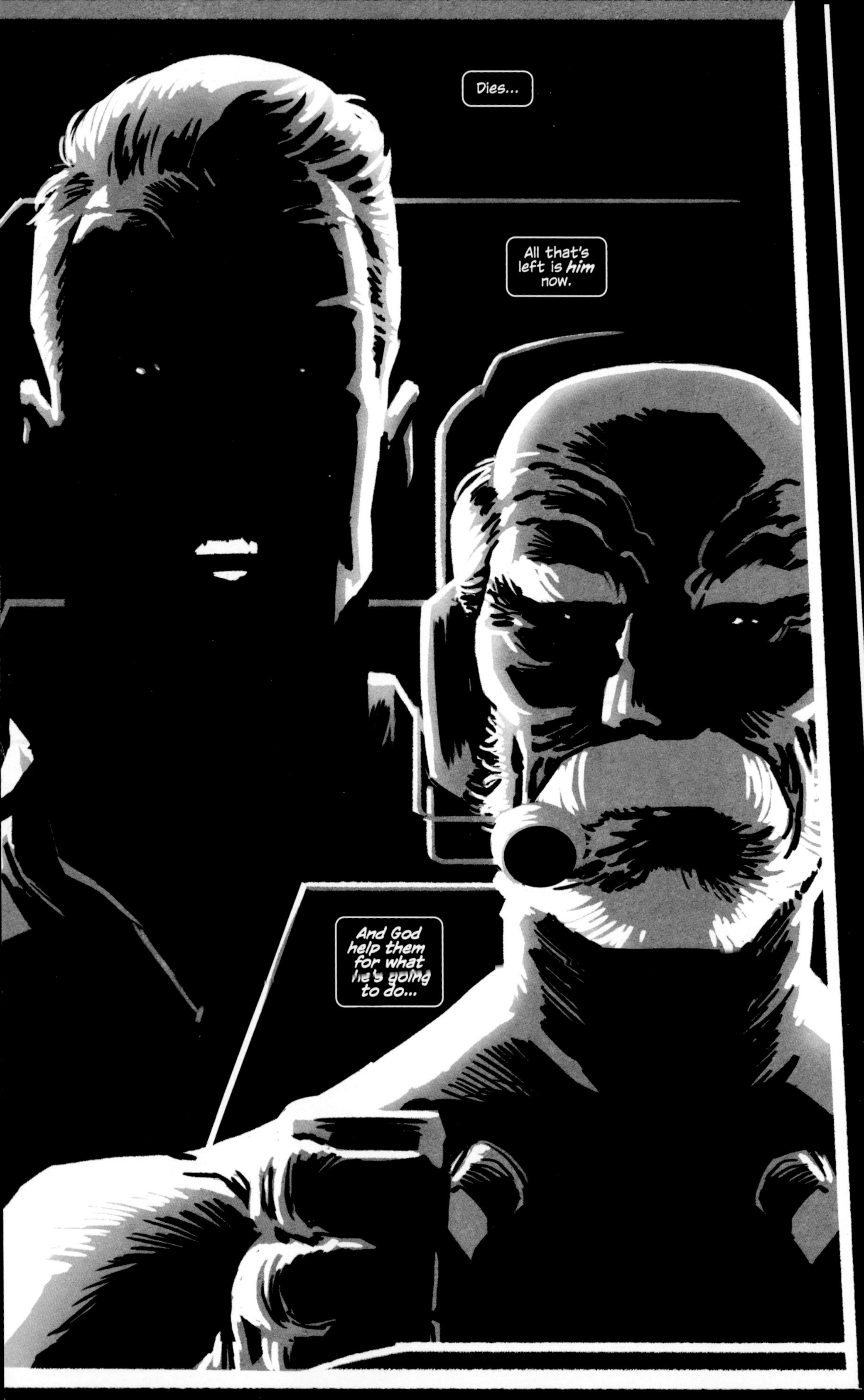
Dies...
All that's left is *him* now.
And God help them for what he's going to do...

"Choke
on
this."

SKETCHBOOK

A peak at some of the ideation that takes place when I create a new story. I generate both and text and very quick sketches to try out ideas on the fly. In this case I filled over 60 pages of story and art before I drew a single panel of Renato Jones.

The original title I came up with was THE MACHINE...

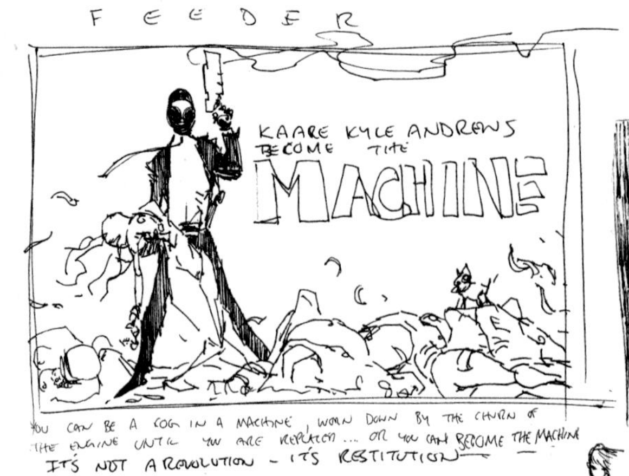

FEEDER
KAARE KYLE ANDREWS
BECOME THE
MACHINE
YOU CAN BE A COG IN A MACHINE, WORN DOWN BY THE CHURN OF THE ENGINE UNTIL YOU ARE REPLACED ... OR YOU CAN BECOME THE MACHINE
IT'S NOT A REVOLUTION - IT'S RESTITUTION

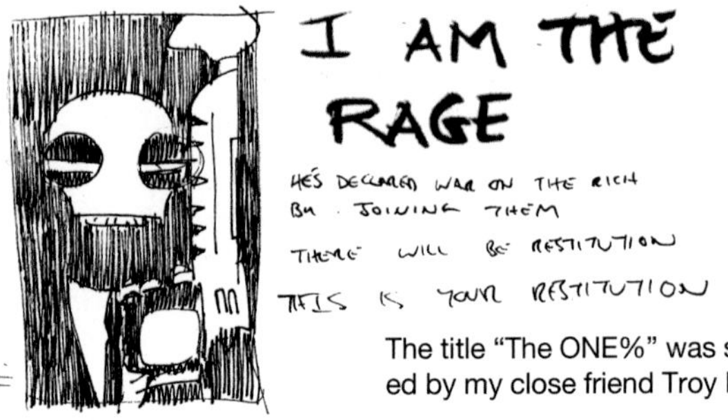

I AM THE RAGE
HE'S DECLARED WAR ON THE RICH BY JOINING THEM
THERE WILL BE RESTITUTION
THIS IS YOUR RESTITUTION

The title "The ONE%" was suggested by my close friend Troy Nixey.

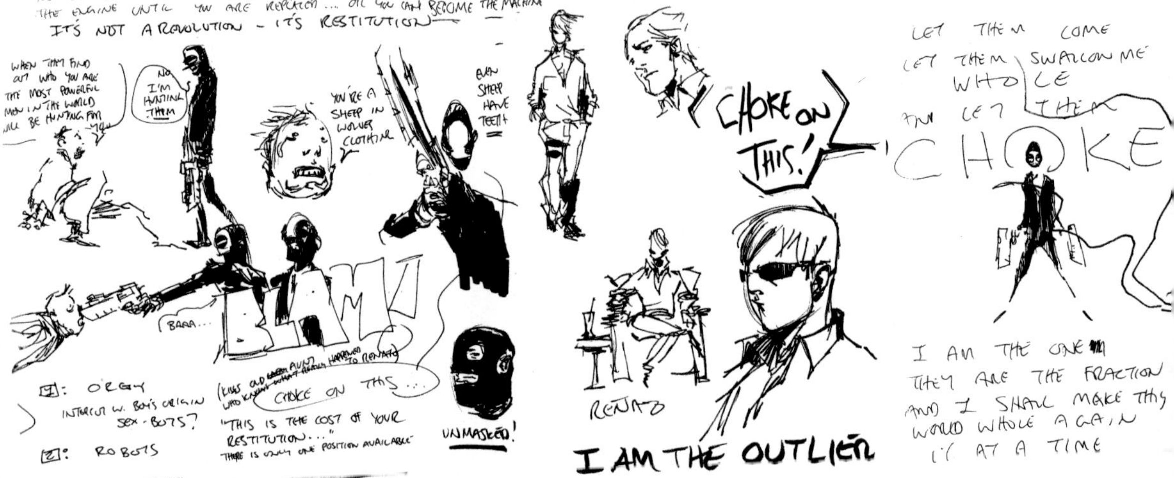

WHEN THEY FIND OUT WHO YOU ARE THE MOST POWERFUL MEN IN THE WORLD WILL BE HUNTING FOR YOU
NO I'M HUNTING THEM
YOU'RE A SHEEP IN WOLVES CLOTHING
EVEN SHEEP HAVE TEETH
CHOKE ON THIS!
LET THEM COME
LET THEM SWALLOW ME WHOLE
AND LET THEM CHOKE
BRAA...
CHOKE ON THIS...
"THIS IS THE COST OF YOUR RESTITUTION..."
THERE IS ONLY ONE POSITION AVAILABLE
1: ORGY
INTERCUT W. BOY'S ORIGIN
SEX-BOTS?
2: ROBOTS
UNMASKED!
RENATO
I AM THE OUTLIER
I AM THE ONE
THEY ARE THE FRACTION
AND I SHALL MAKE THIS WORLD WHOLE AGAIN
1% AT A TIME

Some character names I tried out included, "The Outlier" and "Feeder" before landing on "The Freelancer".

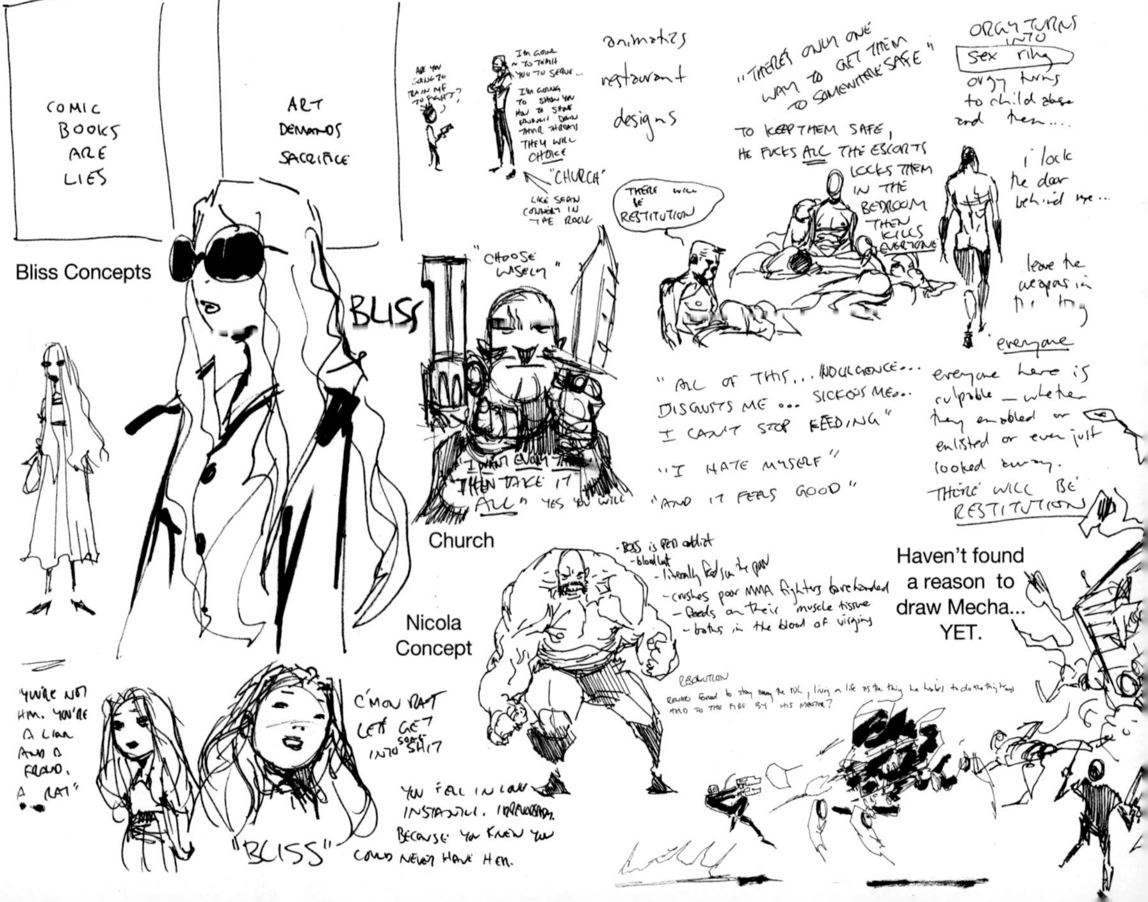

COMIC BOOKS ARE LIES
ART DEMANDS SACRIFICE
animatics
restaurant
designs
"THERE'S ONLY ONE WAY TO GET THEM TO SOMEWHERE SAFE"
TO KEEP THEM SAFE, HE FUCKS ALL THE ESCORTS
LOCKS THEM IN THE BEDROOM THEN KILLS EVERYONE
ORGY TURNS INTO sex ring
orgy turns to child abuse and then...
i lock the door behind me...
leave the weapons in the tray
everyone
THERE WILL BE RESTITUTION
"CHURCH"
BLISS
"CHOOSE WISELY"
"ALL OF THIS... INDULGENCE... DISGUSTS ME ... SICKENS ME... I CAN'T STOP FEEDING"
"I HATE MYSELF"
"AND IT FEELS GOOD"
everyone here is culpable — whether they enabled or enlisted or even just looked away.
THERE WILL BE RESTITUTION
YOU'RE NOT HIM. YOU'RE A LIAR AND A FRAUD. A RAT
C'MON RAT LET'S GET INTO SOME SHIT
YOU FELL IN LOVE INSTANTLY. IRREVOCABLY. BECAUSE YOU KNEW YOU COULD NEVER HAVE HER.
"BLISS"

Bliss Concepts

Church

Nicola Concept

Haven't found a reason to draw Mecha... YET.

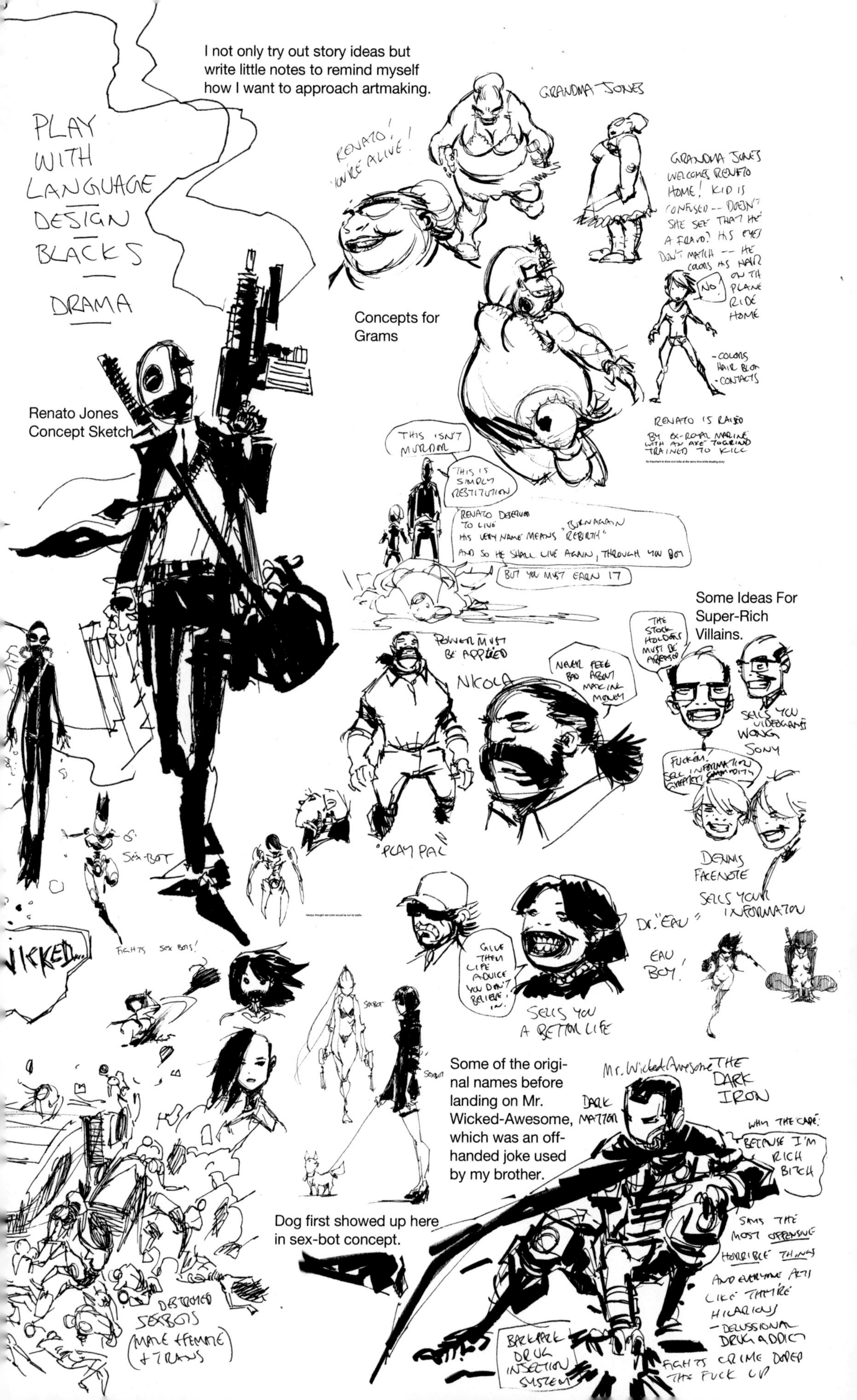
PLAY
WITH
LANGUAGE
DESIGN
BLACKS
DRAMA
GRANDMA JONES
RENATO! YOU'RE ALIVE!
GRANDMA JONES WELCOMES RENATO HOME! KID IS CONFUSED -- DOESN'T SHE SEE THAT HE'S A FRAUD? HIS EYES DON'T MATCH -- HE COLORS HIS HAIR ON THE PLANE RIDE HOME
NO
- COLORS HAIR BLOND
- CONTACTS
RENATO IS RAISED BY EX-ROYAL MARINE WITH AN AXE TO GRIND TRAINED TO KILL
THIS ISN'T MURDER
THIS IS SIMPLY RESTITUTION
RENATO DESERVED TO LIVE
HIS VERY NAME MEANS "BORN AGAIN" "REBIRTH"
AND SO HE SHALL LIVE AGAIN, THROUGH YOU BOY
BUT YOU MUST EARN IT
POWER MUST BE APPLIED
NICOLA
NEVER FEEL BAD ABOUT MAKING MONEY
THE STOCK HOLDERS MUST BE APPEASED
SELLS YOU VIDEOGAMES
WONG
SONY
DENNIS FACENOTE
SELLS YOUR INFORMATION
"PLAY PAL"
SEX-BOT
FIGHTS SEX BOTS!
DR. "EAU"
EAU BOY!
GIVE THEM LIFE ADVICE YOU DON'T BELIEVE IN.
SELLS YOU A BETTER LIFE
Sexbot
Mr. Wicked-Awesome
THE DARK IRON
DARK MATTER
WHY THE CAPE?
BECAUSE I'M RICH BITCH
SAYS THE MOST OFFENSIVE HORRIBLE THINGS
AND EVERYONE ACTS LIKE THEY'RE HILARIOUS
- DELUSSIONAL DRUG ADDICT
FIGHTS CRIME DOPED THE FUCK UP
BACKPACK DRUG INJECTION SYSTEM
DESTROYED SEXBOTS (MALE + FEMALE + TRANS)

I not only try out story ideas but write little notes to remind myself how I want to approach artmaking.

Concepts for Grams

Renato Jones Concept Sketch

So important to draw and write at the same time while studying story.

Some Ideas For Super-Rich Villains.

Always thought sex-bots would be fun to battle.

Some of the original names before landing on Mr. Wicked-Awesome, which was an off-handed joke used by my brother.

Dog first showed up here in sex-bot concept.

LAYOUTS

I lay out entire issues on a single photoshop file. Unlike a mainstream superhero book, I'm not bound to 20 interior pages, plus cover. Instead, I can make each issue as long as it needs. You may think this would make the creation of these issues easier but the reverse is true. Art LIKES restrictions.

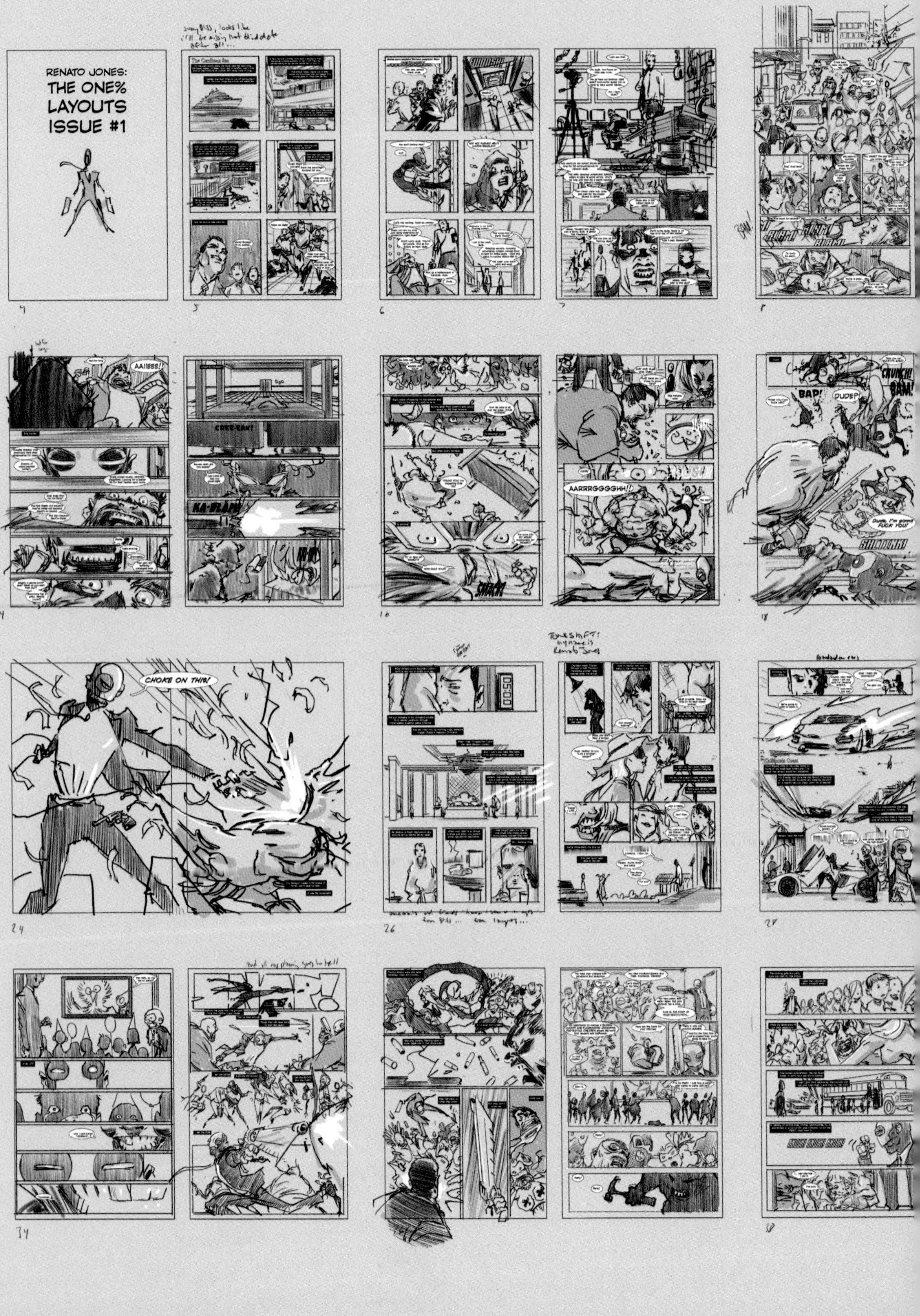

RENATO JONES:
THE ONE%
LAYOUTS
ISSUE #1
AAIIEEE!!
CREE-EAK!
KA-BLAM!
SMACK!
AARRRGGGGHH!!
BAP!
DUDE?!
CRUNCH!
CHOKE ON THIS!

Rules that you can butt up against and break. Chains you can pull free from… But real freedom is harder. And at point, there was a version of the first issue that was 42 story pages long. In a weird way, it seemed like too complete an experience. But it was also too packed. I didn't feel like I was daring enough with my storytelling, either. So I split up this first story into two issues, and lo and behold, all my questions found answers.

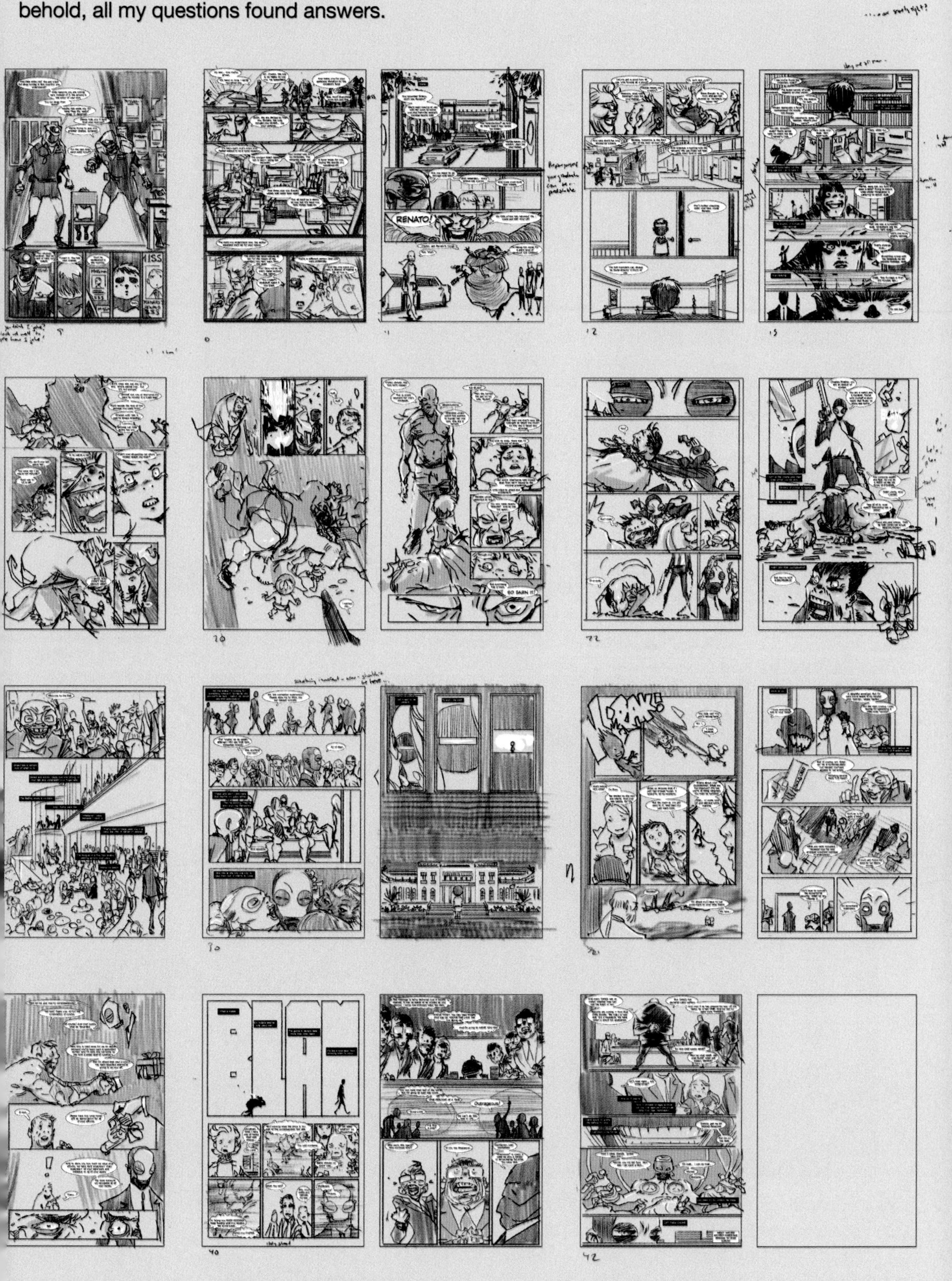
RENATO!

TITLE CARDS

Originally, I thought it would be fun to create double-page animation-style "title cards" and I think I had a good one to start with. But in action, it didn't seem progressive enough. It looked too far back instead of pushing forward and so I let the idea fall away… for now.

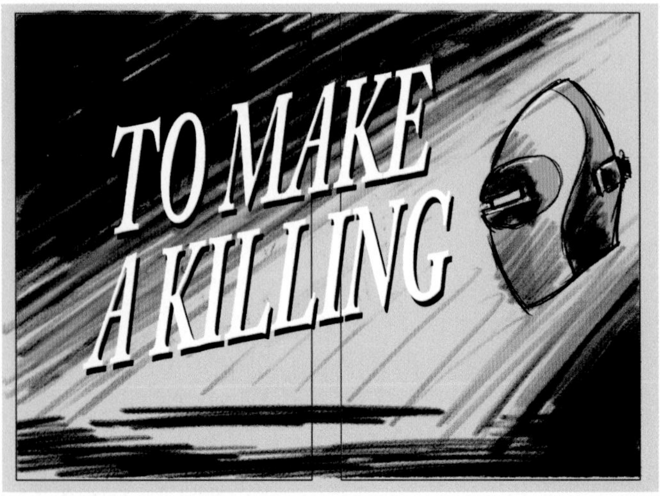
TO MAKE
A KILLING

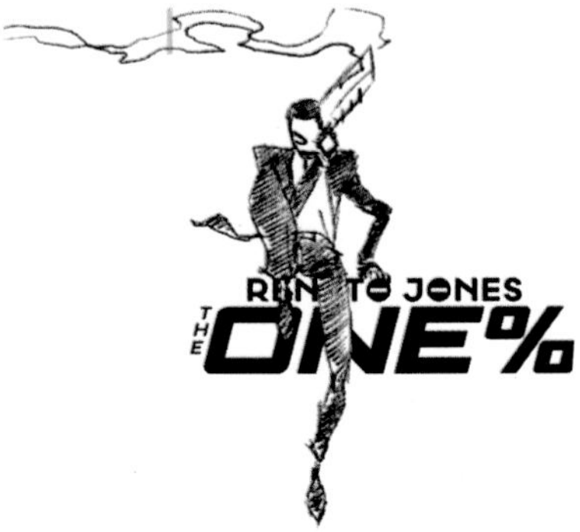
THE ONE%

COVERS

With every cover I design I try to incorporate a certain level of sexuality, fashion, noir, violence and satire. Visually, the cover has to work in two ways, the full image and the front half that is exposed on the comic shelves.

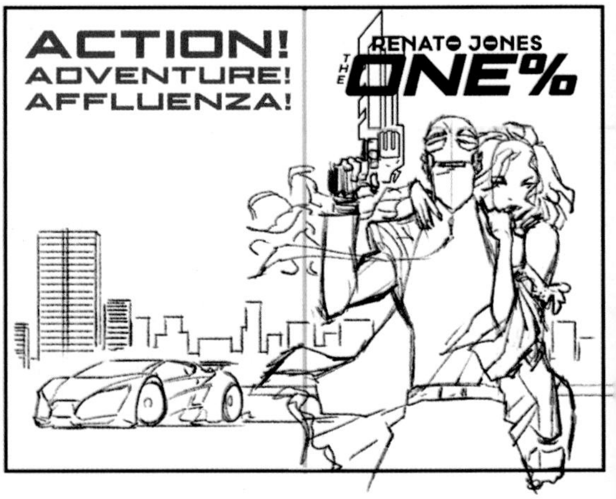
ACTION!
ADVENTURE!
AFFLUENZA!
RENATO JONES
THE ONE%

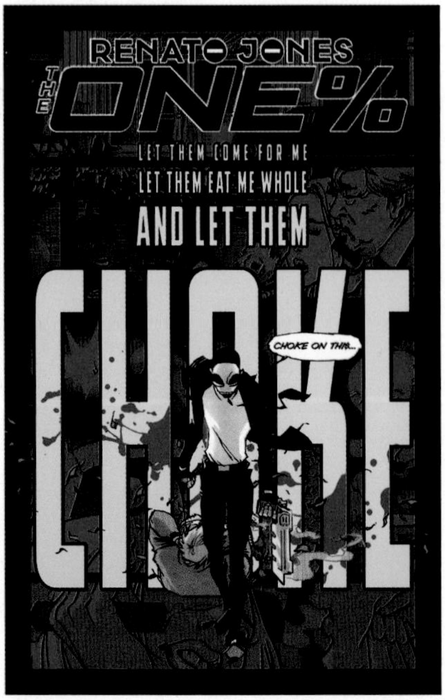
RENATO JONES
THE ONE%
LET THEM COME FOR ME
LET THEM EAT ME WHOLE
AND LET THEM
CHOKE
CHOKE ON THIS...

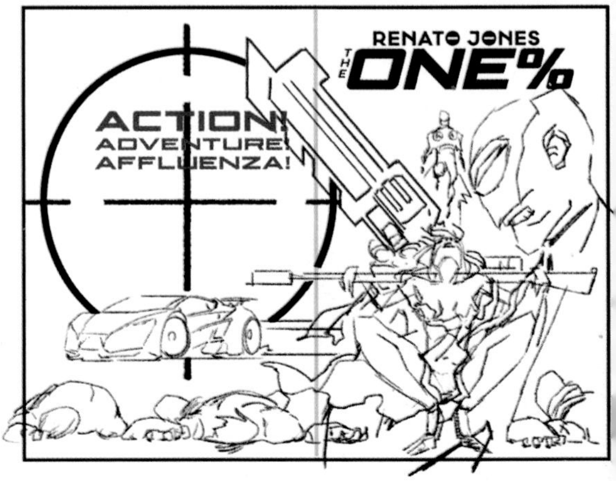
RENATO JONES
THE ONE%

I've always thought it would be interesting to use interior pages as the cover itself. This was an attempt at doing that… not very successful… this time! I'm sure this idea will make its way into a future issue.

TURNS

These kinds of character design turns aren't something I normally do. Renato Jones is a very simple design, but I wanted to really work it out and make sure it made sense.

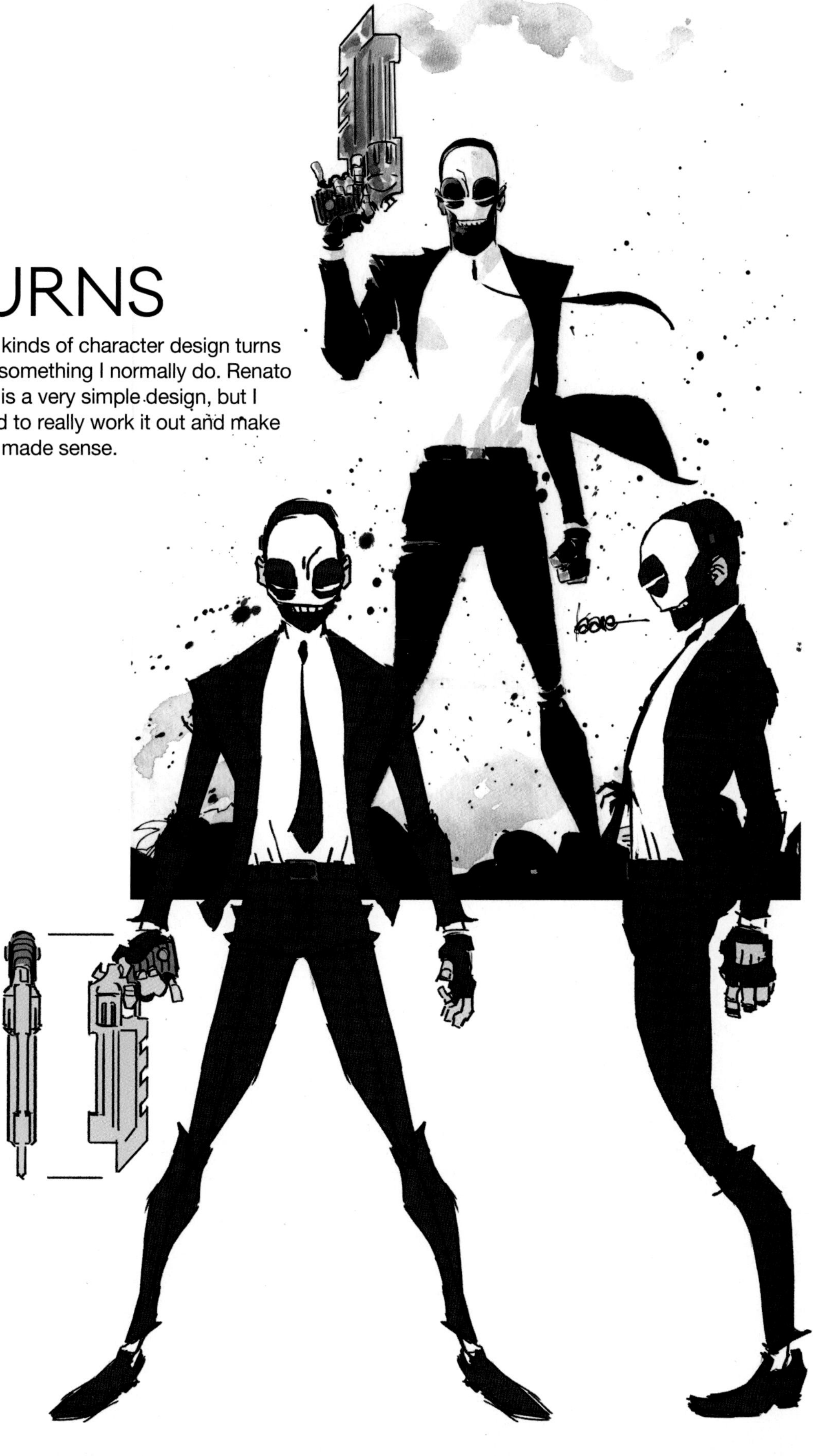

Renato Jones
SEASON 2

RENATO JONES
justicier de luxe

Restitution continues in Season Two of the Most Dangerous Comic on the planet